I0601548

THE FEAR

RAE LOUISE

BLACK ROSE
writing™

The final approval for this literary material is granted by the author.

First printing

This is a work of fiction. Names, characters, businesses, places, events and incidents are either the products of the author's imagination or used in a fictitious manner. Any resemblance to actual persons, living or dead, or actual events is purely coincidental.

ISBN: 978-1-61296-818-6
PUBLISHED BY BLACK ROSE WRITING
www.blackrosewriting.com

Printed in the United States of America
Suggested retail price $19.95

The Fear is printed in Gentium Book Basic

Dedicated to Merlin, Dante and all of the animals
that have brought joy and purpose to my life.

A special thank you to my parents: Mum, for your deranged mind and years of feeding my inspiration with endless horror movies and Grandma's awful books; and Dad, for putting up with it. Thank you, Lizzie, for being a great sister – even though you laugh at my stories and run away when I ask you to proofread. I'm sure I deserve it for making you look at all of those possessed faces during childhood. Thanks, Simon and Woo Woo, for encouraging and believing in me, and generally to all of you guys for the love and support that I pretend I don't need (I do!).

A huge thanks to Philippa Donovan, who was the first person to ever have the misfortune of reading this book. Without her advice, I never would have had the confidence to take it further. To my evil agent, Keith Chawgo – I can't thank you enough for taking a chance on me, for being my friend and for making me bawl with laughter during our ridiculous phone calls. My appreciation also goes to Vickie, Debbie and the rest of my Media Bitch family because you're all so awesome. Finally, to the publishers and everyone who has invested in making this happen, I will be forever grateful. Thank you!

THE FEAR

PROLOGUE

———————————💀———————————

Drip, drip, drip.

It wiggled above him like a drooling baby, mucus sticking to his face. Tiny black dots peered down at him from its wandering tentacles, and the foot frills on the underside of its body were like a pair of grotesque labia.

"Take a deep breath, Mr Wilson." The dentist's mask crinkled around the curvature of his lips, pointy cheekbones making his face appear hollow and stretched.

Billy Wilson mumbled something, but it came out as more of an '*arrg*' sound. The metal clamp felt cool against his swollen gums, and his mouth was drier than ash. The dentist used a forceps to lower the critter; its long, slimy body gliding over his bottom lip. Billy flexed his arms, the leather restraints cutting deeper into his wrists.

"*Ghrrroooar!*" The sound came from his throat this time, saliva foaming like a rabid dog. Bloody head brace – he'd snap his own neck if it meant he could get out of it.

By now, the critter was so close that he could smell the bitterness of its glistening body. The dentist rammed the forceps deeper into his mouth, and Billy screamed harder than any woman or child he knew. After releasing the critter, the dentist removed the jaw clamp and held Billy's mouth shut tight, muffling his cries.

"All finished, Mr Wilson. You have been very brave, indeed."

"*Mmmph! Mmmph!*" Billy's skull was forced back against the padded chair, restricting his movement even more.

The critter slithered over his tongue towards his pharynx. The taste of its secretions was unbearable, and his gag reflex did little to deter it.

Whether the slug would eat its way out of his body before it reached his stomach, he hadn't a clue, but this wasn't your average garden pest: the thing was massive, even longer than his middle finger and at least triple the diameter. Billy wasn't sure it would fit down his throat when he resorted to breathing through his nose, not that he wouldn't welcome suffocation right now. In fact, he wished for it.

Chills built into spasms and the sweat had soaked through his overalls within minutes, but he wasn't sure if it was down to some kind of poisoning or his own shock. The dentist pulled down his mask. His cracked, tombstone teeth were the colour of moldy butter, and a wonky grin melted into his chalky complexion.

"Now for the second part of our procedure," he said, picking up the forceps once more.

Billy watched his tormentor unzip the overalls to expose his shrunken genitals. The dentist turned to a silver tray behind him, blocking its contents from Billy's view – not that he had any desire to see what horrors awaited him. He didn't think it could get much worse until he saw eight spindly legs wriggling frenetically from the palm-sized body clamped between the forceps.

Choking on the slug and his own sobs, Billy closed his eyes, squeezing out the tears. Sharp hooks tugged at the hairs below his navel, moving further down his thighs and, finally, to a place that set off the screams inside his head that were even more deafening than the real thing.

CHAPTER ONE

"For heaven's sake, Lou, settle down!" Mia Reynolds watched her daughter running laps around the table, her hand fastened to the dog's tail.

"Woof, woof, woof!" Louisa yelled. Casey barked happily in response.

Mia said, "How about an ice cream?"

"Yay!" Louisa stopped, swinging her arms up into the air. Casey jumped onto her back legs, as if to mimic the girl.

"Casey, no!" Mia dived across the room as her front paws crashed down onto the table and knocked the crystal wine glasses that she'd carefully unwrapped earlier. They spun on their bases, the nearest to the edge toppling into Mia's hands. She steadied the rest before ordering the animal to its basket.

"What are they for, Mummy?" asked Louisa, as the dog scampered past her.

"Granny Viv gave them to me for my twenty-first birthday. They're very special."

"Why?"

"Because that also happens to be the year you were born, you little monster."

Louisa giggled when Mia tugged one of her pigtails. It was those satiny black curls that defined them as mother and daughter.

"What's all the noise?" Jamie plodded into the kitchen with her iPod, one headphone tucked in her ear and the other draped around her neck.

"Lou's been exciting the dog again," Mia told her younger sister. "We

3

were just about to have some ice creams, do you want one?"

"Nah, too many calories." Jamie flopped onto a chair that was already pulled away from the table, her feet buried in a litter of bubble wrap. Louisa climbed up onto a seat next to her.

"Can I listen, Aunt Jamie?" she said.

"It's for grown-ups only."

"You're not a grown-up."

"I'm as good as."

"What does that mean?"

"It means I'm older than you and there's nothing you can do about it."

Mia chipped in, "Not that you act it half the time."

Jamie glanced up without lifting her head, her hazel eyes flashing a shade darker than usual. She continued to click away on her iPod.

"Have you finished unpacking?" Mia crossed to the freezer and began rummaging through the drawers in search of the Cornettos.

"Yeah, and my room still looks like something out of *Bates Motel*. Smells like someone pissed over a corpse up there."

"Now you're exaggerating. Besides, with all the cash we've saved from the mortgage we'll be able to spruce it up in no time."

"Doesn't change the facts, though. Which room was it that –"

"*Jamie!*" Mia sprang up from behind the freezer door like a crazed jack-in-the-box, her brows drawn together in a stiff V-shape. Jamie didn't say another word.

"Mummy, can I paint my room yellow?" Louisa was too busy popping a sheet of bubble wrap to have picked up on the friction between them.

"You can paint it whatever colour you like, sweetheart." Mia sat down opposite the girls and slid a couple of Cornettos across the table, keeping the third one for herself. Louisa snatched the nearest and tore off the foil as if it was her birthday present.

"Ugh, it's all squishy!" she complained.

"That's what happens when you dawdle around the supermarket." Mia glanced at Jamie while unwrapping her own. "Not hungry?"

"Some of us like being able to see our hips," she muttered.

"Some of us haven't carried a child for nine months."

"Bitch."

"Skeletor."

4

Louisa butt in, "What's a ske-le-tor?"

"It's the opposite to what your mum sees when she looks in the mirror," Jamie replied.

"Oh, shut up and eat the damn ice cream!" Mia laughed, throwing the Cornetto at her. "You'll burn it off in no time – there are a load more boxes that need shifting out of the living room."

***

Mia closed the curtains, the unadorned fabric leaving grimy gloves on each of her hands. She wiped them on the back of her jog bottoms and walked around to the bed. Even the prehistoric furniture that they'd brought over from their previous home made it look like a showroom in comparison to the faded wallpaper and crusty carpet. The house itself was fairly standard: three bedrooms, a compact family bathroom, lounge and kitchen – nothing extravagant, but it was all they needed.

"You all settled, baby?" She pulled the duvet over Louisa's torso so just her head and neck were sticking out.

Louisa nodded, yawning loudly to expose a gap where her two front teeth should have been. Mia sat down on the bed next to her. "I think Mummy's little helper needs a nice long sleep, doesn't she? We've got another busy day tomorrow."

"When will Daddy come and see me?"

"As soon as he gets back from his holiday. In the meantime, I don't want you to worry because nothing is going to change. What did Daddy promise you before he went away?"

"Lots of sleepovers."

"And your dad never breaks a promise, does he?"

"No."

"So, everything's good?"

"Yep."

"That's my girl." Mia kissed her daughter before making the few strides towards the door.

"Mummy ..."

"Yes, sweetheart?" Mia turned before flicking off the light.

"Why is Aunt Jamie sad?"

"What do you mean?"

5

"She cries at bedtime. Is she scared of the bogeyman?"

"Don't worry about Jamie, she's just a bit upset about Grandma leaving. She'll be fine, I promise." Mia smiled unconvincingly. Then she turned off the light, and the child stared through the darkness like it was crystal.

"Sweet dreams," Mia whispered.

"Night-night."

Leaving the door ajar, Mia trudged down the poky landing. The mustard colouring seemed to be a theme throughout the first floor, and she constantly felt like she was walking through a maze of cheese. She stopped halfway to check in on Jamie. Her room was slightly bigger than Louisa's, and the walls were already plastered with posters of various indie bands.

"Fancy a hot chocolate?" Mia said.

"What am I, five?" Jamie continued to thumb through the pages of her magazine. She was lying on the bed in a towel with her slender legs bent up behind her. She'd inherited their mother's tall and graceful figure, whereas Mia had the kind of frame that was built for curves.

"How about a glass of rosé, then – a toast to our new start?" Mia proposed.

"Everything's pretty much the same to me."

"You know what I mean. What's with you recently?"

"What's with *you* trying to play mum all the time?" Jamie glanced up transiently from the magazine. "If you want another kid then go and make one."

"Fine, I get the message. If you change your mind then I'll be downstairs."

Mia closed the door and then headed for the kitchen. Getting across the hallway was like competing in an obstacle course: hurdling over boxes, weaving amongst junk and kicking a path through the ocean of bubble wrap. The whole house, downstairs in particular, was cold and echoed more than it should have done, which Mia put down to the fact that most of the walls were stripped down to their plaster. The only up-to-date room was the lounge with its burgundy carpet and textured wallpaper, all neutrals and beiges that Mia was likely to extend to the hall and landing.

Once she'd reached the kitchen, she squirted some Fairy liquid into the sink and turned on the squeaky taps. Water trickled out with little more force than a stream of urine. Jamie might have been a stroppy cow, but she made a valid point: the house wasn't fit for a bloody caveman.

Casey trotted into the kitchen and began pawing at the back door. "Do you need a wee, girl?" Mia said.

Woof.

Mia unlocked the door and left it open so the dog could get in and out. The late summer breeze felt markedly keen tonight, and she shivered on her way back to the sink. Through the window in front of her, she saw the Golden Retriever disappearing into the night and sighed inwardly. The garden would need clearing out, too, at some point – not that she'd call it that in its present state. More like the Amazon rainforest crammed into a phone box.

She was loading the sink with dirty dishes when gruff barks ripped through the night. "Quiet, girl," Mia warned.

Casey made a deep rumbling sound, like the persistent revving of a car engine.

"Casey, if you don't sh-*iiit!*" Mia glanced up to a pallid face staring back at her through the kitchen window and made an involuntary leap backwards. A dinner plate slipped from her grasp and exploded against the tiled floor, fragments spreading like startled crabs.

It was a tall, middle-aged man with fluffy hair and stubble. The area wasn't exactly known for being plush but, seriously, tramps foraging around in people's gardens – she'd never seen anything like it. The back door creaked in the wind, and Mia realised he could have been through it in no time, inviting himself to a lot more than scraps of food.

A steak knife winked at her from the worktop, bloody juices crusted to the blade. She made a grab for it, pausing once her eyes had acclimatised to the dark. What kind of idiot tried to break into someone's house wearing nothing but their pyjamas?

"Paul? ... Paul!" a voice hollered from outside.

Mia turned off the taps and skulked over to the back door. Casey, who was now crouching at the edge of the lawn, barked when a frizzy-haired woman clambered over the tiny fence that separated next door's garden, overgrown shrubs clawing at her jeans.

"What's going on out here?" Mia demanded, stepping out onto the paving slabs that bordered the house. The concrete felt cool and gritty against her bare feet, and she made an effort to stay close to the door.

"It's okay, he's harmless!" The woman scurried over to the zombie-like man, thorny tentacles trailing after her. "Paul – snap out of it." She vigorously shook his arm. "You've been wandering again, you silly man."

Paul's eyes lit on the full breasts hanging loosely behind Mia's vest. She crossed her arms in front of them to conceal her nipples, which the cold had turned into icicle tips. *Of all the times to be caught braless!* she thought.

"Is he sleepwalking or something?" Mia said, still unsure of what to make of the couple.

"No, he's a bit ..." The woman raised a hand so it was level with her temple and made circles with her forefinger while pretending to be cross-eyed.

"Oh, I see." Mia nodded.

"I'm so sorry, this isn't how I'd planned on introducing myself."

"Don't worry about it. He gave me a start, that's all." Mia turned and clicked her fingers at the grumbling dog. "*Inside.*"

Casey scooted into the house, and the woman continued, "My name's Brenda, I live just next door. This is my brother, Paul."

"Hello, Paul." Mia looked again to the man, who appeared to be mumbling something at the washing line. He was perhaps a few years younger than Brenda, who must have been in her early forties. "I'm Mia, it's nice to meet you both."

Brenda replied, "I hope you didn't think I was being rude, not coming to welcome you sooner. I know how hectic moving house can be and no one appreciates a nosy neighbour. Is it just you and your girls?"

Mia found this to be a bit contradictory, but she answered anyway. "The older one is my sister, Jamie. Louisa's my five-year-old."

"Ah, I thought you looked too young for teens."

Mia chuckled appreciatively.

"Well, I'd better get him inside before he causes any more trouble. If you need anything then give us a shout, my husband cares for Paul so he's usually at home."

"Thanks, I'll see you around."

"Yes – sorry again. Come on, you."

As Brenda escorted Paul back to the fence, he pointed at the house while murmuring to his sister, "Help ... d-de –"

"Not now, Paul," Brenda interrupted, helping him to climb over the fence. She looked like an elf compared to the lumbering giant, and Mia suppressed a giggle.

"I thought I heard voices." Jamie appeared at the back door in her dressing gown. "Who are they?" She nodded at the couple.

"That's Brenda and Paul from next door."

"What were they doing in our garden?"

Mia shrugged. "He's retarded, I think. He appeared at the kitchen window, scared the shit out of me."

Jamie pulled up the collar of her dressing gown, shuddering. "Jeez, this place really is the Bates Motel."

"Well, he seemed pretty freaked out about something." Mia thought she felt someone tweak the hairs on the back of her neck, and she quickly rubbed the sensation away. "Fancy that drink now?"

Jamie nodded, and they went indoors.

CHAPTER TWO

It lingered at the end of her bed. Hunched and skeletal, long hair dangling from its scalp like cobwebs, creating a wispy canopy over its face. A pale nightgown rippled in the draught from the open window.

Mia sat up, squinting as her eyes adjusted to the gloom. "Mum ... is that you?"

Silence.

"*Mum.*" It wasn't a question this time.

The figure slowly lifted its head, as if being roused from a daydream. Its face was fuzzy, featureless. A trick of the shadows – it had to be.

Mia blinked, rubbed her eyes, then blinked again. The snake of dread worming its way through her gut seemed far too embedded for a dream.

Fully alert, she spoke again. "What are you doing here?"

"It's ... your ... fault," a woman whispered.

Mia swallowed, the snake knotting around her heart. "Please, you don't mean that."

"It's your *fault!*"

The form swooped up beside her with its feet hovering several inches above the ground. It thrust forwards its arms to expose the lacerations in its wrists, as if someone had physically peeled back the flesh around its arteries. Mia screamed at the red cascade that saturated her bed sheets.

***

Mia pushed the redial button, chewing her fingernails while she waited for the line to connect.

Beep, beep, beep.

She snapped her mobile shut and plonked it down on the table. "Bloody line is still busy."

"Relax, it's only been ten seconds since the last time you called," said Jamie, with a mouthful of toast. She was slouched in a chair with her feet up on the table, her light brown hair bunched onto her crown like a squashed pineapple.

"What if they're on the phone to the hospital? The police?" *Oh, God, not the police again.* Mia snatched up the phone once more. "Something's wrong, I can feel it."

"Man, it was only a dream," mumbled Jamie.

Louisa stomped into the kitchen, her tiny fists clenched by her sides as if they'd been glued there. "I hate this house! It smells of farts and my bed wobbles."

Jamie almost choked on her food laughing. Mia whacked her legs with a newspaper that had been left on the table, and she immediately retracted them.

"See what you've caused now?" Mia snapped.

"Sorry, but she's got a point." Jamie frowned when Mia grabbed her handbag from one of the worktops. "What are you doing now?"

"I'm just popping out for half an hour. Watch Lou for me, okay?"

"You're not going over there?"

"Ring me if there are any problems. Bye!"

Mia dashed from the house, got into her car and then zoomed off down the road.

***

Mia pulled into the car park of Church View Care Home at roughly 10 a.m. It was a modern, two-storey building set in an L-shape, the neighbouring Woodhouse Moor keeping it secluded from the hustle and bustle of central Leeds.

After locking the Corsa, she headed around to the main entrance and pressed the buzzer on the wall outside. Moments later, a middle-aged lady came waddling into the reception area; a white tunic stretched over her bulging stomach. The women exchanged a smile through the glass double doors, and then a latch was clicked open.

"Hello, Miss Reynolds." The woman beamed at her. "Come on in."

"Thanks, Sally." Mia squeezed past her while she held open the door.

"Would you like to sign in for me?" Sally indicated a clipboard lying on the counter outside the reception booth, which looked more like a dwarf's office.

Mia scribbled her name, the date and time of entry into the chart, before asking the carer, "How is she this morning?"

"A bit more settled than when you last saw her. As we said, it usually takes a few weeks to familiarise themselves with the new environment. She's coping fairly well with the routines, though."

"Great. And there haven't been any accidents or ...?"

"No, we would contact you in such instances. She's in the right place, Miss Reynolds. You have nothing to worry about." Sally's smile was accentuated by the creases in her plump face.

"I know, it's just strange not having her around. I tried ringing earlier but I couldn't get through, then I started to panic and ... well, I guess you see this kind of thing a lot."

"Indeed, I'd be worried if you felt any different. Shall we go and see her, put your mind at ease?"

"Yes, please."

Sally led Mia through the building, where they passed a commodious reception room that adjoined to an even larger dining area via an open archway. Both were decorated with light carpets and floral curtains, a parade of armchairs lining the sitting room – most of them occupied by shrivelled, pale-haired bodies. Crossing the conservatory towards the rear garden, they could still hear the television blaring as if they were on some geriatrics' outing to the cinema.

Eventually, they reached a small courtyard that overlooked the vast expanse of greenery. A gala of colour conflicted with the grimness of the exterior fences, roses and geraniums scenting the summer air, and beyond this the whispering canopy of Woodhouse Moor stretched across the land.

"Good morning, Vivian." Sally spoke to a lady sitting alone on the bench. "You've got a visitor."

Vivian gazed up from beneath hooded lids, the flesh around her eyes and mouth crinkling as she opened her arms wide. "Oh, my beautiful Mia!"

"Hello, Mum." Mia leaned into her knobbly embrace, taking care not to squeeze too tight. Vivian had moved into the care home the previous Sunday, and apart from a fleeting mid-week visit, this was the first opportunity Mia had had to see her mother.

Vivian let go of her and patted the bench. "Sit with me."

Mia did as she was told, suddenly realising the carer had disappeared. "It's lovely out here, isn't it?"

"Yes, I was watching the little birds." Vivian pointed to a wooden construction that protruded from the grass, where tweeting sparrows hopped about on a beach of seeds.

"They look so happy," Mia observed. "Are you happy, Mum?"

She fondled the plait that hung over Vivian's shoulder, what was once a lustrous brown now streaked with grey. Her eyes had faded to a grungy yellow, and Mia felt a tightening in her throat when she thought about how a face she'd known all her life had become almost unrecognisable.

"How's little Jamie? She must be growing up so fast!" Vivian had either ignored the question or, most likely, forgotten it.

"Her name's Louisa. Jamie is your other daughter," Mia corrected her.

"Ah, yes, my little model. She'll be on all the catwalks soon, you'll see. Takes after her mum, doesn't she?" Vivian winked.

"Don't tell her that, she won't be able to get her head through the front door."

Vivian laughed: a deep, husky sound that seemed to jar her shoulders as if she was on puppet strings. Mia could almost hear her bones rattling with the effort.

"Are you looking after the house?" Vivian asked. "I want it cleaned and polished to the brickwork for when I get back."

"We don't live there anymore. We've moved into Uncle Billy's old place, remember?"

"I bet he wasn't too pleased about that? Three young ladies cluttering up the place – he'll end up in here with me!"

"I very much doubt that," Mia mumbled, mainly to herself. "Anyway, I can't stay long because I've left the girls in charge of the house. I'm glad you're feeling better, though."

"Yes, much better." Vivian spoke as if in response to a question.

"I'll bring Jamie and Louisa along next time, they're missing you so much. How do you feel about coming for a visit once we're all settled?"

"Ooh, yes, please."

Mia smiled and reached for the hand on Vivian's lap, tracing her fingers over the shiny pink scar that ran from the side of her wrist to halfway up her forearm. It was shaped like a birthmark and had the waxy texture of a shrivelled tomato. Vivian didn't flinch – it was unlikely that she felt anything at all.

A breath of wind rushed at them from the trees and they sat in silence for several minutes, enjoying the sunshine together while listening to the merry chirping of the birds. It was the most peaceful Mia had felt in a long time.

***

Mia was back in the suburb of Bramley all too soon. Trundling along the quiet streets of Greenway Avenue, a mob of teenage boys flew past on a combination of skateboards and bicycles.

"*Whooo ...*" One made a ghostly whistle as she parked outside her end terrace.

Another yelled, "Fetch an exorcist before it's too late!"

"Where's the *Most Haunted* crew?"

The fourth was so busy gawping at Mia that his front tyre ploughed into the wheelie bin. It crashed onto its side, the lid swinging open and litter strewing the pavement.

Mia switched off the ignition and jumped out of the car. "Pick that up, arsehole!"

The boy swiftly regained control of his bike, and the gang sped away in a blizzard of laughter. Mia straightened the bin and gathered the rubbish bags, stamping on a crumpled piece of paper before it floated away in the breeze. She picked it up and glimpsed the headline at the top of the page. Like the opening to a lover's diary, she couldn't have stopped there even if she wanted to.

Skimming over its contents, she sucked in a deep breath. "You stupid girl," she muttered.

Dropping the bags into the wheelie bin, she closed the lid and then hurried into the house. "Jamie!" she bellowed down the hallway.

No answer.

"Jay?" She poked her head into the living room. Realising it was empty, she turned to make for the kitchen when footsteps thudded down the stairs.

"What's up? Is Mum okay?" Jamie sounded as if she'd raced from the other side of town rather than the few yards from her bedroom.

"She's fine. Where's Lou?"

"On the phone to Nathan. What's happened?"

Mia passed her the sheet of paper. "I found this outside. Do we need to talk?"

Jamie barely glanced over the page before screwing it up again. "I failed a few exams, so what? It's not like I'd be able to afford the college fees anyway, never mind uni."

"I don't care about the results, it's you I'm worried about. If you want to shit all over your future then go ahead, but I'm still responsible for this family."

Jamie groaned and threw her head back in exasperation. "Why do you always have to talk like Mum's dead already? As if selling the house wasn't bad enough!"

"How else would we have funded her care? You did the sums with me, Jay. We barely scrape by on my wage as it is, and this place isn't worth half as much as Mum's old house."

"What if she came back to live with us? I'm old enough to work now, and there's no point in carrying on with my A levels. We could take it in turns to look after Mum."

"Right, because it worked out so well last time, didn't it?"

Memories of that night burned raw in both of the girls' minds: the screeching alarms and the thick, choking smoke pouring into the hallway like a silent assassin. No one had dared to turn on the lights for the fear of causing an explosion, and if it wasn't for a neighbour's horde of fire extinguishers then the whole house might have been incinerated with them in it. Whilst Mia was thankful that the damage had been limited to the kitchen, next time ... well, there wouldn't be a next time.

"It was an *accident*," Jamie pronounced. "She didn't *mean* to do it."

"She threw tea towels over a flaming stove and made a bonfire out of them – she'd be in a prison cell if it wasn't for her condition. I know it sounds harsh, but I've got Louisa to think about."

"Well, if I'd known how crappy it'd make me feel then I never would have agreed to send her away in the first place. Don't you feel the slightest bit guilty?"

"Of course I'd rather she was here with us, but Mum made her decisions a long time ago. This is what she wanted, so don't throw it back in her face when you don't have to."

"I already have, haven't I?" Jamie waved the exam results in front of her. "With these."

"We've still got a bit of money left over from the house. If you can't resit the exams at school then there are plenty of colleges that might be able to help – Mum will never have to know."

"But I know." Big tears welled in Jamie's eyes. "I suck. This whole situation sucks. My life sucks!"

"Jay, come on –" Mia went to console her but she turned and thudded up the stairs, dust puffing out of the carpet beneath her bare feet.

Sighing, Mia returned to the living room and collapsed onto the sofa. She closed her eyes and massaged her temples with her fingers as if loosening the tangles in her brain. Life was supposed to have been a little less taxing without their senile mother to worry about, but this bickering was becoming more and more of a routine. The child she'd helped to bring up all these years was slowly disappearing, and Mia was afraid that one day she'd wake up without a sister or a mother.

"Mummy, Mummy!" Mia opened her eyes to find her daughter standing before her. Soggy Rice Krispies bobbled her pyjama top.

"What is it, baby?"

"Casey won't come out of her basket."

"She's probably still tired after yesterday. I know I am."

"I think she's poorly. Come and –"

"Not now, Lou!" Mia held up an authoritative hand, as if training a hyperactive puppy. Louisa regarded her in silence, a mature awareness in her face.

"Sorry, love." Mia reached for the girl's hand and stroked her teeny fingers. "Mummy's got a bit of a headache, that's all."

Louisa leaned forwards to kiss her on the cheek. "I'll make you and Casey better."

"You're a good girl." Mia patted her on the bum. "Is Dad okay?"

Louisa nodded. "He's coming to see me soon. I told him the house is smelly."

"And what did he say?"

"He said it's because it's old like you."

"Charming! I haven't even hit thirty yet."

"Gina's old. She's got wrinkles."

Mia grinned. "That's no way to talk about your stepmum."

There was a knock on the front door. Standing up, Mia said, "Would you go upstairs and give Aunt Jamie a big hug for me? I don't think she's feeling too well either."

"Doctor Lou today!" said the girl, and she skipped from the room.

Following her into the hallway, Mia noticed a fuzzy red blob through the pane of glass in the front door and wondered why there was a clown outside. Only when she opened the door did the vibrant curls, sunburned nose and white face – which, on closer inspection, she realised was a thin layer of cream – come into focus.

"Howdy, neighbour, how are you settling in?" Brenda spoke cheerfully.

"Er, we're getting there, thanks. Has Paul recovered from his little wander last night?"

"Yes – in fact, a few of the neighbours are coming over for a barbecue this afternoon. It would be fab if you and the girls could join us, everyone's dying to meet you."

"Thanks, you're more considerate than some around here."

"Oh?" Brenda inched her neck forwards, ears pricking up.

Mia shook her head. "It's nothing, just some idiots showing off earlier. Does, er, everyone know ... about what happened here?"

Brenda looked baffled a moment. "Oh, you mean with the last owner? Nah, give it a few weeks and folk around here will have found something else to gossip about."

"You reckon? It's just that I'd like to know what we're getting ourselves into."

"We have very boring lives on this street, that's all. So, we'll see you at about four o'clock?"

"Sure, I'll mention it to the gang. Should I bring anything?"

"No, just yourselves. Bye!"

As Mia closed the front door, there were yelps from upstairs. "Louisa, what have you done? It's all tangled!"

"I'll get the scissors from Mummy."

"No scissors! Just hold it while I – *ouch!*"

Mia chuckled on her way to the kitchen. She took a tin of meaty chunks out of the cupboard and peeled back the lid. "Breakfast, Casey!" she called.

The basket in the far corner of the room was empty. "Casey ..." *whistle,* "where are you, girl?"

Plodding around the table, she spotted two fluffy paws poking out from underneath it and crouched down. "What's wrong, beautiful? Don't tell me you hate this place, too."

Dark, droopy eyes studied Mia. She put out her hand to tickle the dog's chin and received a lick in return. "It'll feel like home in no time, you'll see. How about some grub, eh?"

Mia went over to the placemat next to the basket and emptied the contents of the tin into a steel bowl. She carried it back to the table and went to slide it underneath.

Casey had gone.

CHAPTER THREE

Mia headed next door at 4.15 p.m. People had been arriving for the last twenty minutes, and although she counted less than a dozen in the garden, everyone was still squashed together like sheep in a pen. There was a nanosecond of silence as she and Louisa had stepped outside, which Mia quickly put down to paranoia. The various stares had conjured a flashback of her first day at secondary school, when she'd burst into the assembly hall ten minutes after everyone else and received a rollicking off the headmaster.

"This is Keith and Adele from across the road ... Jim, who lives next door but one ... My husband, Wesley." Brenda babbled away while Mia shook hands, murmured hellos and smiled until her jaw ached.

Louisa tugged Mia's arm while pointing to the far end of the garden. A young boy was dangling a thread of string attached to a twig in front of a tabby cat. The animal writhed on its back, claws swiping viciously at the toy. The tiny bell on its collar jingled playfully.

"That's my nephew, Dillon," Brenda told her. "He's a little older than you. Why don't you go over and say hello?"

Louisa glanced up at Mia as if waiting for permission.

"Go on, then," Mia said, so she pottered over to the boy. They eyed each other up in silence.

"Beer?" said Brenda.

Mia answered, "Just the one, I'm back at work the day after tomorrow."

"What do you do?"

"I'm an events coordinator. I'd have liked a bit more time off but people's special days aren't going to wait, are they?"

"No, I don't suppose so. Let's get you that drink."

Mia followed Brenda to a wooden table, where bowls of nibbles were arranged neatly around a stack of paper plates. Brenda took a bottle of Beck's from a box on the floor, flicked off the cap and then handed it to Mia.

"Cheers," she said.

"You're welcome," Brenda replied. "Will your sister be joining us?"

"I doubt it, she's hiding in her room sulking about ... whatever it is seventeen-year-old girls sulk about these days."

"I wouldn't know, Wesley and I never had children. We were just about to fire up the barby, any requests?"

"Louisa's a burger girl, but I'll eat anything."

"Righty-ho. Have a seat, I won't be long." Brenda gestured towards the table before disappearing into the house.

Mia sat down beneath the parasol – another five minutes in the sun and she'd look like something off a barbecue herself. Louisa and Dillon were now sitting together, taking it in turns to play with the homemade cat toy. She had the same honey-toned skin as Jamie, whereas Mia had inherited her father's fair complexion; although she only remembered this from photographs.

"Phwar, bloody sun is giving me blisters!" Keith slumped into the chair next to Mia, his hairless head dripping like a boiled egg. Sacks of fat burst through the gaps in the chair, and Mia swore she heard one of its legs splintering.

"What brings you to Bramley, lass?" asked the man.

"Convenience, mostly," Mia replied.

"Where are you from?"

"Sheffield."

"Ah, not too far, then. And you're enjoying the new house?"

"It has its advantages." Primarily, the cheap living costs – at least, cheaper than what they were used to.

Keith nodded while fanning himself with a sunhat, sweat dappling his stubby nose. "The wife and I have lived on this street for over twenty years, and the amount of folk who've come and gone from that house recently makes me wonder if anyone will stay."

"I heard it used to be a rental property?"

"Yes, for a short period," Keith confirmed. "It's become quite famous around these parts, especially after what happened to the last owner." He spied Mia over the brim of his hat, as if trying to analyse her reaction.

"Yes, it was very tragic," she agreed.

"Aye, he wasn't here long but he seemed like a nice enough chap. For his ticker to give up on him with no apparent cause whatsoever ... pure bad luck, that's what it was. He must have only been in his forties."

"Forty-eight," Mia said, taking a swig of her beer.

"Huh?"

"Billy was my uncle."

"Your *unc* –" Keith sprang up faster than his weight could cope with and he doubled up coughing, but Mia felt more pity for the saliva-sprayed salad bowl.

"Well, bugger me!" Keith thumped his chest with the side of his fist. "I do apologise, lass."

"It's okay, it's not like we were close. He was more of a distant relative, what with his job and working away so often."

"Still, I didn't mean to go and put my dinosaur foot in it."

Keith's wife ambled over to the table. Her brunette locks were pinned up with a single knitting needle, exposing the grey roots around her crown.

"Hey, Ade," Keith said to the woman, "this is Bill's niece."

"His niece? I say ..." Adele pulled up a chair next to her husband and sat down, her watery eyes fixed on Mia. "Sorry for your loss, lovie. So you inherited the house, did you?"

"Yes – well, sort of. It was left to my mum and she signed it over to us. We're the only family he had, you see, but please don't mention any of this in front of my daughter. She knows Uncle Billy's gone, but I don't want her head filled with ghost stories."

"Of course, but people do talk," Adele warned. "It's such a quiet neighbourhood, and with some of the things that have gone on in that house ..."

Mia recalled Keith mentioning how so many occupants had left and asked, "Such as what?"

"Adele, leave the girl alone!" Brenda reappeared with Paul, and she sat him down in a chair opposite Mia. He'd been shaved since she'd last seen him, and he looked much younger in his khaki shorts and shirt. In fact, he almost looked normal.

"Paul, you remember Mia, don't you?" Brenda spoke in a similar tone that Mia used when talking to Louisa – back when she was a toddler.

Paul scanned for Mia's cleavage, which was now safely concealed behind her Rolling Stones T-shirt. No one else seemed to notice.

"Well, I think we should have a toast on account of our new neighbours." Keith took a glass of burgundy liquid from the table and raised it up in front of him. "Welcome to our town, and may you spend many happy years here. And to poor old Billy, God rest his soul."

Paul's eyes flickered then, a darkness trying to claw its way out of those sterling grey pools like a corpse from a grave. Perhaps it was more pronounced due to the fact that it was the first hint of emotion Mia had seen, but he almost looked like he was coming back to life.

He almost looked haunted.

***

Swish, swoosh ... swish, swoosh ...

It sounded like a dream at first. Distant, yet chillingly real.

A gnawing coldness seeped through the bed sheets, and Mia tugged them up over her shoulders. It wasn't until she felt herself shivering that she realised she was very much awake.

Swish, swoosh ... swish –

The 'breathing' noise ended when she lifted her head off the pillow. She could feel something like ants rushing about on her skin, but it was only the hairs prickling up over her body. She glanced across to the window. The curtains were still, not even the feeblest of draughts. But something had been making the sound. She could sense it in the room with her now, like a billion eyes floating in the darkness.

"Mummy?"

Mia sat up fully, the chill enveloping her like a shawl. She reached for the bedside lamp and winced at its bright yellow glow. The bulb emitted rays of warmth that could have melted her icy flesh.

"Louisa, it's you," she said, sighing. "Is everything okay?"

Louisa plodded over to the bed, her eyes crusted with sleep. "There was someone in my room."

"What?"

"They kept staring at me and I can't sleep."

"It's okay, you must have had a bad dream. Let's get you back into bed." Mia threw back the duvet, but Louisa burrowed into her arms.

"I don't want to go," she protested.

"Don't be silly, you're not a baby anymore. Do you want me to go and check that it's all safe?"

"No, I want to sleep with you!" Louisa clutched onto Mia so tightly that it felt like she had cat claws hooked into her back.

She hoisted the girl onto her lap and looked into her morose face. "What's wrong, sweetheart? This isn't like you at all."

Louisa pouted at the floor, making her cheeks look even chubbier than usual.

"Has Aunt Jamie been telling you stories?" Mia asked her. Louisa shook her head.

"Did you hear something at the barbecue earlier? Has Dillon upset you?"

Adele had warned her that people would talk, and it was only a matter of time before Louisa learned about the house's morbid secret. Mia still shivered whenever she thought about how her uncle had been found in that very room, probably in the exact spot they were in now, a full three days after his heart had ruptured in his chest. Evidently, the neighbours were as perplexed as she was by the abruptness of it all.

When Louisa didn't respond, Mia reassured her, "I know this has been a big scary change, but things will get better soon. I've always kept you safe, haven't I?"

Louisa grunted, which Mia took as a 'yes'.

"So, there's no need to worry. And if anyone says something you don't like then you tell me and I'll sort them out, okay?"

Louisa nodded. Mia pecked her on the cheek, then shifted her across to the other side of the double bed. "You can stay here just for tonight, and no kicking me."

"You snore like a pig."

"Shut it, you."

After tucking themselves in, Mia clicked off the lamp. They were asleep within minutes.

CHAPTER FOUR

"Have you got any plans for today?" Mia flitted about the living room while packing various items into her handbag: her mobile, purse and numerous sets of keys.

"*Ice Age* and jigsaws, apparently," Jamie replied. Mia laughed as she did a jig of mock enthusiasm.

"Well, there's still plenty of tidying to be done. I'd make the most out of Louisa before the holidays are over."

"Oh, that reminds me: Kerry rang last night. She wants to come up and see the new house before sixth-form starts."

"Cool. Any idea when?"

"The weekend, probably. She'll be getting the train up so I told her she could stay over for a couple of nights."

Mia paused. "You do know I've got a wedding to oversee this Saturday?"

"Yeah, I thought Nathan was having Louisa?"

"He's not back from Spain until next week. I did tell you we'd have to juggle things around until I can sort something more permanent, it's not like I can drop her off with Nate or his parents whenever I need a babysitter."

"But I haven't explored the town yet. We were going to go shopping and everything."

"With what, chocolate coins?"

Jamie opened her mouth as if to counter, then closed it while looking despondently at the ground. Mia had to remind herself of their disparate upbringings: their father had died of a brain aneurism when Jamie was a toddler, so she'd been deprived of the emotional and financial security that Mia had been offered. With Vivian's ongoing illness, Mia was the sole earner for the family and showcasing that fact was petty as well as cruel.

"You could always take Louisa into town with you?" Mia suggested. "I'll chuck in twenty quid for a pizza or something. Please, Jay, just this once?"

Jamie deliberated a moment. "Fine, but if this is going to become a regular thing then I want paying for my services – plus the bus fare on top."

"Done. Thanks, sis." Mia clapped her on the shoulder. "I'll see you tonight, and don't forget to walk Casey. She needs perking up as much as the rest of us."

"Will do. Have fun."

Mia shouted goodbye to Louisa and then set off to work.

***

The market town of Penistone sat in the foothills of the Pennines, nestled amid a collar of unspoiled countryside. Mia took her usual route west of the town, car windows wound down, enjoying the daily facial of mountain air. Eventually, the road narrowed and darkened beneath woody pillars and a rustling sky of green. She made a left turn down a private lane that opened up to a sweeping gravel driveway and moderate lawn, which would soon be hogged by vehicles. Mia eased the car around the side of the building to the staff parking area, then switched off the engine.

Taking her handbag from the passenger seat, she locked the doors before heading back to the timber-framed entrance. The reception hall had a cosy oak setting, much of it having been restored along with the stone exterior, but even the various signposts and billboards failed to interfere with its historical charm – one of the many reasons why Mia loved her job.

Just ahead of her, a handful of visitors dispersed and Angela Reed's slick bun jutted up from behind the high-countered reception desk.

"Hi, Ange, sorry I'm late." Mia walked around to her side. "The commute was more of a bastard than I'd thought."

"No problem, your ten o'clock rescheduled for half past – car trouble, apparently."

Mia checked her watch. "Still time for a quick cupper, do you want one?"

"Go on, then, before it gets busy."

The staffroom was situated a few yards down the hall towards the back of reception. Mia put her bag in her locker, made the brews and then returned shortly after. She placed Angela's mug onto a coaster that had been nicked from the gift shop and stood with her own in her hands.

"Thanks." Angela pivoted her chair so she was facing Mia. "So, how are you finding the new place? Have the girls settled in okay?"

Mia let out a long, contemplative breath. "Where do I start? Louisa's convinced the house is haunted, Mum's all over the place and the other day I found out that Jamie failed her AS levels."

"You're joking?" Angela's shapely brows met in the middle, making her face appear thinner than it actually was. "Do you think she's struggling to cope with the move and everything?"

Mia shook her head. "I have a feeling that's what she wants me to think, but this started way before we considered moving. I've tried talking to her about it, but as she's already pointed out, what she does with her life has got bugger all to do with me."

"She's a teenager – my two have been like bulls at a red carpet bash since they hit puberty. Besides, there's still time for her to consider her options. Maybe she could apply to volunteer here for a while, we're always looking for help and it'll give her some experience."

Experience: Angela had forty-odd years of that, in work as well as life. It was her wise counsel that made her such a good friend and mentor to Mia.

The phone rang. Mia sipped her tea while Angela answered, "Godestone Manor, how can I help you? ... It's booking only, a minimum of eight ... Yep, give us a ring when you've decided and we'll sort out a date in the diary ... Thanks, bye."

Angela put down the phone and resumed her conversation with Mia. "I'm sure everything will sort itself out. If worse comes to the worst, stick Jamie on babysitting duties and she'll soon start looking for alternatives."

"Where do you think she is now?" Mia smirked. "I'll tell you something, Ange, if I'm going to be stuck living with my sister for the next fifty years then she can bloody well make herself useful."

More visitors walked into reception: two adults and a young girl, who was wearing ripped jeans, a black vest and lace arm warmers.

"This must be my ten thirty," Mia whispered. She set down her mug and went to greet the family.

"Mr and Mrs Pearson, is it?" she said.

"Yes, that's us," the woman replied. "Thank you for waiting."

"It's no problem at all. My name is Mia, I'm the events coordinator." She shook hands with each of them, saving the girl until last. "And you must be the birthday girl-to-be?"

"Halle." The girl smiled. Her black nail varnish coordinated with the kohl around her eyes.

"It's nice to meet you, Halle. Have you visited Godestone Manor before?"

"No, but my brother came here on a school trip last year. He went on one of the Tudor tours, said it was well creepy."

"You should see it at night." Mia grinned, even though she was serious. "Most of our events take place in the Great Hall, shall we take a look?"

There was a murmur of agreement, and Mia led them down a narrow corridor to the left of reception. The short walk to the Great Hall was like stepping through a portal that whisked them centuries into the past, and Mia felt that familiar swell of pride at the enchantment of it all.

"Gosh." Mrs Pearson studied the high ceiling and timber frames, which were similar to those on the building's front exterior wall. Two long banquet tables stood either side of the room upon a patterned black and white floor.

"It's a work of art, isn't it? Very medieval," Mr Pearson remarked. "Are any of the features original?"

Mia replied, "I'm afraid much of it has been renovated throughout the years, hence the Tudor-Victorian styling. The present owners wanted certain features to replicate what it would have looked like during the fifteenth century, which is when it was first built."

"What about food, decorations and so on for the party?" asked Mrs Pearson.

"We can arrange catering for an additional charge, but things like music and decorations will be your own responsibility. The hall can take a maximum capacity of forty people, so if you're planning on a rave then it might not be the best option, but it is a popular choice for more intimate gatherings."

"I heard this place is supposed to be haunted, is that true?" Halle looked expectantly at Mia.

"I'll be honest with you, I haven't seen anything myself but the manor was once used as a townhouse for the local priors. There've been numerous reports of robed figures wandering the grounds, particularly the old chapel, so it may well have potential."

"What about ghost walks and stuff? That would be so cool."

"It's not something we currently offer, but I'm sure we can sort something out for the night. Have you thought about giving your party a theme? Halloween is coming up in a couple of months, you could have a double celebration if that's the kind of thing you're into."

"Awesome!" Halle punched a fist out in front of her. "Can we do fancy dress, Mum? It'd rock!"

"Let's wait and see how much it will cost to hire the place first." Mrs Pearson turned back to Mia. "Would you be able to give us a quote at all?"

"Certainly. If you'd like to come through to the parlour, I'll dig out some price lists and we can take it from there?"

The family agreed, and Mia led them out of the Great Hall.

***

Jamie took a handful of DVDs from Louisa and slotted them into the cabinet. "Is that the last of them?" she said.

Louisa kicked over the empty box. "All gone!"

"Thank God for that." Jamie closed the glass doors and stood up, yawning. "Does this place seem to drain the life out of you or what?"

Louisa pointed to the dimples in Jamie's knees from where she'd been kneeling on the carpet. "You've got wrinkles."

"It's the fleas, they've sucked all my blood out."

"Eek!" Louisa bounced from one foot to the other, as if stamping on imaginary cockroaches.

"I'm joking, stupid." Jamie took her mobile out of her shorts' pocket and checked the time. She'd only been up for a few hours and her eyelids already felt like they needed pegs to keep them open. "Are you ready for some lunch?"

"Can I play with Cindy first?"

"All right, I'll call you down in a bit - and no misbehaving up there."

"Thank you, Aunt Jamie." Louisa scurried off to her bedroom.

Jamie headed into the kitchen and set the kettle to boil. She poured herself a coffee with extra sugar and then sat down at the table, where the latest issue of *Seventeen* magazine lay waiting for her. She opened it a few pages in and picked up on the article that she'd been reading over breakfast earlier. It wasn't long before her eyelids grew heavier, words blurring into gibberish. Blinking, she turned the page.

Something cool and damp nuzzled her ankle, light breaths moistening her skin. "Hey, Case," she said, without looking under the table.

She giggled when the dog sniffed further up her leg and a rough tongue licked her knee. "Okay, I get it. We'll go for walkies after lunch."

Slurp, lick, lick, slurp ...

Jamie flipped over another page while sipping her coffee. The tonguing intensified, like a cat lapping at a bowl of cream; drool oozing down her shin. Jamie pulled back her leg so it was tucked under the chair. "Casey, give it a rest."

The tongue slithered up the inside of her thigh towards that most sensitive area. She kicked out in a reflex, coffee sloshing over the rim of the mug and splattering the magazine, yet her feet met no resistance. Movement from ahead caught her attention, and she glanced through the kitchen doorway into the hall. Placing the mug onto the table, she might have flinched at the red welt on her hand if she hadn't just seen Casey toddling out of the living room.

"What the f –"

Her legs were thrust apart by cold, gargantuan hands forged by the air itself – an unseen force that could have rivalled that of ten men. Screaming, she jumped up, sending the chair hurtling into the washing machine.

"Lazy bum!" shouted Louisa, from across the kitchen.

Jamie's head bounced up and down, from the table to Louisa and back again until the muscles in her neck felt like an overused springboard. She hadn't even heard her coming down the stairs.

"Oh my god, are you okay?" She scooted over to the girl and held her close, like a child clutching a teddy bear. "What the hell was that? Did you see it?"

Louisa said, "You were moaning like Casey does when she's

dreaming."

"B-but I thought ..." *What, Jamie, the invisible man dropped by for a quick grope?* Logic told her that she must have fallen asleep, but her instincts ... well, she chose to ignore those.

"Holy shit." Jamie raked a hand through her hair, her laughter coming in short convulsions. "I must have been more tired than I thought. Are you sure you didn't see anything weird?"

Louisa shook her head and held up two miniature dresses. "What shall I put Cindy in, red or blue?"

"Er, I dunno. Let's go and try them on her."

Ushering Louisa from the kitchen, Jamie took a final glance over her shoulder. She returned to neither the coffee nor the magazine.

CHAPTER FIVE

Mia watched her mum admiring Louisa as she circled the room, angling her neck to absorb every detail; from the pale ceiling to the peach walls and matching carpet. Furniture was basic and included a bed, wardrobe, chest of drawers and a dressing table that doubled up as a shelving unit, all in a pine finish. A couple of chairs were also dotted about for visiting purposes.

"You've really made this place look like home, haven't you, Mum?" Jamie referred to the family photographs displayed proudly around the television. It was her second time visiting the care home, whereas everything was new to Louisa.

"It'll do for now." Vivian gave her a wily smile. Half the time she didn't know what day of the week it was, yet quite often she would use this 'forgetfulness' to her advantage.

"Lou, why don't you show Grandma the picture you drew for her?" Mia took a sheet of paper out of her handbag and passed it to the girl. She climbed onto the bed next to Vivian and held it for them both to see.

"Aren't you a talented little girl," Vivian praised her. "Is it a picture of the new house?"

Louisa nodded, indicating the three stick figures standing upon a row of green zigzags. "That's me, Mummy and Aunt Jamie."

Vivian studied the picture a while, before glancing at Mia. "You back with Brian, love?"

"What?"

"Brian – Louisa's father. It's about time you started courting again."

Jamie sniggered from across the room, though it was more impulsive than mocking.

"I think you mean Nathan," Mia told her. "Brian was mine and Jamie's dad."

"Oh, that's right. *Brian, Nathan ...*" Vivian spoke as if stamping the names into her memory. She might as well have etched them into sand, for it was only a matter of time before the tide came and washed them away.

"And, no," Mia stated, "Nate and I aren't together."

"Who's that, then?" Vivian pointed to the picture.

Mia leaned forwards to get a closer look, the chair tipping onto its front legs. In the top window of the crayoned house, there was a black outline of a face. It had droopy, O-shaped eyes and its mouth was a hard straight line, the only colour from the paper behind. Mia hadn't noticed it before, having only managed a quick glance in the time gap between arriving home from work and setting off to see Vivian, but the fact that she'd seen a resemblance to Nathan was comical enough.

"That's the shadow man." Louisa answered the question on the verge of everyone's lips. "He comes into my room at night. He's tall and ugly and his breath smells like poo."

Mia swapped glances with her sister, as if they'd developed a psychic bond generated by sheer mortification. Vivian's gravelly laughter filled the bedroom.

"You kiddies and your imaginations!" she said, tousling the girl's hair. "Our family curse, is that – just ask your great Uncle Bill."

"Uncle Billy's gone to hell," Louisa told her.

Vivian's smile melted into her creped flesh, and her eyes hopped between her daughters like frogs on a hot stove. "W-what ...? Billy's *dead?*"

Though Mia's first instinct was to console her mother, they'd had this conversation countless times and it always ended the same way.

"W-when did this happen? Why did no one tell me?" Vivian's lips were quivering now, her eyes barely visible behind the build-up of fluid.

Mia said, "We did tell you. You forgot, that's all."

"I wouldn't forget something like that!" Vivian pushed her knuckles into her eye sockets and let out short, broken sobs. Her body juddered to the point that Louisa was almost knocked off the bed.

"Have I been bad?" the girl asked Mia.

Unwilling to cause her mother any further distress, Mia shook her head. "It's not your fault. Do me a favour and fetch those biscuits from the dressing table, please."

Louisa did as she was told and returned with a tin of Victoria biscuits. Jamie was on the bed now, her arm coiled around Vivian's shoulders.

"It's okay, Mum," she whispered soothingly. "Please, don't cry."

Mia saw the wetness in her sister's eyes but found that her own were dry. For her, it was like witnessing an accident on the television: she sympathised with the victims and might even recoil at the gore, but the screen allowed her to distance herself – similar to her mother's illness – because she knew it was an illusion. She knew the trauma wouldn't last.

Opening the tin of biscuits, Mia let Louisa pick one out for herself and then placed it on the bed next to Vivian. "Have a biccy, Mum, I promise you'll feel better for it," she said.

Vivian gradually moved her hands away from her face, tears glistening in the premature lines on her skin. She took a biscuit between equally damp fingers and had a tiny bite.

"Mmm," she said, munching away like a guinea pig. "Chocolate shortcake – my favourite."

***

"Do you think Mum's going to be okay?" Jamie stood, cross-armed, in the kitchen doorway with her head resting against the wooden frame.

"She's just had to leave her home of twenty-five years," Mia said, while filling the kettle. "It's a big change for anyone, let alone someone in her condition."

"But you said she was fine when you saw her the other day."

"Yeah, as fine as she could have been. You and I both know it's only going to get worse."

Louisa slipped past Jamie on her way into the kitchen and placed an empty glass onto the table. "Mummy, why do cats drink milk?"

"I have no idea." Mia used her thumb to wipe off her daughter's milk moustache. "Maybe it's just the way God made them."

"Can we get a cat?"

"It wouldn't be fair on Casey, would it? You know she hates the things."

"But Casey's this big!" Louisa stretched out her arms to their widest, but in reality the nine-year-old bitch was bigger than her entire body.

"Some people are afraid of spiders and they're tiny," Mia pointed out. "Anyway, hasn't Brenda next door got a cat? I'm sure she'd let you play with it if you asked her nicely."

"That's Dillon's cat. She's called Tabby."

"Oh. Does Dillon live nearby, then?"

Louisa shrugged.

"What's that," said Jamie, "Lou's got a boyfriend?"

"*Pleh!*" Louisa scrunched her features while making a spitting sound, as if she'd just had a taste of her first vindaloo.

Mia fetched a pan from one of the cupboards and laid it on the stove. "Do you want to go and wash your hands, Lou? Tea will be ready in five, it's pasta and meatballs."

"Yummy!" Louisa had already recovered from the boyfriend suggestion.

Jamie said, "Don't pile my plate up, I'm still feeling kinda grotty. You'd get more sleep in Sheffield Cemetery than you do in this place, and it's probably warmer."

"I know it's a little on the creepy side, but we can nip into town on Sunday and pick up some stuff for the decorating. Louisa's back at school next week so you'll need something to keep yourself busy."

"Oh, what a fulfilling life I have," Jamie said sarcastically. There was a chiming sound from inside her jeans' pocket, and she pulled out her mobile. "Kerry's just texted me, are you still cool with her coming over at the weekend?"

"Sure, as long as you behave yourselves around Louisa."

"Course." Putting the phone away, Jamie did a visual sweep of the room. "Where's Casey got to anyway? She usually turns into a stalker at tea time."

"She's been digging up the garden for the last half hour," Mia replied, while stirring the meatballs and sauce. Through the misted window, she could see the dog at the far edge of the garden beneath a crippled elder tree, half-buried amongst a spaghetti ball of brambles. Her front paws raked furiously at the weeds, clumps of soil flying around like shrapnel.

Jamie shrugged. "Maybe she's trying to do us a favour."

"She's scared of the shadow man," Louisa remarked.

Mia turned abruptly. She'd forgotten all about that bloody picture, which Vivian had insisted on sticking to her bedroom wall. "Louisa Reynolds, will you stop this nonsense? You might find it funny but I don't want you talking like that in front of Grandma again, you know she's been poorly."

"But –"

Mia aimed the wooden spatula at her, blobs of tomato sauce splashing the tiles. "I don't want to hear it. Now, go and fetch Casey inside and then wash your hands before tea."

Huffing, Louisa flounced over to the back door, her ponytail swinging rambunctiously behind her. Mia returned to the simmering pan, shaking her head. "What's with her lately? I knew it'd be tough uprooting her, but this ..."

"You really think she's making it up?" Even the rumbling kettle couldn't disguise the solemnity of Jamie's words.

"You know what Louisa's like, she only has to get a whiff of something and it sticks like horse shit. I'm sure that Dillon must have said something to her about Uncle Billy."

"Well, he did die in this house – maybe it's him floating around up there. Louisa wouldn't even recognise him, would she?"

Mia looked at her sister crookedly. "There're no such things as ghosts, Jay."

The kettle clicked as it reached its peak. Despite the muggy air, Mia was gripped by an arctic chill that seemed to be coming from within.

Heading over to the kettle, she mumbled, "And if there is, what the hell am I supposed to do about it?"

CHAPTER SIX

It was late afternoon when there was a lively *rat-a-tat* on the front door. Mia emerged from the kitchen, wiping her hands on a tea towel before greeting the visitor.

"Kerry – I wasn't expecting you for another couple of hours," she said. "I thought I was picking you up from the station?"

"Yeah, I decided to catch an earlier train in case I got lost along the way. I wasn't sure if you'd be back from work yet so I jumped into a taxi," explained the teenager. Her short hair was dyed a deep mahogany, but in the six years Mia had known her she must have experimented with more colours than boyfriends – and according to Jamie, they'd both lost count of those. While her hair matched her vivacity for life, she had the kind of plain features that suited anything.

"Hey, Kez!" Jamie came breezing out of the living room and wrapped her arms around the taller girl's shoulders, as if it was some kind of toll before allowing her through the front door.

Kerry dumped her suitcase down in the hall while gazing around at the half-stripped walls. "Jeez, when you said 'granny pad' I didn't think you meant one that had been dead for fifty years."

Jamie chuckled. "It smelled like it, too, when we first arrived."

"Nice." Kerry wrinkled her nose.

"I was just about to get the tea on, shall I make extra?" Mia asked the girl.

"Yes, please." Kerry licked her lips hungrily.

"Right, you two can make a start on the spuds when you're ready."

"Charming!" Jamie grabbed her friend's suitcase off the floor. "Come on, I'll show you my room. Down in a bit, sis!"

The girls raced upstairs like kids to an ice cream van. Mia headed back to the kitchen and was about to finish washing the dishes when she heard Louisa hollering from outside, "Tabby? Here, kitty!"

Leaving the tea towel on the worktop, Mia went to investigate. "What are you doing, baby?"

"Dillon's lost his cat," said Louisa.

Whistling from next door's garden was accompanied by a rattling sound, and Mia could see a skinny boy tiptoeing about with a tub of Whiskas biscuits. She jumped when Brenda popped up from behind the fence.

"Hello! I don't suppose you've seen a small tabby cat milling about, have you?" She spoke with her wonted gaiety.

"I haven't, sorry," Mia replied.

"Can I go and help Dillon look?" asked Louisa.

"Yes, if it's okay with Brenda?" Mia glanced quizzically at her neighbour.

"Of course, I bet Dillon's fed up of hanging around with us oldies anyway – isn't that right, mate?" Brenda turned to the boy, who grunted and shrugged.

"Go on, then." Mia lifted Louisa over the dividing fence. "And don't go disappearing because your tea will be ready soon. Stay where I can see you, all right?"

"Okay!" Louisa pelted off down the garden with Dillon by her side.

"They seem to be getting on well," Mia noted. "Does Dillon come here often?"

"Yes, my sister and I do shift work up at the hospital so we help her out whenever we can. His dad is in the military."

"That must be hard on them both," Mia empathised. "Strange question, but does Tabby live with you or Dillon? It's just that our dog has been a bit off recently and she's always had a problem with cats."

"Oh, that thing follows Dillon wherever he goes. I don't let it in the house because of Wesley's allergies, but she's usually fine with other animals."

"Must be a territorial thing," Mia decided. "Anyway, I'd better make a start on the tea. I'll be back for Louisa in half an hour or so, but if you get fed up before then just give me a shout."

"I'm sure they'll be fine out here. See you later."

"Bye," said Mia, then she went back indoors.

***

Shuffle, shuffle.

Mia stirred in bed, unsure of what had disturbed her slumber. In her semiconscious state, she became aware of a scratching sound. She didn't realise she'd opened her eyes until the crisp outline of the door cut through the gloom. She couldn't tell if the sounds were coming from inside or outside the room.

She listened harder. There it was again – constant now, like a giant rat gnawing on wood. A loud bang on the opposite wall was followed by muffled giggles. Mia got out of bed and opened the door a fraction. A dark shape lingered by her feet. That explained the scratching.

"What's the matter, girl?" Mia opened the door fully.

Casey trotted down the landing, stopping outside Louisa's bedroom. Mia could hear the dog's short, rapid breaths, and when it started pacing a small patch of carpet outside the door, she sensed an urgency that drove her forwards. The door was ajar, and she gently pushed it open so an estuary of darkness flowed into the room. She felt for the light switch and the shadows soon dispersed, leaving her staring at an empty bed. Bathroom: that was her first thought. But Louisa never relieved herself without turning on the light – not since Casey had developed a habit of drinking loo water. When she'd asked her dad why dogs did this, he'd replied that it helped to scare away the toilet monster that came to bite people's bums.

Mia proceeded to the bathroom, regardless. Moonbeams filtered through the frosted window, as if aiding her search. No sign of her in there.

Turning round, she saw the yellow shaft of light beneath Jamie's bedroom door. She knocked briefly before entering in time to see Kerry shoot up off the inflatable mattress, one hand concealed behind her back. Mia scanned over the bottles of WKD on the bedside cabinet, half of which were empty.

"What is it?" Jamie spoke irritably.

"Lou's not in here, is she?"

"Yeah, she's hiding in the wardrobe with a bottle of voddy." This was followed by snorts of unrestrained laughter.

"I'm serious, she's not in her room," Mia persisted.

"Well, she ain't in here. Have you looked downstairs?" Jamie said.

"Not yet." Mia rubbed her arms as a cold breeze brushed over her. She noticed the curtains swaying and asked, "Why have you got the window open?"

"Sorry, I didn't realise it was illegal."

"Whatever – keep the noise down, will you." It wasn't a request.

Kerry apologised for them both. Mia closed the door and hurried downstairs, scouting the living room and lastly the kitchen.

"Louisa?" The pressure in her chest mounted as she scanned the noiseless room. She slapped the light switch, and the fluorescents pinged to life as if she was standing in some kind of laboratory. Louisa was curled up asleep in the dog basket with her thumb tucked in her mouth. Her heart rate decelerating, Mia went over and gently shook the girl.

"Wake up, baby," she whispered.

Louisa groaned and opened one eye, keeping it squinted as the white beams scalded her retina.

"What are you doing down here?" Mia asked.

"Noises ... in room." Louisa's voice was tired and croaky.

"It was only Jamie and Kerry banging about, I've told them to be quiet."

"Shadow man there."

"No, he isn't. Besides, where's Casey supposed to sleep?"

Moaning again, Louisa hooked an arm over her head and buried her face in the crease of her elbow. Mia didn't know if it was a reaction to herself or the light.

"Come on, you can't stay down here." As Mia hoisted up the limp body, she felt wetness on her arm. There was a huge damp stain on the front of Louisa's pyjama bottoms, and judging by the musty smell it must have been a couple of hours old.

Without a word, Mia carried Louisa upstairs. She peeled off the soggy bottoms, rinsed her down in the shower and then helped her into a fresh pair of pyjamas. All the while Jamie remained in her bedroom, oblivious – or most likely uncaring – as to the hassle they'd caused.

"You can sleep in my bed tonight." Mia guided the dopey girl to her bedroom and lifted the covers while she crawled beneath them. By the time she'd finished tucking her in, Louisa had already drifted off.

Mia made for her daughter's room, where she quickly stripped the bed sheets and gathered them in her arms. Subdued voices from across the landing escalated into high-pitched cackles, accompanied by the occasional thud. No wonder Louisa had freaked out – it sounded like there was an army of poltergeists in the house.

Waddling across the landing with the sheets piled up to her neck, she shouldered Jamie's bedroom door so it swung open. Kerry lay half sprawled on the carpet, her legs hooked over the edge of the bed as if she was sitting on a capsized chair. She tilted her head back as Mia stormed into the room, giving her a skewed glance.

"I'm serious now, will you two shut the fuck up?" Mia snapped. "Louisa's pissed herself."

Jamie spat a mouthful of alcopop back into the bottle. She wiped her mouth before scowling at Mia. "Gross! What the hell has that got to do with us?"

"Because you're making a racket and she's going on about that bloody shadow thing again."

Kerry endeavoured to sit up but swayed with the effort. "What sa-ddo thing?" she slurred.

"Louisa reckons we've got a ghost," Jamie said. "You should have seen the picture she drew for Mum, it freaked us the hell out!"

Kerry sobered. "Oh, great! You could have told me that after I'd left."

Mia rolled her eyes when the girls erupted into maniacal laughter. "Anyway, she's in with me tonight while I put this lot for washing." She inclined her head towards the stagnant heap in her arms. "Don't mention any of this to her tomorrow, okay? With any luck she'll have forgotten about it."

"That makes two of us." Jamie raised the bottle as if to say 'cheers'.

Mia said, "Remember you're supposed to be looking after Louisa tomorrow. I can't afford to get into shit at work."

"All right, killjoy, now get that disgusting shit out of my room."

And Mia did just that, waiting until she'd reached the stairs before cursing to herself rather than at her temperamental sibling. It wasn't often Jamie got plastered, but when she did it seemed to affect her mouth rather than her brain – if she wasn't shouting from it then she was bawling, sometimes both simultaneously. Besides, Jamie was under no obligation to babysit her niece and they both knew it.

In the kitchen, Mia shoved the soiled linen into the washing machine and then loaded it with detergent. The whirring of the barrel started up, and she switched off the light before heading back to bed. Wandering down the hallway, she almost bumped into the silhouette lurking at the bottom of the stairs.

"Jesus!" Mia darted back, hand spread over her chest, but even under the veil of night she could tell that it wasn't Christ.

Before she could say anything more, Jamie fell into her arms, hands clinching the back of her vest. Mia felt her slight form trembling and knew she was crying.

"Hey, there's no need to get upset." She combed her fingers through the girl's silky tresses. "It was a silly argument, we've had plenty of them."

Jamie pulled away and wiped her nose with the back of her hand. "I'm such a bitch." She sniffed, her breath scented like blueberries.

"Yeah, you are," Mia said lightly.

"I'm sorry. Are you pissed at me?"

"Nah, at least one of us still knows how to have a good time. Besides, you'll suffer enough for it in the morning."

They both chuckled and, together, they returned to their beds.

CHAPTER SEVEN

Guests filled the Great Hall, a medley of suits, garish frocks and elaborate hats lined up along the adorned banquet tables. Chatter and laughter bounced off the high walls, but Mia couldn't have felt further from the revelry if she was an astronaut floating around in space. She slid her mobile out of her blazer pocket and checked for any missed calls.

"That's the sixth time I've caught you staring at that thing."

Mia glanced up to find Angela standing beside her with a skyscraper of a wedding cake balanced in her hands. She wasn't required to attend events at the manor but often assisted along with a dozen serving staff. Sometimes Mia thought she got more peace at work than she did at home with her tearaway twins.

Mia tried to smile, but her jaw muscles must have disconnected. "Sorry, I've got this really weird feeling. Jamie had a mate stay over last night and they were hitting the booze pretty hard. Maybe I shouldn't have left Louisa alone with them ..."

"Jamie's a responsible girl, I'm sure she'd have been in touch if there were any problems."

"If you'd said that a few months ago then I might have believed you. Sometimes I feel like I'm living with Jekyll and Hyde."

"If you're that worried then give her a ring, no one will miss you for two minutes."

"Yeah, I think I will. Back in a sec."

Mia took the corridor that led from the Great Hall into reception and continued to the frontal courtyard. She typed the landline number into her mobile. Not long after ringing out, she was greeted by her daughter's voice.

"Hi, baby, it's Mum. Are you okay?" Mia said.

"Yeah."

"What are you doing?"

"Playing cards."

"Are you winning?"

"No, Kerry's cheating."

"Oh, dear. Is Aunt Jamie there?"

"Umm ... she's upstairs."

"Can you take the phone to her, please?"

"She's coming now."

Mia heard a rustling sound, followed by a half-second of silence and then: "Yeah?"

"It's only me, I just wanted to check that everything was okay." A gust of wind crackled into the receiver. Mia waited until it had passed before continuing, "Have you had tea yet?"

"Yep, we ordered a pizza and then hung out in front of the TV. Did you want me to put Louisa to bed before you get back?"

"If she gets sleepy then take her up, but I should be home in a few hours anyway. Thanks again for doing this, Jay, I owe you one."

"Too right. Laters."

"Bye."

Dropping the phone back into her pocket, Mia returned to the manor. Angela made eye contact with her from the opposite end of the Great Hall. Mia smiled and nodded.

***

"Kerry?"

The door handle jiggled. A fist banged against the wood.

"What's going on in there? Why have you locked the door? ... *Kez!*"

Kerry tried to respond to her friend's fraught cries, but her stomach muscles convulsed and that bitterness flooded her mouth once more. In one great heave, half-digested food sloshed into the toilet bowl like diarrhea.

"Jesus, you'd better not be making a mess in there or else my sister will flip." Jamie's voice was low, but stern enough to penetrate the wood

43

between them. "That was her on the phone, she'll be back in a few hours. Did you hear me?"

Kerry dragged her head out of the toilet and used the seat to support her upper body. It felt like there was a block of cement balanced on her shoulders, and her quaking legs threatened to give way. She slumped down against the wall, the tiles like a cold compress against her throbbing skull. Her hair lay pasted to her clammy face, slimy strands adhering to the brownish matter crusted around her chin and mouth. Yet still she shivered in the sub-zero air.

The possibilities streamed through her mind: a stomach bug, delayed hangover – even food poisoning, but she didn't see anyone else honking their guts out. It felt like an acid bomb had gone off inside her; either that or she'd swallowed a match and all of the alcohol from last night had combusted. Unless ...

"Idiot, I told you not to smoke that crap."

Kerry didn't know whether it was her subconscious speaking or an actual voice, but whichever it was had a point. It must have been a dodgy batch – that cousin of hers was heading for a mouthful of fist once she got home.

"G-give me a second," Kerry groaned, her thin voice scarcely leaving the tiny room.

Jamie's incessant knocking told her that she hadn't been heard, which wasn't surprising over the dog's howls, but she didn't try again. As she crawled past the toilet, the chunks of regurgitated pizza bobbing about in a solution of bile and water reminded Kerry of her dad's famous vegetable stew, which she would never look at in the same way again. She groped for the sink and used it to haul herself up. Turning on the cold tap, she slurped a handful of water and swilled out the acrid taste in her mouth. As she spat it into the sink, a fetid stench almost disgorged the remnants of her stomach. *What if something had ruptured internally?* she thought.

Wait ... she sniffed the air ... it seemed to have pervaded the entire room. It engulfed her like the fumes from an exhaust, practically suffocated her. The reek of burning carcasses.

Kerry pressed the back of her hand to her nose, dipping her head in revulsion. That's when she caught sight of her stomach. At first she thought it was bloated – true, it was more or less empty by now – but the muscles could have been inflamed from all the retching. It was like looking into one of those mirrors you see at funfairs that make everything appear warped and distorted.

She slid her hand down to her belly and held it there a few seconds. Ten seconds. Twenty seconds.

"What the ... Oh, God!"

"Kez, what is it? What's wrong?" She heard her friend's voice from beyond the door.

"H-how is this h-happening?" Kerry pressed her stomach harder, as if to flatten the growing bulge. Nothing happened.

Reluctantly, she lifted her T-shirt and staggered back with a short, sharp cry. Her belly had swollen to the size of a football, stretch marks splitting the flesh down from her navel like a burst zip. Wailing now, she attempted to pinch the lesions shut with her fingers but was unable to get a grip on the slippery, crimson-washed surface. If she hadn't fallen into a state of hysteria then she might have puzzled over why she felt little to no pain, but when something kicked against her palm she quickly withdrew her hand.

Oh, no ... oh, Holy-Jesus-Christ!

Her stomach was actually moving, like a tangle of limbs writhing beneath a bed sheet. Something was inside her. *Something* had invaded her body, and it was fighting to get out.

No sooner had the 'growth' spawned than a crumb of reason, or what she deemed as such, formed in the chaos. The nausea, the stretch marks, the chafing sensation in her womb ...

"Not again," she blubbered. "I can't take it!"

Kerry lunged for the cabinet above the sink and tore open its door, bloody fingerprints streaking the paintwork. She rifled through the lotions and potions, flinging them out aimlessly; pausing only to check inside the packet of disposable razors for something more appropriate, before tossing it over her shoulder.

"Shit!" She slammed the cabinet door with such vigour that it bounced open again and the interior mirror, which was already weakened by a crack running through the centre, exploded into the sink below.

A crippling pain zipped through her abdomen, and she keeled onto her knees. She was aware of a resonant hammering over her sobs and put it down to her heartbeat crashing in her ears until she heard a voice bawling from outside, "Kerry, for fuck's sake, open the door!"

The muscle spasms began in her womb, intensifying like a bolt gun entering through the crevice in between her legs. The thing - monster, alien or whatever unholy creature it was - was trying to dig its way out via the easiest way it could.

'Destroy it.'

Kerry's head shot up so fast that she gave herself a crick in the neck. She glanced around to uncover the source of the voice. She couldn't tell whether it was male or female, old or young. They were just words. Inside her head. Maybe even her intuition.

'Destroy it, before *it* destroys you.'

With deep, fitful breaths, Kerry plucked an icicle of glass out of the sink - the longest and sharpest she could find - and stared at the object as though she'd discovered a pistol in her boyfriend's underwear drawer. The walls seemed to close in on her, swamping her in a murky darkness until she was aware of nothing but herself, the weapon and the parasite in her gut. She pressed the tip of the glass an inch or so below her belly button. Through her tears and blood she could just make out the protuberant shapes in her stomach, like tiny fists trying to punch their ways out, because they knew what was coming even if Kerry didn't. It wasn't as if she had a plan - that required a degree of coherent thinking - but at least killing the thing would save her from being mutilated from the inside out.

Squeezing her eyes shut, her hands tightened around the glass shard. The surge of adrenaline made her numb to the smooth, razor edges slicing into her fingers.

Too bad, because it was the only thing that might have stopped her.

CHAPTER EIGHT

Mia arrived at Leeds General Infirmary just after eight, having received a jumbled phone call from her sister over an hour ago. Weekend drunks were already piling up in the A& E reception, and after being directed to the trauma unit, she finally found Jamie and Louisa sitting in the waiting area like a couple of rescued orphans.

Jamie was on her feet as soon as she saw Mia coming around the corner. She met her halfway, grabbing her in a bear hug and holding on as if they were aboard the Titanic.

"I got away as soon as I could," said Mia. "How is she?"

Jamie finally let go of her, red-rimmed eyes averting Mia's stare.

"Oh, no." Mia's voice became husky due to the constriction in her throat. "She's not –"

Jamie shook her head and pointed to a set of double doors to the left. "They took her through there. She's been gone for ages but no one will tell me anything."

"What exactly happened?"

"I don't know, one minute we were having a laugh and then ..."

"Oh, please don't tell me she was hammered – not tonight."

"It wasn't like that, I swear. She just locked herself in the bathroom and started freaking out. Then it went silent and I didn't know what to do, so I called for an ambulance."

"People like Kerry don't start slicing themselves up for no reason." Mia's face hardened, as if the remark had stirred another thought. "Hang on, was all this going on when I called home earlier? Did you get *my* daughter to lie for you?"

47

Jamie swallowed, her voice apologetic. "I kept her out of the way as much as I could, but you know what she's like. I honestly didn't think it was that bad until the paramedics kicked the door in and ... I saw ..."

Mia spat out a breath of air, shaking her head as if to signal that she'd heard enough, before rushing to Louisa. Their last family trip to the hospital was when Vivian had set fire to the kitchen and ended up with second-degree burns, which only contributed to Mia's impatience. She hadn't enjoyed the lingering smell of old food, urine and disinfectant then and she hated it even more now.

"Hi, baby." She crouched in front of Louisa, taking one of her hands while sweeping a loose curl off the girl's face. "Have you got a cuddle for Mummy?"

Louisa glanced up without lifting her head, as if she'd received a phantom touch but could see nothing but the air in front of her. After the night's horrors, Mia doubted her scarred eyes would want to see anything again.

"Mia, I'm so sorry." Jamie spoke from behind them. "I didn't plan for any of this to happen, you've got to believe me."

As Mia turned back to her sister, not necessarily with a response in mind, the double doors to their left swung open and a man dressed in blue overalls stepped into the waiting area. He glanced at both of them in turn, keeping his observation on Mia.

"Are you a relative of Kerry Matthews?" he said.

Mia stood up. "No, I – we're – her friends. Is Kerry going to be okay?"

"Do you have any idea when her parents will be arriving?" The doctor skirted the question.

"Er ... no, I –"

First came the stampede of footsteps, and then two more bodies strode into the waiting area from the same direction in which Mia had emerged only minutes ago.

"I'm Kerry's mother," said a dumpy woman, who was wearing a red trench coat and knee-length boots. Her fringe was swept back into a silver-streaked quiff, as if she was trying to set a trend for older parents.

Lisa Matthews waltzed up to the doctor without acknowledging either Mia or Jamie. Mr Matthews managed a subtle nod behind the shadow of his wife.

"Where's my daughter? When can I see her?" demanded Lisa.

The doctor removed the surgical mask that had been draped around his neck, the material rustling as he twiddled it between his fingers. "We've managed to stop the bleeding and repair any damage to the abdomen. Fortunately, no major organs were hit but there will be significant scarring."

Lisa blinked, although it was so long before she opened her eyes that she could have taken a mini snooze. Then she began scratching her head like a befuddled chimp. "Sorry, doctor, are you referring to damage caused by a fall or ...?"

Mia and Jamie exchanged a furtive glance, while the doctor answered with his usual candour, "We also had to stitch up some minor lacerations on Kerry's hands, which we believe were caused by the glass fragment. This, along with the angle of the entry wound, strongly suggests that the injury was self-inflicted."

It was Mr Matthews who spoke next. "You're saying she did this ... to herself?" His face was more distraught than his tone suggested.

The doctor nodded. "I'm afraid so. Can I ask who it was that called for the ambulance?"

Mia looked to Jamie, which everyone including the doctor took as the answer. It was a few moments before Jamie confirmed this.

"Did or has Kerry ever taken any illegal drugs?" was the doctor's next question.

"No." She answered far too quickly for it to have sounded genuine. "I- I mean, we had a few drinks last night but she was fine this morning – wasn't she, Mia?"

Before Mia could defend her sister, Lisa had already butted in, still pretending that neither of them existed. "My daughter has been brought up to know better than that, and I certainly don't allow alcohol in *my* house."

"I'm not disputing your parenting skills, Mrs Matthews, but Kerry was very delusional when she was brought in to us," the doctor informed her. "She seemed to think something was ... attacking her."

"She was *attacked*?" Lisa practically screeched the word, and there was a noticeable lack of colour in her cheeks. Only then did Mr Matthews extend an arm around her shoulders.

"No, no – that's not what I'm saying." The doctor held up a placating hand. "Perhaps this is best left until Kerry comes around from the anaesthesia, she might be able to give you some clarity. The important thing is that she's going to make a full recovery. The hospital psychiatrist will also need to speak to her at some point before she leaves, but it's just routine. Hopefully, you can have Kerry home in a couple of days or so."

"Oh, thank the lord – and you for all your help, doctor." Lisa clasped both of the man's hands, waggling rather than shaking them.

"May we see her now?" asked Mr Matthews.

"She's being moved to the recovery ward as we speak. I'll get one of the nurses to show you the way." His lips tweaked into a barely there smile, then he headed back to the double doors.

"Oh, and just so you know ..." he waited until he had the couple's attention, "we have done blood tests so if Kerry did take something then it will show up." The last part was directed mainly at Jamie who, ironically, was the only person that didn't notice.

Eyes to the ground, hand over her mouth, Jamie continued to shake her head, as if struggling to accept anything that had happened despite being an eye witness. As soon as the doctor had left, Lisa was virtually on top of the girl, her scarlet face reflecting the colour of her jacket.

"You heard the man," she hissed, lips tight around her clenched teeth. "For Christ's sake, tell them what you know, you silly girl. Did your mother never teach you that those wretched substances can have a lasting effect on the brain? With the condition she's in, I thought you'd be a bit more cautious of such things."

Tears seeped through the gaps in Jamie's fingers and plopped onto the shiny floor. If Mr Matthews hadn't restrained his wife then Mia might not have been able to prevent her fist from pounding the woman's snout. Intimidating a teenage girl was one thing – not least one she was legally responsible for – but to bring *Vivian* into it ...

Mia sidestepped in front of Jamie so she was standing nose to nose with the woman, realising for the first time how short Lisa was. "Back off, will you?" The words were surprisingly even and controlled. "I know this must be a difficult time and I'm sorry for what's happened, but Jamie has had a shock, too, and shouting at each other isn't going to help anyone – least of all Kerry."

Lisa focused her glacial eyes onto Mia, only now they were laced with disgrace that she would dare to defend her drug-dealing sister. "My daughter is in a critical state. I can't ask her what happened, can I? How would you feel if it was your little one?"

"Come on, love, let's not make a scene." Mr Mathews spoke meekly.

Mia said, "I'm not happy about this either, but it was an accident and, to be blunt, the only person responsible for Kerry is Kerry. If she did take something then Jamie hardly forced her."

And if you'd seen what she was necking last night then you'd know she was no flipping amateur, she wanted to add.

Lisa backed off a little, but her face and body remained locked as if cast in an iron shell. Mia continued, "Now, I'm going to take Jamie home. If or when I have any more information then I'll call the hospital straight away. If you could give Kerry our love when she wakes up then we'd really appreciate it."

Jamie objected, "But I want to see Kerry –"

"Not now, for pity's sake, we can come back another time." Mia extended a hand to her daughter. "Come on, Lou, we're leaving."

Louisa hopped off the chair and dawdled over to the group of adults. Mia lifted the girl onto her hip, supporting her with both arms to suppress the temptation to swing for Lisa Matthews on the way out of the building.

***

It looked like there had been a massacre – either that or someone had menstruated all over the floor. Red handprints gripped the edge of the sink, the fragmentary footsteps trailing out onto the landing acting like a backwards projector into the mind's eye. Mia's toenails curled inwards to the point of severing her toes but, in a repulsed sort of way, she was thankful for the overwhelming stench of vomit that acted like an invisible screen, preventing her from entering the bathroom. She'd flushed the toilet several times already, but it felt as though the acidity had singed her nasal hairs.

With the bowl growing heavy in her rubber-gloved hands, Mia went to take a deep breath – stopped herself – then strolled into the bathroom. Kneeling with the bowl by her side, she dipped a sponge into the diluted bleach and then wrung it out over the viscid puddle. The top layer started to dissolve, turning the water a pinkish-red, but the underside remained caked to the vinyl. At least the fumes from the bleach had helped to cleanse her nostrils.

Three bowlfuls later, the only trace of the incident was a faint stain that had retained the shape of the original puddle. It was more an inconvenience than anything, seeing as plans for a new floor would have to be brought forwards. The same went for the landing carpet, although the splodges blended in slightly better with the accumulation of old stains.

"How's it going?" Jamie loitered in the bathroom doorway as if she, too, was a victim to that obstructive odour.

"Perhaps you'd know if you'd bothered to lend a hand." Mia spoke curtly.

Jamie looked as though she'd come face to face with a gangrenous wound. "I ... can't. Sorry."

Mia tore off the gloves and slammed them into the sink to dry off. "You think this is how I wanted to spend my evening, scrubbing up someone else's blood and puke? Louisa's hardly spoken three sentences since we left the hospital, and one of those was to insist on taking a piss in the back garden like some kind of bloody animal." Mia didn't know what was worse: that or the fact she'd allowed it.

"I've said I'm sorry. What, do you want it broadcasting?"

"I don't want apologies, I want an explanation. If there are drugs stashed around the house –"

"Of course there aren't! I'm not some junkie, you know."

"So, if it's not down to drugs then what happened? Why would Kerry do that to herself?"

Jamie lowered her gaze, preventing the answer from gleaming through in her eyes. Her lips were apart but no sound came out, as if she was trapped in conflict with her own thoughts. "Kerry went through some stuff a while back – last Christmas. I thought she was over it, but maybe she just hid it well."

"What stuff?" Mia crossed her arms while waiting for a reply. "Come on, I had your back this evening. The least you can do is explain to me how that girl ended up in the state she did."

Another hesitation, and then: "She might have taken something."

"Might?"

Jamie finally met Mia's probing glare. "She got her hands on some weed, okay – from that dickhead cousin of hers. I didn't even know about it until last night."

"Last night ..." The admission jolted Mia's memory. "So, not only were you hammered but you had your heads in fucking Timbuktu?"

"Kerry made a couple of joints but I didn't touch the stuff – that's why the window was open. It was barely enough to get Louisa high, so unless it was spiked with something then I'm as clueless as you are."

"Christ, Jay." Mia turned from the girl, arms flopping hopelessly by her sides. "Well, Mrs Holier-than-thou is going to love it when those blood results come back. What am I supposed to do if she turns up here, shouting the odds? There's no way she'll accept that her 'little angel' was responsible for any of this."

"I'm not asking you to stick up for me," Jamie muttered.

"But I always will because, for some daft reason, I trust you. You do know that?"

Jamie nodded.

"Then, a bit of reciprocation would be nice. If you've got a problem, not necessarily with drugs but with anything, then the only way we're going to keep what's left of this family together is if you talk to me. You're my sister and I'll do whatever I can to support you."

Jamie's eyes melted to the warmth of Mia's tone, and for one brief second, Mia thought she might crumple to her knees in an overflow of tears and confessions.

"There isn't anything, I swear," Jamie said.

With a sigh, although she was about as satisfied as an empty stomach, Mia gave a languid nod. "Right, well, if you're too much of a wimp to help me out here then you might as well get off to bed or whatever it is you're planning on doing tonight."

Without saying anything, Jamie receded from view. A few seconds later, Mia heard the sound of her bedroom door clicking shut. She spent the next ten minutes scrubbing the toilet and bagging up the shards of broken mirror from the sink. A part of her wondered if they'd get a visit from the police tomorrow, especially if Kerry maintained that she'd been attacked. Still, the paramedics had had to literally force open the bathroom door – something else she'd need to get fixed – and it would have taken Spider-Man to climb up through the window.

Mia shook her head, her empty laughter suffusing the bathroom as if it was coming from someone else. She started to gather everything to take downstairs when there was a sharp prick in the sole of her foot.

"Ouch!"

She lifted it off the ground to discover a glass diamond tipped with blood. Hopping about, she looked for somewhere to place the items before eventually setting them down on the floor. As the blood tears dripped from the puncture wound, she balanced herself by holding onto the edge of the bathtub. She swung her leg over the top of it to prevent more staining on the vinyl, and her ankle fell into the grip of a talon-like hand.

Mia didn't have time to scream – to do anything, no matter how futile – for one almighty wrench brought her splashing into the crimson water. The edge of the tub jabbed into her spine, sending a bolt of pain coursing through her. She opened her mouth in a reflexive cry, allowing the bitter liquid to flood her lungs.

Something clambered on top of her, weighting down her shoulders with those long, knobbly fingers. Mia lashed out blindly, her hands entwining themselves in what felt like straggly seaweed before they came upon something hard and leathery ... then something squidgy, about the size of a ping-pong ball ... there were two of them.

Her oxygen-deprived brain swelling against the sides of her skull, Mia buried her thumbs into the thing's eye sockets. A tinny wail vibrated through the water like seismic waves. As her shoulders were freed, she fumbled for the sides of the bathtub and heaved herself up, choking and gasping noisy lungfuls of air. If keeping her eyes shut was an option then she would have done, but as she blinked away the redness that stung her eyes, the droopy breasts flapping about over an almost fleshless ribcage was the last and possibly most grotesque thing she expected to see. Even in her frantic state, Mia knew that whatever it was straddling her was far too light, too emaciated for the ferocious strength it possessed – in human biology anyway.

But there was more incredulity to come, for when it moved its hands away from its pain-creased face, Mia's instincts to pummel the thing – along with a single definable emotion – vanished for one standstill second.

"*Mum ...?*" She barely spluttered out the word before the she-monster hissed and lunged at her again, splayed hands aiming for her throat. It may have had Vivian's face, but that's as far as the likeness went. If there was a single doubt in her mind otherwise then she wouldn't have done what she did next.

Bunching her fingers into a fist, Mia thumped it in the cheekbone. Unaware and, frankly, uncaring as to the damage she'd caused the recoiling freak, she dragged herself out of the bathtub.

"Jam –" she began to shout, but her foot skidded on the waterlogged floor and she toppled onto her front, forehead smashing into the vinyl.

Through the cloud of black and white sparkles dancing before her, Mia could just make out something slithering over the edge of the bathtub, like a serpent that had swallowed a bag of bones. Next came the freak's head, which seemed to be jutting from its neck at a sickeningly unnatural angle – had she really hit it that hard?

A torso appeared, and she realised the 'serpent' had actually been an arm. It wasn't just the head that appeared deformed; all of its limbs were twisted out of alignment. Every joint buckled and bent as though it had been in a horrendous car accident. Even with the weeping willow hairdo veiling its face, Mia couldn't forget the dripping features she'd laid eyes on a moment ago; after all, they'd been engraved into her memory since birth.

As the thing that posed as her mother scuttled towards her like a contortionist crab, hands and feet squelching in its own puddles, the flurry of questions – what was it? Where had it come from? Why was it there? Was it even real? – were obliterated by two gut-munching fears. Fears that would soon be alone, unprotected and, worst of all, oblivious.

"D-don't ... hurt ... them."

It was the last thing Mia said, before unconsciousness swept over her like a black sail.

CHAPTER NINE

An interminable screeching resonated through Mia's skull like vibrations from a power drill. Her hands flew up to her ears, and she could feel her temples throbbing from the headache.

"Shut up!" Mia pounded the alarm clock with the base of her fist. It slid off the bedside table and clattered across the floor, the sound fizzling out as if a dying wasp was trapped inside the mechanism. It took her longer than usual to adjust to consciousness, although the silence did nothing for her head. Wiping the drool from her chin, she caught the luminous digits of the upturned clock. 10.30 a.m.

"Bollocks." Mia sprang up in bed like a resurrected corpse, but the sudden wave of nausea dragged her back down. It was her first day off work since they'd moved and she was supposed to be making a start on the decorating, but it felt like she'd been on a week-long pub crawl.

Placing a hand on her forehead, she winced and sucked a sharp intake of air through her teeth, making a kind of hissing sound, and gently prodded the swollen lump. Gradually, memories of last night slotted together like pieces of a nonsensical puzzle: Kerry, the hospital, the abundance of bodily fluids decorating the bathroom and ... Vivian?

"Oh, God." Mia rose again, this time using her elbows for support. She shook her head, slowly at first, but as the memories whizzed through her mind like scenes from a horror film, the action became so vigorous that it sparked something close to a migraine.

The creep in the bathtub. The hideously dislocated limbs. The blood-dyed water.

A nightmare, she assured herself. Her anxieties regarding Vivian must have infected her subconscious. It happened to everyone, especially when stress was added to the equation. The imagination had a habit of amplifying situations, making things seem worse than they actually were.

Almost instinctively, she threw back the bed sheets and checked the sole of her right foot. There it was, as real as she was sitting there now: the blood-crusted wound from where she'd stepped on the glass. But that would mean it hadn't been a dream at all. It meant ...

Holy shit, it had actually happened!

Mia half leaped and half stumbled out of bed, her heart entangled in her bowels, and pelted from the room. She burst into Louisa's bedroom, concerned more by the prospect of an empty bed than startling the girl, but was soon reassured by the little body cocooned in the duvet and the sound of her soft, rhythmic breaths. Mia backed out of the room and tiptoed further down the landing, hugging the wall as if she was being forced to walk a rickety plank.

Stilling her breath, she peeked into the bathroom. The bowl and cleaning products from last night lay in a pile exactly where she'd left them. Not only that, but there wasn't a footprint, puddle or single droplet of evidence that attested to the freak's existence. As for the bathtub: empty. No blood. No naked Vivian. Mia realised for the first time that not only was she wearing yesterday's clothes, but apart from the sweat patches around her armpit and cleavage areas, they were otherwise unblemished.

"Jesus Christ, what's wrong with me?" she said, running her hands down either side of her face.

Mia puffed out her cheeks and blew the air through her mouth, more a sigh than an exhalation, then plodded into the bathroom. After filling the sink with warm water, she peeled off her vest and washed herself down, casting sporadic glances at the bath and each time expecting to see Vivian glaring back at her. She dried herself with a towel and then returned to her bedroom, topless, where she changed into a baggy T-shirt and a pair of jeans. On her way to the door, she caught her reflection in the full-length mirror and almost smiled. As with most of her tops, the material was significantly strained over her double Ds and drew the focus away from the post-baby bump that she'd never bothered to tone up, creating the illusion of a tiny waistline. Adjusting her fringe so it covered the purple dune on her forehead, not unmindful of how pasty she was looking, Mia headed downstairs.

In the kitchen, she made herself a black coffee and a round of toast and then took everything over to the table. Although she didn't particularly enjoy how the silence seemed to exacerbate those nerve-shredding memories, dreams or whatever the hell they were, she thought it best to let the girls sleep in a while longer. She wasn't sure she had the energy or patience to console a traumatised five-year-old – not without a few more caffeine spikes anyway – and Jamie would probably be too ashamed to show her face until next month.

However, fifteen minutes on, her mug was still half-full and the toast looked about as appetising as cardboard slathered with jam – or thick, glutinous blood. Unable to stomach the sweet aroma, Mia pushed away the plate with more force than intended. She closed her eyes as the porcelain smashed against the floor. She might have gone ahead and hurled her mug at the nearest wall if it wasn't for the knock at the front door.

"Who the balls is that?" She spoke as if there was someone else in the room. Scraping back the chair, she stood up too quickly and had to grip the edge of the table until she'd stopped swaying. Part of her wanted to hide until the person at the door had buggered off; but another part of her was desperate for some human interaction, whether it be a sales creep, Jehovah's Witnesses, charity collectors – anything that made her feel a bit more ordinary. A bit more sane.

Mia scurried down the hallway before the visitor disappeared. She went to release the latch on the front door but found that it was already unlocked. *Christ, was that how the mutant had got into the house?* she wondered. She couldn't remember dragging herself into bed, let alone whether or not she'd locked the place up. But there was no way a monstrosity like that could have walked in and attacked her without someone having heard the fracas in the bathroom.

Mia opened the door, cautiously at first, until she saw the freckled face staring at her from the doorstep.

"Hello." Brenda's light, sympathetic tone immediately betrayed the reason for her visit. If it was anyone else, Mia would have slammed the door so hard that they'd be feeling the aftershock for weeks.

"Blimey," Mia scanned up and down the street, "I'm surprised the entire population of Bramley isn't queuing around the block."

"Oh ..." The woman's smile withered away. "I-I'm sorry, I didn't mean to ... I'll come back another time."

"I'm kidding." Mia grinned, although it didn't evince the humour she'd hoped for. "You are here about last night, though?"

"Yes, sort of. I just wanted to make sure you were all okay. No one has sent me over, I promise." Brenda raised one of her hands in a scout's honour.

"Jamie's friend had an accident, but she's going to be fine," Mia explained. "We're more shaken up than anything."

"Yes, I saw someone being wheeled into the ambulance but I wasn't sure who it was. I'm a nurse up at the hospital, you see. In fact, I've got a shift in a few hours so if there's anything I can do?"

"Thanks, but I'll probably be taking Jamie to see her at some point today – that's if she ever decides to get out of bed."

"Oh, she left in a taxi about half an hour ago. Didn't she say anything?"

Mia cast a backwards glance up the stairs, as if she had the gift of X-ray vision. That explained why the door had been left off the latch. "Are you sure it was Jamie?" she said.

Brenda nodded. "She walked right past the window. I hope she wasn't on her way to the hospital, visiting hours aren't until later this afternoon. She did have a couple of bags with her, though."

"Bags?" Mia frowned. It was possible that Jamie had gone to see Vivian, maybe taken her some food or personal items, but that didn't explain why she hadn't left a note or something.

Mia felt herself pale – she'd become translucent if she wasn't careful. "How did she seem? I mean, was she upset or ...?"

"I honestly couldn't tell you." Brenda viewed Mia in a way that made her wonder if she *was* starting to vanish. "Is there a problem?"

"Well, we did have words last night ..." Mia shook her head, assuring herself as much as Brenda, "They were probably Kerry's bags. I doubt she'll want to show her face around here for a while. Jamie must be dropping them off at the hospital."

Brenda nodded, although she couldn't possibly have understood what Mia was rambling about unless she or her pals had been snooping at the hospital. "I'm sure she'll come home when she's ready. Hasn't she got a mobile you can try?"

"I'll give it another hour or so, she'll only get pissed off if she thinks I'm checking up on her. Do you fancy coming in for a coffee?" Mia hoped it hadn't sounded as desperate out loud as it had done in her head.

"Now?" Brenda studied her wristwatch for longer than necessary. "Umm ..."

"Never mind, you need to get ready for your shift –"

"No, there's plenty of time. I'd love a coffee, thanks."

Mia stepped aside while Brenda entered – or rather, shuffled – into the house. Keeping her head still, her eyes rotated in their sockets while she drank in the surroundings, as if it was her first time visiting. She followed Mia into the kitchen closer than a shadow and almost trampled over the shards of plate, which might as well have been a heap of bones for the perturbation that came over her face.

"I always was a clumsy oaf," said Mia, silently wondering where the toast had gone. No one needed a poltergeist with Casey in the house. "Did you ever find Dillon's cat, by the way?"

"Not yet, the poor lad's gutted. God help us if it turns up dead somewhere."

"I'll be sure to keep an eye out for it." Mia flicked the switch on the kettle. "How do you take your coffee?"

"Milk no sugar, please. Same as my tea, simple me." Brenda's laughter waned when Mia flexed a querying brow. "It's just something Paul used to say."

"I see." Mia cleared up the broken plate before making the coffees, then they both sat down at the table warming their hands on the mugs. The house was becoming more and more like the North Pole each day, and Mia reminded herself to check all the windows at some point. The draught must have been coming from somewhere.

"So," Mia broke the lingering silence, "what exactly happened to Paul if you don't mind me asking? Was he born that way?"

"No, he was perfectly normal until a couple of months ago. The doctors think it was a mental breakdown, but I doubt we'll ever know for sure. He's like a zombie most days, God bless him."

"I know how you feel."

Brenda's eyes dilated with interest, and Mia continued, "My mum's suffering from early-onset Alzheimer's, that's one of the reasons we moved up here. I'm not saying we're in the same situation as you and

Paul, but I can resonate with how helpless it makes you feel."

"Sorry, I didn't realise. So Billy was your mum's brother?"

Mia nodded. "Jamie and I have been looking after her these last couple of years, but it got to the point where we had no choice but to put her into residential care. She was becoming a danger to herself and we were all suffering for it."

"I guess I'm lucky in that sense." Brenda watched the swirls of vapour rising like spectres from her mug. "Wesley is brilliant with Paul, and we can always send Dillon back to his mum when he's having one of his off-days. If you're ever in need of a babysitter or just fancy a break then Louisa would be great company for the boy."

"Thanks, I might take you up on that." Mia chuckled.

As the women sipped their coffees, Mia thought now might be a convenient time to reveal the real reason why she'd invited Brenda into her home.

"So, how long have you lived on the street?" she asked her neighbour.

"A little over two years. Paul joined us after his breakdown."

"Do you happen to know anything about the previous owners of this house? I know it was rented out for a while, but Keith mentioned that no one stuck around for very long."

"That's right." Brenda kept her eyes on the mug, scratching the animal print motif as if in an attempt to distract herself from something. "It was students mainly, but they never stay in one place for very long. As I recall, the landlord initially bought the house for his daughter but she ended up moving into her boyfriend's flat."

"So my uncle bought the house off him?"

"No, it was sold to a middle-aged couple with two kids. They'd planned on making renovations, so it was a bit of a mystery when they up and left one night. The house didn't get much interest after that. I know your uncle got it on the cheap – not that there's anything wrong with that," Brenda quickly added, but it hadn't even occurred to Mia to take offence.

"Why did they leave?" she asked, intrigued.

"No one knows exactly. There was a falling out between the parents. Things got nasty – physical, I reckon, from some of the things we used to hear through the walls. I suspect they'd been having marital problems since well before they moved here, though. Anne always seemed very wary around Mike, but then I didn't know them well enough to make a judgement."

"And they never mentioned anything strange happening in the house? Were they ever frightened or did they have any concerns?"

Brenda's hands stiffened around the mug, and she kept her gaze level on Mia. "What sort of concerns?"

"Well, with the way people have been acting, you'd think we'd moved into the Amityville house or something. I thought it was because of what happened to my uncle, but then Keith said some stuff and now this ..."

Brenda shrugged, but Mia swore the action was forced. "As I said the other week, there's nothing like a bit of gossip to liven up someone's day. You know how stories escalate and the facts get lost along the way."

"Okay, let me put it another way: would *you* live here?"

"I'm sure it would make a lovely home for any family given the chance," was Brenda's eventual response.

That would be a circumlocutory 'no', Mia thought.

"You said the last couple that lived here were making renovations, does that mean the house was like this when my uncle bought it? He never planned on finishing the decorating?"

"I suppose it was more a case of he didn't get a chance to. I've only been in the house once before and it doesn't seem to have changed much."

Mia opened her mouth to enquire some more, but took a swig of coffee instead. If the house's history was that catastrophic then, surely, someone would have warned her by now.

"What about the original owners?" Mia gazed around at the worn, discoloured tiles. "Going off the décor, I'd say it must have been someone's home for generations."

"Crikey ..." Brenda propped one of her elbows on the table and stroked her chin with her spindly fingers. "I do recall Keith mentioning a man, Edward something. He died just before we moved in next door. Apparently, he was one of the oldest residents on the street." She pondered a while longer, eventually shrugging. "You'd have to ask him or Adele about it, they'll be able to tell you a lot more than me."

Mia shook her head briskly. "I don't want to feed the gossips around here anything else, for my family's sake more than anything. Let's just put it down to curiosity."

"How about I talk to them? Adele often pops around to the house and she can waffle for Europe. I wouldn't even bring your name into it."

"You'd do that?"

"Of course, what are friends for?" Brenda smiled.

"Thanks, I'd appreciate that. Shall I crack open some biscuits to go with these?" Mia nodded at the mugs and stood up before Brenda could reply. She was on her way to the cupboard when a floorboard creaked from above.

Brenda jolted so violently that her knees whacked the underside of the table, creating a mini tsunami in the mugs. Mia noticed that she'd hardy touched her coffee.

"That must be Louisa stirring," she said, bending to ferret through the biscuit tin. She stumbled when it felt like her brain had slid forwards, pushing against her skull and almost bursting through the lump on her forehead.

"Are you all right?" Brenda enquired.

"Yeah, I took a bump to the head last night. I woke up this morning not knowing where the hell I was – that's bleach fumes for you."

"Shall I take a look? You have to be careful with these things, concussion can cause all sorts of problems."

Like hallucinations? Mia wondered. Perhaps she'd seen the thing in the bathtub after she'd hit her head and was suffering from temporary amnesia. She'd have contemplated a trip to A&E if it didn't mean risking another confrontation with the Matthews'. Besides, she needed to get to the shops before they closed and Louisa started her new school tomorrow. Plus, she didn't fancy leaving Jamie on her own.

"I'm sure it's nothing a couple of paracetamols won't fix," she replied, at last. "What do you prefer, digestives or party rings?"

"Christ, I haven't had party rings since I was a kid. Paul and I used to get through packets of the things, I'd go berserk if he ate the pink ones." Brenda seemed to have forgotten about Mia's injury, a distant smile softening her pointy features.

"Louisa's the same." Mia took the biscuits anyway, if only to kindle her new friend's memories. "By the way, you never told me how it happened."

"What?"

"Paul's breakdown. Can I ask what caused it?"

"Oh, post-traumatic stress."

"Really? From what?"

More creaks and squeaks from above, followed by the padding of tiny footsteps. Brenda shivered while rubbing away the goosebumps on her bare arms. "*Brr*, did it just get colder in here?"

***

Jamie gazed down at her friend's sleeping face. If it wasn't for the frame of mahogany locks then she might have blended in with the white pillow beneath her head. Reaching across the bed, Jamie combed away the strands that were stuck to her face. Kerry hated her dimples, but right now it was the only bit of personality she had.

The action roused her friend. Her head rolled to the side, eyes opening woozily. She murmured something that didn't even sound English.

"Kerry?" Jamie leaned closer to her, speaking softly. "It's me, Jay. Are you ... Do you know where you are?"

Kerry's hand slid down to her stomach and she cramped up, as if forgetting she had a wound there.

"Sshh," Jamie whispered, over her friend's groans. She glanced through the cubical window to check that no one had been alerted, but all seemed clear. "What the hell were you thinking, getting off your tits like that?"

"W-why are you whispering?" said Kerry.

"Because I'm not exactly supposed to be here. I told the receptionist I was your cousin and that I'd been asked to bring some clean clothes for you. I figured it'd be easier if I came here than your parents having to pick your stuff up from mine. Have they spoken to you yet?"

"Briefly – they know about the dope. I'm surprised they let you in here."

"They didn't, I waited for them to leave and then snuck in. I had to make sure you were okay, you loony."

Kerry went to laugh but her face puckered up, as if the action was painful. "Sorry if I got you into trouble, but I swear I didn't take anything last night ... at least, I don't think I did. Everything's so fuzzy."

"The paramedics reckoned you were hallucinating pretty badly. Do you remember any of it? What you were saying?"

Kerry found her stomach again, as though it would help to prompt last night's memories. Her eyes closed up, tears catching in her dark lashes. Jamie clasped her hand as a bulk formed in the back of her throat. "I'm sorry, I should have known what this is really about. Is that what the weed was for? To help you forget about ... you know ... the *mistake*."

Kerry shook her head, sniffing loudly. "It was meant to be a laugh, that's all. I thought I'd put that shit behind me, but last night it felt like it happened all over again. I was convinced of it."

"What do you mean?"

"I felt it. *Inside*."

Jamie winced at the crushing pressure on her hand, acrylic nails eating into her flesh.

"I was imagining it, wasn't I? Tell me it isn't real." Kerry pushed back the bed sheets and hoicked up the papery nightgown so it bunched around her waist.

"Kez, what are you –"

"Please, look. Tell me if you can see it. I-I can't ..." She twisted her head so she was facing the wall.

Jamie slowly lifted the gown and peeked underneath it, her own hands shaking even though she had no idea why. There was a bandage taped to the area below Kerry's navel with a deep red splodge in the centre. "I don't get it, what am I supposed to be looking for?" she said.

"Something – *anything*. The fucking thing tried to rip me open!"

Jamie took another look before shaking her head. "Everything looks fine apart from the obvious. Trust me, whatever you saw, it was in your head."

Kerry let her hands flop onto her forehead, one on top of the other, and her face had turned a ghoulish green. "Oh, God – my parents. What if they know? Is there any way they can find out?"

"You've still got your legs, haven't you?"

"For how long? Shit, they'd disown me if they realised what a disappointment I really am. Promise me you'll never say anything, no matter what?"

"Like you even have to ask."

Neither of them heard the cubical door opening.

"What are you doing here?"

Jamie swivelled round in the chair. Lisa was glowering down at her like a frumpy version of the Grim Reaper.

"Mum, don't start," Kerry moaned. "This isn't Jamie's fault."

"I don't care whose fault it is. You need to rest."

Jamie stood up, her movement as awkward as her response. "I just came to drop off Kerry's stuff. I'm going now."

Kerry hoisted herself upright. "No, you don't have to –"

"It's fine," Jamie cut in, "Mia will be wondering where I've got to. See you later."

"Cool, I'll text you when I get home," Kerry promised, but Jamie was already leaving the cubical.

She didn't make it very far before a low, stony voice called after her, "I know what you were up to last night."

Her head advised her to keep walking, but instead she stopped and turned in the corridor. Lisa was only a few feet away before she continued, "Kerry's blood test results have come back. Still, I guess that doesn't matter now you'll no longer be around to lead her astray."

"So, what's your problem?"

"Excuse me?"

"You heard, you miserable old bag. No wonder Kerry was so desperate for a weekend away from you." Jamie wouldn't usually have been so bold, but Lisa's reaction was more unexpected than combative.

"Well," she crossed her arms over her hefty bosom, "that's more or less answered my next question. I always knew you were lacking in the parental guidance department, but there are more positive ways of gaining attention."

"Is that what you think this is?" Jamie gave a short laugh. "Jeez, my mum knows Kerry better than you and she's senile!"

"There's no point in denying it, I know all about your sort. Next time you decide to get high, for God's sake, do it on your bloody own."

"What, like you've never messed around with the stuff?"

"Actually, I've done nothing of the sort."

"You should give it a shot, it might loosen up your ass so you can pull that walking stick out of it."

Lisa's eyes broadened almost to the width of her glasses, her jaw sagging in wordless astonishment. Jamie turned and flounced from the building, a smug grin tugging at the corners of her mouth. She'd waited a long time to say those words, and boy it was worth it.

CHAPTER TEN

The front door slammed shut, footsteps tramping down the hallway. Mia glanced up from the television as Jamie entered the living room. She slumped into the armchair as if she'd just popped down to the local shop for a can of coke. Huddled in Mia's arms, Louisa didn't even acknowledge her presence.

No one spoke for the first couple of minutes. The only sound came from a dispute on television, which might as well have been switched off for all the attention it was getting. Then, out of nowhere: "Kerry had a miscarriage."

Mia looked at Jamie again, only this time her gaze hovered. "What?" she said, having heard it perfectly well the first time.

"She got pregnant last Christmas. I'd planned on going to the clinic with her, but it was too late."

Mia sat up straight and lowered Louisa onto the floor. "Go and fetch me a chocolate bar from the kitchen, Lou – and one for yourself."

The girl toddled off, glancing at Jamie on her way out of the room as if knowing full well that she wasn't being sent away purely for chocolate. Mia's feet found the carpet as she shifted to face her sister.

"I take it her parents don't know?"

Jamie shook her head. "It proper shit her up. Last night must have been her brain's way of telling her that she's not over it. It's almost like she was trying to cut it out of herself."

"Cut what out?"

"I'm not sure exactly. I should never have let her smoke that stuff."

"At least we agree on something. Is that where you've been, the hospital?"

"Yeah, I borrowed some cash for the taxi fare. I'll pay you back."

With what, kindness? Mia thought. "So, what did Lisa have to say?"

"The usual. I basically told her to take the stick out of her arse."

Mia laughed through her nose so it came out as more of a snort. "What is that woman's problem?"

"Me." Jamie glanced towards Mia for the first time. "She found the pregnancy test in Kerry's PE kit when she went through it for washing. I guess Kerry panicked and I was the first person she thought of."

"She told Lisa it was *yours?*"

Jamie nodded. "The first I knew about it was when Lisa confronted me. That's twice I've taken the rap for Kerry now."

Mia tutted, shaking her head at the ground. "The sneaky bitch."

"I don't care anymore. Louisa will be okay, won't she?" Jamie asked earnestly.

"She's had to cope with a lot recently – we all have. But she's a resilient thing, thank goodness."

Louisa returned to the living room right on cue. She handed Mia a Curly Wurly before clambering back into the warmth of her lap.

"Where's mine?" said Jamie.

"Get your own, fatso."

Jamie gave an exaggerated gasp. "You'd better not talk to the kids at your new school like that or else you'll get a fat lip," she joked.

Louisa stuck out her tongue while unwrapping the chocolate bar. Jamie used the arms of the chair to haul herself up. "I'm going to take a shower, rinse the stench of hospitals off me."

Before she'd reached the door, Mia said, "You didn't hear anything strange after you went to bed last night, did you? Any bangs or shouts?"

"Dunno, I was listening to my iPod until gone midnight – couldn't get thoughts of you know who out of my head. I almost had a heart attack when I found you passed out in the bathroom."

Mia froze, her teeth half-sunk into the caramel. "Huh?"

"I got up to go to the toilet and you were fast asleep. Don't you remember me helping you into bed?"

Mia shook her head.

"God, and you call me a piss head," Jamie finished.

"I didn't have a drink last night."

"Really? I assumed you'd got fed up and decided to get wasted. Everything is okay, isn't it?"

Seeing the disquiet in her sister's face, Mia replied with a mouthful of chocolate, "All that drama must have knackered me out. Go on, have your shower and then I'll make us some lunch."

"Okay, I won't be long." Jamie smiled, and then she headed upstairs.

***

"Paul, get inside. The poor lass will have you done for harassment if you don't learn to keep your eyes in your skull." Wesley Clarke manoeuvred his brother-in-law into the house with a firm but gentle force, closing the back door behind them. They were relatively equal in size and build, the decade between them giving Wesley a slight disadvantage to the younger man's brawn. No matter how dense Paul appeared on the outside, practically everything had been taken from him but that.

"What's he done now?" Brenda finished buttering her sixth round of bread and then slapped it onto the growing stack.

Wesley replied, "I caught him gawping at her next door again – Jamie, is it? She was wandering around the house half-naked, gave him a right eyeful."

"Oh, Paul, you're old enough to be her dad!" Brenda scolded. "As if that family hasn't got enough going on without you spooking them."

"Problems?" Wesley arched his dark, pipe-cleaner brows in a curious manner.

"Their mum isn't doing so great, and with some of the questions that Mia was asking about the house earlier ..." Brenda glanced at Paul, who was sloshing his glass of juice like some wine connoisseur, then whispered to Wesley, "Let's just keep him away from that place, especially after what happened last time."

"You're the boss." Wesley slinked up behind his wife, pressing himself against her while slipping a hand up inside her nurse's tunic. She smacked it away before it found her tiny breasts.

"I'm serious," she said. "Life is tough enough for Mia, and that Jamie seems like a bit of a rebel as well."

"So you didn't tell her about Paul's ... encounter?"

Brenda hesitated. "I'll bring it up if or when the time is right, and I can assure you that isn't now."

"Okay, but Billy was her uncle and secrets don't stay that way around here for long. All she has to do is look into the matter and she'll be banging on the door like, well, a woman who wants to know what happened to her uncle."

"And I'd tell her that we know as much as she does. We've got nothing to hide, Wes."

"I know *we* haven't. What about him?"

They both turned to Paul, who was already surveying them through fathomless eyes. Brenda smiled at her younger brother. "Do you want pickle on your sarnie?"

CHAPTER ELEVEN

"Are you going to be all right, baby?" Mia crouched so she was level with her daughter, and suddenly the classroom felt more like a football field; the ceiling so far away that it could have been the sky.

Louisa nodded zealously. Mia would have been doubtful it wasn't the first time she'd seen her smile since the night of Kerry's accident. Miss Barker took the girl by her hand. "Do you want to say goodbye to your mummy before we get you settled in?" Her voice was light and sweet, and she had a permanent smile sewn across her delicate features.

However, Louisa's attention was on the cluster of children sitting in front of the whiteboard. Mia stood up without disturbing the girl. If she'd known it'd be this easy then she wouldn't be lugging around the great puffy bags under her eyes.

"I'm going to be at work all day, but I've got my mobile on me in case there are any problems," Mia informed the teacher. "We've been having some issues at home and Louisa hasn't exactly been herself. Did I mention that her aunt would be picking her up this afternoon?"

"Yes, that's not a problem. I'm sure we're going to have lots of fun today, aren't we, Louisa?"

The girl gazed up at Miss Barker, who looked like she was barely out of school herself, and flashed her a gappy grin. The teacher led her over to the other children, and Mia blew her a goodbye kiss before making her way back to the car, which was parked on a street not far from the school gates. She was about to fire up the engine when her mobile went off.

Ferreting through her bag, she located her phone amongst the clutter. 'Nathan' flashed up on the screen. *About bloody time*, Mia thought.

"You're back, then," she answered.

"Um, yeah." *Pause.* "Sorry I've not been in touch sooner." *Pause.* "Had a lot on."

"You and me both," Mia murmured. "Good holiday?"

"It was okay. Uncomfortably hot as usual."

"And Regina's family?"

"Still don't understand a word I'm saying. The kids can communicate better than me."

Mia smirked. A duck had better communication skills than Louisa's father, though it hadn't always been the case. Not between the two of them anyway.

"How's the little monster?" Nathan asked, with a bit more enthusiasm.

"Fine, I've just dropped her off at school. She seemed happier there than she does at home." Mia flipped down the sunshade mirror and took a compact foundation out of her handbag.

"Bollocks," Nathan groaned, or it might have been a yawn. "I was hoping to catch her beforehand, wish her good luck and all. What was all that business with Jamie and her mate about?"

"Didn't you read my text messages?" Mia said, dabbing the powder puff over the bruise on her forehead. It was concealed quite well now some of the swelling had gone down, thanks to a combination of icepacks and ibuprofen.

"Er, briefly," Nathan replied.

"Forget it, everything's sorted now. Are you picking Louisa up this weekend, or would it be easier if I dropped her off at your place?"

"Hmm ..." Nathan clucked his tongue, "might be a bit tricky this weekend –"

"For pity's sake, Nate!" Mia slammed the sunshade up loud enough for it to be heard on the other end of the line and chucked the foundation into her bag. "As if the upheaval of moving wasn't bad enough, you go swanning off to another country and then expect me to break the news that she won't be seeing you for another fortnight. Don't you know how busy I am?"

"Well, if you'd let me finish, I was going to say that I'm not back at work until next week. I can pop up sometime within the next few days *if* that's okay with you?"

Mia relaxed into her seat a little, silently cursing the man for being so reasonable – and the smugness that came with it. "I guess it'll be good for Louisa to see that nothing is going to change," was all she said.

"Right, I'll have a word with Regina and let you know a day and a time. She might want to bring the boys up one day after school, depends on her schedule."

"Great." Mia spoke flatly. It wasn't that she had a virulent hatred for Nathan's wife; she could just think of much more interesting ways of wasting her energy.

Hanging up the phone, Mia started the car and gripped the steering wheel. Sometimes she thought she must have dreamed the night Louisa was conceived and her real father was out there somewhere, waiting to be found. Sadly, although Nathan got his priorities muddled on occasion, the term 'two peas in a pod' could have been invented for him and Louisa. He wasn't a bad bloke, but how Regina had shared a house with him for the past year, she couldn't begin to imagine.

"Poor cow," Mia muttered to herself. Reversing out of the side street, she swung the car round and set off for work.

***

"Come on, Case, what's wrong with you?" Jamie dangled the lead in front of the dog's face. "Don't you want walkies?"

Casey gazed vacuously at her owner with her tongue lolled out, panting feverishly. She ducked back when Jamie reached into the wardrobe.

"Look, I don't like living in this shithole either but you don't see me moping about. Stop hiding and get out of –"

Had Jamie blinked at that precise moment, she wouldn't have seen Casey's head lurch forwards, mouth snapping shut like a crocodile's jaws and narrowly missing her fingertips. She leaped backwards so her feet became tangled in a screwed up dressing gown on the floor. Arms flailing, she whacked a photograph off the television stand and clumsily descended, her elbow crashing into the glass frame.

With a groan, she pushed herself into a sitting position and examined the clear triangle sticking out of her forearm. Her gut contracted, forcing bile up into her throat, which she reluctantly swallowed back down. She pinched the glass between her forefinger and thumb and gently tugged it free, watching the trapped blood ooze from the gash. Dropping it onto the photo frame, Jamie focused on the wardrobe and could just make out a shadowy blob cowering amongst the clothes that swung from their hangers.

"Stupid mutt!" She scrambled to her feet with a hand cupped over the dripping wound. Any more stains like that and the house really would start to look like a crime scene.

Hurrying along the landing, she grabbed a wad of toilet paper on the way past the bathroom and pressed it against her arm, but by the time she'd reached the kitchen it had already soaked through. She crossed to the sink and held her arm under the running water. Surprisingly, the pain wasn't too bad considering the profuse bleeding, which must have had something to do with the adrenaline.

Jamie wrapped a tea towel around her arm and then lifted the medicine box down from the top cupboard. There was only a sliver of plaster dressing left and a couple of loose blister patches.

"Damn it," she muttered, as the stinging began. She could have hit an artery – or a nerve. Flashbacks of Kerry invaded her thoughts, and she could see no other option than to get help.

Jogging down the hallway, she grabbed her keys and slipped out through the front door. There was a Renault parked outside Brenda's house, but she wasn't sure which one of the couple it belonged to. She knocked anyway, and it was Wesley who answered.

"Hi, is Brenda in?" Jamie had to arch her neck to look up at the man.

"She's at work, won't be back till later tonight. You okay, there?" Wesley studied the homemade bandage.

"I'm not sure, I've cut myself pretty badly. Mia said Brenda was a nurse ...?"

Wesley stepped outside and took her arm without invitation, gently lifting a corner of the tea towel. "*Ugh.*" He sprang back, cringing like a schoolgirl at the sight of worms.

Jamie felt the acid clawing its way back up her throat. "Is it that bad?"

"I can't tell. Come on in so I can take a proper look."

Jamie did as she was told and waited until he'd closed the door before following him into the kitchen. It wasn't much different from their own in terms of size and layout, but the modern units, small breakfast bar and clinical décor made it bright and homely and everything theirs wasn't. In fact, as soon as she'd entered the house it was like wading out of a cold, murky swamp into a sun-bathed meadow.

Wesley instructed her to sit down while he fetched a first aid kit from the cupboard under the sink. He brought it back to the table and picked various items out of the box: swabs, bandages and an assortment of plasters. He saw Jamie watching him and said, "The advantages of having a medical professional in the family."

Pulling up a chair opposite her, he rolled up the sleeves of his shirt. He had black hair that was mottled with grey and more stubble than she'd usually find acceptable, but it suited him in a Wolverine-ish sort of way. If she squinted, there was even a vague resemblance between the two men.

This time Wesley didn't wince when he removed the tea towel from around her arm. Instead, he unwrapped a swab and began dabbing away the blood that had congealed around the wound. Jamie squeezed her lips together and whimpered, glancing away so he wouldn't see the tears that threatened to spill from her eyes.

"Sorry." Wesley gentled the action. "Give me a kick in the shins if I'm too heavy-handed, won't you?"

"It's just me being a wuss." She peered at him over her arm. "Do you think it'll need stitches?"

"The bleeding seems to be slowing down by itself. If you want, I can clean it up for you and then drive you down to A&E?"

"No way, I'm sick of that place."

Wesley nodded, as though he'd already guessed as much. "What happened anyway? Don't tell me – you were practicing your karate moves."

"No, I fell on some glass when I was trying to get the dog ready for a walk. She's been hiding in my sister's wardrobe all weekend."

"Is she sick?"

"We're not sure, but if she doesn't cheer up soon then we'll have to get her to the vets. She's never gone for anyone like that before."

"Well, they say animals don't respond well to change. The nearest surgery is about a five-minute drive away, I'll get you the details after I've done this. We've had to take Dillon's bloody cat enough times."

"Thanks."

After giving the injury a few moments to dry, Wesley applied some

Steristrips to it and then wrapped her arm in a small bandage. "All sorted," he said. "Keep it dry and covered for tonight, you don't want to risk reopening the wound. You can check for signs of infection tomorrow, but I reckon you'll live."

"With a great big scar? *Attractive*."

"Nah, it'll make you look tough. I'll just clear this lot away and then I'll have a hunt for the wife's address book."

Wesley replaced the first aid kit into the cupboard and then collected the used swabs and wrappers, which he dropped into the pedal bin on the way out of the kitchen. Jamie rotated her arm back and forth to inspect the dressing. Neat job – better than she could have done anyway.

"'Ello."

Jamie turned in the chair. Paul came shuffling into the kitchen with his slippers dragging along the tiles as if he was on roller skates.

"Oh, hi," she replied.

Paul was transfixed by her arm.

"I had an accident," she said, hiding it under the table. With the way his eyes seemed to be boring holes into her soul, Jamie felt like crawling under there herself.

"Y-you okay?" Paul stammered.

"Yeah, Wesley's been helping me."

Paul continued to stare. Jamie shifted in her seat, clearing her throat if only to break the uneasy silence. She doubted the dude was even capable of holding a conversation.

"B-but ... are *you* okay?" Paul asked again.

"It's a bit sore, but –"

Paul moaned and started tugging his hair as if trying to wrench it from his scalp. Jamie watched him from across the room, unable to close her mouth.

"Not that, not that," Paul said. "It's ... there. Always ... there." He shook his head, groaning and chuntering away to himself.

Hearing footsteps from the floor above, Jamie realised she'd been left all alone with the retard and slipped out of the chair. "I'll go and get Wes-"

"*Naaargh!*" Paul launched himself across the room, grasping her shoulders in his king-sized hands and almost lifting her off the ground. "Have to get out! Can't stop it!"

"Get off me, you weirdo!" Jamie yanked at his hands, but her fingers were lubricated with sweat and slid down his arms; her nails leaving red tracks beneath the wispy hairs.

"Leave, leave, *leeeave!*" Paul's voice morphed into a thunderous growl which, even for his Herculean size, was unearthly in every sense of the word. One glance into those eyes – if you could still call them eyes – left Jamie virtually immobile.

Everything was gone: the colour, the humanity, the soul. It was as if his pupils had dilated to the circumference of his eyeballs and left nothing but big black, hollow wells. Then he was upon her. His jaw stretched open, thick lips fastening around her mouth like a faeces-smeared plunger – he literally tasted of shit. Jamie gagged when an elongated tongue slithered towards the back of her throat, tickling her uvula. When a warmish liquid filled her mouth, she was convinced she must have bitten down.

The more Jamie panicked, the harder she choked, and her knee jerked up into Paul's crotch with a will of its own. She pushed back on his chest the second he'd loosened his hold on her, using the man's own strength to tear herself free. Vomit sprayed over his T-shirt like an orange tie-dye pattern, and only then did she realise that she hadn't chewed off his tongue after all.

More hands grabbed at her from behind. She wheeled round so fast that she clouted Wesley with her elbow and almost toppled over in a three-hundred-and-sixty-degree spin.

"Whoa, take it easy!" Wesley tried to stabalise her but, trapped between the two giants like a schoolyard game of Piggy in the Middle, Jamie clambered over the table in a frantic attempt to evade them both.

"It's okay, lass, no one is going to hurt you," said Wesley, without pursuing her. "Why don't you sit down and I'll make you some sweet tea, eh?"

"*Tea?*" Jamie squawked. She used the back of her hand to wipe the sick off her chin. "W-what's wrong with you p-people?"

"It's a misunderstanding, that's all. Paul … he's not used to strangers." Wesley focused on the whimpering retard, who was standing in the middle of the room flapping his arms like a malfunctioned chicken. Other than that, he'd reverted to his normal self.

"I really think you should sit down." Wesley edged slowly towards

Jamie. "You might have lost more blood than we thought."

"Don't come near me, you freak!" Jamie sidled around the perimeter of the table, clinging onto its edges as if walking the brow of a cliff top. "Just let me go. I won't say anything to anyone, I swear."

Wesley frowned for the first time. "What is there to say?"

Jamie had no answer. *Was that a threat?* she wondered. They could have been a Satan worshipping voodoo family for all she knew, and that was something she definitely didn't fancy having to explain to the cops.

"Shut up – just shut up!" Jamie yelled to no one in particular. "Please, let me out of here. I just want to go home."

"Of course, no one's stopping you," Wesley answered. "But –"

It was too late: Jamie had scarpered.

CHAPTER TWELVE

It wasn't long after Mia had pressed the doorbell that Wesley answered, an awkward smile restricted to his lips only.

"You'd better come in," he said, as if he'd been expecting her.

Mia entered the house and closed the door behind her. She followed Wesley down the hallway where the air was heavy with Mediterranean spices. "Sorry, did I disturb your tea?" she said.

"No, Brenda was just about to dish up." Wesley extended an arm towards the living room. "Do you want to come though? I assume you're here about your sister."

"Yes, but I won't keep you for long. It's just that I came home to find her in a bit of a state and Paul's name was mentioned. I couldn't get much sense out of her but ..." Mia scratched the bridge of her nose. "Man, this is awkward."

"Who is it, Wes?" Brenda popped her head around the kitchen door and glimpsed the couple in the hall. "Oh, Mia ..." She scurried towards them like a mad cook, oven gloves draped over one arm, ladle in hand. "I'm so sorry, I was going to nip around after –"

"It's fine, really," Mia assured them both. "I'm not here to have a go, I just wanted to clear things up. Is it true that Paul made a move on Jamie today?"

"I wasn't here, but Wesley saw everything – didn't you, love?" Brenda prompted her husband.

"Well, yeah, sort of." Wesley's dark eyes flitted between the two women. "She'd hurt her arm so I offered to patch it up for her. We got chatting and she mentioned something about the dog playing up. I went to get her the details for the vet's surgery – you know, from your address book?" He glanced at Brenda, who confirmed with a nod.

Mia said, "She came around here?"

Wesley nodded. "She was looking for Brenda. Anyway, when I came back downstairs she and Paul were ... well, Jamie had chucked up all over him. I thought it was a reaction to the injury – delayed shock or something."

"And what did Paul have to say about it?" Mia enquired.

"He insisted that he was trying to help her. Maybe she'd gone dizzy and fallen over, poor thing was whiter than a ghost when she left here."

Mia's brows sagged over her eyes. "Strange, I don't know why she'd freak out over something like that."

"Do you want me to fetch Paul so you can ask him yourself?" Brenda offered.

"No, that isn't necessary. I'll have another word with Jamie later, but maybe it's best that they stay away from each other for now."

"Of course. Paul can be a bit heavy-handed sometimes and he does get flustered easily, but he'd never hurt anyone. I wouldn't let him around Dillon otherwise," assured Brenda.

"I understand, it's the same with my mum. I hope Paul's okay."

"Thanks, Mia – and give Jamie our apologies, won't you?"

"I will. Enjoy your tea." Mia said goodbye and then showed herself out.

***

Mia knocked on Jamie's bedroom door before opening it a crack. Her sister was lying on the bed in a foetal position with her back to the door, exactly how Mia had found her upon returning home from work twenty minutes ago.

"Hey." Mia wandered inside and planted herself on the bed next to Jamie. "I've spoken to Brenda and Wesley. They seemed genuinely upset about what's happened."

Jamie sniffed and wiped her eyes with the pads of her fingers. "I bet they still covered for that freak, didn't they?"

"He's not a freak. He's ill, just like Mum is."

"You're sticking up for him now?"

"No, but you haven't exactly given me much to go off. Are you positive that he attacked you because Wesley seems to think he was trying to help?"

Jamie's head shot off the pillow, and she glared at Mia over her shoulder. The glow from the bedside lamp reflected in her eyes so it looked like they were on fire. "He grabbed me, okay? Practically ripped off my arms and then shoved his disgusting tongue down my throat."

"Okay, so show me."

"Show you what?"

"If he was that forceful then you must have bruises."

"No ... I mean, it all happened so fast. He was different."

"Different, how?"

"I don't know, it's like he changed. His face, his voice ..." Jamie closed her eyes as if to block out some ghastly images, and she turned from Mia once more. "He was *evil*."

Even though the last part was barely audible, that word – 'evil' – reverberated through Mia's skull as if someone had blown a trumpet into her ear. Her own experiences blitzed through her mind with such intensity that she could have been reliving them right there and then, but she fought to cling onto logic – for all their sakes.

"Are you saying that Paul had some kind of psychotic episode?" Mia said, as if to strengthen her own belief. When Jamie didn't reply, she leaned across the bed and put a hand on her shoulder. "Come on, sis, we used to be able to tell each other anything."

"What's the point? You obviously don't believe me – I bet you're already wondering if I'm high. Whatever happened to Kerry is happening to me, I know it."

"Kerry did a stupid thing and she suffered for it. You've had a shock, you're bound to be skittish for a while. After Mum tried to burn the house down, I was afraid to boil an egg in case it caught fire. I had no trust for the woman whatsoever, even though I knew she'd never do anything to deliberately harm us."

"What are you saying?" Jamie asked her.

"We both know that Mum didn't have a clue what she was doing that night. Chances are, what happened with Paul was just another misunderstanding – a one-off – but if you want to take it further then that's up to you."

"What, by going to the police and telling them the retard next door tried to touch me up? I'd be laughed out of town."

"Well, yeah, when you put it like that," Mia concurred. "With the way Brenda mollycoddles him, I bet the chap hasn't been able to get within six feet of a woman since his episode. He probably thought his luck was in."

"Piss off, Mia!" This time Jamie swung her whole body round and whacked Mia in the face with a sequinned scatter cushion. Mia dived back as the tiny discs scratched her face, scrabbling for the edge of the mattress before she rolled off it.

"I was kidding – Jesus!" She wrested the cushion out of Jamie's grasp. "What the hell is your problem? If I didn't know you better then, yeah, I probably would think you were on something."

"Because I'm such a failure, aren't I? Unlike you with your perfect job and your perfect life. You're so busy running around acting like a total control freak that you don't have a clue what's really going on." Shadows thrown from the lamplight inked the creases in Jamie's face, a canvas once so flawless that now looked so weary. So withered.

"What are you talking about?" Mia scowled. "Where's all this coming from?"

"It's coming from the fact that you call yourself my sister but you obviously don't know shit about me or my life. All you care about is bullying me into going along with your crap decisions!"

"Those 'crap' decisions are what have got us out of debt and kept you from the clutches of social services all these years." Mia got up off the bed and pointed an accusing finger at the girl. "I might have initiated the move to Bramley, but you agreed that it was the best option. Come to think of it, you seemed pretty desperate for a new start. What exactly are you running away from, eh?"

Jamie disregarded the question. "I was talking about the four of us: me, you, Mum and Louisa. You're always going on about family, but it means nothing without her."

"Look, we've been over this a thousand times and to be honest, Jay, it's getting kind of boring. I love Mum just as much as you do, but she's also the reason I could be standing here arguing with a pile of fucking ashes."

"Yeah, well maybe that's exactly what I deserve!" Jamie rolled back onto her side, punching the lumps out of her pillow before letting her head flop on top of it.

And that was it, end of conversation. Mia hesitated a while before stepping towards the bed with a hand outstretched to her sister. She was desperate to pry some more, to reassure Jamie that she was loved and that everything was going to work itself out, but consoling her was almost as pointless as trying to reason with the girl. As Jamie had indirectly pointed out, she didn't want another mother. She *needed* her sister. Mia wasn't sure she knew how to balance the two.

Without a word, she dropped her arm and headed downstairs.

CHAPTER THIRTEEN

"Don't do that, might be something fragile in there," Nathan hinted to his daughter.

Louisa stopped shaking the box and held it to her ear, as if listening for a clue.

"I think it's a bit small for a pussycat, Lou," Mia joked.

Finally, Louisa tore off the bow and carefully removed the lid. She looked up to Nathan, eyes glittering with as much intensity as the object in the box. "For me?" She gasped.

"Who else?" Nathan replied, the self-satisfaction oozing from him. He looked even more like Louisa with his fresh tan, although his hair was more dark brown than black. It had a coarse texture, the type that developed a kink once it reached the length it was at now. Clearly, he hadn't bothered to get a haircut during his fortnight in Spain.

Mia took the necklace out of its package, afraid the girl would snap the delicate chain, and displayed the heart-shaped pendant in the palm of her hand. "Wow – special occasions only, I think," she said.

"Can I put it on, Mummy?" Louisa pleaded.

"Course you can, princess." Nathan beckoned her over to the armchair. "C'mon, give it here."

Louisa snatched the necklace and dashed over to her father. He fastened it around her neck before opening the locket and pointing to the two halves. "See," he said, "this is where you can put pictures of the people you love so they'll always be close to your heart."

"Like you and Mummy?"

"Whatever you like, you could even put a photo of Casey in there."

Clicking the locket shut, he whispered just loud enough for Mia to hear, "It's not like you can tell the difference between her and your mum anyway."

Louisa giggled while covering her mouth with her hand. Then she rushed back to Mia to flaunt her gift.

"Very pretty." Mia glanced at Nathan, the remnants of a scowl still shaping her forehead. "Must have been expensive?"

"Worth every euro." He winked.

"What did you get, Mummy?" Bored of the necklace already, Louisa picked up the wooden object next to Mia and gave it a thorough inspection.

"It's called a maraca – your dad's idea of a joke, I think."

"What's it for?"

"You play music with it, like the tambourine bells you use in your school plays."

Louisa picked up its twin and shook the instruments more vigorously. "Jingle bells," *rattle,* "jingle bells," *rattle, rattle,* "jungle all the way! Oh, what fun –"

"God, will someone shut her the hell up!" Jamie tossed the television remote onto the coffee table. "I can't hear myself think."

"All right, there's no need to snap." Mia seized the maracas and placed them on the side unit away from Louisa. Nathan's smile quickly broadened into a grin. Mia mouthed the word 'bastard' at him.

"Can you stay for tea?" Louisa asked her dad.

"Er ... if it's okay with your mum?" He looked hesitantly at Mia, who answered her daughter rather than Nathan.

"I suppose so. And seeing as Daddy's wallet is so fat at the minute, I reckon he'd treat us all to a takeaway if you asked him nicely."

"Not for me." Jamie heaved herself out of the sofa. "I'm going to my room."

"Fine, I'll leave any leftovers in the fridge," Mia said.

Nathan watched the teenager stomp from the room. "What's up with her?" he said, once Jamie had left.

Mia gave a lethargic sigh. "She's had a bit of bother with the guy next door, it's not as big a deal as she's making it out to be."

"Do you want me to have a word?"

Mia laughed spontaneously. "Since when did you become so macho?"

"I meant with Jamie."

Mia's face straightened, her right brow levitating up by her hairline. "Christ, has all that sunshine revived some of your brain cells? You haven't been this attentive since … Oh, God, don't tell me you and Regina have finally taken things to the next stage?"

This time it was Nathan's turn to scoff. "Do me a favour, the boys are a handful enough – especially with their dad being in the nick. Besides," his focus returned to Louisa, "no one messes with my girls and gets away with it."

"I hate to break it to you," Mia cupped her hands over their daughter's ears, "but a drunken romp on the back end of a college dare doesn't technically make me *yours*, does it?"

Nathan grinned as Mia got up off the sofa.

"What's so funny?" Louisa wanted to know.

"Nothing, princess. So, where's good to eat around here?"

"We had some leaflets come through the letter box the other day. I'll dig them out," said Mia, and then she was gone.

***

"Thanks for letting me come over tonight." Nathan stepped onto the path that ran alongside the picnic blanket of a front lawn. "I know you're busy getting the house sorted and whatever, but I do appreciate it."

"You're welcome," Mia replied. "But, seriously, no more lavish gifts or else Louisa will start expecting more and more."

"Yeah, sorry about that." Nathan scuffed the toe of his trainer against the doorstep. His hands were tucked into his pockets, head bowed. "Didn't realise how hard it'd be."

"What?"

"All these miles between us. It kinda feels like I've been taking the last five years for granted."

Mia had to stop herself from putting a comforting hand on the man's shoulder. Even with these flares of maturity, he still couldn't dissociate himself from the awkward nineteen-year-old she'd met in what seemed like a lifetime ago. Mia had found it endearing at the time – comical, even – but after Louisa's birth it had become a case of she'd grown up too quickly and Nathan hadn't grown up at all. It was also the reason she hadn't been on a date since.

"Nate, can I ask you something?" Mia pulled the front door shut while moving towards him.

"Yeah?"

"How does Louisa seem to you – in herself, I mean?"

"Fine, all things considered. Great, in fact."

Mia gave a feeble nod. "She does seem brighter after starting school. It's just that she's been saying and doing some really unusual things since we moved. I was seriously beginning to regret having done all this."

"Probably just anxiety," Nathan said. "I'll have a chat with her at the weekend."

"I thought you couldn't have her?"

"Regina's got this work's do that I was supposed to be going to, but I think I'll give it a miss after today. Like you said, we need to get Lou back into a routine."

"I bet Regina will love that."

"She'll understand. Are you still okay to drop her off on Friday, or shall I pick her up after school?"

"I haven't got any appointments so I should be able to finish work a bit early. I'll text you if it's going to be a problem."

"Cheers. And go easy on Jamie, yeah?"

Mia wondered if he'd had a personality transplant in Spain and that was the reason he'd been unable to afford a haircut. "Is there something you know that I don't?" It was a serious question.

Nathan answered, "As I said, family is more important than anything now. See you Friday."

After a cursory goodbye, Mia wrapped her cardigan around her front and folded her arms to stop it from blowing open. As Nathan's car shrank into the distance it seemed to tow away her very soul, leaving behind a cold, empty husk. A part of her wanted to scream at him for abandoning them because, pathetic as it was, he was the only reminder she had of home – their *proper* home – and the contentment it had offered. Of course, there was Angela and the girls from work, but they had their own lives and their own families to deal with. Jamie and Louisa were all she had now, and she was all they had. Failing them wasn't an option.

Mia stood there a few minutes before retreating into the house. She jogged upstairs and popped her head around the bathroom door. "You almost finished in there, Lou?"

"Yep." Louisa scooped a handful of bubbles out of the bathwater and blew them so they sprayed up into her face.

Mia pulled a towel from the rail hanging over the door and laid it on the toilet lid. "Shout me when you're ready to get out, okay? I'll go and find you some clean pyjamas."

Leaving the girl splashing away, Mia wandered into Louisa's bedroom. As she reached the chest of drawers, something crunched beneath her slipper. She stepped back, lifting her foot off the carpet. "Oh, shit!"

She picked up the locket that Nathan had bought for Louisa. The delicate hinge was split down the middle so it had broken in half. Mia clearly remembered putting the necklace back into its box when Louisa had got undressed for a bath, and this was on top of the chest of drawers exactly where she'd left it. She checked inside to find that the chain was also missing.

Getting onto her hands and knees, she searched the surrounding floor, feeling beneath the drawers and finally under the bed. Something glinted at her from the shadows. With her chest almost flat against the carpet, she stretched out her arm as far as it would go to reach the object.

"What the hell ...?" She dangled the chain in front of her face and fingered the broken link. It looked like it had been yanked from around someone's neck.

However, the necklace wasn't the only thing she'd discovered stashed under the bed. Mia fished out a yellow collar – the same one she'd seen Tabby wearing at Brenda's barbecue the other week. She thought the crusty stains around the bell must have been mud until she held it under the light and saw that it had a reddish tinge.

Pushing herself onto her knees, she noticed someone hovering in the bedroom doorway and looked at her daughter as if she was the devil's spawn.

"Is this Tabby's collar?" she said, wanting to hear it from the girl's own lips. But not a sound passed through them.

"Louisa, why do you have this? Do you know what happened to Tabby?"

"I found it."

"Where?"

"In the garden."

"Why didn't you say anything?" As Mia stood up, the girl seemed to physically shrink. She'd almost forgotten about the broken necklace and held up the items as if presenting evidence at a murder trial. "If you know where Tabby is then you need to tell me because Dillon's very upset that she's gone missing. And what happened to your new necklace? Daddy spent a lot of money on that."

Louisa shrugged in that same elusive manner. Mia could believe this to an extent – there was no way she could have reached up to the chest of drawers by herself. "Sweetheart, I'm not mad at you. Just tell me what –"

"No!" Louisa turned and fled from the room. It was the fastest Mia had ever seen her move in her life, but she'd caught up with the girl in just a few strides. In the grab for her shoulders, she ripped the towel clean off her body.

"Louisa Reynolds, don't you dare run away from me when I'm speaking to you!" Mia jerked her round so they were facing one another. "Tell me what you did to that cat or else I'll get Brenda over here and you can explain it to her yourself."

"I didn't do anything! I hate you, bitch!" Louisa's arms flailed violently, the redness spreading throughout her face until it looked as though she'd stuck it in a nettle bush. Mia was too taken aback to reprimand the girl. Neither she nor Jamie were as cautious as they should have been with language, but if that was the case then she'd have picked up on it long before now.

"Louisa, stop this right now!" The more Mia tried to restrain her, the fiercer she struggled, kicking and punching as if she no longer recognised the woman who had birthed her. Louisa was screaming so loudly that neither of them heard Jamie come stomping out of her bedroom.

"What the hell is going on out here?" Jamie glanced at Mia and the naked girl in turn, bewilderment eating through the vexation in her face.

Louisa spat at Mia before finally squirming free. She pelted over to Jamie and hugged her legs, lung-drawn wails resounding through the landing. Mia slumped back into a crouch, half oblivious to the spittle dribbling down her cheek.

"What's she done this time?" Jamie looked as shocked by Louisa's behaviour as Mia was with her own. Her entire body trembled – it felt like her nerves were trying to burst out through her pores and she had no concept as to why. It wasn't that she was angry at Louisa. She was angry at *everything*.

"I'm sorry," Mia whispered. "I'm so, so sorry."

She retrieved the towel and went to cover Louisa, then lifted her up and hugged her so tightly that she could feel her tiny heart thumping as if it was coming from inside her own chest.

Leaving Jamie staring after them, she carried the girl back to her bedroom.

CHAPTER FOURTEEN

Blood-smeared drapes covered the banquet tables, which were accessorised with a grim selection of cobweb-dusted candle sticks, snot cocktails, oozing cupcakes and an insect-ridden buffet. As if Godestone Manor wasn't spooky enough in its usual fifteenth-century splendour, tonight it looked like the set of a gothic horror film.

A ghostly woman approached Mia in the entrance to the Great Hall, her heavy gown rustling behind her. A band of stitches crisscrossed around her neck, and through the white face paint Mia recognised her friend's features.

"Who do you think you are, *Angela* Boleyn?" Mia joked. "The boss really will have your head if you get stains all over the tour costumes."

Angela flicked a gloved hand through the air between them. "Nah, it'll wash out. They're in need of an update anyway, it might persuade the tight git to put his hand in his pocket." She forced a plain white gown and bonnet into Mia's hands. "Don't think you're getting away with it either."

Mia held the robe by its sleeves and let the flimsy material unravel in front of her. "What am I supposed to be, the ghost slut of Godestone?"

"Better than looking like a prostitute – good luck getting those baps into a corset. The teenage lads here will think it's Christmas."

"Gee, thanks." Mia took off her jacket and slipped the nightgown over her vest and pencil skirt.

"Wow, this is totally awesome!"

The women turned to find a purple-haired witch bouncing around in front of them. She was wearing a long black dress with a pointed hat and a fake, pimpled nose.

Mia smiled at the girl. "Happy Birthday, Halle. We hope you have an amazing night, and take lots of pictures because you're only sixteen once."

"Yes – thank you, thank you!" Halle gave the hostesses a quick hug and then skipped off with a trail of minions behind her.

"Just think," Angela said, "you've got all this to come."

"That's if Louisa ever decides to speak to me again," Mia mumbled at the ground.

"She'll come around, they always do. A bit of TLC and she'll have forgotten all about it."

"I know, but that doesn't excuse how I reacted." Mia folded her jacket and draped it over her arm. "Anyway, I'd better go and bob this in the staffroom. I'll pick up some more champagne on my way back."

Mia headed to the back of the manor, where she hung her jacket in the staffroom before fetching a couple of champagne bottles out of the kitchen. It was on her way back to the Great Hall that she glimpsed something sweeping up the staircase to her right. She came to a halt mid-stride, angling her neck so she could peer into the blackness above.

"Excuse me," she called, edging towards the stairs. "Hello ...?"

No reply. The staircase was more or less opposite the main entrance, so any cars that pulled into the driveway were bound to bring the shadows to life with the glare from their headlights; and even over the music and clamour from the party, Mia would have heard footsteps moving at that speed. But there were no signs of any vehicles having approached from outside.

"Coming through!"

Mia gasped when a zombie nun whooshed past her, the champagne bottles almost slipping from her grasp. "Hey, wait!" She tugged them back and stuffed the bottles into their hands, too preoccupied to discern whether or not it was a guest. "Keep the top-ups going, and no underage drinkers."

Her gaze fixed on the stairs, Mia climbed over the rope barrier and hurried after the shadow. Upon reaching the first floor, she scanned up and down the T-shaped corridor. To her left was the large family hall, which spanned over almost half of the upper ground. She couldn't see into the room fully, but the landing was all clear. She glanced in the opposite direction. There, at the far end of the corridor, something pale and vague loitered in the gloom. If it hadn't been fancy dress then she'd be standing in a puddle of her own urine right about now, whereas a few weeks ago she'd have searched every room without so much as an erect hair.

Clearing her throat, she spoke in an assertive voice. "Excuse me, but this area is off-limits. I'm going to have to ask you to return to the party."

Silence. If it was one of the staff then they would have answered her by now. "Didn't you hear me? You can't – hey!"

The figure disappeared into one of the bedrooms, almost as if it was floating. It wasn't until Mia followed that she noticed the door was firmly closed. No one could move that stealthily – at least, no one human.

Get a grip, Mia, she scolded herself. Teenagers and their hormones, that's all it was.

"Look," she said, barging the door open, "if you think you can sneak up here for a quick fumble then –"

But the room was vacant. Bed untouched, furniture in its place – nothing out of the ordinary. She even checked under the duvet before collapsing on top of it with her face pressed into her hand, giving an unforced chuckle. She had developed something of a delirious imagination since the bump to her head, and just looking at herself now ... well, if the thing she'd been pursuing had been some kind of apparition then, chances were, it was running upstairs to get away from her.

"Come on, only a few more hours to get through," Mia told herself. She removed the bonnet to neaten her hair and then got up off the bed. There was a flock of rowdy teenagers downstairs and they weren't going to entertain themselves.

She was passing the window when she caught movement in her peripheral vision. First she noticed the colour, pale as the moon in the black of night. And it was moving – no, swaying – like a sheet that had snagged on a branch in the wind. Wandering over to the window, that's exactly what she thought it was initially. The large oak tree climbed higher than the building itself, contorted boughs casting shadows that stretched across the lawn like the devil's fingers. In the dull lights from the manor house, she was able to discern that the object swinging from the tree was the very same thing that had led her upstairs in the first instance.

Mia took a wobbly stride back from the window, her breaths caged in her lungs. She blinked twice, praying the image would have vanished, but each time she opened her eyes it became plainer.

The feet suspended a metre or so above the ground, the pendulous arms and the rope entwined around a flaccid neck. Then there was the face ...

Mia's brain flipped into overdrive. *Oh God oh God this couldn't be happening it wasn't real had to be a delusion please please please don't let it be true!*

But it was, and after a third blink she was still there.

Vivian.

Hanging. Suffocating. Dying.

"Oh, no," Mia wept. "No, no, *no!*"

She dropped the bonnet and took off to the stairs, her mind overwrought with what her eyes had witnessed. On the sprint through reception, she cannoned into Angela and knocked a stack of tin trays out of her hands so they crashed and clanged against the floor. After skidding on several of them as if they were toboggans, Mia regained her footing and burst out through the main entrance regardless of her friend's cries. Racing around the side of the building to where the staff car park merged with the back lawn, a part of her still expected the body to have disappeared. But there it dangled, as real as the great oak itself.

"Mum! Oh, shit – oh, *Christ!*" Mia looped her arms around the cold, waxy legs and heaved up the bulk with all her might, hoping it would take some of the strain off Vivian's neck; but she was crying so hard that it seemed all of her effort was put into that.

"Don't do this, Mum," she wailed. "You can't be gone – I won't let you. Come back to me, damn it!"

Mia forced her eyes up to Vivian's face, where her swollen tongue lolled out from the side of her mouth. Even in the shadows she could see that her eyes were open – open but not *seeing*. It was the old rope swing coiled around her neck, but Mia couldn't begin to fathom how someone of her age and condition had climbed up there without a ladder.

"Mia!" Hearing shouts from behind, Mia turned to see Angela tearing across the lawn, holding her dress up around her scrawny thighs.

"Angela, help me! We've got to get her down!" Mia was sweating from the exertion of supporting the body, which in reality couldn't have weighed more than seven or eight stone.

Angela froze just a few feet away. Her head was bent backwards, and a hand crept up over her mouth.

"Ange!" Mia screamed. "For Christ's sake, if you're not going to help me then call an ambulance now!"

"I-it's too late, hun." Angela tried to draw her away, but Mia might as well have been bound to the shrivelled legs. "Please, stop. There's nothing we can do."

"What are you talking about? She might still be alive!"

"Mia." Angela gripped her face and gently turned it so they were facing one another. "I'm sorry, but she's gone."

"B-but ... she can't be." Mia's voice rattled in her throat, salty tears dripping over her lips. "Ange, it's my mother."

"Your mo – *what?*" Angela said, after rethinking the statement. She looked up at the inanimate form again, this time shaking her head. "No, you're confused. Your mum's perfectly safe."

"Safe?" Mia pointed to the limbs that dangled above them like a sick party decoration. "You call that shit safe!"

"It's not what you think. How would Vivian have got all the way here from Leeds, eh?"

"*Are you fucking blind?*" Mia was screeching now. "She's right –"

Glancing at the body again, it was swathed in shadows so thick that she could scarcely make out the features that had a moment ago been obscenely clear. The dressing gown, slippers and straggly hair were all the same, but somehow she knew that none of them belonged to her mother. It was as though, for one ephemeral moment, her worst nightmare had become reality.

"I ... I ..." It was all Mia could utter.

"Sshh, it's okay." Angela pulled Mia into her embrace, lightly patting her back. "I'm sorry, I didn't realise how bad things had got with your mum. For you to think she'd do something like this ... well, it's no wonder you haven't been yourself lately."

"But I could have sworn ..."

"Come on, let's get you inside and find something to treat that shock. One of the staff can call for an ambulance while I deal with the guests. It looks like the party's over for tonight."

Mia broke away, drying her eyes with the sleeve of her nightgown. "You go ahead, I'm staying here."

"Are you sure?"

Mia nodded. "We don't want any of those kids wandering back here. And for Christ's sake, Ange, find something to cut her down with. I don't care what the cops say, I'm not leaving her like this."

With a nod, Angela dashed back to the manor. Mia sank to her knees, dampness from the grass soaking through the cotton nightgown. Her legs felt too weak to hold her upright, never mind carry her back to the house. She still felt like she'd wake up in bed any second, not knowing whether this had all been a dream or reality – just like the incident in the bathroom, which she was still unable to banish from her thoughts.

Dream or reality, the nightmare went on.

**

A floorboard moaned from just outside the living room. The streetlamps barely penetrated the thick curtains, and it was only by chance that Mia spotted the silhouette peering around the open door.

"Hey." She spoke from the armchair.

A bright glow doused the room, and Jamie was standing with her finger on the light switch as though it was some kind of detonator. "Shit," she said, with a gasp. "I heard noises down here and I thought ... never mind. Why were you sitting in the dark?"

"I was just thinking." Mia draped her hand over the arm of the chair. A glass hung loosely from her fingers. "How's Louisa been?"

"Fine, I think. She still won't talk about what happened last night." Jamie wandered further into the room and flumped down on the sofa. "Decided to bring the party home, did you?"

"Huh?"

"It stinks of vodka in here."

"Sorry, it's what you had left over from the weekend. I'll get you some more."

"After what happened to Kerry, I'm never touching the stuff again." Jamie yawned while kneading her eyes.

Mia brought the glass up to her mouth, paused a second, then traced the rim back and forth along her lower lip. "I think you're right about this place," she said.

"What?"

"First Louisa, then Kerry – even the bloody dog can sense that something isn't right."

Jamie watched her gulp down the dregs like it was water, a drop of unease sinking into her features. "Don't tell me you think we've got a ghost? My sister, the skeptic."

"Ghosts are one thing, evil is another. If whatever happened to Uncle Billy is linked to the house then what's to say the same thing won't happen to us?"

"I thought he died from a heart attack?"

"But why here? Why now? He spent half of his life digging up archaeological sites around the world, so no one can say he was unhealthy. And if his death was suspicious," Mia leaned over to position the glass onto the coffee table, "then someone around here must know something about it."

Jamie looked alternately from the glass to Mia, shuddering as though that feeling of unease had dispersed into her bloodstream. "Did something happen tonight or what?"

Mia slouched back in the chair. Everywhere she looked reminded her of that poor dead woman: the patterns in the carpet could have been faces, drops from the chandelier hung like sparkly bones and the curtain ties could easily have been made into nooses. She made a mental note to move them so they were out of reach from Louisa.

"There was an incident at the manor," was Mia's eventual response. "A death, to be blunt."

"Someone from the party?" Jamie seemed more curious than anything, and Mia had already decided that she wouldn't go into details as to how or why she'd been the one to discover the body.

"No, it was some random old woman. Both the police and paramedics agreed that it was most likely a suicide, but it can't be a coincidence, can it?"

"What's that got to do with Uncle Billy or the house?"

"I don't know," Mia answered honestly. "You should have seen her, Jay – she was in her night clothes, for Christ's sake. It's like she just woke up and thought, 'I don't want to live anymore. Goodbye and amen.'"

"Maybe she was a nut job, there are plenty of them around."

"But why walk all the way to Godestone? Why tonight when everyone was going to be there – when *I* was there? Even if she lived nearby, don't you think it's a bit convenient?"

"What did the police say about it?"

"Not much. She didn't have any ID on her so it's just a case of asking around, finding out who might know her and where she lives." Mia combed a hand through her hair and brushed it back off her makeup-free face. "Whatever the reason for taking her own life, she's cost us a hell of a lot of money. The guests were pissed about having to leave, and we'll be closed to the public until the police have finished investigating."

"On the plus side," Jamie added, "at least it's something to tell the tourists."

Mia managed a quiet chuckle, although it probably would appeal to some grim bastards. Jamie stood up and went over to her, balancing herself on the edge of the chair.

"Want another voddy?" she said, snaking an arm around Mia's shoulders.

"I'd better not."

"You sure? It'll help you to sleep."

"I'll be fine once the shock has worn off. You go back to bed."

Kissing Mia's crown, Jamie made for the door.

"Jay?"

"Yeah?"

"Have you been ... *seeing* things recently?"

"Like what?"

Mia shrugged. "Stuff you know isn't possible but you're convinced of it anyway."

Jamie's eyes dropped a millimetre or so, just enough for Mia to have noticed, before she replied, "You definitely need more sleep."

"I guess so. See you in the morning."

"Night."

Clasping her hands over stomach, Mia let her head roll back against the cushions and exhaled a blustery sigh. She was even more determined to find out what had really gone on in this house, not just concerning her uncle but all those before him, and Brenda was her starting point. Plus, she never had got around to explaining what had happened to Paul that was so traumatic it had decimated half of his brain function.

Mia's thoughts soon turned to his alleged attack on Jamie. Although the teenager had been unable to make sense of the incident herself, she maintained one thing: that Paul hadn't only looked deranged, he'd looked evil. Just like the Vivian clone in the bathtub.

"Holy crap." Mia shot upright in the chair, her fingertips denting the padding. Her body so rigid that she could have been welded to the frame itself.

Louisa ... the thing she claimed to have seen in her bedroom ... the picture she'd drawn for Vivian. As the memories cycled through Mia's mind, it was as if a denseness had infused the air and she suddenly felt like an extraterrestrial in a laboratory full of scientists. Like *she* was the intruder and her every move was being analysed. Her gaze roamed to the empty glass on the coffee table. She picked it up and took it into the kitchen, pouring what remained of the vodka down the sink and then heading promptly for bed.

CHAPTER FIFTEEN

Louisa trudged across the school playground with her feet dragging along behind her. No outstretched arms, no rucksack bouncing up and down and not a ghost of a smile on that morbid face.

"Hey, baby, did you have a good day at school?" Mia spoke as brightly as her mood would allow.

Louisa stopped to look up at her. "Where's Aunt Jamie?" she said.

"She's at home. I'm taking you to your dad's for the weekend, remember? I've packed your bag so we're all ready to go."

"Miss Reynolds?" a voice called from the school entrance.

Mia glanced around to see Miss Barker approaching them. "May I have a word?" she said, without a greeting.

"Is there a problem?" Mia asked her.

"Not a problem as such, but there has been a small incident today that's left me a little concerned. Have you got time for a quick chat?"

Mia glanced at her watch. Another thirty minutes and she'd hit the rush hour traffic coming out of Leeds. "It would have to be very quick. What's it about?"

"I think it might be easier if I showed you. Would you like to come inside?"

"All right, if it's that important. Come on, Lou." Mia took her daughter's hand, and they followed Miss Barker back to the school. Once they'd reached the classroom, Louisa was instructed to wait in the activity area at the back while the teacher fished an A3 sheet of paper out of her desk drawer.

"Now, it's probably nothing," Miss Barker passed the sheet to Mia, "but the kids were doing some artwork this afternoon and Louisa painted something quite disturbing."

Glancing over the image, Mia's face turned whiter than the paper in her hands. 'Disturbing' was one word for it. The thing was so inconceivably bizarre that she thought it was coming to life, but it was only the painting quivering in her hands.

"Miss Reynolds?"

"Huh?"

"I asked if this meant anything to you."

"What?"

"The picture."

"Oh." Mia's gaze returned to the painted tree. The colours and blending were actually quite marvellous – they must have been for her to recognise it as the oak from Godestone Manor. She might have been proud if it wasn't for the robed woman hanging from one of the branches.

"I, er ..." Mia didn't have an excuse, although any would have been better than the truth – whatever that may be. There was no way Jamie would have told her niece about the suicide, and even if Louisa had been listening in on their conversation last night, Mia had mentioned nothing about the hanging.

"Do you know who this woman is?" Miss Barker pointed to the image. "Have there been any deaths Louisa knows of, or might she have seen something on the television?"

"Not that I can think of." Mia looked into the teacher's dubious face. "What was the assignment anyway?"

"They were to choose a past experience – a family outing, for example – and explain to the class why it was special to them."

"And what did Louisa say?"

"Nothing, I took the painting away before any of the other children started asking questions. She refused to do another one, and when I asked why she'd drawn it, she said she didn't know." A pause, and then: "Louisa also talks about her grandmother a lot. I understand she no longer lives with you?"

"That's right. Are you saying this has something to do with my mum?"

"Well, as I'm sure you know, children can be very unsettled by change. I do get the feeling it might be affecting Louisa more than she's letting on."

"I thought she was doing well at school? At least, that's the impression you gave me last week."

"Yes, very well. She's bright, sociable, enthusiastic – that's why I was so shocked when she came up with something so macabre."

"I see." Mia gave her back the painting, mainly because she could no longer stand to look at it. "Well, thanks for bringing it to my attention. I'll have a word with my sister, she often minds Louisa while I'm at work. Teenagers and their horror films, eh?" Mia gave a casual chuckle, but was silenced by a disapproving arch to the woman's brows.

"Yes, well, do let me know – and have a lovely weekend," she said.

"You, too." Mia turned and headed for the door, calling Louisa on the way out. Before leaving she stole a quick glance at Miss Barker, who was still studying the grisly painting.

***

Coming off the A61 fifty minutes later, Mia glanced at her daughter in the rearview mirror. "If you carry on brushing like that then Cindy won't have any hair left," she warned.

Grooming the doll's golden mane, Louisa didn't look up once. Mia had put off talking about the painting that Miss Barker had shown her, seeing as Louisa had been so excited about going to stay with her dad, but she'd been unusually quiet on the drive down to Hillsborough in Sheffield. As Mia pulled into Whitby Lane, she couldn't skirt the issue any longer.

"Sweetie, do you know why Miss Barker wanted to talk to me earlier?"

No response. She glanced back into the rearview mirror. "Lou, will you answer me, please?"

"No."

"No, what?"

"I don't know why she wanted to talk to you."

"Well, she showed me the painting you did in class today. It wasn't very nice, was it?"

Louisa shrugged.

"Look, I know I got a bit cross with you the other night and I'm very sorry, but it's only because I want to help you. If you say you don't know where Tabby is then I believe you, but that picture could have upset a lot of children."

"Don't care."

"Maybe not, but if you don't explain to me why you did it then I'll turn the car round and we'll go straight back home."

"No!" Mia heard a clattering sound as Louisa hurled the doll against the back of the driver's seat.

"Then, tell me why you drew that horrible picture," she repeated calmly.

"I didn't."

"Well, Miss Barker said you did. And she thinks you're sad because Granny Viv doesn't live with us anymore."

"Miss Barker's a liar and her pants are on fire!"

Easing the car to a stop outside number twenty-one, Mia applied the handbrake and twisted to face Louisa, whose arms were folded right up under her chin.

"Are you worried about Grandma? Is that who the lady in the picture was supposed to be?" Mia spoke hopefully. Anything was better than having a psychic daughter, but Louisa's glare was anchored to the floor; her chin jutted defiantly.

"Fine," Mia unclipped her seatbelt, "if you're going to be difficult about it then we'll see what Daddy has to say."

Not the most fearsome of threats, but it was all she had. She got out of the car and fetched Louisa's overnight bag from the boot, then let her daughter out of the back door. On the path up to the house, Mia noticed that Nathan's four-by-four wasn't on the drive and her mood fractured even more. A minute or so after knocking, Regina answered the door. Thick raven waves tumbled over her shoulders, and her dark skin was blemish-free even with minimal makeup. She looked like Pocahontas in a pinny.

"Hi, Lou Lou." The woman deliberately greeted the child first, ruffling her hair as she dashed past her.

"Fuck off!" Louisa yelled, while disappearing into the house.

Mia wanted to laugh and cringe at the same time, more so the latter when Regina's deprecatory stare became like a chronic disfigurement.

"Don't ask," Mia said, handing her the overnight bag. "Nathan about?"

"He's just popped out for some on-ions." If it wasn't for the Spanish twang in Regina's accent, her hoarse 'smoker's' voice would have made her beauty seem like a mere illusion. Mia could see why Nathan had allowed himself to be bludgeoned into marriage so soon, but then there was nothing like a good dragon to keep him in check.

"Can I give him a message?"

Mia noted how the woman hadn't invited her to wait inside, but for some reason it annoyed her more than usual. "No, I'll ring him later tonight."

"Anything impor-tant?"

"I'm not sure yet."

Regina glowered at Mia as though she was purposely trying to be cryptic. Standing there on the doorstep like Queen High and Mighty, Mia could have laughed out loud. Regina's parents had emigrated to England when she was ten, and by the time she'd hit her early twenties, she was already married to a criminal and pregnant with her first child; therefore, it was no surprise that Mr and Mrs Cabello had fled back to Spain soon after.

"I'll let him know." Regina was already beginning to close the door. "Thanks for bringing Louisa over."

"No problem. Bye."

Back on the journey towards Leeds, the ache in Mia's jaw felt like she'd been clobbered with a mallet. One day she'd ask Pocahontas what her problem was. While she was at it, she might ask Nathan why he'd become such a dull, reticent shell. Then there was Jamie's apparent personality disorder and Louisa's obsession with dead things. And Brenda and Paul and –

"Bloody secrets!" Mia belted the steering wheel with the palm of her hand. Her thumb caught the horn and the car veered to the side. She received several hand gestures from other drivers and responded with a few of her own, then reduced her speed from forty to thirty. The longer it took her to get home, the better.

Home ... Mia scoffed. That was a joke in itself.

***

Dusk was setting in fast by the time Mia arrived in Bramley. She let herself into the house and almost walked straight back out. She thought something was burning at first, but that only masked the smell of stale dog farts.

She traced the odour into the kitchen and found Jamie hunched over a pan on the stove, stirring furiously. Mia went over for a gander, crinkling her nose.

"What in the name of God is that?" she said.

"It's supposed to be korma."

"Korma? It looks like Casey threw up in the pan." Mia picked up an empty food tin and inspected the label.

"I must have had the heat too high. Can it be saved?"

"The pan or the food?"

"Both."

Mia took over the stirring, using the spatula to prod the sticky paste, then turned off the hob. "Nice thought, sis. I'll rustle us up a salad or something, I'm not in the mood for cooking."

A quarter of an hour later, they sat down to tea in front of the television. It was even quieter in the house without Louisa to entertain them. Almost too quiet.

"So," said Jamie, stuffing a forkful of lettuce leaves into her mouth, "what happened at work this afternoon? I take it the police have finished investigating."

"Yeah, we'll be reopening as usual next week. Angela and I have had to cancel a load of bookings, which the boss isn't too pleased about."

"Did you find out who the old woman was?"

"Just some local – Missy Gibbons, her name was. Apparently, her daughter said she'd been suffering from depression ever since the death of her brother."

"That sucks," Jamie sympathised, while stacking as many tomato cubes as possible onto the prongs of her fork. "Hey, I've been doing some research into Leeds College today."

"Oh, yeah?" Mia cocked her head in interest.

"It says on the website that they're pretty flexible with entry requirements, depending on what it is you want to study. I might even be able to do a couple of exam resits on the side."

"Have you got a course in mind?"

"I thought an apprenticeship might be cool. Plus, the fees won't be as high."

"An apprenticeship in what, culinary skills?"

Jamie laughed, and the inelasticity in Mia's own lips made her realise how long it had been since she'd smiled. "Whatever I do has got to be better than sitting cooped up in here all day, even if it means getting a job. I will start paying my way around here."

"I'm glad to hear it," Mia said, half-joking. "Has Kerry been in touch since she left the hospital?"

"Not really," Jamie grunted. "Did you get a chance to speak to Brenda about our other little problem?"

The thought of Louisa's painting staunched Mia's appetite, but with Jamie eyeing her from across the room, she forced her food down with a smile. "Not yet."

"Do you really think we should be worried?"

"I honestly don't know, but the sooner we find out what's going on around here, the sooner we can do something about it. Whatever's happening to Louisa is more than temper tantrums, and I have a feeling it's only going to get worse. She's already told Regina to fuck off."

"Someone had to," Jamie said, before adding a bit more seriously, "Couldn't she just be copying something she's heard?"

"But from who?" Mia thought out loud. She'd been agonising all day over whether or not to share her thoughts about Paul's involvement in the strange phenomena, but the man was under constant surveillance by either Brenda or Wesley – unless they were in on the whole thing as well.

"Jay, remember the night when Kerry cut herself up?" Mia said.

"How could I forget?"

"Are you absolutely positive that no one could have got into the house, maybe influenced her in some way?"

"I'm pretty sure I'd have noticed someone legging it up and down the stairs." Jamie swallowed her food. "Where's this coming from anyway?"

"I'm just trying to rule out a few things. Do you fancy seeing Mum tomorrow?"

"Yeah."

"Cool."

They finished their teas in silence.

***

A jarring scream tore through the house. Mia's head was off the pillow in an instant, her heart like a throbbing jelly in the back of her throat.

"Lou –" she began, but common sense apprised her that it couldn't have been her daughter because she was forty miles away.

Scrambling out of bed, she tore down the landing to Jamie's bedroom. Dawn penetrated the curtains to create a murky half-light, and Mia's gaze was drawn to the bed where the sheets smothered a thrashing body like cling film.

"Jesus." Mia dived over and attempted to pin down the girl's arms, but they wrestled with her defiantly.

"Get off me!" Jamie was screaming. "Please, don't – please, stop. *Pleeease!*"

"Wake up, Jay, you're dreaming." Mia tried shaking her instead, but the wailing only got louder. Afraid she might disturb the neighbours, Mia grabbed a glass of water from the bedside table and chucked its contents over her sister's face.

Jamie gasped and sat up, her chest heaving and water dripping onto her sweat-stained vest. The first time she looked at Mia, there wasn't an inkling of recognition in those green eyes. "W-what ... Mia?"

"Christ, Jay." Mia placed the empty glass back onto the table and switched on the lamp. "No wonder you're so tired if this is what goes on every night. What the hell was that about?"

"I-it was nothing. Just a stupid nightmare." Jamie picked the wet strands of hair off her face and then straightened her ponytail, using the corner of the duvet to dry herself off. With a noisy sigh, she let her arms flop down in between her legs. That's when Mia saw it: the thin red slash running diagonally across her wrist.

"What's this?" Mia lifted Jamie's arm and was able to verify that it was a small cut – or a scratch. There was another, larger mark a bit higher up, but Jamie yanked back her arm and hid it beneath the duvet.

"Have you quite finished poking me?" If it wasn't for the dramatic overreaction, Mia would have thought little of it.

"How did you get those marks?"

"Casey did it when I tried to take her for a walk the other day. Is that okay? Can I go back to sleep now?" Jamie's tone fluctuated between ridicule and rage.

"Do you want to talk about it?"

"I *said* it's nothing, are you deaf?"

"I meant the nightmare. With the shit that's been going on recently I thought ..." Mia left the sentence unfinished. She'd leaped out of bed so quickly that she hadn't had a chance to think about anything, and perhaps it was best left that way.

"Just go back to bed, yeah?" Jamie flipped over her pillow so the damp patch was facing the mattress, then she pulled the covers up over her shoulders.

Before turning off the lamp, Mia positioned the clock so she could see its ticking face. It was six forty in the morning. There was no point in going back to bed, it had taken her long enough to drift off the first time around. She stood up and made for the door, pausing to ask Jamie, "Are you sure you're okay?"

There was no answer.

CHAPTER SIXTEEN

"Jay, are you ready yet?" It was the third time Mia had called up the stairs, but there were still no sounds from above.

"Jamie!" She rested a hand on the banister. "I thought you were getting dressed, not knitting a whole new –"

Jamie came clumping down the stairs in her jog pants and hoody, jostling past Mia as if she hadn't seen her standing there. "I don't feel up to seeing Mum today," she said.

"Great, you could have told me that half an hour ago. What's wrong anyway? Is it because of what happened this morning?"

"I'm tired, okay? I don't want her to see me looking like crap."

"You look fine." Mia pursued her into the kitchen. "I don't particularly like seeing her stuck in that place either, but we've got to stay positive – for Mum's sake as much as ours."

"I'm not saying I'll never visit her again, just not today. Quit flapping, will you?"

"Fine, I'll tell Mum you're sick. But don't go blaming me the next time you show up there and she can't remember your face."

"Oh, piss off," Jamie grumbled, and Mia did just that. There was no point in quarrelling with the girl when she was in one of her moods, and she certainly wasn't going to expose Vivian to those negative vibes. Just because she was senile didn't mean she was stupid.

Stomping down the hallway, Mia heard Jamie curse again, only this time it was at the toaster.

***

Vivian was sitting in an armchair staring vacantly out of her bedroom window. The view from the second floor spanned out over the rear garden, and even on this dismal afternoon, the flowerbeds stood like technicoloured soldiers; trees and shrubbery all whispering like a choir in tune.

Mia was shown into the room by one of the Church View carers, who had already informed her that Vivian was having one of her 'bad' days. She walked straight over to her mother and pecked her on the cheek. "Hi, Mum, how are you today?"

Mia perched herself on the windowsill opposite Vivian, careful not to obscure her view. She might as well have been picking out her own grave plot for the look of resigned hopelessness that seemed to have beaten away what little plumpness remained in her cheeks.

"Jamie's sorry that she couldn't make it, but she sends her love." Mia spoke again. "She's been throwing up all morning – dodgy curry, I think."

"Curry?" Vivian flashed her a sidelong glance.

"Yeah, it tasted even worse than it looked."

Vivian snorted. "Lying whore, you'll have to do better than that."

"Pardon?"

"If Jamie has food poisoning then why aren't you ill as well?"

Mia had no excuses. Alzheimer's had stripped her mum of many things: her sense of humour, her motherly instincts and even chunks of her personality. Although Mia had grown used to this unpredictability, glimmers of the old Vivian were becoming more a burden than a blessing because each time she grew hopeful and, each time, she was left heartbroken and disappointed. It was a cruel ploy of the fates, having to say goodbye to her mother all over again, and Mia dreaded this even more than the disease itself.

Mia decided to switch tactics. "Louisa is settling in brilliantly at her new school. She's spending her first weekend with Nathan and Regina since we moved."

Vivian nodded, but it was only to gesture the window. "Chilly out there, is it?"

"It's not too bad. Uncle Billy's house is freezing, I was thinking about getting someone in to give it the once-over." In fact, she'd been considering it for some time in the hope to eliminate any supernatural theories. Better they found something than nothing at all.

Vivian's eyes constricted a little, and she looked at Mia with a despondency that hit her right in the chest. "Wasn't there long, was he? Poor chap finally found somewhere he could settle down and then he went and left me – his only sister. Still, I expect I won't be far behind him."

Mia stroked her mum's arm and gave a sympathetic murmur, both surprised and relieved that today she was aware of her brother's departure. But she had a feeling the relief wouldn't last for long.

"Did Uncle Billy ever talk to you about the house?" she asked Vivian.

"In what way?"

"I just wondered if he liked living there and what he thought of the neighbours. I know we weren't the closest of families, but you had more contact with him than Jamie and me."

Twiddling her fingers on her lap, Vivian looked to the window once more, as if her memories were out there somewhere, waiting to be reclaimed. "Bugs," she said, at last.

"What, Mum?" Mia leaned closer to her, having thought she'd misheard.

"Creepies – he hated them. The kids at school used to call him Billy Bug Squasher, ever since Daddy locked him in the shed as punishment for breaking Grandnanna's urn. I hadn't heard him squeal so much since that time he had a bad tooth pulled out by the dentist."

Interesting, but what has that got to do with the house? Mia wondered. Probably just another childhood memory creeping in amongst the haze.

"Is it chilly outside?" Vivian regurgitated her earlier question.

Mia smiled cheerlessly. "It's not too bad. Do you want to take a walk, get some fresh air? They tell me you haven't been out of your room in a while, and I know how much you love the garden."

Vivian snarled, a cruel kink to her upper lip. "You want me to freeze to death, don't you? Can't be bothered with me anymore."

"You know that's not true. We love you very much."

"She doesn't – that lying little bitch. I should have had an abortion when I had the chance."

"*Mother.*" Mia accented the word by deepening rather than raising her voice, not that it made a difference to the woman. "Jamie would be gutted if she heard you talking like that."

"Well, who wants a baby at thirty-nine? I only kept her because of

Brian. She was a mistake."

"Lou wasn't planned either, but now she's here I couldn't imagine life without her."

"Who?"

"Louisa, your granddaughter."

Vivian scowled, but her lips were still fixed that wicked sneer. "What are you talking about? You're too young for children, silly girl. How would you know anything about motherhood?"

Sighing, Mia shook her head. "Never mind, I can see that you're not up for visitors so I won't stay for much longer. Is there anything I can do before I go? Anything you need?"

Vivian waved a hand in dismissal before letting it drop onto the arm of the chair. Mia kissed her on the cheek and then headed for the door. "Bye, then," she said, before leaving.

Vivian poked her head around the back of the chair. "Bye, love. Don't forget to let Billy out of the shed, it was an accident and Granny Wilson can always have a new urn."

"Don't worry," Mia replied, "Billy will be fine. We'll *all* be fine."

One of those promises was a lie. Mia hoped it wouldn't soon become two.

***

Jamie wasn't home when Mia got back from visiting Vivian; neither was Casey. She must have taken the dog for a walk which, considering their mother's current frame of mind, was probably better than having had a change of heart and found her own way to the care home. Mia couldn't blame her sister for wanting to escape the house for an hour or so – she'd only been there a couple of minutes and it felt like the rest of the planet had abandoned her.

Mia headed into the kitchen and switched on the kettle. It was still warm so Jamie couldn't have been gone for long. While the water was boiling, she rang Nathan's mobile. Regina answered, so Mia quickly hung up with the intention of trying again later. She'd already informed him of the tragedy at Godestone but hadn't yet had a chance to mention the painting that Louisa had done at school, and the last thing she needed was Regina's silent criticism.

She let the tea bag brew a good five minutes before sitting down at the table with her phone staring up at her, willing it to ring. Perhaps she'd been a little hasty in ignoring Regina; after all, anyone's voice was better than no one's. Even the humming of the freezer sounded like a bulldozer in the chronic silence. How Jamie spent all day indoors without losing what was left of her sanity was a miracle, only it had taken this long for Mia to realise it.

Eager to get her blood circulation flowing, she carried the mug over to the kitchen window. Outside, the hole that Casey had been digging in the back garden was even bigger than the last time she'd seen it; soil scattered over the newly mowed lawn. Mia shook her head and slurped her tea, wincing when she realised she'd forgotten to add the sugar. Nevertheless, it would take more than a sprinkle of Silver Spoon's to prepare her for the task ahead. Brenda had set off to work early that morning, which meant she was on a day shift and would be back in plenty of time for Mia to bombard her with questions about the house; about Paul and his PTSD.

Mia reached over to switch on the radio, setting the volume to about halfway. How she longed to hear Jamie's grousing, Louisa piping about one thing or another and her mother repeating facts and statements like a senile parrot. Even though the air was persistently cold, the atmosphere somehow felt heavy; suffocating. It was like being trapped in a crowded lift, except there were no people. No signs of existence. Nothing but her in this empty, isolated tomb.

***

Louisa watched Jack Summers pushing around his toy fire truck, its plastic wheels leaving track marks in the navy carpet. He parked it to one side while he took a couple of cars and smashed them into one another, tossing them into the air as if they'd been blasted from the force of an imaginary explosion.

"Boom!" he roared, as they clattered to the floor. He returned to the fire engine, wheeling it round in frenzied circles. "*Nee-nah, nee-nah, nee-nah!*"

Louisa picked her Cindy doll up off the bed and pottered over to him. She'd been sitting there for ages and he still hadn't invited her to join in.

He never did.

"Can we play, Jack?" she asked the boy, who was a couple of years older than herself.

"No."

"Why not?"

"Because it's *my* toy. Dad got it me for my birthday." Jack clutched the truck possessively to his chest.

"He's not your real daddy," Louisa stressed.

"He will be soon, my mum told me. My daddy, my daddy!"

Louisa glowered at the boy, blood gushing to her cheeks. "Shut up and let me play!"

"I don't like playing with *girls*." Jack ripped the doll out of her hands and chucked it onto the floor, then he drove the fire truck over Cindy's grinning face.

"Stop it!" Louisa made a lunge for the doll, snapping back her hand when the wheels nipped her fingertips. "Ouch, I hate you!"

"I hate you more, and your stupid Cindy."

"When you come to my house, the shadow man is going to kill you."

The truck plopped out of Jack's hand and tumbled onto its side. He stared up at Louisa as if she was a giant about to trample him to death, the whites of his eyes gleaming beneath her shadow.

"I'm telling!" he said, leaping to his feet.

Louisa waited until he'd reached the door before grabbing the truck and marching after him. As he scrabbled with the handle, she raised the toy high above her head and then brought it crashing down onto his skull.

CHAPTER SEVENTEEN

Approximately two hours after Jack Summers had been rushed into hospital, Mia arrived in Hillsborough. She parked the Corsa on the street outside Nathan's semidetached and then knocked on the front door. He answered a few seconds later with his youngest stepson, Liam, balanced on his hip, one arm supporting him from underneath.

"Thanks for coming," he said, taking a step back so Mia could enter the house.

"Where's Louisa? Is Jack okay?" she asked him.

"The doctors want to keep him in overnight for observations, but it's looking like a bit of swelling and maybe some concussion."

"All that from a toy truck?"

"There was some blood on his bedroom door handle so he must have slipped and hit his head. Louisa pretty much confessed straight away, so I haven't given her too much of a hard time."

"Is Regina still at the hospital?"

"Yeah, this one was getting grouchy so I said I'd bring him home while I waited for you to collect Louisa. Sorry you've had to come all the way down here again, but Gina kind of insisted."

"It's no problem, I'm just glad Jack's going to be okay."

Two and a half-year-old, Liam, stretched out to Mia, grinning inanely. Nathan used both arms to support the wriggling boy. "'Ello, Auntie Mi Mi," he chirped.

"Hello, trouble." Mia clasped his tiny fingers while sticking her tongue out. Liam gurgled and chuckled, totally unaware of what had happened to his older brother – or what could have happened if Louisa had hit him that little bit harder.

"Lou's just through here." Nathan nudged the living room door open with his bare foot, and Mia hurried past him. Louisa was sitting cross-legged in front of the television.

"Hi, baby, your dad's told me what happened." Mia crouched next to her. "Why on earth did you do it?"

"Jack was being horrible to Cindy." Louisa spoke as if her actions were perfectly justified.

"Cindy's made from plastic, Jack isn't. You can't go around attacking people like that."

"But he's trying to take Daddy away."

Mia coiled an arm around Louisa's shoulders, but her affection wasn't requited. "Sweetheart, you know Daddy's got two families now. You've got to learn to share him, but that doesn't mean he loves you any less."

Nathan added, "Your mum's right, Lou. You'll always be my special girl."

"But you're going to be Jack and Liam's proper dad soon and then you won't want me!" Louisa burst out.

Mia shot Nathan a backwards glance. "Is there something I should know?"

Transferring Liam onto his other hip, Nathan indicated the adjoined dining room with a bob of his head. "Through here," he said, shuffling through the broad archway with his oversized jeans dragging along the spotless carpet. Mia waltzed after him, making sure Louisa was in her sight at all times. She'd trust a stray dog over the girl right now.

"Well?" she said to Nathan. "What's the big secret?"

Nathan set Liam down on the floor, then his hand disappeared into his bushy mane as he scratched nervously at his scalp. "The thing is, well, Regina wants me to adopt the kids."

"Okay. And you didn't think to mention this sooner?"

"I was going to tell you when I brought Louisa back on Sunday. I thought we could explain it to her together, only Regina went and blurted it out to the boys last week. I had a word with Louisa and she seemed cool with it, so I didn't think there'd be a problem."

"Cool?" Mia placed emphasis on the word. "News like that would mess with a teenager's head, let alone a five-year-old. Trust me, I live with both."

Nathan shrugged while watching the toddler waddle about the dining area. "We've been married for six months now, and it's not like their biological dad gives a damn. Regina seemed to think it was for the best."

"Well, congratulations and all, but if Jack was taunting Louisa about something like that then it's no wonder she flipped. And if your wife is thinking of banning her visits then you can bloody well sort it out because Louisa needs stability now more than ever."

"Why are you making it out to be my fault?" Nathan raised his voice without sounding angry. "I know the kid's got a temper, but you said yourself that her behaviour has been getting out of control lately."

"You don't know the half of it," Mia mumbled.

"What's that supposed to mean?"

Liam was now hanging off his stepdad's leg in a babbling endeavour to steal his attention. Louisa's motive might not have been too dissimilar in the beginning, but Mia knew it was going to take a lot more than kisses and cuddles to remedy whatever was happening to their sweet girl.

"Did you get a chance to speak to Louisa about what we discussed the other night?" she asked Nathan.

"Kinda."

"And?"

"I asked her if she liked the new place and how she was getting on at school, tried to keep it casual. She didn't say much apart from how everyone seemed happier at the old house, but isn't that to be expected?"

"That's what I thought until I picked her up from school yesterday," Mia began, and she went on to tell Nathan about Louisa's painting; the sleepless nights and the bedwetting, which was becoming more and more frequent as the nights passed by.

"Maybe she's feeling a little unbalanced," Nathan tried to reason. "She's been through a lot more than most five-year-olds, and she knows Vivian isn't well. If she overheard you talking about the suicide and put two and two together then –"

Mia shook her head vehemently. "I've been mulling over it all night, Nathan. There's literally no way Louisa could have known about what happened at Godestone, certainly not in so much detail as to go and paint a bloody picture of it."

"So, what's the alternative?" Nathan asked simply.

"Why don't we go and find out?"

And so, the two of them returned to the living room like detectives preparing for an interrogation. Nathan settled Liam on the play mat with some toys while Mia went and knelt by Louisa. They hadn't devised a plan as such, just to coax the truth out of her as quickly and painlessly as possible.

"Sweetheart, your dad and I want to talk to you about something very important." Mia started without Nathan. "We need you to tell us why you drew that picture at school. You know, the one with the tree and that poor lady?"

Louisa shrugged, which was about as much as Mia had expected. Nathan sat down on the sofa behind them and lifted the girl onto his lap. "You know you did a bad thing today, don't you?" he said.

"Nate," Mia hissed, but he held up a hand to placate her.

Louisa nodded, and Nathan went on, "I was cross with you at first, but what happened when you told me the truth about what you'd done to Jack?"

"You gave me hugs."

"That's right, because lies are bad and all they do is get you into trouble. Sometimes secrets can be bad, too – especially when they make you feel sad. Understand?"

Louisa nodded again.

"When you're hurting inside, your mum and I feel it as well. You don't want that, do you?"

"No."

"Well, the only way we can fix the problem is if you talk to us. I promise we won't be angry."

Wise. Mature. Astute ... Mia wondered if it was Nathan sitting opposite her and not another figment of her imagination.

Louisa said, "If I tell, the shadow man will get me."

"The *what* man?" Nathan looked to Mia's whitewashed face. "Do you know what she's talking about?"

Mia felt the contents of her stomach evaporate there and then. Even if she was ready to disclose her own experiences and fears, she wouldn't have got far as Louisa continued, "He used to hide from people, but now he's strong and he's not scared anymore. He's old and grumpy and he hates us all."

"Oh, sweetheart." Mia clasped Louisa's tremulous hands in both of hers. She was so little, so vulnerable, and to think of her suffering in silence all this time caused the anger to swell inside Mia until she thought she might self-combust.

"What does this man want?" She couldn't disguise the gravity in her voice.

Another hesitation, and then the build-up of words came more freely. "He's stuck in the house and he wants to get out."

"Did he make you paint that picture?"

"No."

"But it's got something to do with the shadow man, hasn't it? Maybe something he told you ..."

From the corner of her eye, Mia could see Nathan's frown etching itself deeper and deeper into his forehead, but he retained his composure as promised. Chances were, he didn't have a clue how to react, and if Mia was honest with herself then neither did she.

"I don't know why I did it," was Louisa's response. "He makes me see horrible things in my head. I don't like him, Mummy. Can you make him go away?"

"Of course, you don't have to be afraid anymore. Was he the one who hurt Tabby as well? Were you scared that I wouldn't believe you?"

"He said if I told, the men would come and take Casey away."

Nathan chimed in, "Who or what the hell is Tabby?"

"It's next door's cat, she went missing a while ago. Casey must have snapped and attacked her or something." Mia concentrated on her daughter. "Louisa, do you know this man's name? What he looks like? Do you recognise him from anywhere?"

Louisa shook her head. At least there was a good chance Paul could be absolved from the equation, unless he'd threatened the girl in some way. Mia didn't know which of the scenarios was worse.

"Is he a real man like Daddy or ..." *here goes*, "is he invisible like Casper the ghost?"

"A gho –" Nathan couldn't bring himself to utter the word. "Jesus Christ, what is this? What the bloody hell is going on?" Even though he kept his voice hushed, there was a sense of urgency in it that caused Louisa to clam up once more.

Ignoring him, Mia reassured the girl, "It's okay, we're not angry with you. Just tell me where I can find this man."

"He's at home."

"What, now?"

Louisa nodded. "He's always there. Sometimes he watches us but no one else can see him. He said to keep it a secret because you wouldn't believe me and you'd send me to a home for naughty girls like you sent Grandma away to the madhouse."

"My god," Mia whispered, glancing away to hide the surfacing tears. She felt a hand touch upon her shoulder and looked into Nathan's pitiful face.

"There you have it." He spoke gently. "She's overwhelmed, confused even. This is about one thing: A-T-T-E-N-T-I-O-N." He spelled out the last word.

"Haven't you been listening to a word she's said? There's something in the goddamn house. Something –" She stopped herself, realising she didn't have a word to describe the thing that had been tormenting her only daughter. 'Evil' had been used on more than one occasion, and there was no longer a trace of doubt in Mia's mind that that was what it was.

"Mia, you're not making any sense." Nathan's voice hardly reached the tumult in her thoughts. "Who is this guy you're all so scared of?"

"I-I don't know but ... everything that's happened ... it's all real, Nate. This thing has been worming its way into our lives for weeks. It wants to destroy us, just like it destroyed him."

"Who?"

"My uncle." Mia gazed up at Nathan as the realisation dawned on her. "Billy didn't just die. Something caused that heart attack. I think he was ... *murdered*."

***

Jamie let herself into the house and unclipped the lead from Casey's collar. "There's a good girl, see what a bit of fresh air can do?" she said, ruffling the dog's sheeny coat. She'd definitely lost some weight over the last few weeks, but then none of them had had much of an appetite recently.

Casey tilted her head to the side while panting furiously, tongue drooping from her mouth. "Phwar!" Jamie made a fanning motion with her hand. "Go and have a drink, your breath reeks worse than a sewer."

As the dog trotted off into the kitchen, Jamie slung her hoody over the stair banister and then plodded into the living room. The television was off, sofa unoccupied.

"Mia?" she called, backtracking into the hall. She could see from where she stood that there was no one in the kitchen and bellowed up the stairs, "Hey, we're back! You up there?"

No reply. *She must still be at the care home,* Jamie figured. After the way she'd spoken to Mia that morning, she wouldn't have blamed her sister if she never came home.

She returned to the living room and switched on the TV, then collapsed onto the sofa with a tub of Pringles that she'd picked up from the local shop. Chomping away, she reached for the remote control and skipped through the Freesat channels. Man, she was beginning to loathe daytime television. She'd give anything to be back in a classroom during one of Mr Hodge's brain-melting history lessons.

"Boring, boring, boring –"

Slam!

Jamie shot up, Pringles flying everywhere and the remote bouncing halfway across the carpet. She couldn't be sure over the noise from the telly, but it had sounded like a door being flung shut.

Licking her fingers clean, she scurried into the hallway. "Jesus, you scared the –"

Jamie was greeted by an empty silence. Moving only her head, she glanced from left to right as if waiting to cross a road. She crept over to the front door, made sure it was locked and then retreated to the living room. A peek through the bay window revealed that it definitely couldn't have been Mia because her car wasn't outside. She couldn't recall leaving a window open, but the house was as draughty as a cave sometimes. There was no other explanation apart from ...

"Casey, you shit," Jamie grumbled. She started to gather the Pringles off the carpet when there was a loud scrape from above. She slowly looked up to the ceiling, her heart beat accelerating. There it was again: a heavy jarring sound, as if the furniture was being lugged around in her own bedroom.

"Oh, God." Jamie covered her mouth with her hands as if to stifle her breaths. She glanced around fretfully, not knowing whether to run or hide – either way, she wasn't leaving without Casey.

With light, nimble steps, she tiptoed into the hallway. The dog was already at the bottom of the stairs glaring upwards, shoulders hunched; a continuous growl escaping through her gnashed teeth.

"*Psst* ... Casey," Jamie whispered, even though the intruder must have been well aware of her presence. She clicked her fingers as quietly as possible. "Please, don't bark."

The dog lowered its torso even more. Her growls intensified into deep, jagged snarls. *Who or what in the name of Satan is up there?* Jamie thought. Casey was well known for her hatred of cats, but it must have been a bloody big one to hurl the furniture around like that.

"Casey, shut up and get over here. We've got to – *no!*" Jamie lunged forwards when the dog hurtled up the stairs at a missile speed. No way was she going up there after her – Casey had four sets of nails and dagger-like canines to defend herself with, and if she was going to tear rashers out of the trespasser then Jamie didn't want to be around to witness it.

She'd just reached the front door when there was a crash and numerous thuds from upstairs. The shrill whine that came immediately after caused her hand to freeze on the door handle. Turning her head, she peered up into the dimness of the landing. The tautness in her chest and throat prevented her from calling to the animal – from even breathing. A gentle tug on the handle reminded her that she'd locked it earlier. She reached for her keys, which she always dumped on the telephone table no matter where she'd been. They weren't there.

Jamie circled on the spot, scanning the ground in case they'd fallen off, but the keys seemed to have vanished. Flattening herself against the door, all she could hear was a voice inside urging her to find another way out of the house and wait for help; but Casey's image in her mind's eye could just as well have been her own child staring back at her through the lens of a camera.

"Damn it!" Jamie thwacked the door with her elbow.

In the end it was pure adrenaline that led her back to the telephone table. She picked up the dog lead and coiled the ends of the chain around each of her hands to make a sort of garrotte, which she tugged multiple times to test the tension. What she intended on doing with it, she had no idea – especially if the supernatural was involved. How could she kick an ass that, technically, didn't exist?

Gulping down her nerves, the lead taut in her hands, she gingerly treaded the never-ending staircase.

CHAPTER EIGHTEEN

"Come on, Lou, it's time to go." Mia hooked her hands under Louisa's armpits and lifted her off Nathan's knee. "Have you got her bag ready?" she asked him.

"Wait – that's it?" Nathan rose sharply. "You can't tell me you think some creep murdered your uncle and then just take off!"

"What am I supposed to do? Princess Regina has made it perfectly clear that Louisa isn't welcome here, and I assume that extends to the rest of us as well."

"But –"

"Mummy, I need to get Cindy from upstairs," Louisa broke in.

"Okay, hurry up." Mia was about to follow her out when Nathan caught her arm.

"Are you losing it upstairs or something? I love that kid, too, but she's obviously got issues and you running around after her like this is exactly what she wants. Think about it a second: murder is one thing, but *killer ghosts* ..." Nathan left Mia to entertain the notion for herself.

"Look, if you'd seen some of the things I have ... if you'd felt what I've felt ..." She finished by shaking her head, a stinging sensation in her eyes that usually came before tears. Trying to explain was a waste of time and effort, both of which were vital if she was going to face whatever was to come next.

"So, what," Nathan tailed her into the hallway, "you're going to pop down to the local church and get some old codger to perform an exorcism?"

"If that's what it takes." Mia stopped to bellow up the stairs, "Chop,

125

chop, Louisa!"

"*Mia.*"

She glanced at Nathan once more, taken aback not only by the seriousness of his tone but the sensitivity that exuded from it. Louisa's entrance into the world may have created a hindrance between them, made their lives more complicated than either of them wanted or needed at the time, but here was a glimpse of the friend she'd known and cared about all those years ago. It was a shame, Mia thought, how it had taken such dire circumstances to spark some passion back into the man.

"Trust me, I know how all of this sounds," Mia said. "But I will do anything to protect my family, and if that makes me crazy then I'll just have to live with it."

"I didn't say you were –" Nathan was interrupted by Louisa galloping downstairs with the Cindy doll swinging by its hair. Mia spotted her bag in the hall and slung it over her shoulder before steering Louisa towards the door, but it was as if her toes had grown roots beneath the floorboards.

"What are you waiting for?" Mia stared down at her. "We're going home now."

"Can I stay with Daddy?"

"What?" Mia released her slightly, now unable to move herself. "You can't stay here, you've got school on Monday."

"I don't want to go – please, Daddy?" Louisa hugged the doll close to her chest, and her dark eyes expanded in a cartoon-like fashion.

Nathan looked from the girl to Mia. "Maybe I can talk to Regina, persuade her to let Louisa stay a couple more days. Just until you've had a chance to sort things out."

"And have her treated like a goddamn problem child? I don't think so. From now on, I'm not letting her out of my sight."

"I'm just trying to show some responsibility," Nathan argued. "I thought that's what you wanted?"

"I don't expect you to understand any of this, as long as you're there for Louisa if and when she needs you. I've already made the mistake of not believing her and I don't intend on making it again."

"Dada, dada!" Liam piped from the living room. Nathan rushed back to the door, his head disappearing through the gap.

"Hang on, mate, I'll be there in a minute." He half-turned to face Mia. "Look, you know you can call me at any time. Whatever's going on with Louisa, it's nowt we can't fix."

"It looks like you've got enough to worry about here," she replied. "Say bye to your dad, Lou."

Nathan bent down for a hug off his daughter, but she passed by him with little more than a grunt. Mia let herself out of the house and marched to the car with Louisa trotting after her. After strapping themselves in, she started up the engine and left Whitby Lane. She waited until they were back on the main road before trying to formulate a plan, but it seemed the consternation of it all had paralysed her thinking. Only one person had the answers Mia needed, and she was sitting in the back of the car gazing out of the window like something fresh off a mortuary slab.

"You okay, sweetheart?" Mia asked Louisa.

A muted voice from behind her answered, "I want Daddy."

"I know, but he's got a lot to deal with right now. Jack's very poorly, and he can't leave Regina and the boys no matter how much he wants to."

"Does he hate me?"

"Of course not – you must never think that, you hear?"

Louisa nodded glumly.

"Now, I know you're scared but I'm going to ask you one last question and I need you to think very carefully about it. If I wanted to meet this shadow man, what would I have to do?"

"You can only see him if he wants you to. What does 'cock teaser' mean?"

Mia's eyes locked onto the rearview mirror for so long that she almost missed the next turning. The little face staring back at her in the reflection was so innocent, so unsuspecting that she couldn't possibly have conceived such a term. "W-what ... Where have you heard that?" Mia asked.

"It's what the shadow man calls Aunt Jamie. And he uses naughty words."

"What words? It's okay, you can tell me."

"He said ..." Louisa nibbled her bottom lip. "He said Aunt Jamie is an 'effing slag' and he's going to sort her out."

Mia threw a swift glance over her shoulder, half expecting Louisa to be giggling away as if it was all a big odious prank. But she wasn't laughing, and Mia could tell by her face that it was the gut-scrambling truth.

Mia gulped twice, then her eyes were back on the road. She pressed down harder on the accelerator pedal and gripped the steering wheel until her fingers ached and her knuckles were bloodless.

For once, home seemed all too far away.

CHAPTER NINETEEN

Five … four … three steps left.

Jamie had nothing left to swallow, her mouth was that dry. She slackened her hold on Casey's lead as the metal rings ate into her skin and left red imprints in her hands, at the same time wishing she'd chosen a more functional weapon. Better yet, she should have called the police as soon as she'd heard the disturbance upstairs, but Casey's image drove her forwards until she'd reached the landing.

On this dull mid-afternoon, only a squint of daylight passed through the tiny window at the end of the corridor. She thought about calling for the dog, but it would only draw attention to herself. God, she hoped Casey was okay. Jamie hadn't heard so much as a sniff out of the animal for well over two minutes, and her dread was soaring like liquid mercury. A quick search for the cause of the bangs she'd heard earlier revealed nothing overtly suspicious. She was pretty sure the noises had come from her bedroom, which was the first door on her left.

With the chain looped around her hands, Jamie realised she'd be at a disadvantage if she used them to open the door. Someone might be hiding behind it, waiting for her to sneak past them. Waiting to leap out and do whatever it was they planned on doing with her weak, defenceless body.

Screw this, Jamie thought, turning back the way she'd come from. A whimper from her bedroom snatched at her collar like an invisible hand, and she was in front of the door before she'd even willed her legs to move.

"Right, you bastard!" Raising her arms in front of her, she drew her knee up to her chest and was a second away from booting the door with her trainer when Icona Pop blasted from her shorts' pocket.

"Shit!" She jumped back in an uncoordinated half-spin, almost toppling over her own feet. For a reason she had no time to consider, she made a sprint for the bathroom and bolted herself inside. She fumbled for her mobile, her back pressed against the door for extra stability should the intruder try to force it open.

"Mia?" she answered.

"Jay, where are you?" came her sister's distant voice.

"At home, where the hell are you?"

"Are ..." *crackle*, "okay?"

"What?"

"Listen, you ... trouble. Get out ... wait for me ... Brenda's."

"I can't hear you, the line's all fuzzy." Jamie's voice dropped to a whisper. "I think there's someone in the house. Did you get that?" She pressed a finger to her other ear, as if it would help to make things clearer. "Hello? Mia?"

"*... danger ...*"

More static, a bleep and then silence.

Jamie checked the screen. No signal. "Ah, crap, not now!"

Waving the phone above her head, she made small circles around the room but there was no improvement. Great, now the cops really were out of the question. She placed the dog lead on the side of the sink and decided to try one last tactic before escaping the house via one of the windows if she had to.

Clearing her throat, she returned to the bathroom door and assumed a dominance that was restricted to her voice only. "That was the police on the phone! Leave now and you might have a chance, I won't stop you. Just don't hurt my dog!"

The reply of total silence made her feel even more foolish and confused. 'Danger': that was Mia's last word before the phone had mysteriously cut out, and she'd also mentioned Brenda's name. *Oh, God, it couldn't be her freak brother coming to finish what he'd started last week, could it?* Jamie fretted.

Having given up waiting for a signal to return, she typed a brief text message to Mia in the hope that she'd call the police upon receipt of it. Something caused her to stop mid-sentence. She wasn't sure what, how or why, but it was that feeling you get when you just *know* someone's behind you, even though you haven't seen or heard them. When your flesh starts to creep and every nerve ending tingles, every hair stands erect in warning of what your mind is slow to detect – kind of like ESP or whatever they called it.

Then came the stench, like someone had dug up a graveyard and set fire to the multitude of corpses: the decay, the burning of flesh, rags and hair. At the same time it was an odour far too putrid to have been human, let alone natural. She glanced down expecting to see smoke pouring through the gap under the door, but soon realised that it wasn't coming from outside. It was there with her. In that very room.

Whatever you do, Jamie told herself, *don't turn around*. They always did this in the films and she always screamed at them for being morons. Only here and now did she learn that shrugging off one's curiosity, no matter how bowel-destroying it was, was a physical impossibility.

With the phone wobbling in her hands, she rotated her head as far to the right as it would go. Before the rest of her body could follow, her screams were already resounding around the confines of the bathroom. The *thing* – and that's all her petrified brain would allow her to perceive – loomed over her. A dense, juddering shape that was so black it was as if night had fallen in that very room. It emanated a chill that crept through her rather than around her, and Jamie didn't know if she was shivering because of that or sheer, bone-locking horror.

A pale globe appeared near the top of the shadow, with two dark rings in the centre and some random, discoloured blobs a few inches below. The curves and angles of a human face appeared, and ...

Holy shit, the blobs were actually teeth!

The grooves in the phantom's face looked like they'd been sculpted from melted wax, and the yawning motion of its jaw was accompanied by a sharp, scratchy hiss. The frosty breath on her cheek – the realisation that the monster was real – galvanised Jamie into action. She prised open the lock on the bathroom door before pelting down the landing, half-blinded by tears of horrified despair.

A figure blocked the stairs, and the collision sent her reeling backwards. She attempted to turn at the same time she descended, enabling her to scramble away without stopping. Instead she blundered forwards several feet before crashing to the ground, the rough carpet grazing her elbows and forearms. Even without having identified the stranger, their physique had been too tall, too scrawny for it to have been her sister. When she stared up into that pitted face, saw the leering dark eyes and the wetness on those thin lips, everything came to a transitory standstill. The agony in her chest felt like her heart had fallen into a trauma-induced spasm – she didn't realise it was because she'd stopped breathing.

The man flexed one of his legs in preparation to move forwards, eyes brimming with dark desire.

"No!" Jamie kicked out at the air between them.

The smirk spanned across his face, infecting the rest of his features.

"W-why are you ... How did you ..."

No matter how many questions clogged in Jamie's mind, she could only wrestle with her words. She'd have put the whole thing down to insanity if she hadn't blinked and found the man still standing there, exactly as he had been all those months ago. Same grungy tracksuit, the same whiff of stale alcohol and the same red rings around those cadaverous eyes. Jamie should have left the party there and then. In fact she shouldn't have been there in the first place, but it made her feel big. Clever. Cool.

It turned out that she was none of those things.

Jamie quailed when the man raised a spindly arm, but it was only to feel the back of his skull. Then he gazed down at the deep red fluid on his hand, dribbling through his open fingers. "Look at what you did to me, you whore," he snarled.

Jamie shook her head while scrabbling away on her elbows and feet in a half-crab position. "This isn't real," she murmured, as if hearing the words would make them so. "You couldn't have found me. Something's messing with my mind!"

The man cocked his head to the side, giving himself a lopsided grin. "Perhaps." His hand slid down to his belt buckle. "Shall we find out?"

All it took were those four words and Jamie was on her feet, stumbling in the opposite direction to the stairs with a demented cry. This time she bypassed the bathroom on account of the floating wraith, the next room in line being her sister's. Hearing the clomping of boots behind her, she had no time to barricade herself inside and headed straight for the window, yanking the latch with such savagery that chips of paint flaked off onto the windowsill; but it was jammed with years of grime and damp. Then she saw something that fuelled a last surge of desperation.

"Hey – up here!" Jamie rapped on the glass before waving her arms around frenziedly.

Outside on the front, Wesley was leaning into the boot of his car with just his long legs visible from the window. If he'd heard her then he didn't acknowledge it, but another face stared up at her from the pavement: pale, vacant but, most importantly, seeing.

"Paul! *Heeellp* –" A hand was clamped over Jamie's jaw, tobacco-stained fingers probing her mouth and choking her with their stench. The man's bristly skin felt like sandpaper against her cheek, and the memories it conjured left Paul's face a blur through her tears.

"Please," Jamie's whimper was muffled by the hand, "d-don't hurt me."

"Like you hurt me?" a voice rasped in her ear. In the window, Jamie caught a faint reflection of her attacker and the two black, whirring spheres – almost like storm clouds – where his eyes should have been.

"It was an ... a-accident. I swear –"

"Accident or not, your guilt made sure I'd catch up with you in the end, Jamie. Don't pretend like you don't want this, you goddamn slut!"

Clutching a fistful of her hair, the man wrenched Jamie away from the window and thrust her downwards onto the unmade bed. She bounced on her front, gripping the duvet to stop herself from rolling over the edge of it. Then she glanced back at the window expecting him to pounce on her.

The man had gone.

Jamie's momentary relief was superseded by a gut-whisking dread. It was as if she'd imagined the whole episode, from the noises upstairs to the tainted breath on her face. *Could that be why Paul had failed to react?* she wondered. Why he'd looked at her as though *she* was the crazy one?

"Oh, God," Jamie wept, her voice little more than a squeak. "What's h-happening to me?"

Her gaze darted about the soundless room, tears rolling down her cheeks. It struck her that now might be her last chance to do what she should have done right from the very beginning: run.

Maintaining rapid scans of the room, she started to shuffle towards the edge of the bed when a powerful force slammed her back down – the same unseen entity that she'd encountered in the kitchen weeks ago. As if the memory had appeared above her on a giant neon screen, those invisible fingers – like glaciated blocks of air – brushed up her thighs until they, too, became immobilised and she lay spread-legged on the bed.

Terror pumped though her, along with an incurable hopelessness. It was happening all over again, only this time it couldn't have been a dream, and if it was then there was no one to wake her. Jamie had never felt anything so malignant, so impure in all her life; and when her top rolled up over her breasts, the hows and whys suddenly seemed a million light years away.

Sobbing, she attempted to tug her T-shirt back down but the force moved up to her wrists in a cold, vice-like grip. Jamie watched her own arms wrestling with the air in front of her, the sight so surreal that she still thought she must have been imagining it. They were soon pinned down either side of her head, preventing her from covering herself as rough hands groped and rubbed; kneading and caressing her as if she was a lump of dough. It wasn't until she observed the dips and contortions of her reddened flesh that her brain was finally able to comprehend what her body felt as incontestably as she existed.

A crushing weight on Jamie's chest reduced her breaths to shallow grunts. Inside, her screams were so deafening that they might have been in competition with her thumping heart, but it seemed even her tear ducts were frozen. Next came the slimy, leech-like sucking sensation on her neck and the cold, foul air that almost gassed her to unconsciousness, for which she might have been grateful for. Especially when the buttons on her shorts popped open, a couple of them pinging off onto the bed.

This is it, Jamie thought. In fact, it was her only thought at that moment in time. She didn't need to see the entity to understand the pleasure it was getting out of her nakedness, for she could feel it in its touch and its aura of sadistic depravity; but still she closed her eyes, squeezing out the last of her tears. The fight was over for her, mentally as well as physically. All she could do now was shut down, force her mind to another place and wait until the nightmare was over. Wait until the presence had satisfied itself in whatever fashion it desired. Whether or not Jamie would be alive by the end of it no longer mattered to her, because the damage was irreversible. It wasn't just her modesty she'd lost that afternoon.

Most of all, she'd lost her sanity.

***

"Come on, pal, make yourself useful." Wesley dumped several bags of shopping down by Paul's feet. He took the remaining groceries out of the boot of the car before locking it up.

"Paul," he echoed. "What planet are you on, Mars?"

Paul continued to ignore his brother-in-law, too engrossed by what he'd seen to acknowledge anything else. Wesley eventually drew up beside him and followed his eyeline towards next door's top window.

"Christ, how many times do we have to tell you to leave those lasses alone? *Oi* ..." He clicked his fingers in front of Paul's face. "What's with you, eh? If it's action you're after then I'll load up the laptop while your sister isn't around. It's nothing to be ashamed about, us blokes all have needs. That's what you told me once upon a time."

Paul gave him an absent stare. There wasn't a flutter of interest in his face, which was more dishevelled than usual: whiskers prickling out in all directions, brown hair looking like he'd just walked off a beach.

"Look," Wesley spoke through a sigh, "you know how Brenda worries about you. She already thinks there's something funny going on in that house, and you stalking everyone who lives there isn't helping matters. Is this about Billy Wilson?"

A keen awareness rose in Paul's leaden eyes – something he tried with all his will to conceal from the man before him.

"I know you feel shitty about what happened, but you've got to let it go," Wesley insisted. "Now, how about we get this lot unpacked and then I'll clean you up a bit? You're never going to find a woman looking like a bleedin' scarecrow!"

With a deep chortle, he slapped Paul on the shoulder, at the same time noticing that his jumper was on back to front. "Have you been walking around the supermarket like that? Christ, Bee would kill me."

Still laughing, he proceeded down the garden path towards the house. Paul glanced up to next door's window again, only this time he saw nothing. He wasn't unused to the deceptiveness of his eyes these days; after all, the scars inflicted on that grisly morning would never fully heal. But the look on young Jamie's face ... the twisted, gaping jaw and eyes so wide that even from a distance they'd looked like black specks on the surface of a full moon ... that wasn't just a girl waving to say hello. She'd been trying to seize his attention, to call for help. That face had been the very definition of horror. He knew because he'd seen it once before, only the face had belonged to someone else. And it would be branded in his memory until the day he died.

"Come on, mate," Wesley called from the house, a dozen shopping bags suspended from his arms. "I'll get a brew on, you look like you could use one."

Picking up the bags by his feet, Paul went inside.

CHAPTER TWENTY

It was coming up to four o'clock by the time Mia arrived home. She parked the car in its usual space outside the house and remained in the driver's seat a few moments, just staring out of the window. It looked so ordinary from the outside – no more or less remarkable than those surrounding it, if not a little neglected. It was the kind of house she'd pass by without even noticing it, not like some old tumbledown mansion or abandoned hospital – places one would expect to be teeming with the dead. Godestone Manor was a prime example, yet she'd sooner spend a week in there alone than another minute in that house.

"Right," Mia took the keys out of the ignition, "I'm just going to see if Aunt Jamie is in and then we'll all sit down for a chat, okay?" She turned to find that Louisa was already staring back at her, and probably had been doing for some time.

"Don't go, Mummy." Mia wasn't sure if it was a plea or a demand.

"I have to, but I'll be right back. Promise." She managed a smile, but Louisa's face remained impassive. Despite her daughter's age, Mia sometimes forgot how perspicacious she was, not to mention brave. She'd already faced an adversary that left Mia in paroxysms of shivers just thinking about.

"Are you okay to wait in the car for a minute?" Mia said.

Louisa nodded, so Mia got out of the car and locked the doors – to keep Louisa from getting out as much as preventing someone from getting in – then she made slow, steady strides towards the house. Even from halfway down the garden path, she could see that the front door was ajar. Mia's heart drummed at a speed she was unable to keep up with, but with Louisa's eyes hot on her back, she forged ahead. Rolling the sleeve of her jacket over her hand on the perchance there'd been a break in, she tapped the door so it swung open. She couldn't hear any sounds from the television but decided to check the living room anyway. As soon as she saw the tub of Pringles on the floor, her joints locked up, one foot in front of the other. She'd been unable to make out much of their earlier conversation apart from a jumble of half-syllables and static, but hopefully Jamie had legged it after her warning and simply forgotten to lock the door.

Mia searched the kitchen before heading upstairs. "Jamie?" She spoke rather than bellowed her sister's name for the first time.

No answer – not a sound to denote anyone's presence, burglar or not. The only place Jamie could have gone to was one of the neighbour's houses, and Mia knew that Brenda was back from work because her car had been parked a little further down the road. The fears and possibilities skimmed through her mind and, one stair from the landing, she thought she heard a noise. It was so indistinct that she had to pause to listen again.

Scuffle, scuffle, scratch.

Mia stretched out her neck to peer down the landing. She couldn't tell which room, if any, the sounds were coming from.

Sniffle, sniffle, pant.

Mia jolted when Jamie's bedroom door squeaked open an inch. It quickly dawned on her that if someone had forced their way into the house then there was every chance they might still be there. With Jamie. Right now.

"Oh, no." Mia moved promptly, yanking the door handle. It would only open a crevice. Something was wedged behind it.

"Jamie?" She shouldered the door as visions of her sister's cold, battered corpse dominated her thoughts. "Jamie!" *Ram.* "Open the goddamn –"

The door finally gave way. Mia shrieked when a furry blur scooted past her, claws snagging at the carpet as it careened downstairs. She would have sworn at the dog had her heart not leaped into her throat and acted like a cork, preventing anything from escaping. After a few calming breaths, she eased her way into the room.

A lamp was lying on its side on the floor, the shade skewed but undamaged. The bedside table it had fallen from, as well as the bed itself, looked like they'd both been dragged away from the wall and left randomly in the centre of the room.

"What ... the ... hell?" Mia pulled back the door to expose the obstruction: a plastic shoe rack that had been wrenched from its hanging place, flats and sandals scattering the carpet. No wonder Casey had left in such a panic – there was no telling how long she'd been in there, or how she'd become trapped in the first place.

Mia reversed out of the room, and there was a sudden clicking sound. At the far end of the landing, her own bedroom door slowly creaked open, as if it was inviting her inside. There was a time when she'd have deemed this impossible, but right now all she cared about was finding her baby sister.

Mia gradually approached her bedroom and slinked though the open door, still being careful not to touch anything. Even when she saw the dainty feet hanging over the end of the bed, she couldn't – she *wouldn't* – allow herself to believe what her gut was hinting at. Then came the splayed legs and the naked torso.

"Oh, God!" Mia's hand flew up over her mouth, while she used the other to cling onto the doorframe as her knees crumbled. Her liquid eyes traced the recumbent form of her sister, from the torn knickers that barely concealed her ladyhood to the pert breasts bared for the whole of Bramley to see.

Mia continued to shake her head, her hand welded to her jaw. She couldn't even cry for the fear of plummeting into a deep hysteria. The shock fomented a numbness that seeped through to her bones, and she dragged her gaze up to Jamie's face. A face that was tilted directly towards her, eyes open to their utmost, as if she was making a silent plea for help. Mia had never imagined that the dead could look so helpless.

Letting go of the doorframe, she shambled across to the bed. "Oh, Jamie," she whispered, the words so quiet that she wasn't sure if she'd imagined them. Her hand drifted over the girl's inert form but froze before making contact. *Could this just be another illusion?* It was a fleeting thought, but a thought nonetheless. She'd lost the ability to distinguish fact from fantasy a long time ago.

Mia was whisked back to reality upon seeing the purple-red marks on Jamie's thighs. It was as though someone had dunked their hands into a tin of paint and printed them onto her flesh. The scratches on her arms had also multiplied since she'd glimpsed them earlier that morning, but it was the crescent-moon dents just above her right breast that left Mia recoiling in mortification. Their circular patterning had all the signs of human teeth.

"Mia."

The voice came as a rush of air. Mia glanced back to Jamie's face and saw her own dismay mirrored there. She hesitated for maybe a second, making sure the whisper had been real, before leaning closer to the girl. "J-Jamie ...?"

Jamie's mouth opened slightly, as if restricted by a loss of mobility in her jaw. Slowly, her lips formed the faint words: "H-e-l-p m-e."

"Sshh, I'm here now." Mia's hands were still hovering in front of her, not that she had a clue what to do with them. She couldn't understand why Jamie wasn't moving. Why she was lying all rigidly, as if something was bearing down on top of her.

"I-it's okay. You're okay. Everything's going to be –"

It was when Mia reached out to touch Jamie that something – and she had absolutely no idea what, for she'd heard nothing behind her – wrenched her backwards with a preternatural strength, as if she was attached to a bungee rope that catapulted her all the way out onto the landing. She crashed into the banister and rebounded onto the floor with a yelp and a cry. Her hand fell to her lower back, fingers like daggers stabbing at her spine. She shifted her legs to make sure there was no significant damage before hoisting herself up onto all fours. Mia didn't sense the presence looming over her until the area was bathed in darkness, and she looked up without knowing what to expect. It wasn't long before her facial muscles flexed and rippled beneath the skin, tugging her features into a relentless glare.

"You," she said, climbing up the banister to ease the throbbing in her back. "What are you doing here? How did you ..."

Paul regarded her with that wooden face, which Mia had convinced herself was a mask – a façade to conceal his inner corruption. Then she saw the object he had clutched in his right hand, and everything fell into place. She guided her eyes back up to his face, which was now set with a palpable dread.

"You," hiss, "sick," spit, "twisted fucking pervert!" Mia launched herself at the man, arms thrust out in front of her like battering rams; the tenderness in her spine erased from her mind.

Paul's stocky form was propelled into the wall with astounding ease, and the camera *click-flashed* as it clattered to the floor. Mia beat him repeatedly with the downsides of her fists, catching his shoulders and arms as he used them to guard his face. Screaming away, the image of Jamie's naked, abused body scorched into her retinas, Mia thought she'd never be satisfied until Paul's blood decorated the landing so he could never harm another woman again.

It wasn't until her aching arms forced her to a respite that Mia realised she was sobbing, her breaths laboured and spittle frothing in the corners of her mouth. Paul was huddled against the wall like a child cowering from its drunken mother. The fact that he wasn't fighting back, or even trying to restrain her, didn't fragment the scarlet mist that caused her whole body to tremble. She snatched up the camera and wrapped its plastic sling around her wrist for a more secure grip.

"See how you like being made to feel helpless, you fucking animal!"

Paul shrieked as she swung the weapon back over her head. A second before her arms came plunging down, a voice bawled from behind, "Mia, no!"

Mia turned her head abruptly. Her fingers twitched around the camera, willing her to cave the pervert's skull in. Jamie was standing in the bedroom doorway with the bed sheets clutched to her chest in order to protect what was left of her modesty.

"It ... w-wasn't him," she stammered.

"What?" Mia frowned, turning some more. "But he –"

"Paul didn't do this to me. No one did. It was *no one!*" Jamie slumped down against the open door, her fatigued body folding in on itself until she was curled into a ball. Forgetting about Paul, or even understanding what her sister was ranting about, Mia dropped the camera and rushed to comfort her.

"It's okay, you're safe now." Mia embraced her tightly, feeling heavy tears soaking into the material of her top. "I'm so sorry, Jay, I should have been here. This is all my fault." Her own tears seemed to have evaporated now, and even her rage had been conquered by the innate urge to protect those she loved most.

Jamie clung onto the flaps of Mia's jacket, strings of drool and snot stretching from the denim like an alien excretion as she looked up at her. "It's real, Mia. There was n-nothing I could do. I wish it had killed me!"

"No, don't say that. Whatever's happened, I promise you we'll get through it, but first I need to get you some help. I'll call for an ambulance–"

"No!" Jamie fought against her. "Please, Mia, don't make me go. They'll think I'm crazy!"

"Okay, okay – calm down." Mia held Jamie's head to her bosom while glancing over at Paul. He hadn't moved an inch since her outburst, all hunched and stiff like a petrified cat. A tiny cut had appeared on his cheek from where she'd nicked him with the jewels on her ring.

"I don't know what the hell went on here," Mia spoke to him gravely, "and right now I don't give a damn. Unless you want me to stick that camera where the sun doesn't shine then I suggest you get Brenda over here now. We need her help."

Without replying, or a gesture of any kind, Paul clambered to his feet and then scarpered from the house. Jamie's howls had exhausted to snivels by now, and Mia could feel the vibrations from her body infecting her own. Her gaze returned to the discarded Nikon. Keeping hold of Jamie, she reached across the landing to pick up the camera. She found the 'on' button and took a couple of seconds to figure out the controls. The image that popped up on the screen next caused Mia's chest to flatten in a rapid expulsion of air, a sort of anti-gasp that she was unable to recover from. It was a distance shot of Jamie on the bed, exactly how Mia had found her with only one difference. Straddling her sister's body, hunched over, there was a foggy silhouette that looked like it was composed of smoke. From the region in which a human's shoulders would have been, two slightly darker lines extended down towards Jamie's throat.

Mia tossed the camera away and watched it roll across the carpet as if it was a hand grenade, ready to explode with truths and horrors that would blow apart their lives forever. She and Jamie remained locked together until Brenda's voice called up the stairs three minutes later.

CHAPTER TWENTY-ONE

Mia sprang up from the chair as Brenda entered the kitchen. "Is she okay? Can I see her?"

"Most of her injuries are superficial cuts and bruises. I've given her something to help her relax, so she might feel drowsy for a while," Brenda replied.

"That's it? She didn't say anything? Did you manage to find out if ... if she was ..." Mia couldn't even contemplate the extent of the abuse, but when Brenda shook her head, she knew the thoughts must have invaded her mind also.

Laying her medical bag on the table, the furrows in Brenda's face seemed to have enhanced since she'd first found the traumtised teenager. With only the ramblings of a madman and little more from Mia to go off, Brenda had taken them around to her house where she'd tended to Jamie's wounds. Wesley was busy minding Paul and Louisa in the living room, and the fact that neither of them had questioned Jamie's refusal to go back home left Mia even more curious about the Clarke family than before.

"Have you thought about reporting any of this to the police?" Brenda asked.

"What's the point? I know what it looks like, but this was no ordinary assault. A *person* didn't do this to her." Mia hung her head, squeezing the bridge of her nose between her fingers and thumb. "Christ, why didn't I listen to Louisa? She tried to tell me time and time again, but I didn't want to believe it."

"Don't go torturing yourself." Brenda strolled around the table and snaked an arm around Mia's shoulders, massaging them with her bony fingers. "Physically, Jamie's going to be fine. It's her emotional state we need to focus on now."

Looking at her new friend, Mia felt the beginnings of a smile tweak across her lips. Brenda was more a comfort than she'd ever truly know. Mia allowed the woman to guide her back to the chair and waited until they were both seated before saying, "What am I supposed to do now? What do I tell Louisa? How can I help Jamie?"

"Are you sure you don't want me to call the police?" Brenda's tone was soft, encouraging. "I couldn't have done an intimate examination on Jamie even if she'd let me, but I don't think it's as bad as it looks. I'm not sure she knows what happened herself, but the police will have people that specialise in this kind of thing: doctors, counsellors – whatever she needs."

Mia shook her head. "Jamie would never agree to it. It's like she said, one word about what's been going on in that house and she'd be locked away – and I don't mean in a prison cell."

Brenda allowed her gaze to drop a moment. "I know you probably don't want to hear this, but some of the cuts on Jamie's arms and legs look to be a few days old. In fact, I'd say they were more like scratches."

"I know what you're thinking – trust me, it crossed my mind as well. But what about the bruises on her thighs? The bite marks on her chest? Jamie couldn't have done that to herself."

"As I said, the police can arrange for swabs to be taken. They can search for fibres, DNA – anything that might help with finding a suspect. Isn't it worth it, if not for peace of mind?"

"But they won't *find* anything because there was no *suspect*," Mia reiterated forcefully. "I was there, Brenda. The same thing that has been terrorising my little girl has violated my sister, and there was fuck all I could do about it."

Brenda put a hand on Mia's arm, a silent act of unity. "I won't pretend to understand what's going on either, but what's important is that you're all here and you're safe. That's down to you, Mia."

"Are we safe, though?" Mia slid the Nikon across the table to a nonplussed Brenda, having brought it with her to return to Paul. "Your brother had this on him earlier. When I found him skulking outside the bedroom like that I thought ... well, you can probably imagine."

And from Brenda's equanimity, she must have already taken this into account after seeing the state of the young girl. "Paul's weakness is his mind, not his body. He'll be fine."

"Still, it's no excuse for what I did. This thing seems to be bringing out the worst in all of us and I will apologise to Paul, but first you need to take a look at the photos on there."

Picking up the camera, Brenda did as she was commanded. "I don't understand," her eyes jumped from the screen to Mia, "all I see is a hallway."

"Keep going. The pictures come in five-second intervals. They follow a path all the way up the stairs until they get to my bedroom."

Brenda continued to skip through the images, and then: "What in the name of ..." She brought the screen up closer to her face, squinting her eyes. "What *is* that?"

"That's your suspect. Now do you see why we can't go to the police?"

Brenda studied the photo of Jamie and the ghostly shape a while longer, rotating the camera in her hands as if trying to find a clearer angle. "Maybe it's a trick of the light – a shadow or something."

"It's no shadow: I know it, you know it and Paul knows it." Mia pointed to the camera. "That looks like an expensive piece of equipment, not the kind of thing meant for taking holiday snaps. Paul intended to catch something on it today, and while I can't figure out how he knew, I'm pretty certain it has something to do with my uncle."

The determination in Mia's voice alone was enough to convince Brenda that she wasn't leaving until she had something close to an explanation. With a long nasal sigh, Brenda set down the camera and pulled a small silver item out of her trouser pocket. She placed it next to the camera, and Mia glanced at the key and her neighbour in succession. "What's this?" she said.

"I took it from Paul earlier. I honestly didn't know he still had it."

"What do you mean, 'still'?"

"He was the one who found your Uncle Billy."

And there it was: half the mystery solved with one simple declaration. It also explained why the key had looked so familiar, but Mia knew it couldn't be that simple – nothing ever was. "Why didn't you tell me this before?"

"Because I knew you'd have questions and Paul is still fragile. He barely came back from that day, we might not be so lucky a second time around. This is the first time he's stepped foot in that house since ..."

Brenda dipped her head, tears glinting in the shadow of her unruly curls. Mia assuaged her temper; after all, she knew better than anyone how important it was to protect those you loved.

"It was the house, wasn't it?" Mia concluded. "That's what made your brother the way he is, just like it killed my uncle. Paul knows what happened, doesn't he?"

Brenda sniffed while dabbing her eyes with the backs of her fingers. "Paul dropped by the house to see Billy one morning, it was nothing unusual. The next time I saw him, he wasn't my brother anymore."

"He and Billy were friends?"

Brenda nodded while giving a light, reminiscent chuckle. "They bumped into each other when Paul was visiting us one day and it was like seeing two long lost brothers being reunited. Paul's always had a fascination with the paranormal, and what with all the relics Billy had acquired from his expeditions, I guess they kind of bounced off each other."

"Did my uncle have similar experiences to what we've had in the house?"

Brenda didn't need to think too hard. "Paul did mention that Billy had been having these ... visions. It was odd things, like food turning moldy when it was fine, maggots raiding the cupboards; creatures trying to get in through the windows at night. I remember one time he claimed to have woken up to a house full of wasps and went to stay with Paul for a whole week after pest control had checked the house and found nothing. Naturally, Paul was convinced it was down to demonic activity but I insisted that he'd seen too many horror films."

Mia chuckled along with her neighbour this time, although Brenda was still perched on the edge of her seat, twirling her wedding ring round and round on her finger as if hoping to make herself giddy. "Anyway," she went on, "Paul helped Billy to set up some equipment: motion sensors, cameras, thermometers and so on. He'd been wanting to conduct an investigation ever since rumours about the house became public knowledge. He got his wish, for all the good it did."

"Did they find anything?"

Brenda shook her head. "Nothing concrete. Billy's work meant that he didn't spend a lot of time at home – that's why he gave Paul a key, just in case of emergencies. Maybe that's why things didn't progress as quickly as those before him."

"You mean this kind of thing has happened to other people? And you never said anything?"

"I'm sorry, but you seemed to have enough going on in your lives without some lunatic turning up on your doorstep spouting ghost stories. Remember the girl I told you about, whose father bought the house for her just after Wesley and I moved in?"

Mia nodded.

"Well, she was the first to experience things: shadows, objects moving by themselves, cold spots – your average haunted house stuff. There was an article about it in the local paper, so it's not like it was a big secret. It became more serious when she claimed that something had tried to drown her in the bathtub."

"And this girl didn't see what attacked her either?" Mia said.

"No, I spoke to her parents myself when they came to clear the house out. The poor girl wouldn't even walk down the street, she was that traumatised. What made it worse was that she had a phobia of water – something about not being able to swim. I figured she must have fallen asleep and –"

"*Oh my god.*" Mia bounced to her feet, causing the chair to tip onto its back legs and rock tauntingly. She rested a hand on the table to support her upper body, which felt heavier than a sack of sand.

"Impossible ..." she gasped, as if halfway through a marathon, "... has to be."

"Mia, what is it? What's wrong?" Brenda stood up as well, purely out of instinct.

"Kerry – my sister's friend. She was terrified of getting pregnant."

"The one who was rushed off in the ambulance?"

Mia nodded. "That's why she did it. The house ... somehow, it made her believe. And my mum said something about Uncle Billy being locked in a shed when he was a kid. That he developed this irrational fear of –"

"Bugs," a frail voice cut in from behind. Paul was standing in the kitchen doorway, his shoulders almost as wide as the frame itself.

"Paul, how long have you been there?" Brenda made hurriedly to her brother.

"*Bugs.*" His tone had developed a note of agitation.

"Yes, bugs. What about them?" urged Brenda.

"He's talking about my uncle," Mia answered for him. "Billy had a phobia of insects, just like Kerry and the pregnancy. Like ..." In all the chaos, Mia had forgotten about the dreams and visions of her mother being so close to death. She was the person who'd kept the family together after their father had passed away, and with her gone it would all fall onto Mia's shoulders. Whatever dark presence had invaded their home, evidently, it knew more about all of them than they knew about themselves.

Brenda slowly faced Mia, a fair brow merging with her hairline. "Are you implying that this ... thing ... is preying on people's fears?"

Although Mia hadn't quite decided on a theory yet, she knew there was too much evidence to discount this one altogether. She drew her focus back to Paul, speaking solemnly. "I understand how difficult this must be for you, but my family's lives depend on it. Is whatever attacked Jamie tonight the same thing that murdered my uncle?"

The man responded with a slow but assured nod. Mia asked him the same question that Louisa had been unable to answer. "Why is it doing this to us?"

Paul's eyes were drawn to the ground as if they were magnets. Brenda gently rubbed him in between the shoulder blades. "It's okay, you're safe here with us. Tell Mia what this thing wants."

Gradually, his eyes rose in the same direction to which his finger pointed: directly at Mia. Even if Wesley hadn't entered the kitchen at that precise moment, Mia wasn't sure she would have wanted to hear any more.

"Hey, we've got some company here," Wesley announced.

"Jamie ..." Mia converged with her sister in the middle of the room, the last ten minutes receding to the back of her mind. "What are you doing down here? You're supposed to be resting."

Jamie gazed at her with that wan expression, her eyes sunken in shadow and mascara staining her cheeks. The woollen blanket draped around her shoulders made her look even more aged and frail. "How can I do anything when I feel so rank?" Her voice was empty, defeated.

"You're welcome to use our bathroom if you want to clean yourself up," Brenda offered. "Wes, go and fetch Jamie a towel from –"

"Oh, no, you've done enough for us already," Mia insisted. "Thank you for everything, I won't forget it. We can't stay here forever, though."

"What?" Jamie snapped, suddenly alert. "You expect me to go back to that place after this? Mia, look at the state of me!"

Mia held Jamie's arms on the off chance her frustration would prevail. "I'm not going to let anything else happen to you – ever. It'll have to kill me first."

"And what if *it* does? What'd happen to us then? What about Louisa?"

"Maybe she's right," Brenda sympathised with the girl. "I'd offer to let you stay here, but we haven't got much space with Dillon staying over. I could ring around the local hotels and see if any can squeeze you in for the night?"

"Please, Mia," Jamie begged, before Mia had a chance to consider their options. "I'll sleep on the streets if I have to, you know I'm not kidding."

"Fine, but it's just for tonight. I'm not being made bankrupt by something that's too cowardly to show itself. You and Louisa can stay here while I go and get some of our stuff together."

"On your own? Mia, you can't!" Jamie's eyes were wide and watery, lips quivering even more feverishly than the rest of her.

"Wesley will go with her – won't you, hun?" Brenda glanced at her husband, who'd suddenly turned whiter than Jamie.

Before the man could decline, Brenda was already dragging Mia down the hallway. They spent a good while skimming through the phone book, making calls and enquiries as they went along. Twenty minutes later and sixty quid less off, the Park Inn Bed and Breakfast had been booked and the car was packed up.

Outside in the porch, Brenda gave Mia a hug that was so tight it crushed the breath from her lungs. "I'm so sorry we couldn't do more to help," she said. "If you need anything – anything at all – then you only have to ask. Wesley and I will always be here."

"Thanks, Brenda." Mia patted the woman's back, red curls tickling her face. "I don't know what I would have done without you tonight."

As they parted, Brenda said to her, "I know it sounds cliché, but have you thought about getting the house blessed by a priest? I'm not a religious person myself but anything must be worth a try."

"Yeah, maybe." Mia didn't admit that she'd already toyed with the idea. "Since we're being honest with each other, there is something else I've been meaning to tell you. It's about Dillon's cat ..."

Brenda crossed her arms with a deflating sigh. "Why do I get the feeling I'm not going to like this?"

"I found her collar in Louisa's bedroom a few days ago, it had blood on it. Earlier today, she confessed that it had something to do with our dog. Unless she or Casey buried the body then I can only assume that foxes must have sniffed it out, but I'm willing to pay for a new one if –"

Brenda shook her head before Mia could finish. "Don't worry about the cat – or Dillon. To be honest, it's probably best that we leave him with some hope that she'll return."

"Okay, whatever you want." Mia started to back away from the door. "By the way, did you ever get a chance to speak to Keith about the house? You mentioned one of the original owners last time we spoke – Edward, I think you said his name was. I just wondered if you'd found out anything else about him."

"No, after the incident between Jamie and Paul, I didn't anticipate you popping around for a chat and a cuppa anytime soon." Brenda hesitated, a profound dread flashing across her face. "You don't think Paul's actions that day were linked to this as well, do you? Living next door is one thing, but the thought of that monster coming into my home ..."

Mia remembered what Louisa had said about the shadow man being trapped inside the house and reassured her friend, "If that was the case, I think you'd know about it by now. If you could find out from Keith what the deal was with this Edward guy then it might at least help us to uncover a source. My mum always taught me that to solve a problem you have to go back to the beginning, let's hope that applies the supernatural as well."

"Of course, I'll ring you as soon as I've heard anything." Another hesitation. "Mia, about what happened to Jamie tonight. If you're right about this thing feeding off people's fears then, well, there has to be a reason why it did what it did?"

It was the same question that had been stewing in Mia's mind all evening, and she decided to go ahead and tell Brenda everything; after all, it could be the last chance she got to unburden herself. "Jamie's behaviour these last few months has become more and more erratic. Something happened to her, Brenda, and if the house picked up on it so easily then why couldn't I? What does that say about me – as a sister, a guardian, a *person?*"

"People have a habit of hiding things from those who are closest to them, I see it all the time at work. Maybe now isn't the best time to go shovelling up the past. I'm sure Jamie will open up to you when she's ready, anyone can see that you love her as if she was your own daughter."

Mia gave a hollow smile. "Let's just hope she sees it, too."

***

Mia gazed up at the ceiling, one hand tucked beneath her head and the other sprawled over her belly. Every so often, lights from passing traffic outside would slink through the curtains and throw indistinguishable shadows across the paintwork so it looked like the ceiling was actually moving. She closed her eyes to settle the dizziness, reopening them when Louisa stirred beside her. The girl had given no indication that she knew what had happened to her aunt, but then Mia wasn't aware of the full details herself. All she knew was that if it hadn't been for Paul, she might no longer have a sister. Even after the way Mia had treated him, Brenda had still offered to take Casey in for the night, which was another worry off their minds.

To her left, Jamie was sleeping soundly thanks to whatever drugs Brenda had pumped her with. Mia regretted not having asked for a pill or two herself. What a trio they were, huddled together in the double bed like battered women in a refuge – the receptionist's face when they'd checked in had said enough. Perhaps that was what had disinclined Mia to ring anyone else for help. Angela, for one, was always good in a crisis; but as Brenda had pointed out earlier, their problem was spiritual and therefore required the skills of a spiritual person. Mia wasn't going to risk exposing anyone else to this evil, not least those she was closest to.

Wondering what the time was, Mia glanced across to her mobile on the bedside cabinet, but she wouldn't have been able to reach it without disturbing the girls. It must have been past midnight by now. She'd promised to have come up with a plan by morning, but as the hours dragged on that promise was closer and closer to being broken.

Face it, Mia, she admonished herself, *you can't do this alone - the circumstances forbid it.* She pushed away the bed sheets and climbed slowly and precariously over Jamie, wincing at the pain in her lower back from where she'd fallen - or rather, been thrown - into the banister. It hadn't been too bad until the bruising had set in, or maybe it was more a case of she hadn't had a chance to think about it until then. Even now she could feel that cold, indomitable force surging through her, and she suspected it was something that she'd never truly be rid of.

Jamie moaned and stirred a little, but Mia couldn't tell whether her eyes were open or closed in the darkness. "Mia?" she murmured.

"Sshh, I'm just nipping to the loo. Go back to sleep," Mia whispered. The silence that followed made her wonder if Jamie had woken up at all.

Tugging the covers back into place, Mia picked up her mobile and tiptoed into the en-suite, closing the door behind her. She'd already made a call to Church View to check that her mum was okay which, most likely, was exactly what the entity had wanted, but it was worth it for sanity's sake. Nathan had also texted her numerous times, but she'd put off replying for the fear of pushing Jamie into a deeper psychosis. The last thing her sister needed was to listen to her ordeal being relayed over and over again.

She found Nathan's number in her contacts and hit the dial button, pacing the room while it rang out. She almost shrieked when she glimpsed a haggard wraith floating past her, but it was only her reflection in the mirror above the sink. Mia paused to study herself, massaging her cheeks with her free hand as if to test their plumpness. She was starting to look old, and she couldn't decide whether it was due to lack of sleep or the pounds that she'd been rapidly shedding. With her hair looking like something Casey had dragged in from the garden, Mia might as well have just crawled out of her own coffin. She couldn't remember the last time she'd eaten a good wholesome meal - probably not since her mind had become an auditorium of nightmares that kept her consciousness alert even in sleep.

It was over a minute later before the ringing ended, and a croaky voice answered, "Hello?"

"Hey, it's me. Can you talk?" said Mia.

There was a shuffling sound from Nathan's end of the line and then a scrape, as if something was being moved across a hard surface. "Mia, it's the middle of the night."

"I know, but it's urgent. I need you to come over to the house tomorrow – take the day off work if you have to. And, Nate, you might want to pack an overnight bag."

CHAPTER TWENTY-TWO

Easing the car along Greenway Avenue, the first thing Mia saw was Nathan's four-by-four parked outside the house. It was nine fifteen in the morning; persuading Jamie and Louisa to return home with her had turned out to be more of a challenge than a request, but the assurance of Nathan's presence seemed to have soothed them as much as it did Mia. She'd slept a lot easier with the knowledge that she had someone to support her. Someone who cared about her family as much as she did because they also had something to lose, although Mia would admit this to no one but herself.

As they drew nearer to the house, Mia saw Nathan leaning against the car bonnet with a phone glued to his ear. His lips were flapping angrily and he had a discernible squint to his eyes, although this might have been a reaction to the sun. He hadn't sounded too impressed by the demands she'd made last night, but on this occasion Mia couldn't blame him – especially seeing as she hadn't wanted to discuss matters in too much detail over the phone. Just the knowledge that Louisa was in danger had been enough to get him there, and no one could judge him for that.

Mia parked up behind Nathan's car and stepped out onto the pavement just as he hung up the phone. "You're late," he pointed out, purely for the sake of it.

"Sorry, the girls were –" Mia glanced over her shoulder expecting Jamie and Louisa to be behind her. Instead they remained in the back seats, each gazing out of their own window. They'd been like that since leaving Leeds a quarter of an hour ago.

"Thanks for coming." Mia thought it wiser not to blurt everything out on the street in full view of an audience. It wouldn't be long before word got around that the residents of number twelve were, yet again, experiencing strange phenomena. "That Regina on the phone?" she said.

"Who else?" It was a rhetorical question.

"How did she take you coming up here?"

Nathan shrugged while cramming the phone into his back pocket. "Where've you lot been all night anyway?" He waved at Louisa through the car's windscreen. "Jeez, someone's in a mood. You going to tell me what this is about?"

"Yeah, once you've helped me get those two inside."

An unwonted seriousness descended over Nathan's face. "I take it this has got something to do with what Louisa was talking about yesterday. Is it that bad?"

"No," Mia replied. "It's worse."

***

Nathan listened to Mia's recount of events over the last few weeks with unexpected tranquillity, acknowledging every now and again with a pensive nod. The dreams, the visions and her conversations with Brenda: Mia was careful not to exclude a single detail, saving Jamie's assault – by far the most brutal occurrence – until last. Only then had the doubt in those muddy brown eyes snowballed into something close to disbelief. He'd asked questions and Mia had answered to the best of her ability, but this was also met with skepticism. A skepticism which she knew from experience could only be cured by the eyes; by the dread that swept through your gut like rolling thunderclouds, and the prickly cold that cut through skin and muscle until it became a living part of you. 'There must be a logical explanation,' Nathan would keep saying, over and over again until Mia wanted to slap the furrows out of his face.

Seconds ticked by into minutes. Neither of them spoke for a while, not because they had nothing to say but because they didn't know where to start. Nathan brought the mug up to his lips and winced at the cold brown liquid.

"Any chance of a fresh one?" he said, as if their previous conversation had never happened. Mia went to stand but Nathan raised a hand in gesticulation for her to stop. "Actually, you can scrap that."

Silence again. Nathan set down the mug and watched the tea lapping at the sides until it became still once more. Noise from the television drifted in from the living room, where Mia had told the girls to wait while she spoke to Nathan, ensuring that they yell for help if anything should happen: a groaning floorboard, an unexplained draught, a flickering light bulb – literally *anything*. Exactly how much Louisa was aware of, Mia was afraid to even speculate, but that didn't mean she needed to hear a conversation about it all.

"You're sure it's not drugs?" Nathan asked Mia for the umpteenth time. "I mean, after what happened with her mate –"

"If Jamie was on drugs then we all must be, it's as simple as that. Have I ever given you a reason not to trust me?"

"No."

"Then, don't stop now. Whatever did this to Jamie was dark, it was hostile and it was the most terrifyingly evil thing that I've ever felt in my life. I couldn't be more shocked to find out it was all down to the devil himself."

Perhaps the reference to Satan was taking it a bit too far, but it delivered the exclamation mark she needed. Nathan took a stealthy look around the room, as if a thousand snipers had him in their sights. It felt as though the house had been listening in on their every word and was as curious as Mia to witness the man's reaction. It may have been her imagination, but Nathan's presence did seem to have brought about a lightness in the air. Now it felt like she was choking rather than suffocating.

"So, let's say this spook is as real as you and I." Nathan spoke at last. "Louisa seems to think it can't leave the house, right?"

At least he's keeping an open mind, Mia thought. "Yeah, so?"

"Then, wouldn't the obvious answer be to leave? I know it's a bit extreme, but in your eyes these are extreme circumstances."

"You think, if it was that simple, we wouldn't be long gone? You know our predicament, Nate. Most of the money we got from Mum's house went towards her care, and even that wasn't as much as it should have been thanks to her pyromania. There's no way I can afford to rent anywhere half decent until Jamie starts earning."

"So, sell this place. Speak to the bank, ask about getting a mortgage. I could try and scrape together a small loan without Regina finding out, but it won't be much."

"I appreciate the gesture, but given the reputation of the house, getting rid might be harder than it sounds. It could be months until anyone's stupid enough to take a gamble on it, and we can't stray too far from Mum."

"Would it help if I had Louisa for a while? Jamie can stay with Kerry, and you've got mates."

Mia shook her head while leaning back in the chair. "Kerry's parents would sooner welcome a serial killer than they would Jamie. I know you're trying to help, Nate, and believe me it does make sense in the short-term. I can't just pull Louisa out of school with no indication of when she'll be back, though. I'll certainly look into our options financially, but splitting up the family has to be a last resort."

"Better that than ending up like Billy," Nathan pointed out.

Mia didn't know what peeved her most: the fact that he was being so rational about the situation or the complete stalemate she was facing. Looking through the kitchen window, she noted the peacefulness of nature and yearned for it to flow through the house; cleanse it of this demonic force.

"Brenda reckons we should get the place blessed." It was more a reflection than a statement.

Nathan answered, "Go for it, if you think a crucifix and some holy water is going to solve anything."

Mia shrugged. "Depends on what it is. Why it's here. What it wants from me. In any case, I'm positive it has something to do with the original owner of the house. Brenda said he'd lived here for most of his life, so he couldn't have suffered what we've been through."

"Where is he now?"

"He died a couple of years ago. Who knows, maybe the old bastard just wants his house back." Actually, that sounded a lot less absurd in her head than it had done out loud.

"And it's preying on people's fears, why, to get rid of them or something?" Nathan hypothesised.

"Maybe – which begs the question, why the hell was it attracted to Jamie in the first place? She hasn't spoken a word to me about what happened, but Brenda and I have got a pretty good idea and there must be a reason for it."

"Not necessarily." Nathan repositioned his mug in order to avoid Mia's glare. "I'd have thought it would be any female's worst fear to be ... you know ... abused like that. Maybe Jamie was just unlucky."

"Unlucky?" Only Nathan was capable of making an act so heinous sound so trivial. Mia swiped the mug from under his nose, and he watched her cross over to the sink where she tipped away its contents.

"You're not believing a word of this, are you?" she said, turning to face him again.

"It doesn't matter what I believe. This is about our daughter and I'll do whatever it takes to make her feel safe. For all we know, what happened to Jamie could just be another one of those hallucination thingamajigs. Who's to say this ... *force* ... has got any real power at all?"

"Did you forget the part where I was launched across a room?"

"If it can do that then why hasn't it killed you already?"

"That's what I need to figure out." Mia returned to the chair and leaned across the table on her forearms. "What's your worst fear, Nathan? How would you feel if you had to live with it every second of every day?"

"What if I'm not afraid of anything?"

"Then, I guess you must be immune. In which case, you can stay here and watch the girls while I'm out – and I *mean* watch them. Follow them to the bathroom if you have to."

"Where are you going?"

"Work, then town. Brenda texted me the address of a local church this morning, there's no harm in getting some advice. I doubt the estate agents will be open on a Sunday afternoon but I'll swing by anyway."

"Okay, but I thought Godestone was closed until tomorrow?"

"The staff will be getting it ready for reopening, and it's the only day the boss is guaranteed to be in. I'll ask about having some more time off, but if it comes down to it then Louisa will have to stay with you until this mess is sorted out. If there's a chance we might lose our home then I can't afford to lose my job as well."

"Understandable. Dare I ask if there's a plan B?"

"Honestly? I haven't a bloody clue." Mia stood up once more, this time tucking her chair underneath the table. "Promise me you'll be careful, and ring me if there are any problems."

"I will, but I can guarantee you that there'll be no need."

"I wouldn't be so cocky if I were you. Just don't trust everything you see because this thing will sniff out your weaknesses whether you know about them or not. Look at Kerry, she didn't last two nights in this place."

Nathan smiled coolly. "Like I said, we'll be fine."

After a long and laborious goodbye to Jamie and Louisa, both of whom had acted as though she was leaving for another continent, Mia had finally managed to escape the house with a little help from Nathan. As she made for her car, she caught Keith's cumbersome form waddling across his drive on the opposite side of the road like Mr Blobby dressed in a tweed suit. She thought about nipping over to query him about the house, assuming Brenda hadn't already done so, but was discouraged by the questions she might receive in return. Instead, she quickened her pace towards the car and prepared to duck out of sight when the decision was wrenched from her hands.

"Yoo-hoo, Miss Reynolds!"

It was too late to pretend she hadn't heard the voice calling out to her, for she'd already glanced up to see Keith waving a chunky arm over his head. A smile was too much of a strain on her facial muscles, so she raised a hand in greeting. It wasn't until he shouted again that she realised he was beckoning her over. Taking the opportunity while it presented itself, she tootled across to number fifteen.

"Is there something I can help you with, Keith?" Mia decided to cut out the bullshit for him.

"Just a friendly chat, we haven't seen you around much recently. How are those girls of yours doing?"

"They're good, thanks. We all are."

The grooves in Keith's face appeared to multiply in depth rather than quantity. "I say, Ade and I did have a fright when we saw the ambulance pull up the other week. Nothing serious, I hope?"

"No, just a careless accident."

"Jolly good. And you've settled into the house well enough?"

"Yes, er, come to think of it, I was planning on speaking to you about that at some point."

"Go on," Keith prompted, with a slight gleam in his piggy eyes.

"It's just that I've been clearing out the attic and, er, I came across a box of junk containing some unopened letters." Mia had no idea where the lie had spun from. "They're dated a good few years back so I doubt they're of any importance, but they're addressed to a man named Edward. I wondered if you knew who he might be?"

"Edward Perkins? Oh, aye, he used to own the house – bit of a queer one, was old Ed. I can't think why his stuff would be lying around after all this time, though. His younger sister was supposed to have cleared the house out after he passed away."

"Oh. Lived there long, did he?"

"Yes, the man took his first and last breaths in that house. He wasn't a very sociable fellow, but his sister regularly checked up on him. Apparently, he never fully recovered from the time he served in the army during the Second World War. Then again, with some of the things those lads must have witnessed ..." Keith gave an exaggerated shudder, his flabby cheeks vibrating like ripples through water.

"You mean like post-traumatic stress?" Mia asked him.

"Not stress as such. He just became somewhat of a hermit, particularly after the loss of his mother. I wouldn't want to guess the full story, but the house was an absolute state – constantly ill, he was. By God, he used to kick up a fuss whenever someone from the authorities came by. There was talk of having him committed to a psychiatric hospital, but as fate would have it, he died shortly after that."

"And you say he died in the house?"

Keith nodded. "He was found at the bottom of the stairs in a pool of his own blood, skull cracked open like a melon." He pummelled his hand with his fist, the *thwacking* sound causing Mia to flinch. "Whether or not it was an accident or he threw himself down, well, I guess only old Ed knows the answer to that."

"I see – how awful." It didn't sound heartfelt, even to herself. "So, is there any family you know of who I could pass the letters over to? Any kids or grandchildren?"

"No, there was only his sister. Lord knows where she disappeared to."

Afraid that Keith would see the disappointment in her face, Mia focused on the ground, at the same time marvelling at how the man's gnome-sized feet could possibly support the twenty-odd stone of blubber. It seemed her only option was to rely on the faith of the holy church, and she was beginning to wish she'd said her prayers at night.

"Thanks, Keith. Enjoy the rest of your day." Before she knew it, Mia was inside her car and starting up the engine. If Keith had bid her goodbye then she hadn't heard him.

Adjusting the rearview mirror so it pointed over her shoulder, she saw Keith's wife, Adele, come breezing out of the house wearing a long floaty skirt and mint blouse. It looked like they were off to a party or something – maybe even a wedding. *If only my own life was full of such joyous celebrations,* Mia thought.

She repositioned the mirror before taking a last glance at the hellhole she refused to call home. Jamie's grey face hovered at the living room window, and in front of her Louisa's head was just visible above the windowsill like some kind of grotesque ornament. Mia didn't wave – didn't even smile properly. None of them did, for the time for fakery and lies was over. Now it was about one thing and one thing only: survival.

***

Angela glanced up from behind the reception counter as the sound of Mia's pumps squeaked against the polished floor.

"Hey, I didn't expect to see you today," she said, shoving a can of Mr Sheen behind the desk. "Come to lend a hand?"

"Not exactly," Mia replied, without stopping. "Is he in the staffroom?"

Angela nodded, her gaze fastened to Mia as she strode by with a brisk and restless air about her. She paused outside the staffroom, dread sneaking through the fatigue that was fighting to overwhelm her, and knocked on the door before entering.

Quade Sims was sitting at a large circular table, the type you might find at a store's garden sale. One elbow was propped on the tabletop, and he held a mug near to but not touching his lips. In front of him lay an open folder that was at least double the thickness of the man's arm. Mr Sims was the manager and co-owner of Godstone Manor, which his partner, professional as well as personal, had purchased as a wedding gift for his beloved six years previously. Mia had been interviewed for the position of Events Coordinator by Quade himself, who came in every Sunday without fail to review the company books, events and transactions; as well as general overseeing of the property.

"Miss Reynolds, what a pleasant surprise," Quade greeted her.

"You won't be saying that when you hear what I've come to ask you."

Mia couldn't believe she'd said that out loud. When Quade failed to respond, she explained, "We've been having some personal issues at home. I know I've only just had time off for the move, but I'm going to need a little more."

Quade stared up at her through the steam spiralling from his mug, like an evil magician preparing to cast some dark sorcery upon her. "Haven't I been lenient enough with you?" he said, as if whatever excuse she came up with would have been unacceptable.

"Yes, and I appreciate that." Mia knew better than to follow up with a 'but'.

Satisfied with the response, Quade gave a modest nod. Then he took a long and theatrical slurp of his coffee before placing the mug onto the table and closing the file in front of him. Mia watched the man draw his lofty form up to its full height – he could have had a balloon stuffed up his shirt, his belly was that overhung. He tugged his blazer around the paunch as if mindful of its unsightliness, then finally spoke again.

"I heard you've been having some trouble with your little one?"

"She's, um, not coping too well with the recent changes. In fact, she's not coping at all."

"Well, I'm sorry to hear that, but it seems to me that if it's not your mother causing you issues then it's the child, and if not her then it will be something else. From now on, unless it's a case of life or death –"

"My sister was attacked yesterday," Mia blurted out. It wasn't that she'd planned on telling him, but it was as close to the truth as she could get without sounding like a raving lunatic.

Quade continued to move his lips even though no sound came out. Loose skin wobbled under his chin like a shrivelled testicle. "*Attacked*, you say? Where? By whom?"

"At home. Someone broke in. I've never seen her in such a state, I'm afraid of what she might do to herself." It wasn't wholly a lie.

"Have you contacted the police?"

"I'm working on it, but Jamie's too scared to talk to me about it, let alone a bunch of strangers. I just don't want her going through something like this alone."

"No, of course you don't." Quade ran a hand over his slick grey hair. "Well, had you brought this to my attention sooner, I might have shown you a bit more sympathy. You may be a critical part of our team, Mia, but

I'd rather have you here bright and healthy with your mind on the job, not scaring away the public. Have you even slept?"

Mia shook her head. Quade deliberated no longer.

"Well, after the tragedy we had here the other week and all you've been through recently, maybe you're due some compassionate leave."

"No, that's not what I'm asking for." Mia strode purposefully over to the table. "If you could just give me a couple of days – a week at most – to sort out my family then everything will go back to normal and I won't ask you for anything like this again. Please, Quade, you know how much I love working here."

Quade smiled then, so it must have been genuine. "I admire your dedication to this place, and I have to admit that it wouldn't be the same without you. But if you did need more time off then we'd only be replacing you on a temporary basis."

"I just need a few days and that's my final answer. I'll still be on my mobile, so if you want to pass any clients over then I'll do whatever I can to help."

"Fine, I'll take over any appointments you have personally, but I'm afraid there'll be no more flexibility after that. You know I can't be seen to show favouritism."

"I understand. Thank you, Quade."

And so, five minutes after arriving at Godestone Manor, Mia was on her way back to the car; her anxieties merely postponed. There was no guessing how long it would take to purge the house of its evil presence, or even if it was possible. Losing her job and her home she could just about cope with, but if anything happened to Jamie or Louisa … well, there wouldn't be a point to living.

"Everything okay, hun?" Angela's voice brought Mia back to the present.

"Er, yeah, I'm sure it will be." Mia advanced towards her friend, who was wedging open the entrance doors to let some fresh air into reception. "Listen, I won't be back in work until midweek. Quade has offered to cover my appointments so you're best directing people to him for now."

"No problem. Is there anything I can do to help?"

If it was anyone else then Mia would have advised them to snoop into someone else's business, but one of the reasons she respected Angela so much was because she genuinely cared. She was like the mother hen of

Godestone's little family.

"That depends." Mia glanced behind to check that Quade hadn't followed her out of the staffroom. Then she walked back to the desk with her friend, speaking in a discreet voice. "How much do you know about the paranormal?"

"In what sense?" Angela said.

"In the sense that something – something *non*-human – is trying to tear my family apart. That it's been brainwashing Louisa; attacking my sister. That the guy next door witnessed what it did to my uncle and ended up losing his frigging marbles for it, and now it's trying to get to me by threatening my mother." She hadn't meant for it to pour out like that, but the release was like breaking wind.

The slight flutter in Angela's brows was only visible because the rest of her face was like concrete. She surveyed Mia through slitted green eyes, as if she'd suffered from a temporary bout of amnesia and was trying with all her determination to recognise the woman in front of her.

"Did you tell Sims what you just told me?" she said, after an age.

Mia shook her head.

"Thank God for that." Angela ducked behind the reception counter. She stood up a few moments later with a tatty folder that she'd plucked from one of the drawers.

"You think I'm crazy, don't you?" said Mia.

"Not at all." Angela opened the folder and licked her thumb before flipping through the plastic wallets. "In fact, with all these experiences you've been having it kind of makes sense. And from what you've told me about Louisa, well, supernatural beings are supposed to be attracted to kids, aren't they?"

"Uh ... they are?" Mia could hardly contain the relief, confusion aside, that left her awash with a new sense of hope.

Angela nodded in that same composed manner. "More so than adults anyway."

Her hand left the folder to find Mia's, and for a glimmer of a second it was like having Vivian right there in front of her. "Mia, why didn't you say anything? You know I'd never judge you."

"After the way I acted that night of the suicide, I thought you'd be hesitant to believe another word I said. That and the fact I was scared shitless."

"Of what?"

"That I was going mad. That people would think I wasn't coping. That I'd be putting everyone I care about in danger if I got them involved. Christ, I've been working in this place for almost five years and not once have I felt anything close to a ghostly presence. If I was going to encounter something then I'd have put money on it being here, not in my own bloody home."

"Do you know what it wants? You hear stories about places being haunted by troubled spirits, but in most cases they don't mean you any harm; they just need help to move on."

"All I know is that it's cunning, unpredictable; a trickster. It knows – no, it learns – exactly which keys to press and then it plays you like some demented fucking piano." Mia didn't realise how hard she was squeezing Angela's hand until she saw her blueing flesh, but the woman still regarded her with that placid expression.

"Well, don't think for a second that you're losing it," Angela said. "You're one of the most strong-minded people I know. If you say there's something going on in that house, no matter how inexplicable, then there *is* something going on. Where are the girls now?"

"At home with Nathan. I've tried persuading Jamie to ring around her friends, see if she can crash with them for a few nights, but she's convinced that they'll all think she's nuts. She doesn't trust anyone right now, including me."

"What does Nathan have to say about it?"

"He's trying to be supportive, but I can see in his eyes that he thinks it's more psychological than supernatural. A neighbour has passed on the details of a local church, Saint Margaret's. That's my best bet right now, but what if they can't help us, Ange? What this thing did to Jamie ..." Mia let the sentence trail off, sparing both of them the sordid details. "It could kill her next time – kill all of us."

"I have another idea." Angela returned to the folder and flicked briskly through various papers and wallets.

Mia drew up curiously by her side. "What are you looking for?"

"Remember the psychic fair we had here last summer? Of course you do - you were the one who organised it," she added, almost as an afterthought. "I heard that some of the clairvoyants were pretty impressive, and if you think about it they deal with the spirit world on a day-to-day basis. I don't know if any of them are still local, but I kept all of their business and contact details in here. Maybe they'll be better equipped than a priest to deal with your kind of problem."

"Yeah ... you're right. That's great." The longer Mia ruminated over the idea, the more favourable it became. She wasn't surprised that it hadn't occurred to her sooner; after all, her indifference to the supernatural applied to all things associated with it.

Angela continued to rifle through the folder until she found what she'd been searching for. She dipped a hand into the plastic wallet and pulled out a wad of leaflets and business cards. "Right, let's see what we've got." She spread them out in front of her. "Liz White, astrologer – no good." This card was pushed to one side. "Agnes, clairvoyant and tarot reader. Duncan Lowe, clairvoyant medium – he's based in Leeds."

She passed a leaflet over to Mia. The words 'Secret Realm' followed by an address were printed across the top in luminescent letters on a midnight blue background. "It says he owns a shop just outside the town centre. Maybe you could drop by on your way home," Angela suggested.

Mia skimmed through the other information on the page, including services, stock lists and general details about the company. She couldn't even remember having met this Duncan Lowe and replied to Angela, "I doubt it'll be open at this time, assuming it's still there."

"There's only one way to find out." Angela shoved everything back into the plastic wallet and then handed it to Mia. "Here, you might as well take the lot. Go through them at home, talk to Nathan about it. I assume he'll be sticking around for a while?"

Mia shrugged, trying a little too hard to sound nonchalant. "Depends on the wife."

"In any case, make sure you keep in touch. I don't doubt for a second that you can beat this thing, but if you need anything – even a sofa for the night – then you mustn't hesitate to ring me. I know it's not much, but ..."

"It's something. Thanks, Ange." Mia leaned in for a hug, which her friend gladly returned. She could think of nothing more daunting than being left alone in that house, although if the entity really did thrive off fear then it should have been quite easy to lure it out using its own sadistic compulsions.

Once she was back in the car, the first thing Mia did was check her mobile. There were no missed calls or messages from Nathan, which could only be a good thing. She contemplated dropping by the care home on the way through Leeds, but the demon – assuming that was the correct term for it – was well aware that Vivian was her Achilles' heel, so to speak. Whether it could leave the house or not was immaterial, for that hadn't stopped it from screwing with their minds so far.

As she started up the car, Mia faintly wondered if Jamie would confide in Nathan about why the presence had developed this fixation with her. Aside from the victim herself, there was only one other being on this earth who was sure to know her secrets. Mia planned on asking it sometime in the near future. Right before she drove it back into the infernal hell it had spawned from.

CHAPTER TWENTY-THREE

Mia guided the car to a stop outside Saint Margaret's Church, leaving the engine chugging away. It didn't look like your archetypal place of worship, more like a well-kept community centre or small block of flats. If it wasn't for the giant metal cross stuck to the side of the building then she'd have driven straight past it. There were no stone carvings, no pointed roof and spire or brilliant stained-glass windows that even a non-religious person like Mia could appreciate; just four brick walls on an ordinary residential street. It should have been less intimidating than some dark, looming monstrosity, but something stopped her from going inside and she wasn't sure what. Certainly not the fear of being perceived as crazy – she was well past that. Maybe it was because she'd never stepped foot in a church before and couldn't shake visions of her flesh hissing and smoking like a rasher of bacon on a barbecue as soon as she walked through the door.

"Idiot," Mia said out loud, as if to knock some sense into herself. She'd never understood why churches were regarded as places of comfort: full of people confessing their sins, praying for the sick and wounded, unloading their burdens and mourning over the deaths of loved ones. But while convincing herself of all the reasons not to enter, she knew it would have been foolish to discount the chance that someone in there might be able to help.

"Please, God, help me to save my family and I'll worship you forever..."

Mia giggled, as if she'd been listening to someone else. It was the first time she'd prayed in her life. She felt no better for it.

When the main door to the church swung open, Mia swore her bowels loosened. A sign – it had to be. God had heeded her prayer. He was inviting her into His home. It was a miracle.

Mia watched as a middle-aged man emerged onto the exterior path. He had grey streaks running from his temples to the back of his head, as if someone had swept a paintbrush over his dark hair. He was wearing a white robe that sat over the top of something else dress-like and stood sideways on to the entrance. One by one, a train of people exited the building: some young and some old; some smartly dressed and others more casual. Mia even spotted a woman carrying a baby.

Of course, she almost slapped her forehead, *it was Sunday – there'd probably been a service.* Damn it, she could have snuck in amongst the congregation and got a proper feel for the place. She counted at least twenty people filtering out of the church, most – if not all of them – shaking hands with the stripy-haired man. Mia noticed a white collar around his neck, although the robes had more or less given away his identity. Similar to the church itself, the priest wasn't quite the relic she'd expected, but then she'd learned the hard way that there was nothing predictable about the town of Bramley.

The congress people gradually started to disperse, some disappearing down side streets while others got into cars parked nearby. *Now's my chance,* Mia thought. If she caught the priest while he was on his own then she could spare herself a profusion of embarrassment, for it was likely that every one of those people – maybe even the priest himself – was well acquainted with the horror tales concerning number twelve Greenway Avenue.

Mia was about to open the car door when two more bodies departed from the church. The first was a thin lady wearing a floral skirt, whose tallness was a misconception due to the short, fat bald man by her side.

"Oh, bugger!" Mia did a sideways dive onto the passenger seat, the hand break jabbing into her side while the seatbelt practically garrotted her. Of all the people she could have bumped into, *why* did it have to be Keith and Adele? Even if they hadn't spotted her, all they had to do was recognise the car and she'd be busted.

After some time, Mia forced her gaze up to the window and half expected to see Keith's giant sweaty face beaming down at her, but there was only the pastel sky. She pushed herself up while rubbing her side to check there was no physical damage from the hand break. Then, keeping her shoulders stooped and her head low, she refired the ignition and sped off down the road without looking back.

***

Mia's next stop was the high street shop that Angela had recommended from the list of psychic contacts. Based on Penny Street, the shop's exterior was less pretentious than the leaflet had portrayed. It had a simple name sign above the window, which Mia had been peering through for way too long now while pretending to admire the display of gothic ornaments: skulls, dragons and fairies which, ironically, were still more inviting than Saint Margaret's. She could see a handful of customers browsing inside the shop, one hippy-looking woman – or man, she couldn't tell – but otherwise Mia wouldn't have looked too out of place.

She walked around to the door. It squeaked in protest as she pushed it open, as if to alert the entire street of her presence. A musky waft of incense pervaded her nostrils, heavy but not offensive, although she couldn't see anything burning. She responded to the various glances with a retiring smile and headed over to the bookshelf as if she knew exactly what she'd come in for. She soon found herself skimming over the unusual titles: *Palmistry for Beginners*, *The Dream Dictionary*, *Secrets of the Angel Cards*. Mia had never heard of angel cards before, but she already felt like she was being conned. If these things were so easy as to learn from a book then wouldn't everyone be doing it?

Voices drew her observation to the till area at the back of the shop. Behind the counter there was an open doorway that led off into a secret chamber. A hand came through the beaded curtain, parting the strings down the middle as a girl emerged from the dingy space beyond. Following her out was a man dressed in a psychedelic shirt and matching turban, the patterning mostly a blur due to Mia's eyes being unable to focus. The wooden beads clicked and tapped in a soothing melody as the man let them fall back into place.

"Many thanks for your kind custom, madam, and don't forget to purchase that Lottery ticket." The shopkeeper pointed a finger at the girl and made a clucking sound with his tongue, winking as she waved him goodbye. The mention of gambling alone was enough to alert Mia, and she was beginning to wish she'd stuck with the church.

The girl hurried over to her friends, and they drifted towards the exit in a chattering cluster. None of them looked old enough to have left school, never mind buy a Lottery ticket.

"Can I help you, miss?"

Mia glanced at the man in the turban and was even more dazzled by the eyes that stared back at her. He could have had ultraviolet lights fitted behind the sockets, they were so bright, and for a reason unknown to Mia, she shook her head and replied, "Just looking, thanks."

The man nodded and started fiddling with the till. Mia sauntered over to the central table on which collections of stones, gems and crystals were arranged in their individual baskets. There were small cards in front of each one to label the different types, but it was all meaningless to Mia.

Always conscious of the shop owner's eyes upon her, she'd spy him every so often and then roam to another section of the shop like it was some ridiculous game. A painful squeak sounded more like a squeal in the ongoing silence, and Mia glanced at the door to see that the last customer was just leaving.

"If you're going to pinch something then I won't stop you, but remember karma and the Threefold Law," the man said to Mia.

She put back the item she'd been fingering without even realising what it was before heading over to the counter. "Are you Duncan Lowe?" she said.

"I could be anyone for you."

"Excuse me?"

"I said yes, who are you?" The man's lips curved into a charming smile. His white teeth gleamed like a pearl necklace and were further enhanced by his bronze complexion. The blond fuzz on his chin barely passed for a goatee, and though the turban made it difficult to tell, he must have been around Mia's age if not a little younger.

"I was, er, recommended to you by a friend." Mia spoke hesitantly. "It's kind of awkward, really. I don't even know if you'll be able to help me."

"There is no question that can't be answered by the tarot, my dear."

"Oh, no, I'm not here for a reading. It's a little more ... practical than that."

Mr Lowe leaned forwards with his elbows propped on the counter, chin resting on his knuckles. "Now I am intrigued."

"Well," Mia began, "I know you're probably used to dealing with spirits and things but what about, like, hauntings?"

"Who is it that you think is being haunted?"

"Me. Well, my family. I feel ridiculous even talking about it –"

As if he didn't need to hear any more, the man held up a hand to silence her. The flesh on his palm was several shades lighter than that on his face, and Mia couldn't decide whether he'd lounged on a sunbed for too long or fallen face first into a puddle of mud. Although the suspiciously smooth skin made it clear that makeup was involved.

Mr Lowe nodded his head, slowly at first, and then with more vigour. "You came to the right place. Here's what will happen: we'll start with a reading, just so I can tune into your aura. Don't be afraid to open up your mind and soul to me. That will allow me to better assess what might be troubling you and why, then we can take things from there. Comprende?"

"Er, I guess."

"Splendid, the cards should tell us all we need to know. Thirty-five quid, is that okay?"

Mia was sure the last part had been deliberately sped up. If she wasn't convinced by him before then she was even less so now, but the bloke did have to earn a living from this and she was running out of options.

Mia delved in her handbag for her purse and eventually presented him with her debit card. "You do accept cards?" she said, as he looked disappointedly at the plastic.

"Machine's a bit temperamental, that's all."

"Oh." She rifled through the purse some more. "Sorry, I've only got thirty on me."

"Go on, then. Seeing as it's your first time and these are exceptional circumstances, I'll give you a discount – but I expect you to spread the good word."

"Thanks, that's very kind of you." Mia handed over the cash, which went straight into the back pocket of Mr Lowe's combats.

He walked over to the beaded curtain that he'd come through with the young girl earlier, gesturing the doorway with a sweep of his arm. "Ladies first."

The back room was about half the size of the main shop and included a dinky sink unit and a kettle that looked like it had been bought from a car boot sale. *Must have been the equivalent to a staff canteen,* Mia mused.

"Can I get you anything: tea, coffee?" asked Mr Lowe, as if reading her thoughts. Mia hoped he wasn't telepathic as well.

"No, thank you," she replied.

Overall, the room was relatively plain apart from a small circular table in the centre, a sparsely stacked bookshelf and various abstract paintings hanging from the ruby-coloured walls. Mr Lowe seated himself on a stool by the table and indicated the chair opposite, which looked like it was made from matchsticks. Mia sat down gingerly, waiting until its joints had stopped creaking before placing her bag down by her feet. On the table there was a loose pile of tarot cards, their discolouration and tattered edges giving the impression that they were well handled; as well as adding a touch of authenticity. When the psychic started shuffling the deck, Mia was surprised at their size and thickness, which must have been double that of normal playing cards. Also displayed on the table was a crystal ball mounted on a claw-like stand.

"Don't worry, it's just for show," Mr Lowe admitted, having caught Mia eyeing the object.

He cut the cards into three piles, then laid them on the table and instructed Mia to pick one. She pointed to the middle stack. Mr Lowe pushed everything else to one side, reshuffled her chosen selection and then spread the cards out into a line, facedown.

"Now choose three cards and place them in front of you without looking," he told Mia.

She took a few moments to study the cards, trying to guess which ones were 'good' and which were 'bad', despite having no idea what was hidden on the other side. After a while, boredom set in so she picked the last card at random. From left to right, the psychic labelled them as 'past', 'present' and 'future'.

"Right." Mia nodded, completely absorbed.

"If you'd like to turn over your past when you're ready," said Mr Lowe.

Mia flipped over the first card. There was an image of what appeared to be a jester on the front with the word 'Fool' written underneath it. She looked to the man with an eager mixture of dread and anticipation.

"This card indicates decisions that have been made, perhaps in haste or which you've come to regret," he explained. "It may be connected to another person, or as it is a past card, you could be the affected one."

Even though it was vague, Mia instantly linked this to her mother and the decision to put her into residential care. She couldn't ignore the thrill that raced through her because, ashamedly, she wanted to believe it. She *needed* to believe it, because without a problem there could be no solution, and without a solution they were all doomed. A friend had once told her that dabbling with psychics was like gambling: once you thought your luck was in, you kept on going. Mia recalled snubbing the notion, yet here she was hooked on one card.

Without giving anything away, Mia went to turn over the next card when Mr Lowe slammed his hand down on top of it. She almost expected a resounding '*Snap!*' to follow.

"Wait." He put two fingers to his right temple, as if attempting some form of mind control. "They're saying something but ... I can't ... quite ..."

"Who is it? What's going on?" Mia sat erect, her impatience starting to simmer. Mr Lowe finally looked up, not at her but beyond her, as if someone was standing far back in the distance. Mia would have turned round if her neck muscles weren't as stiff as a horseman's riding crop.

"I'm picking up some vibrations," mumbled the psychic, eyes shrinking into indigo slits. "There's a presence around you. Someone is trying to communicate."

"Is it the thing that's been haunting us? Has it followed me here?"

Mr Lowe shook his head. "It's someone you know. A relative."

Mia thought hard, biting into her bottom lip. Uncle Billy – it had to be. Maybe, just *maybe*, he held the secret to vanquishing this evil.

"Whoever it is, they're here to warn you but a dark force is blocking them." Mr Lowe closed his eyes. "*Harrruuum* ... Come into the light, my dear ... *Harumwaaah*."

Mia was on the very tip of her chair, her eyes bolted to the meditating psychic. She might have laughed under different circumstances, but right now she was so fascinated that she could think of nothing beyond that moment.

"Mia ..." he whispered. *Holy crap, she hadn't told him her name!*

"W-what are they saying?" Mia asked.

"I'm not sure. I think it's related to the first card – yes, definitely. Something you did in your past is burdening you now. That's what is causing this disturbance, this haunting."

Mia cast her thoughts back to the dreams and hallucinations that had been plaguing her this last month. How the entity seemed to be getting stronger and more violent by the day, as if their suffering provided some sort of nourishment for it. There was no cushioning the facts: this was about one person and one person only.

"Oh, God – it's my mother, isn't it?" she said.

"Yes!" Mr Lowe exclaimed, eyes still firmly shut. "She's here with us. Whatever happened between you two, now is the time to let it go. That's all she wants."

"B-but that's not possible, my mum isn't –" Mia felt a tide of nausea wash over her, and the whole room felt like a ship being tossed about on the ocean's tempestuous waves. Either the psychic had got his spirits muddled up, or she was already too late.

"*Harrruuum ... harumwaaah-gagaaa ...*" His chanting was becoming more and more farcical, and his face wasn't much better. The creases in his fake tan, bronzer or whatever the hell it was were starting to look more like plaster cracks, and he must have had more kohl pencilled around his eyes than Mia did. But he couldn't have been a fraud – a little eccentric, maybe – but he'd been so accurate up until now. So convincing. He'd known her name, for Christ's sake.

The same name that was printed across the front of your debit card? a niggling voice sounded from the back of her mind.

Mia swallowed, the tiny, rage-fuelled convulsions in the back of her throat causing her voice to waver. "Does my mum have any messages for my father?"

"Let me just ... Oh, yes, I can hear her clearly now. She says that she misses you both very much, but it's time to stop grieving. Time to –"

Rising from the chair, Mia swiped forth her arm and batted the cards, along with the crystal ball, off the table. The 'psychic' opened his eyes with a start, watching the cards flutter about the room and then almost toppling off the stool when he saw her towering over him.

"You lying little shit!" Mia spat, her forefinger only centimetres away from his nose – he actually went cross-eyed looking at it. "You're lucky I don't sue your ass, do you know that? Fucking conman."

The man elevated both arms in an act of surrender. "Hey, lady, I'm just the messenger. I can't control what –"

"Give it up, dickhead, my mum's very much alive –" *for now*, "– it's my dad who's been dead for years. Enjoy ripping people off, do you? Preying on their emotions?" Mia cackled at her own stupidity. "Christ, you're no better than the thing that's invaded my home."

"I get that you're pissed, but I was trying to do you a favour. Folk find it comforting when they think their loved ones are watching over them and you're no exception. I saw your face when you turned over that first card."

Boy, he's good, Mia thought – in a scheming and immoral sort of way. Had her mind not been in such disarray then she'd have sussed him out from the beginning, but desperation was a bastard and so was he.

"Do you know what?" she said, grabbing her handbag off the floor. "It's my own fault for being such a gullible idiot. You enjoy your pathetic existence and I'll stick to sorting out my own problems, but don't think I'm leaving here without my thirty quid back."

"Come on, give an idiot a break." Mr Lowe spread his arms out in front of him, legs astride the stool. "Everyone has to earn a crust, right?"

"Fine, if you won't give it back then I'll take something from the shop and flog it online. Good luck calling the cops." Mia turned to storm out.

"Whoa, hold it!" Mr Lowe jumped off the stool and made a grab for her arm, but somehow his hand became entangled in the straps of her handbag.

"Let go!" Mia whirled round and shoved him away with the length of her forearm. He skidded on the crystal ball, and the unanticipated attack sent him reeling into the bookshelf. Several titles were propelled from their shelves but, miraculously, both unit and man were saved by the sturdiness of the wall behind. Straightening himself up, he clutched his wonky turban as if it encased his brain.

"I-I'm sorry ..." Mia could only gawp at the man, whose line-riddled face generated a flashback of the night she'd blown up at Louisa. It was as if the evil she'd been cooped up with for so long was slowly contaminating her, and she had no idea how to stop it.

Taking the notes out of his back pocket, Mr Lowe offered them to Mia while being careful to maintain the distance between them. "Look, you seem like a reasonable-ish lady and I'm not that bad a guy really. Take the cash, I'm sorry for any distress I've caused you but, please, you can't take this any further."

"Oh, really?" Mia crossed her arms while transferring her weight onto her right leg. Just when she was beginning to feel sorry for the prick...

"The truth is, this is my Uncle's shop. I'm just covering for him while he takes some time off. He's, um, not been well. It's stress related."

Mia narrowed her eyes. "Are you telling me you're not Duncan Lowe?"

The man shook his head. "The name's Max; Duncan, my uncle, lives in the flat above the shop. So you see, I can't be responsible for him losing his livelihood – which is totally legit, by the way. I was just trying to raise a bit of cash, pay off some debts. I never set out to hurt anyone."

"And the cards – that was all bullshit, too?"

Max bowed his head, looking up at her sheepishly. "I read people, not cards. Everyone's made decisions they come to regret at some point in their lives, right? That's what got me into the shit I'm in now. I gambled away half of my parents' worldly possessions, they chucked me out and so here I am. Pathetic, I know, but that's me."

"You expect me to believe that sob story after what you've just pulled?" Even as she spoke, there was something about this man that convinced Mia he was harmless. Perhaps it was the whimsical air about him, or those beautiful clear eyes in which she could see her reflection as though she was looking through glass.

"I don't expect you to do anything, but it is the truth," Max vowed.

"Well, sorry to hear that, but you're not the only one with issues." It was sincere even though she couldn't have sounded more patronising if she tried.

As she turned to leave, Max said, "Wait, you said you had a problem with a haunting?"

Mia faced him again, purely out of curiosity. "What of it?"

"I know it might feel like it right now, but you ain't alone. My uncle has helped people like you up and down the country, and he doesn't charge fees for stuff like that."

"He actually deals with spirits – even malevolent ones?"

"He's a clairvoyant medium: basically, a channel between the living and the dead. Look him up if you don't believe me, there are plenty of articles about him. He's a good guy – gifted, nowt like me. Can't say I envy him for it, though, some of the shit I've witnessed." Max shivered in emphasis, and Mia caught herself doing the same.

Moving towards him, she said, "All I know about hauntings is what I've seen on TV, but I doubt this is like anything he's come across before."

"You said it's malicious, right?"

"I think 'evil' would be putting it tamely. It's already attacked my sister, and I'm afraid that my daughter will be next. I just don't want to put anyone else in danger."

"Can I ask how old she is – your sister?"

Mia took a moment to consider what and how much she should tell the man who'd lied to her face, as well as cheating a schoolgirl out of her pocket money and probably ripping off half the city. Yet he was also the first person, professionally speaking, who had the faintest clue of what she was going through. Someone who could empathise with her because, for them, it was a part of everyday life. And searching beneath all those coatings of fake tan, Mia began to see a face far too attractive to have been anything but innocent.

"She's seventeen," Mia told him, but Max looked as though he'd already predicted the answer. He didn't say anything, which perturbed her all the more.

"So, do you have any theories?" she queried.

"Well, bearing in mind I'm no expert and Uncle Duncan would probably shoot me for advising his clients ... going off what I've learned over the years and things I've heard him talking about ... I'd say it could possibly be a poltergeist but, most likely, we're dealing with a demon."

"Okay." Even Mia had been able to figure that out, but Max seemed impressed with himself. "What exactly is a demon and how do I get rid of it?" she said.

"Depends."

"On what?"

"Religion, history, mythology. I don't think there are any scientific explanations for these sorts of things, but they do tend to go for the adolescents first. Especially the screwed up ones."

"What makes them such easy targets?"

"Because they're younger, weaker; more vulnerable and less likely to put up a fight. It's the same with kids, only they're generally a lot less emotional than teenagers."

"So it's normal for demons to sense people's fears?"

"In a manner of speaking. Is that what you think it's doing?"

"It seems that way, and we're not the first people to have felt a presence in the house. I think it might be connected to a man who used to live there. Ever since he passed away, there've been stories of unexplainable attacks on people. I heard it almost broke up one couple's marriage."

"Hmm ..." Max dipped his brows, pursed lips pointing to one side. "Spirits certainly can be troubled, but a demon ... well, they're a separate book altogether. They aren't usually people at all, more like entities."

Mia considered this a moment, then shook her head. "I don't get it, are you saying it couldn't possibly be someone who once lived there?"

"I'm saying they never had a human form like you and me – at least, none that Uncle Duncan has ever mentioned. They're just evil forces, usually without any reason for existing aside from possession of a human, hence why they're so rare. You don't know of anyone having messed around with a Ouija board, do you?"

Demons, Ouija boards, possession – what would it be next, *werewolves?* Mia shook her head once more, this time reminding herself that everything she and her family had witnessed was definitely not down to fantasy. "Not that I'm aware of. I could ask my neighbour, he's encountered this thing as well. In fact, he and my daughter are the only two people I know of who've actually seen it."

"So it hasn't manifested in its true form yet?"

"Not unless its true form is my mother's identical twin." Mia rethought the question. "What do you mean, 'yet'?"

"Like I said," Max spontaneously decided to start gathering the books that had fallen from the unit, "you're better off speaking to my uncle about it. I don't know a whole lot about demons, but I do know they can be a bastard to shift. Duncan ... well, these things take their toll on him. It's like every time he deals with one, it takes a piece of his soul."

He placed the books haphazardly onto their shelves, then glanced at Mia while adding, "Not that I'm trying to freak you out even more than you must be already."

"It's okay, I know exactly how he feels. When will your uncle be back in the shop?"

"His coach is due in tomorrow morning. If you want to leave your number then I'll make sure he calls you ASAP."

"I'd appreciate that, as long as it's not going to be a problem."

"Nothing's too much trouble for my Uncle Duncan."

As Mia reeled off her mobile number, Max jotted it down onto the back of an envelope that he'd found on the bookshelf. "Just so you know," she warned, "if this is a wind up then I'll be back, and I'll bring my demon with me."

"I don't doubt it," Max answered, with a half-grin. "Is there anyone else at home? Mum, Dad, boyfriend ...?"

"There's going to be someone staying with us for a while, but otherwise it's just the three of us."

"Great." A dreamy smile touched his lips. He saw Mia watching him and shook his head, face square once more. "I-I mean it's good that ... I'm glad you have someone –"

"Bye, Max." Mia saw herself out of the room, back through the shop and towards the exit.

"Hey, Mia ..." She turned to find the man standing behind the counter, as if he'd been there all along. "Don't leave anyone alone in that house, okay? Just because it's struck once doesn't mean it won't try again, especially if it thinks you're vulnerable. Sorry I couldn't be more helpful."

Mia smiled at him. "You've done fine."

The door whined, and then she was gone.

CHAPTER TWENTY-FOUR

Nathan carried the plates of risotto over to the kitchen table and laid one down in front of Mia. Even though it smelled as delectable as it looked, the colourful mélange of peppers and herbs like some kind of scattered rainbow, her stomach felt like it was shrinking into itself; recoiling from the food as if convinced it was poisoned.

"Thanks," she said, as Nathan took a seat opposite her. The flowery apron he was wearing rustled as he sat down, and Mia let out a soft chuckle.

"What's so funny?" asked Nathan.

"I was just thinking, we've known each other going on eight years – even produced a child together – but the two of us haven't once sat down to a meal. Excluding all those nights at the kebab shop, of course."

Nathan laughed while stirring the risotto with his fork to help it cool down. Mia dunked her cutlery into the mush and licked off the sauce with the tip of her tongue. "Mmm," she murmured, more surprised by its taste than the little skip in her appetite. Louisa was always crowing on about how Daddy was a better cook than Mummy, and Mia started to wonder if she'd been underestimating him all these years – in more ways than one.

"Hey ..."

Mia glanced up to meet Nathan's pensive stare.

"Do you ever wonder what might have happened if it wasn't for that night of passion?"

Mia almost spat out her food laughing. "*Passion?*" she squawked. "I don't know what the hell you were on back then, but I wish you'd given me some."

Nathan rolled his eyes playfully. "I just meant to say where would our lives have taken us? Would we have kept in touch or gone our separate ways? Maybe we'd have got together properly, imagine that?"

"Please, not while I'm eating." Mia stuffed her mouth with another forkful of risotto, waiting until she'd swallowed before saying, "With the way you're prattling on, anyone would think you're disappointed that we didn't make a go of things."

"I was just thinking out loud. There's something about the silence here, it sends your mind to places you never thought existed."

Mia didn't like the sound of that – not one bit. She washed out her mouth with a big slurp of wine and then tactfully changed the subject. "Have you made up with Regina yet?"

"More or less. She'll get over it."

"Did you tell her about what's been going on here?"

Nathan stopped chewing, arched a brow. "You honestly think she wouldn't be banging the door down if I told her I was here ghost busting?"

"Then, why does she think you're here?"

"Burglars." He grinned at his own guilefulness. "I told her you were waiting for an alarm system to be installed and that you wanted me nearby in case anything happened. It's not too far off the truth if you think about it."

"You mean she doesn't know you'll be staying here tonight?"

Nathan shook his head. "I said I'd booked into a bed and breakfast. You know what she's like, can't get her head around a man and a woman just being friends."

"Well, you can't blame her when that woman is the mother of your only child." The wine glass was back in Mia's hand before she'd even realised it. "Isn't it funny how we drifted apart after Louisa was born, yet five years down the line you're married with two illegitimate kids? Regina must be giving you a lot more than I ever could."

Nathan shrugged, his attention back on the food. "I'm content and that's a lot more than some people can say. There are days when I feel like running away, but if I'd done that five years ago when Louisa was born then it would have been the biggest mistake of my life." He followed up with, "Don't get me wrong, I love Regina and the boys, but marriage was more about making them feel secure. Besides, would you have said no to that crazy shrew?"

Mia shook her head despairingly. "No wonder Regina's so bloody possessive. If you being here is going to cause problems then you could always take Louisa back to your place like we planned. I know Regina's still upset with her over what she did to Jack, but this is no place for a child right now."

"That's funny, because I've been here all day and there hasn't been a whiff of anything out of the ordinary. Maybe the spook has got guy issues or something."

"I'm sure it's quaking in its imaginary boots." It was more scornful than sarcastic. Mia took another sip of her wine, which seemed to be going down a lot faster than the risotto. "Did Jamie say anything while I was out today?"

"About what?"

"You know what." She glared at Nathan over the rim of her glass. "This is probably the worst time for an interrogation, but it's been playing on my mind all day. I have to know what happened to her."

"If it's any consolation, she's been acting anything but the victim. I got my ears chewed off earlier for rustling a crisp packet too loudly, that's typical Jamie if you ask me."

Rather than anger at his ignorance, Mia gave a resigned sigh. "It's called denial, Nathan, and the deeper she buries it, the harder it'll be to reach her."

"Why don't you let me try?"

"No offence, but if she won't talk to me or Brenda then what makes you think you'll have any luck?"

"Maybe you're too close to her. Think about it, you've become a lot more than her big sister these last couple of years and we can all see how run down you are. Would you want to burden Vivian with something like that?"

"No, but she's my mother and if I had a problem then she'd want to know about it. Wouldn't you if it was Louisa?"

"Well, Jamie obviously doesn't see it like that. Maybe she'll talk to me if I promise not to say anything. You don't want her ending up like Kerry the stoner, do you?"

Jamie wandered into the kitchen, and a rapid silence ensued. "What are you two whispering about?" It was almost an accusation.

Mia noted that she was wearing a baggy jumper, presumably to hide the cuts and bruises on her arms and chest, mainly from Louisa but also from Nathan. Mia, herself, had seen the way he looked at her sister: like someone in need of a few weeks on the psychiatric ward.

"We were just discussing our next move," Mia lied. "You can still take up Brenda's offer, you know, if things are getting too much for you. She said you're welcome to crash at theirs, at least until we've made a decision about the house."

"So that retard can pester me with his camera all night? No, thanks, I'll take my chances with you lot. Besides, what makes you think I'll be any safer there than I am here?"

Mia couldn't argue with that. Jamie scraped the remains of her risotto into the dog's bowl, asking, "Has Casey still not eaten?"

"No, the poor thing's wasting away. I'll get the vet's number from Brenda tomorrow."

"Oh," Nathan clicked his fingers, "is that the redhead from next door? She popped around earlier, said she had some information and that you'd know what it was about."

"And?" Mia prompted.

"That's all she'd tell me, but she seemed pretty rattled about something. Maybe I gave her a shock answering the door instead of you."

"I bet she's spoken to Keith. It doesn't matter, I bumped into him earlier."

"What did he say?" Jamie left her plate on the side and approached the table, inquisitiveness breaking through some of the gloom that dulled her pretty face.

Mia did plan on telling her about Edward Perkins and the whole fear theory, but if Jamie already felt pressurised to tell the truth then there was a risk of her becoming even more withdrawn. Especially if she found out the attack had been carried out by some bitter, decrepit old man.

"He talked a bit about the house's history, but I think we should wait and see what the psychic has to say rather than taking the word of some old gossip," Mia answered slickly.

Louisa came pottering down the hallway with her empty bowl. She entered the kitchen and studied the three faces in turn.

"Hey, sweetie, you all finished?" Mia took the bowl from her while stroking the girl's ebony curls.

Louisa nodded.

"Was it good?" Nathan asked her. She nodded again.

Mia said, "Daddy's going to be having a sleepover in your room tonight, won't that be nice?"

"What, I'm not taking the couch?" Nathan almost looked disappointed.

"With this thing lurking in every nook, cranny and shadow? No way, we've come too far to start taking risks now." Mia still felt uneasy whenever she mentioned the demon, knowing it was there. Watching. Listening. Plotting. It was like being on some reality TV show and the house was bugged with secret cameras.

Looking back to Jamie, she said, "We'll take your room if that's okay? Mine's strictly off-limits after what happened."

Jamie nodded in agreement, her body trembling at the recollection. Mia had a mental flash of her nude, helpless form on the bed and closed her eyes to dispel it from her thoughts.

"Can I at least pinch your mattress?" Nathan said to Mia. "Beats sleeping on the floor."

"Take whatever you want, but do *not* leave Louisa on her own at any point during the night. If she tells you there's something in the room then you come and get me, right?"

"Yes, boss. Now, finish your flipping risotto. I've put a lot of effort into that."

To everyone's astonishment, it was Jamie who started laughing at Nathan's American pronunciation of the word 'risotto' so it sounded more like '*riz-o-doh*', whether it had been deliberate or not.

"You eat it!" Mia scooped a clump of rice onto her fork. With a quick flick of her wrist, the grains flew across the table in all directions. Nathan closed his eyes as the rice clung to his lashes and stuck to his T-shirt like spitballs.

Loud, hysterical laughter rumbled through the room. A drunken merriment usually reserved for Christmas parties or work dos, tears flowing like wine. In fact, the scene bordered on insanity and even Nathan appeared to be contemplating them as if they were total strangers.

But Mia knew they were all weeping inside.

***

"For Christ's sake, pick up, you bastard." Regina's ear was crushed beneath the phone, her diamond stud practically lacerating her lobe. She glimpsed the clock on the mantelpiece while pacing the large living room. It was ten fifteen in the evening. She hadn't had so much as a text message from her husband since tea time and was desperately trying to ignore the 'Christmas card' scene in her mind: Nathan, his daughter, his daughter's mother and that slut sister of hers all snuggled around the fire having a drink and a laugh together. He'd always put Louisa first, and while a part of Regina respected and admired him for that, the provoking voice would always be there in the back of her mind, taunting her insecurities. The voice that maintained she, Nathan's biological daughter, meant more to him than his wife and stepsons put together. That if they were being held at gunpoint, he would sooner save Louisa than all three of them.

After an eternity of ringing out, someone picked up. "About bloody time!" Regina barked, stopping dead in the middle of the room. "What, are you too busy playing happy families to speak to your fucking wife?"

In the next few seconds, all Regina could hear was the sound of her own breaths gusting down the phone. Finally, a voice answered, but it wasn't the voice she'd expected.

"Daddy isn't here right now."

"Louisa? Oh, sh –" Regina slammed a hand over her mouth to stop herself from cursing again. "Sorry, darling, just pretend you didn't ... Hang on, why are you answering your dad's phone? Is he still there?"

No reply.

"Lou Lou?"

"Aunt Jamie's sad."

"Oh. Okay. So, where's Nat – I mean your father?"

"In the bedroom."

"What's he doing in there?" Regina's fingers started to cramp up, making it even more difficult to loosen her grip on the phone. She kept having to remind herself that it was a five-year-old on the other end of the line. "Louisa, whose bedroom is he in? How long has he been there? Where's your mum?"

More silence.

"I'm not angry with him, darling, I just wanted to say goodnight before I go to bed."

"Daddy doesn't want to talk to you. He said you're a crazy shrew and he's going to come and live with us. Bye, bye, Gina."

The line cut out. *Crazy shrew ...?* "Crazy shrew!" Regina boomed it the second time around.

She immediately redialled, her fingers almost missing the number keys, they were that shaky. This time it went straight to answer phone. "Damn it!" She slammed the phone onto the coffee table and swapped it for a tumbler of whisky nearby. She went to take a sip, but her raging breaths wouldn't allow it.

"What the heck does he think he's playing at?" Regina carped to herself. She wouldn't usually have taken the word of an infant, and after Louisa's attack on Jack the other day, the kid obviously had behavioural issues. But if Nathan really cared about his family then he'd have been at home comforting his wounded stepson, not off chasing burglars.

Burglars ... Regina realised how stupid that sounded.

She stomped into the kitchen and poured the last few drops of whisky into the sink, then busied herself scrubbing the glass clean. Even if she hadn't been drinking, she was in no fit state to drive all the way up to Leeds, and she didn't think it would be fair on the boys to drag them out of bed. Fortunately, working alongside her best friend, who owned a small cosmetics company, Regina had the flexibility to take time off as and when she needed it.

She had her back to the door when Jack Summers shuffled into the kitchen, rubbing his crusty eyes. "I heard shouting," he said.

"I spilled my drink, that's all. Go back to bed, son." Regina kept on sponging the glass. Her arms worked furiously, like a serial killer hacking up body parts.

"My head hurts," the boy complained.

"It will do for a while. You're not feeling sick, are you?" Regina peered at him over the breakfast bar.

Jack shook his head.

"That's a good sign. Go on up to bed and I'll bring you an icepack and a mug of hot chocolate."

"When's Dad coming home?"

"That's what I'd bloody well like to know." Plonking the glass onto the draining board, Regina ushered her son back to the staircase.

She waited until he'd disappeared before swiping the home phone from its stand in the hallway. She dialled her friend's number and was soon greeted by a woman's voice.

"Hey, Nell, am I okay to slip off work early tomorrow afternoon?" said Regina. "I've got some urgent business that I need to take care of, and I might need to borrow your car."

***

Louisa placed her dad's mobile phone back onto the bedside table where he'd left it charging earlier. She tucked her knees up to her chest and looped her arms around them so she was huddled up on the bed. Her breath frosted in the air before her, as if winter had come early and compacted itself into that tiny room. She made a conscious effort not to look into the farthest corner. She didn't want or need to see it to know that it was there: the *thing* everyone whispered about when they thought she wasn't listening. People didn't understand that talking about the monster, worrying about how it was going to hurt them, only made matters worse. Louisa couldn't understand it herself, but somehow it *knew* she was afraid of it, just like it knew everything about everyone. It also had no intention of leaving.

She took her cup from the bedside table and held it over the phone a second or two, water sloshing about in her quaking hand. Then she tipped it upside down and watched the liquid cascade over the device. There was a persistent *tap, tap, tap* as the water dribbled over the edge of the table and made dark soggy patches on the carpet.

Floorboards creaked just outside her bedroom. The door burst open and something huge and unwieldy blundered in from the shadows of the landing. Louisa jolted, the empty cup slipping out of her hand and rolling into the puddle on the floor. It was only her dad lugging in the mattress from her mum's room.

"Phew!" Nathan panted. He let the mattress flop down next to the bed with a resounding thud. The old springs twanged inside the polyester, dust clouds blasting into the air. There was barely enough space to open the door now, it was that cramped.

Nathan grinned at Louisa with one hand pressed against his lower back. He was wearing a T-shirt and shorts, and his socks were pulled halfway up his calves. "I bet you're not going to give up the bed for your old man, are you?"

His eyes moved across to the bedside table and almost tripled their size when he spotted the wire protruding from his waterlogged phone. "Shit, Louisa!" He yanked the plug from the wall socket and grabbed the Blackberry, rubbing it vigorously with the end of his T-shirt. "Jesus, what happened? You could have been electrocuted!"

"I knocked my cup over," said Louisa.

Nathan tapped the keypad frantically. "Ah, shit, I think it's broken."

"It was an accident Daddy really it was I didn't mean to do it." The flood of words came without respite.

"S'pose it's my own fault for leaving it there in the first place. There's nowt we can do about it now."

Louisa watched him dismantle the phone. He blew the individual components and then placed them on the windowsill. "We'll leave them to dry off, see if I can fix it in the morning. Regina will probably be in bed by now anyway."

"I'm sorry, Daddy."

"It's okay, princess, I'm just glad you didn't get fried." He crouched in front of her and brushed his hands over her goosepimply arms. "Man, you're freezing. Is it really that cold in here?"

Though her breath was no longer clouding the air, Louisa still shivered. "Will you stay with us forever?" she whispered.

"You know I can't, but I'm going to do everything I can to help you and Mum. Soon, all this bad stuff will go away and you won't have to worry about the shadow man ever again."

"Why not?"

"Well ..." Nathan scratched the back of his head and leaned back on his heels, "it's your Aunt Jamie. She's sick, see? There's something wrong with her brain and she's making up all these stories to scare you. We both know ghosts aren't real, don't we?"

"But Mummy said –"

"You let me worry about your mum. I reckon I know how to make Jamie better, but let's keep it as our little secret for now, okay?"

"Okay."

Nathan pecked her on the forehead. "Now, let's get some rest. Something tells me it's going to be an eventful day tomorrow, but all will be back to normal soon enough. I can promise you that much."

As he set about making up the mattress with the fresh sheets that Mia had given him, Louisa glanced back to the murky silhouette that slowly melted into the wall behind. She swore it was grinning.

CHAPTER TWENTY-FIVE

When Mia awoke naturally, both her instincts and the undisturbed silence told her that something wasn't right. She wasn't quite sure of what until she rolled over and saw the unoccupied pillow next to her. Her hand shot across the bed, and she patted down the mattress to check there was no one hiding under the duvet.

"Jamie?" She elevated herself onto one elbow and scanned all four corners of the bedroom, eyes like a raptor hunting its prey. Her sister was nowhere.

Mia swung herself out of bed and dashed onto the landing in her cami vest and shorts. Passing the bathroom, she saw that it was also vacant. She hovered outside Louisa's room and listened to the sound of Nathan's guttural snoring from inside. She decided not to disturb them – it was light outside but she had no idea what time it was.

Mia hurried downstairs and eventually found Jamie in the kitchen, kneeling by Casey's basket. "There you are." She tried not to sound too relieved. "What are you doing down here?"

Hearing a whimper, she proceeded across the room. The tiles were like icecaps beneath her bare feet. Casey was slouched in her basket with a skinny paw lying flat in Jamie's hand, fur matted with blood.

"What happened?" said Mia, crouching next to them.

"I don't know, I came down for a drink and just found her like this."

Mia tried parting the dog's fur to inspect the wound, but she recoiled with a yowl.

"Looks like she might have caught it on something," Jamie noted.

"Or she's been fighting." Mia indicated the red flecks beneath Casey's chin.

"Fighting with what? Oh, no, you don't think ..."

When Mia returned Jamie's stare, it was like peering at her own reflection in a pool of liquid horrors. "Let's not jump to any conclusions – at least, not until Duncan has been to check the place out."

"Can we at least take her to the vets like you promised?"

"I need to sort out appointments with the bank and estate agents first. If it turns out that there's no hope for us living here peacefully then we need to have some sort of contingency plan in place." Mia stood up and went to switch on the kettle. "I'd better ring Brenda as well, see if Keith told her the same thing he told me."

"I think she said that she was going to be on a night shift. I doubt she'll even be home yet."

"Oh." Mia took her mobile from the side unit anyway. "Maybe she's left me a message, then."

"Are you planning on taking Louisa to school this morning?"

"Yeah, it's better than her hanging around here all day. Hopefully, it'll help to take her mind off things." Mia glanced across to her sister. "How are you holding up anyway? Did you sleep much?"

Jamie projected a look that didn't demand words.

"I know it's a stupid question, and I can understand why you don't want to talk about it right now. Repressing what happened will only make things worse, though."

"Nothing *happened*."

Mia's stare became even more muddled. "You mean it didn't –"

"Stop it!" Jamie rose without warning, fetching a couple of mugs from the rack next to the sink and slamming them shakily onto the worktop. "I-I can't remember much, and I don't want to either. All I know is that if Paul hadn't barged in when he did ..." She twisted her head fractionally towards Mia, modulating her tone. "I just want things to go back to normal so I can forget it ever happened, is that so wrong?"

"Of course it isn't." Mia couldn't say much more than that, apart from the fact that Jamie's wish would never truly be granted. "Just tell me what I can do to help and I'll do it."

"Well, for starters, I wouldn't mind going to see Mum before that psychic bloke gets here." Jamie spoke as if the memory had already been eradicated. "I feel like I haven't seen her in ages."

"*No.*" It came out sharper than intended. Mia saw the bewilderment in the younger girl's face. "I'm missing her, too, but it's best that we keep as much distance between her and us as possible."

"Why? What aren't you telling me?" Jamie approached Mia, the nine years between them certainly not depicted by their equal heights.

"I just don't want to put her in any unnecessary danger. You know as well as I do that this thing preys on people's insecurities, and Mum's more vulnerable than us lot put together."

"Has it threatened her or something?"

"No. Just pour the brews, will you?" Mia ordered, as the kettle rumbled to its boiling point. "Let's not give this leech any more negativity to feed on."

A while after switching on her mobile, a couple of voicemails buzzed through. The first was a message from Brenda from late last night:

'*In case I didn't get a chance to speak to you anytime soon, I thought I should let you know that I've had a friend from medical records check out Edward Perkins's file. I don't know whether it's good news or bad news, but I think you might be on to something. The man was diagnosed with agoraphobia over twenty years ago – he literally couldn't leave the house. No wonder the chap went stir-crazy.*' There was a sound of papers being shuffled. '*Oh, and something else you might be interested to know is that Edward's sister, Missy Gibbons, committed suicide recently – hung herself, apparently. She lived in Penistone, isn't that where you work? Anyway ...*'

The message babbled on a while longer, but all Mia heard were the words 'good luck' followed by 'see you soon' and then a beep to signal the end of the message. Keeping the phone to her ear, she found herself gazing through the kitchen window as if there was nothing but solar space on the other side of the glass – an uninvestigated, black nothingness. She could have been beamed up onto a spacecraft and she'd be none the wiser.

"Mia ..." Jamie's voice dragged her back to earth. "Are you deaf?"

"Huh?"

"I asked if you wanted tea or coffee." Jamie stood with the tea and coffee tins displayed in each of her hands.

"Oh. Yeah, thanks. I'm just going to ..." Mia drifted from the room without completing the sentence, her innards feeling like they were trailing along behind her through thick sludge. Edward's condition had come more as confirmation than a surprise, but that poor, harmless old lady – his sister, who'd looked out for him all his life – suspended from the oak at Godestone Manor like some kind of trophy ... If that was a coincidence then Mia was Queen of Narnia.

It was with a grade of hesitation that she listened to the second voice message:

'Hello, this is a message for Mia,' came a clear and consistent voice, which would have sounded robotic if it wasn't for the northern twang. 'It's Duncan Lowe from Secret Realm here. I believe you spoke to my nephew yesterday about a haunting. Please call me on this number or feel free to drop by at the shop any time after four o'clock this afternoon. I may be of some assistance.'

End of message.

Mia checked the clock on her phone. 8.02 a.m.

The next eight hours would be the longest of her life.

***

The shop was deserted when Mia arrived at precisely one minute to four. There was a closed sign on the door, but it had been left unlocked as if specifically for her. A man from behind the counter glanced up as the door gave its customary squeak, which startled Mia even more than the first time she'd entered. Strolling through the shop, her nostrils seemed to have familiarised themselves with that musky fragrance – it was almost soothing. It wasn't until she was close enough to see those luminous teeth that she realised it was Max grinning back at her.

"Madam, what a pleasure it is to see you again," he said, standing up as if she was royalty or something. His complexion was still dark but more olive than tango, and he no longer looked like something from the Madame Tussauds. More of his stubble also showed through, and his sandy hair was trying to leap from his scalp in all directions.

"I see you've ditched the turban," Mia said.

"Er, yeah, sorry again for our little misunderstanding." As Max swept a hand through his unkempt mane, Mia noticed a symbolic tattoo on his inner bicep and then another, smaller one became visible above the waistband of his jeans. Tugging his T-shirt down, the man grinned at her again. Mia was sure the action had been premeditated and bit her lip in hot, tingly vexation. While she wasn't unused to male attention, she'd had neither the want, time nor energy to do anything about it – until five seconds ago.

"Oi, Uncle Dunc! There's someone here to see you," Max called through the beaded curtain, before his attention was on Mia once more. "You survived the night, then?" She could tell by his face that his concern was genuine.

"Yeah, it was surprisingly uneventful. To be honest, that makes me even more nervous as to what will happen next."

"If you ask me, it knows exactly what's coming and it's shitting its pants. Seriously, my uncle is like kryptonite to these things. You'll be glad you found us."

"Even if I was almost cheated out of thirty quid," Mia reminded him. The man had an annoying tendency to make the most extreme circumstances sound like something from a spoof movie, which reminded Mia very much of another male she knew. That alone should have been as much a deterrent as she needed.

Clunky footsteps advanced from the next room, and Max smacked a finger to his lips as if begging her to keep his misconduct a secret. The curtain jangled as a short man poked his head through the beads.

"Hello, Mia." He spoke in the same smooth tone as his voice message. He had a dark, slicked back ponytail and similar facial hair to Max, although he was quite a bit older.

"Hi, there," she replied. "Thank you for getting in touch so quickly."

"It's no problem, Max was very insistent that you needed my help."

"Really?"

"Oh, yes – worryingly so."

Mia wasn't sure if Duncan was teasing his nephew, but a quick glance at the rugged stranger showed that he was as carmine-faced as she was.

"Do you want to come through?" The psychic was smiling now.

"Er, yeah." Mia found her way behind the counter, squeezing past Max in order to reach the curtain. His natural odour wasn't overwhelmed by whatever spray he was wearing, and Mia did well not to sneak a peek at his sturdy torso.

That was, until he whispered to her, "No mentioning the turban shit. We had a deal, remember?"

Mia raised a playful brow. "You do know that your uncle's psychic?"

"Good point."

Max went to follow them into the back room when Duncan stepped in front of him. "Not you," he warned. "Stay here and tidy the shop up."

"Yes, Dad," Mia heard the younger man reply, before Duncan showed her to the table on which the tarot deck and crystal ball had sat previously, only now there was nothing.

"I must apologise for my nephew," said the psychic, dragging up a stool and slouching on top of it. "He has his mother's heart and his father's foolhardiness. He'd be a fine man given the right guidance."

Mia responded with a weak chuckle. She was certain this man had just had a glimpse into her thoughts. Before she could say anything, Duncan clasped his hands together and rested them on the table, tiny blackcurrant eyes peering at her through his rounded spectacles.

"Now, then," he said, "tell me everything you know about number twelve Greenway Avenue."

***

Jamie bent over to put the juice carton back into the fridge. When she stood up to turn round, Nathan was standing behind her.

"Shit!" She staggered back, her left heel booting the fridge door so the contents inside rattled and clanked.

"Sorry, I thought you'd have heard me coming in," said Nathan, laying his car keys on the table. "Weren't you supposed to be out getting some fresh air?"

"I can't walk the streets forever, can I?" Jamie glanced beyond him into the hallway. "Where's Louisa? Did she get on at school okay?"

"The teacher said she was a bit quiet, but it's hardly surprising. I've told her to watch some television while I get my stuff together."

"You're leaving already?"

"I've got a family at home in case you'd forgotten. Besides, once Mia knows the truth she'll drop all this demon crap and we can all get on with our lives, can't we?" There was an edge to the man's voice that Jamie couldn't quite decipher. She tried to walk around him but his arm shot up to create a blockade between her and the exit, hand pressed firmly against one of the cupboard doors only inches away from her face.

"Do you have any idea what you're putting your sister through with these fabrications of yours?" Nathan asked her candidly.

"What do you mean?"

"Come on, love, it's just you and me now. There's no need to bullshit, and pretending to run errands all day so you can avoid me isn't going to work forever. Mia would have my guts on a plate if she found out I'd left you alone just now, even if it was only for ten minutes, yet here you are safe and sound. What does that tell you?"

Only then did Jamie's frustration bubble to the surface, the vehemence of her response startling even herself. "Get lost, Nathan, you have no idea what's been going on around here. In fact, why *are* you here? Mia doesn't need your worthless ass – she never has."

"I'm here for you and Louisa because, apparently, you're in serious peril. We both know what this is really about, though, don't we?"

"No ... y-you're wrong." Jamie shook her head, as if it would help to reinforce the words. "That's all in the past, I swear."

"A bit convenient, though, isn't it? Anyone would think you wanted Mia to find out about our little secret, especially with the way you've been acting these last few months. She already knows something's up."

"You can't say anything – not now. She'll lose it with both of us!"

Casey started yapping from beneath the kitchen table, as if championing her owner. Not the loud, sonorous barks she was capable of at her full health but weak, strained sounds – as though her lungs were set to collapse.

Nathan ignored the animal. "Can't you see that she's already losing it? She's gone to seek out a psychic – the Leeds equivalent to Derek bleedin' Acorah. I was hoping to talk some sense into you before it goes too far, because you and I both know that he's going to come all the way here and find nothing."

"Then, why persuade Mia to move house? She's been running around all day trying to find out about loans and stuff. You put those ideas into her head, not me."

"So I panicked, can you blame me? I didn't think for a second that she'd actually go through with it. Besides, now I've had a chance to process everything it stands to reason that if – and that's an astronomical *if* – there was something to be scared of then I'm pretty sure I'd know about it by now."

"I'm not bullshitting you, I swear!" Jamie's voice rose to a whine.

"Forget about the past for a minute, stuff has been happening to Mia as well – to all of us."

"Mia's under a ton of pressure, anyone can see that, and I know for a fact that Louisa's too petrified to sleep. Do you know what happens to people with severe sleep deprivation?"

Jamie shook her head and stepped back as the gap between them shrank smaller and smaller.

"I had a mate once who became convinced the streetlamps outside his house were UFOs – no one ever let him live it down. That's what's going on here, and your lies are only adding to the problem. I've been patient enough, but if you think I'm going to let you turn my daughter into some fucking freak show then –"

Woof, woof, grrr! Casey protested.

"Shut it, mutt!" boomed Nathan.

The dog glared up at him, lips pulled back over her teeth to expose their pink gums. Jamie focused on the doorway ahead, afraid it might vanish so she'd be trapped in that room forever. If she'd had issues with men before tonight then she might as well have been allergic to them now.

"God, why did I have to come over that night? We wouldn't be in this situation if I'd told Mia the truth from the beginning." Nathan started tugging the collar of his shirt, sweat diamonds glittering on his forehead and dripping from his fringe. His other arm was still blocking Jamie's path, and although he wasn't particularly well built, he was still a lot bigger than her.

"Nate, it isn't your fault –"

"Damn right, it aint!" he roared, his face taut with anger. "Has it not occurred to you that you might have brought it on yourself, you little tart? You went to that party knowing exactly what you were getting yourself into and now it's on my conscience as well. *Quiet, Casey!*"

The dog retreated under the table, ducking back its head like a frightened tortoise while keeping its eyes pinned on the man. Nathan continued to fiddle with his collar, hooking a finger inside his shirt as if trying to loosen a noose around his neck.

"W-why are you being like this?" Jamie spoke charily.

Nathan puffed out his flushed cheeks, fanning himself with his own breath. Dark patches appeared under his arms as if by magic, and the smell of his deodorant was tainted with musty sweat. Even his shadow felt like it was smothering her.

"Why is it so damn stuffy in here?" Nathan grumbled. "There's more fresh air in a bloody coffin."

"What's wrong with ... Oh, no ..." Jamie tried to back away but found that she was already squashed against the worktop. She extended an arm to maintain the short distance between them, aware that he could probably shatter every joint before she could scream for help.

"Nathan, please, l-let me past," she begged him. "I need to get out of here now."

"You're not going anywhere until you admit that this whole thing is a ploy for attention."

"You don't understand, it's *here*. I don't know how, but it's getting to you just like Mia said it would."

"Huh?" Nathan's brows slanted inwards, shading his eyes. "What are you on about, you mad cow?"

"She warned me about this – about you. She said if anything happened or I didn't feel safe then I should take Louisa and run."

"There's nowt," *pant*, "wrong with me. Just need to ... catch breath."

"Daddy, are you poorly?" Neither of them had heard Louisa approaching the kitchen.

"No, sweetheart. Go back and watch the telly." Nathan spoke without facing the girl.

Casey's barking had intensified to roars by now, and he shielded his ears with his hands as if there was a metal file grating away at the insides of his skull. He staggered sideways with a drunken kind of giddiness, and for a second Jamie wondered if he'd actually been pushed.

"Daddy –"

"Not now, Louisa. *Caseywillyoushutthefuckup!*" Nathan swivelled round, kicking a chair so it was flung across the room.

The dog shot over to its basket, paws skidding on the tiles like a scene from a cartoon as the chair somersaulted into the opposite wall. Louisa broke into long, whiny sobs.

"Screw this!" Jamie elbowed her way past Nathan. "Come on, Lou, we're out of here."

Nathan turned to his daughter and clenched a fist in response to his own mindless outburst. "Shit – sorry, darling, Daddy didn't mean to shout. Just, er, make sure Casey's okay, will you?" He marched after Jamie, leaving Louisa gawping after them from the kitchen.

"Jamie, wait!" Nathan caught up with her at the bottom of the stairs. He grabbed her shoulder, fingers scrunching the sleeve of her blouse.

"Get off me!" As she wrenched back her arm, the material ripped at the neckline and the top button came flying off. Nathan looked even more aghast than Jamie as she streaked up the stairs, yelling, "I'm going to get our bags, and if you try to stop me then I'll tell Mia and she'll kick your ass!"

"Please, Jay – just stop a second!" Nathan pursued Jamie onto the landing, the stampede of footsteps sounding like it was coming from an army. He charged into Mia's bedroom in time to see her pull two pre-packed rucksacks out from under the bed.

"What's this? What on earth are you lot playing at?" Nathan snatched the bags out of her hands and threw them onto the bed. The tendons running through his arms were as taut as piano strings, and if he punched a wall then his fist would surely go through it. Jamie couldn't help picturing the mess it would make of her face either.

"Brenda's just next door. I'll scream if you hurt me," she threatened.

"I'm sorry, okay? I didn't mean to scare you. Christ, I don't know what's wrong with me."

"You're crazy, that's what's wrong with you! If you care about Louisa at all then you'll let me get her as far away from here as possible."

"Come on, there's no need for that. You know I'd never lay a hand on her – or you." Nathan advanced towards Jamie, letting his hands glide up her arms before they closed tentatively around her. Jamie resisted at first, not fully trusting the man but too frightened to be alone.

Locked in embrace, neither of them noticed the blue Ford parked opposite the house. Nor the face louring up at them from the driver's seat, straight through the bedroom window.

CHAPTER TWENTY-SIX

Duncan Lowe sat with his arms resting on the table, the fingertips of each hand pressed against their opposites. He surveyed Mia over the rims of his glasses as she sipped the tap water that he'd poured for her. She'd been rambling on for at least twenty minutes, and combined with the anxiety and constant perspiring, she had a mouth like the morning after a night on the town.

Apparently, Duncan had read about the house in one of the local newspapers some years ago, which Mia presumed was regarding the young girl that Brenda had spoken of, and he'd been waiting for someone to seek him out ever since.

'Why did you never approach any of the previous owners or tenants?' Mia had enquired at one point, to which she'd received the oblique reply:

'I didn't think it was my place to interfere with the natural order of things.'

Mia didn't know exactly what that meant or even if she believed it, but exorcising demons must have been a daunting task for any man or woman, whether it was their job or not.

After several moments dedicated to forethought, Duncan asked her, "How much do you know about the spirit world, Miss Reynolds?"

"All I know is what Max told me yesterday. Until a few weeks ago, anyone who came to me with complaints about being harassed by a rapist demon would have got directions straight to the nearest loony bin."

Duncan seemed neither surprised nor offended by the revelation. "Did Max explain to you the difference between a spirit and a demon?"

"He just said that spirits used to be people, whereas demons come from something else. That's why I'm so confused as to what this thing is; how or why it exists."

"Well, without going into too much detail," Duncan parted his hands in gesticulation of his words, "spirits and even poltergeists can simply be the residual energy of a person or animal. They may be trapped between worlds for all manner of reasons: unfinished business, in which they need help to complete a task; tragic circumstances, such as murder – or it may be a case that the spirit doesn't know it's dead and is therefore unable to move on. Many people live side by side with them for years and never have any problems, but some hauntings can be more troublesome depending on the nature of the spirit. More often than not, they're after one thing: attention."

"So, what exactly are we dealing with here? Is it demonic like Max said?"

"There are myths – rumours, really – that a very powerful spirit can evolve into something much worse. It progresses, if you will, as we humans grow and age through life. The only difference is that a demon of this breed requires a host as it is unable to generate its own energy, so instead it must absorb it. In a sense, it uses us as batteries – you follow?"

"I think so." Mia was too preoccupied to have been overtaken by dread. "How do ordinary demons come to exist, then, if not through people like this one?"

"Let's think about it in simpler terms: have you ever considered the possibility of angels?"

"You mean do I believe in them?" Mia asked herself the question as much as Duncan. "To be honest, I'm not sure what I do and don't believe anymore."

"Well, whatever image comes into your mind when you hear the word 'angel', a demon will be the polar opposite to that. Frankly, what you see in films and read about in books – the concepts of heaven and hell – it's all loosely based on fact. While goodness attracts positive energy, evil and sin attract the negative far easier."

"But if the thing in my house was once a person then it must have some humanity left in it. Can't this 'evolution' process be reversed so it becomes a harmless spirit again?"

Duncan gave a regretful sigh. "There are some questions that even I can't answer. Sometimes spirits lose all sense of who they were and where they came from, as with people. Even the most kind and loving of us can become corrupted should we choose the wrong path in life."

Mia only had to think of Jamie to resonate with that. "So, how common is this demonic advancement?" she asked the psychic. It was the first time she'd used the word 'demon' without feeling like she'd flushed her sanity down the drains.

"It is extremely rare," Duncan admitted. "I've never encountered it myself, but I do know of a friend of a friend who has successfully dealt with this kind of thing. Sadly, they're no longer with us; and of course there's been little research into the topic, but the fact that you've been able to establish the demon's motive is a positive sign. Having said that, this man ... Edward ... must have been subjected to some deep psychological trauma and despondency in his life."

Like that's an excuse, Mia thought. "Great, so now we've established a cause, what do we do about it?"

Duncan continued to study her as if weighing up a response, or just didn't have one. Mia noticed that his face had the same circular contour as his glasses, which only seemed to magnify the puffiness under his eyes. The longer she observed him, the more transparent it became that the wrinkles in his face were not the results of age or exhaustion alone, but to a constant scrunching of his features – like laundry that had been dumped in a basket and forgotten about for weeks. It seemed Max wasn't exaggerating when he'd said that work had taken its toll on the man.

"Look," Mia shifted on the rickety seat, "you said in your message that you could help me. If you want to come to the house, test out your vibes or whatever it is you people do then I can take you there right now."

Duncan removed his glasses while replying in a collected manner, "Miss Reynolds, I'm afraid –"

"It's Mia, and I'm begging you." She lifted her bag onto the table and rummaged through it frantically. "I'll pay you, just name your price."

Duncan raised a hand, nose turned up as if she'd handed over a plate of rotten sushi. "I don't want your money. God gave me this gift for helping people, not for profit. I've known this day would come for a very long time."

"Then, what do you want?"

"Nothing, I was merely going to say that there's no need to conduct an initial investigation in this instance. What we must do will either work or it won't, but beware that these things are seldom resolved on a permanent basis."

"What are you saying?"

"That, unlike your average lost spirit or poltergeist, there is nowhere for demons to go. There's no light to follow, no eternal resting place. Should we exorcise the demon successfully, it will be down to you to keep it at bay."

"Me?" Mia realised she was clutching the straps of her handbag as if it was the safety harness on the world's most extreme rollercoaster. In fact, she felt like she'd been stuck on the thing nonstop for weeks. "But I'm just an ordinary woman. A mother."

"Miss ... Mia," Duncan corrected himself. "How exactly do you think I'm able to tell you all of this now? The dark energy has been festering for so long that it's practically growing off you like mold. The more it drains from you, the more pungent it becomes. Demons have a habit of latching onto their targets, and that's exactly what it has done to you. That you've coped with it for so long tells me what an extraordinary psyche you must have, which is exactly what we need if we're going to defeat this demon."

"So, basically, it's using me as some kind of escort? How is that even possible?"

"Edward might have been housebound when he was alive, but with all the power he's accumulated these last few weeks - not to mention the years before that - there's no saying what he's capable of now, or the lengths he'll go to in order to gain his freedom. It won't be long before he attempts complete possession."

There wasn't a single atom of Mia that sought to understand the term 'possession' - at least, not until it was crucial for her survival - so instead she cut straight to the conclusion. "What do you propose? And when will it happen?"

Replacing the glasses onto the bridge of his nose, Duncan pressed his knuckles flat against the tabletop and used them to push himself up, as if the effort of standing was too great a strain on his knackered joints. He really could have passed for a seventy-year-old.

"Tonight, my dear. We finish this tonight, because I can guarantee you that it will do everything in its power to prevent what's coming. In fact ..." his eyes circled the air around them, "it knows exactly what you're up to."

***

Regina tightened her grasp on the steering wheel, arms locked at the elbows; the dark skin on her knuckles fading to a ghostly white. She hadn't a clue what she was doing outside number twelve Greenway Avenue, or what she might find – probably nothing and she'd end up looking like the neurotic wife as usual. Her plan had only got as far as dropping the boys, Jack and Liam, off at their grandparents' house and then jumping into the car – it wasn't as if stalking people was in the 'skills' section of her CV. But something had compelled her to make the fifty-minute journey from Sheffield to Bramley, and her conversation with Louisa last night had only been a percentage of it.

Regina was about to get out of the car when movement from one of the upstairs windows stopped her. In the rearmost of her thoughts she was aware that she was most likely staring up into someone's bedroom, but she was concentrating more on the head of dark waves bobbing about behind the glass. She couldn't make out much more than a silhouette in the light from the dimming sky; nevertheless, it was a silhouette she recognised. She'd been sleeping next to it every night for the past twelve months.

The second person in the room was harder to distinguish, mainly because she couldn't actually *see* anyone. She knew there was a female present because she'd heard them shouting – Christ, the whole street could probably hear – and Regina figured there must have been a window open somewhere. Mia had a temper all right, but she'd never lost it with Nathan like that. At least, not in front of her and certainly not in front of the kids. Come to think of it, a quick scan of the road showed that Mia's car was nowhere in sight.

It was then she saw her husband reach out to the second figure, who had now come into view. Regina blinked, her eyelids like windscreen wipers removing anything that might have distorted her vision, but she was soon to learn that her eyes weren't the problem; it was her mind's inability to accept what she was witnessing.

"What the ..." Regina leaned forwards until her nose was pressed against the driver's window and she physically couldn't get any closer.

She had a sudden flashback of the row – or 'misunderstanding' as Nathan had termed it – that had broken out between the couple earlier on in the year. All those text messages Regina had found on his phone and the secret calls that he thought she was too brainless to check for – who wouldn't have suspected an affair? Admittedly, she had found it strange that he hadn't bothered to delete the evidence; plus her husband was no James Bond in the charisma department. But that obviously didn't matter to Jamie, nor did the fact he was married.

"You two-faced little whore," Regina spat, not knowing whether she was more sickened or insulted. Before she could decide which, the couple were thrust together as if by some ungovernable magnetic force. Her husband's lips sought the girl's, and she responded with that same insatiable desire.

Hot acid tears raced down Regina's cheeks. *The dirty bastard, how could he? Right there in front of the window for the entire street to behold!* Her foot depressed the accelerator pedal as she envisioned ramming the car through the living room window so the entire front wall and ceiling came tumbling down, burying the pair of cheats beneath a heap of rubble; but fortunately the engine was switched off. Besides, she wouldn't be satisfied until she had his balls for earrings and her tits for Christmas tree decorations.

By now, Nathan's hands were all over the teenager. Not lovingly as he touched his wife but driven by steaming, unadulterated lust. Groping rather than caressing, squeezing rather than playing; slipping up into her blouse like a killer probing for body parts to sell on the black market. Regina watched his lips trace down the curve of her neck, following his hands to one of her exposed breasts and then ... *oh, no – not that!*

When Nathan's head disappeared beneath the window frame and the girl rolled her head back in delight, even with the restricted view, Regina had to look away. The slapper was probably having a right laugh about this with her mates, while Nathan must have thought himself a fucking king: wifey at home taking care of the house and the boys, washing his skiddy underpants and cooking his meals. Loving him as any good wife should love her husband, while all along he had some deluded seventeen-year-old tending to his sexual needs, with her perfectly tight body that had yet to be spoiled by stretch marks and varicose veins.

With a growl of unrestrained fury, Regina sprang from the car like a caged lioness being released into the wild, slamming the door shut and leaving the keys swinging from the ignition. She charged across the road and hammered on the door with her fist, completely insensitive to the bruising of her knuckles. She tried pushing down on the handle but the door was sealed fast. *Of course*, Regina mused, *they wouldn't want Mia barging in on their sordid pursuits, would they?* She almost laughed when she imagined the dumbfounded horror on their faces when they rushed downstairs to find her on the doorstep, and she didn't doubt that Nathan, at least, would try to deny the whole thing – make out that she was going crazy, just like last time.

Well, what Regina had witnessed that afternoon was worth far more than any confession.

CHAPTER TWENTY-SEVEN

Bangs from downstairs ricocheted through the house.

"Open this door, you bastard!" *Thump, bash, thud.* "Open it now or, by God, I'll break it down."

"What the hell?" Nathan slinked over to the bedroom window. Peering onto the street outside, he could see no one. Until his wife stepped into view and glared up at him from the front garden.

"I see you, Nathan Summers!" she barked.

"Shit," Nathan muttered, and for a reason he had no time to contemplate, he yanked the curtains closed.

"Who is it?" said Jamie, as the banging reached a crescendo.

"It's Regina. What the bloody hell is she doing here?"

Drying her tears, Jamie went over to the window and peeked through a split in the curtains. Nathan swept from the room and descended the stairs two at a time before unlocking the front door. So stupefied was he by his wife's presence that he almost forgot to dodge when she took a swing at him.

"Jesus Christ!" He restrained her by making a sort of lasso with his arms as she lunged at him again, thick black tresses cascading over her enraged face.

"You cheating scumbag, I knew something was going on!" cried Regina.

"What are you talking about? How long have you been here? Are the boys with you?"

"No, thank God. And don't pretend that you care about them – in fact, never mention their names again. You don't deserve them and you certainly don't deserve me!"

"Calm down, woman." At the same time Nathan released her, he managed to push her back to create enough space between them so he could put out his arms to guard himself. "Gina, listen to me. I know what this looks like, but if you'll give me a chance to explain –"

"Explain what? I saw you with my own eyes, pawing at each other like a couple of randy hyenas. I should have gone with my instincts all those months ago, but I fell for your excuses and your lies because I'm such a bloody fool!"

"Nate, what's going on?" Jamie appeared at the top of the stairs, and Regina's eyes instantly fell to the tear in her blouse that exposed her lacey bra strap.

"Oh, here's the little skank now." Regina waited until she'd reached the hallway before pointing an unbending finger at the girl. "I bet this was all your doing, wasn't it? Oh, yes, I remember those text messages: 'I need you, Nate. Please, can I see you? My sister can never find out.'" She spoke in a childish whine, before refocusing her anger onto Nathan. "What, couldn't you resist making the comparison between her and Mia? Or was it more a case of you couldn't have the woman herself so you settled for the next best thing?"

"*Huh* ...?" It was all Nathan could utter for a while, his perplexity reflecting in his silence. "I told you they'd had an intruder. I'm here to watch over things, that's all. Why don't you come inside before you make even more of a scene?"

Regina folded her arms, speaking in an even louder voice. "I don't care who's watching, I've got nothing to be ashamed about."

Jamie intervened, "For Christ's sake, Nathan, tell her the truth and put her out of her misery."

"You know, if you were a decade older I'd slap you so hard that you'd feel the sting every time you looked at another married man," Regina threatened. "And to think, I actually felt sorry for you when Nathan spouted all that rubbish about the abuse."

"Shit, you *told* her?" Jamie looked at Nathan as though he'd strangled a newborn kitten in front of her. "I thought I could trust you!"

"So that much is true, at least," Regina said, before Nathan could reply. "You thought you'd jump in there while she was vulnerable, is that it? I don't know which one of you I should throttle first."

"Stop it, both of you!" Nathan felt like they were in a school playground as he stepped in between the two women. "Let's all just cool down and –"

A shrill cry blasted from the depths of the house, and all three heads snapped in the direction of the sound. "Oh, God – Louisa!" Jamie shrieked.

"What?" Regina stood on her tiptoes so she could see past them into the hallway. "You were about to have it off with that poor girl in the house?"

"Oh, shut up, Gina!" Nathan was first to take off towards the kitchen, followed by an equally frantic Jamie, leaving Regina stranded on the doorstep.

First he saw the blood. Volumes of it splattered up the kitchen cupboards, coating the floor as if there'd been a squabble over the ketchup bottle. Nathan's eyes roamed continuously from left to right until he was able to see over the far side of the table. In the middle of the room, almost blending in with the gore, there was a tiny body curled up like a foetus. His mutilated daughter.

"My god ..." He could have mouthed the words, they were so faint – or maybe it was because his senses had numbed themselves almost to the point of oblivion.

Casey crouched back in the corner with a feral glint in her eyes, the fur on her back bristling up. She snarled at Nathan, well aware of what punishment was about to be bestowed upon her; teeth dripping with the blood of his only daughter.

"You savage fucking beast!" Nathan screamed.

"No!" Jamie reached out to pull him back, but he was already charging across the room like some kind of machine. He went straight for the scuff of Casey's neck, grabbing the meagre rolls of fat with both hands. There was a bone-splintering crunch as he rammed the dog's head into the tiles, a hailstorm of teeth flying out of its skull.

That was it, over in an instant; but still Nathan repeated the action, over and over again until the cracks turned to squelches and his hands were crimson. Even his shirt looked like one of those blow-paint pictures that kids did at school. Jamie gazed down at the pulverised mess, her eyes and mouth agape. Neither of them heard the three other people that came bursting into the kitchen until there was a strangulated cry from behind.

Nathan turned in time to see his wife vomit all over the floor, whereas Mia was halfway across the room before her brain must have calibrated to the gorefest before her. The following minute of deathlike silence could have lasted a whole hour, and Nathan remained as paralysed as the rest of them, his emotions oscillating between breathless shock to just about everything his drumming heart was able to withstand. Casey was only recognisable from the body of golden fur lying limply by his side and the chunks of brain, bone and Lord knows what else scattered about the place. If it wasn't for the muffled wails coming from another heap on the ground then Nathan would have forgotten all about his daughter.

"Louisa!" Mia dropped her handbag and did a lunging skid on her knees, swiping the girl up in both arms. "Baby, are you okay? Are you hurt?"

Even as she patted Louisa down, Nathan couldn't believe she was standing there at all. Red splashes garnished her school uniform and her body shook with sobs, but that only contradicted everything he'd seen. Everything he'd felt and even believed.

"What ... have ... you ... done?" Jamie whispered.

Nathan shook his head, only the whites of his eyes shining through the blood mask. "I-I had to. Casey ... she attacked ..."

"She's fine, you idiot!" Mia yelled at him. "Louisa's *fine*."

Everyone else, including Nathan, continued to stare at the grisly scene as if they'd witnessed a horrific accident and God had pressed pause. He slouched back against the wall with his knees bent at right angles, hands clasped behind his head. Even if he wanted to protest, to explain, there simply weren't any words.

"It's not the girl's blood." A man crouched over Casey's body and ran his hands through her fur as if she was merely sleeping. He seemed unaffected by the mush that made the entire kitchen smell like a butcher's shop, and Nathan guessed it could only be the psychic that Mia had spoken of.

"What do you mean?" Mia asked him.

"There are wounds all over the dog's body and limbs, but none on its back. The child must have been in the wrong place at the wrong time."

"S-something attacked Casey?" said Jamie. She and Mia looked at one another as if they both already knew the answer, and Nathan was also beginning to understand his own actions for the duration of that night.

"I'm saying she attacked herself," Duncan stated. "If your dog had a particular fear then it may have been accelerated under the demon's influence – unbearably so. Quite simply, she flipped."

Jamie staggered then, as if someone had taken a sledgehammer to her kneecaps and the bone had disintegrated. Regina caught the girl, supporting her by enfolding an arm around her waist and acting as a pillar for her to lean against. Jamie buried her face in the shorter woman's bosom, and Nathan was surprised when Regina lightly, albeit grudgingly, patted the girl's head. Mia sat Louisa down on a chair by the table, having to literally peel her off like melted wax. Then she dragged Casey's basket over the carcass so just her bushy tail poked out from underneath it.

"Is someone going to tell me what the hell is going on?" Regina's voice was unusually brittle. "Who are *you?*" She glared down at the psychic.

Mia interjected, "Regina, will you please sort your husband out while I see to Louisa. Duncan, if you wouldn't mind getting rid of the body then there's cleaning stuff under the sink." They weren't requests.

"Of course," Duncan replied.

Nathan sat with his knees pulled up to his chest, lips quivering to the point they appeared to be dancing and huge tears building stubbornly in his eyes. He felt a hand on his shoulder and looked up to see Mia standing over him.

"It's not your fault," she whispered. "Now, for pity's sake, snap out of it."

Returning to Louisa, she lifted her off the chair and carried her away.

CHAPTER TWENTY-EIGHT

"I've brought you some fresh clothes, sweetheart." Mia laid a jumper and some leggings on top of the radiator and then helped Louisa to dry off with a towel. The girl had been shaking like a jelly all the while Mia had sponged her down in the shower, and not once had Casey been mentioned – not that Mia was looking forward to explaining why she'd had to witness her father beating the animal to a bloody death. As far as Louisa was concerned – or any of them, for that matter – it might as well have been a family member that Nathan had slaughtered. The only reason Mia hadn't grieved was because tears equalled weakness, and for her that was not an option.

"Darling, I'm so sorry I wasn't here when you needed me," Mia went on to say. "That man downstairs is here to help us and I promise that, from now on, I'm going to keep you safe no matter what it takes. You do believe me?"

Louisa nodded, the light in her dark eyes fighting through her despondency even after everything that had taken place. That alone gave Mia all the hope she needed.

"Oh, excuse me." Regina was partially visible behind the bathroom door. "I thought you'd have finished in here by now."

"We're almost done," Mia replied. "I'll get Louisa dressed in her bedroom."

"No, it's fine. I'll wait." Regina retreated as swiftly as she'd appeared. Mia pursued her onto the landing, keeping one foot wedged in front of the door to prevent it from closing behind her.

"Thanks for what you did back there – with Jamie," she said. "I appreciate you looking after her."

Regina waved a hand in acknowledgement, a mangled tissue clutched between her fingers. Mascara was smudged under her eyes, and she avoided eye contact with Mia for as long as possible.

"How's Nate holding up?" Mia said.

"He's, er, still in shock, I think. I've never seen him so ... I can't believe that he'd ... Nathan moped about for a whole day after Jack's budgie died, gave it a burial service and everything. I laughed about it at the time, but *this* ... it just doesn't make sense." Regina shook her head in bewilderment.

"Regina, what were you three arguing about earlier?" Mia couldn't keep her curiosities a secret any longer.

"Huh?"

"When Duncan and I pulled up in the car, you were on the doorstep screaming like a banshee. Usually you go out of your way to avoid me, yet here you are. Why?"

"I've never cared for you much, I'll admit that, but I realised a long time ago that you're not the real threat. You never were."

"Are you talking about Louisa? Come on, she's just a kid. She didn't ask to be born."

"*Jamie.*" Regina spoke condemningly, some of her usual brusqueness returning. "I thought I knew my husband well enough to know that he wouldn't take advantage of vulnerable girls, but maybe he's still a teenager at heart. Maybe it's my own fault for bullying him into marriage so early on."

"Hold up, are you saying what I think you're saying? Surely, you know as well as I do that that's a total perversion of common sense."

"But the evidence was there: the phone calls, the text messages. Nathan told me she'd been having some trouble with a boy and that you couldn't find out about it. I convinced myself that's all there was to it until I found out he stayed here last night, and after what Louisa said on the phone –"

"You spoke to Louisa? When?"

"It doesn't matter." Regina shook her head. "She only confirmed what, deep down, I already knew. I thought I'd drive up here and catch the dirty sod out for myself, and boy I saw all right."

"Saw what?"

"Him and her. Together. Right in that room over there." Regina pointed to the furthest door on the landing.

Mia knew all too well how withdrawn and secretive her sister had been of late, with her fluctuating temperament, and she couldn't deny that Nathan had been more interested in Jamie's well-being than his natural solicitude allowed. One thing she could be certain of, however, was that if she suspected there was an ounce of truth in Regina's words then she'd have confronted them already.

"Look," Mia said, having assembled her thoughts, "we both know how much Nathan adores Louisa and he'd never do anything to jeopardise her happiness. Besides, he's way too stupid not to have been caught out sooner."

Regina chuckled while blowing her nose into the tissue. "You obviously have a lot more faith in my husband than I do."

"That's half the problem. I don't know what you think you saw today, but if Nathan and my sister were having some kind of relationship then, trust me, I'd know about it. This house has a habit of messing with your head, it's –"

"The demon, I know. Mr Lowe has explained it to me as best as he could."

"You seem to be taking it a lot better than Nathan did."

"I'm not saying I believe it, or that I don't have questions. But I do know what I saw and felt tonight, and the thing that murdered Casey was *not* my husband."

"That's exactly why you can't blame him for this. Regina, if you want to help Nathan then you'll get him and Louisa as far away from here as possible. Now this thing has got his claws into him and it understands his weaknesses, it will use them to hurt you and everyone else he cares about."

"If things really are that bad then why did you get Nathan involved? Why put him in even more danger?" There was an inclination of blame in Regina's voice that reminded Mia they would never be the best of friends, but at the end of the day they were both fighting for the same cause, the same family, so nothing else mattered.

"I involved him because he's Louisa's father and, as much as you loathe me for it, it's his duty to protect her as much as it is mine," Mia defended herself. "Now, are you going to help me or not? Because I'd sure as hell do the same for you and your kids."

It was with some reluctance that Regina finally nodded, perhaps for Nathan's sake more than any of theirs. After a brief but heartfelt thank you, Mia returned to the bathroom.

***

Duncan Lowe positioned himself at the bottom of the narrow staircase. Even if the walls hadn't been so stark, even if they'd been decorated in luscious lilacs and splendid silvers, the atmosphere would always be cold. Desolate. If he closed his eyes he could have been sinking deep beneath the ocean's waves, the pressure building in his chest, head ready to explode; that knowledge of impending death. Every now and then he would fight his way to the surface and gulp for air, feel the sun's rays warming his skin, but it was only the house taunting him. Demonstrating its control and relishing every millisecond of it. The more Duncan connected with that evil, the more he tried to understand and even reason with it, the higher that barrier between worlds was raised, allowing the darkness to drip into his consciousness like water from a leaky tap.

Duncan felt a progressive weakening in his ankles and knees, as if he'd been wading through quicksand for several hours and his body was finally giving in to fatigue. He gripped the unvarnished banister, rivulets of sweat trickling over his brow bone and splashing the floor, which suddenly seemed a million miles away. In fact, it didn't look like a floor at all – more like a vast, swirling abyss. A few years ago he'd have been better able to withstand this fiendish being, challenge it even; but at the moderate age of fifty, he could have been a few generations older in mind and spirit. He'd had his fair share of demons and every one of them remained imprinted into his memory, which in turn made them a part of him. Now it felt as if those demons were awakening once more, that this hellish force had summoned them to gang up on his subconscious. A force which he never expected to encounter in this life or the next.

The whispers accumulated with speed and were soon encompassing Duncan like a roaring windstorm: swearing, cursing, bullying and goading – all as voices inside his head.

"Sticks and stones may break my bones, but *you* will have to do a lot better than that." Duncan continued to scan the hallway, eyes narrowed from both the throbbing ache behind them and the sweat raining down his forehead.

'*You will not beat them down so easily.*' The statement came in the form of a thought rather than words, for he knew the demon was listening. '*Tonight, this family is under my charge. Remember, I can get to you just as easily as you can get to them.*'

Once again, Duncan felt himself floating to the ocean's surface, gulping lungfuls of air while bobbing about in the golden light from the sun. The room no longer seemed to be spinning and his migraine had blunted somewhat, but he knew it wouldn't be long before that unruly current dragged him back down. Next time he might not be so lucky as to resurface.

"Mr Lowe ..." A distant voice intersected his thoughts.

'*I will not heed your taunting, demon.*'

"Hello – Duncan?"

It was as if someone had turned up the volume on a radio. A hand landed on his shoulder and he whirled round, for a second not recognising the fair-faced young woman that stared back at him.

Mia said, "Can I get you some water? You look like you're ready to collapse."

"No, thank you. I was just attuning to the house's energy, I'm perfectly all right."

"Have you picked up on anything yet? What it wants from me?"

"Perhaps." Duncan's focus shifted to the stairs, and he began the slow and vigilant ascent. Mia traipsed after him several paces behind, as though afraid something might pounce on them from the shadows. The very thought prompted Duncan to flick on the lights once he'd reached the top of the stairs, and he ventured down the landing with the feeling that something was leading – or guiding – him.

He stopped outside the first room and peered inside, dictating out loud what his senses were picking up on. Then he repeated the procedure for every other room on the landing. "There has been much activity up here, but the energy is most concentrated in this area." When Duncan indicated the door adjacent to the bathroom, Mia looked as if a weight had dropped into the pit of her belly.

"That's my daughter's bedroom," she revealed. "As far as I know, the demon hasn't done anything to harm her like it has done with the rest of us."

"That's because it has no need to. Children are naturally more sensitive to the spiritual realm than adults." Duncan traced a hand over the door and its frame, absorbing their vibrations into his own energy. "As we grow older and become more attuned to the complexities of life and human emotions, we find less need to rely on instinct and intuition; therefore, our psyche develops a wall around it – a block to what we may be unable or are too afraid to understand. Many of us don't care for the supernatural and so will never encounter it. Others, like yourself, may just be unlucky."

Duncan moved on to the bathroom, and Mia followed him as always. "Something happened to you in here," he reflected. "You were scared – terrified. I'm sensing some kind of struggle ..."

In that fragment of a second, Duncan had a glimpse of something that was neither creature nor human slithering out of the bathtub. Mia regarded him as though she, too, had felt the psychic link between them.

"Holy Christ, that thing was real?" she said.

"As real as your mind made it. That's how demons attack – once they've established a connection, that is. As I said, its ultimate goal will undoubtedly be possession. This generally happens in stages and always begins with an invitation."

"Max mentioned Ouija boards, is that a possibility?"

"Ouija boards, witchcraft, Satanism – anything that creates a doorway, no matter how accidental. Sometimes our own emotions are as much a hook as they need: grief, anxiety –"

"Fear," Mia concluded.

Duncan needn't have said any more.

"I was right, wasn't I? All this is because of Edward's agoraphobia and what he endured in the war. Keith said it turned the old bastard insane."

"Mia, you have to remember that it is no longer a man; it's an entity, the remnants of his suffering and his pain. Technically, it no longer has an identity so it uses your own imaginations and fears to shape shift into whatever form you allow it to."

"I don't care who or what it is anymore, I just want rid of it." Mia looked at Duncan fretfully. "We *can* get rid of it?"

"That depends on what stage it reaches. The second and most

common is infestation, in which the demon makes itself known through things like temperature changes, odours and the movement of objects and furniture. Currently, you're experiencing phase three: oppression. This would explain the phantasmagoria you described: the dreams, delusions and other mental and physical abuse."

"What's phase four?"

"Four is the last and what we're aiming to avoid. By the time oppression kicks in, we've already begun to doubt ourselves and everything around us. The mind becomes so fragile that it has to shut down, providing an open gateway for the demon to take control and thus possession occurs. That's where the more conventional exorcisms come in, similar to what a priest would perform."

"What about Paul next door? The guy is practically a zombie. If he's been left open to attack then why doesn't the demon take over him and do whatever it set out to do?"

"Because this one doesn't want just any host." Duncan moved slowly towards Mia. "Edward Perkins spent a large portion of his life feeling scared, isolated, defenceless. You, on the other hand, he sees as a challenge. Your natural energy is some of the most vibrant I have ever seen; you've already accomplished and overcome so much in your life, yet you still don't realise how strong you are. But as with all demonic attacks, first it must break you down piece by piece. It has already preyed on your insecurities and failed, so now it's going for the source of your strength – those you love and care about most in the world. Your family."

"*Family* ..." Mia looked as if the word had summoned more thoughts, more anxieties. "What about Missy Gibbons, the woman who committed suicide? Surely, he wouldn't have killed his own sister just to get at me."

Duncan took a little longer to answer this time. "It is practicable for a demon to enter the mind of a more vulnerable person, albeit temporarily – the sick, the elderly and even the mentally unstable – but it's more like brainwashing than possession. Until it's been banished from our plane, it will always have a connection to its victims or those it has affected."

"How is that possible if the demon can't leave the house?"

"Because it latches onto them, the same way it's latched onto you. Remember, a living, breathing human being gives it the strength to overcome such obstacles, but in this particular case I do feel that there is something else binding it to the house. Something physical, which it can't remove by itself."

"Like an item?"

Duncan closed his eyes a moment, lids wrinkling up. "I'm not sure, the demon is going to great lengths to block my senses. If you come across anything strange or significant then you mustn't remove it from the house unless you plan on taking it to consecrated grounds." He reopened his eyes to look at Mia. "Think of it as a shackle, a leash preventing the demon from being able to roam the open world. I don't know if someone has purposely hidden it, but this item is the link between Edward's body and soul and he will stop at nothing to protect it."

"So, if we were to find the item and bury it at a church, that would mean an end to all of this?" There was an optimism about Mia that Duncan hadn't yet encountered.

"Technically, yes, but locating the item may be more problematic than it sounds. Plus, if you don't face the demon now while you're still strong then there's a chance that the darkness could follow your family wherever you go. You'll be walking magnets for negative energy, and who knows what you could attract next? Whether or not you wish to take that risk is up to you."

"I suppose it depends. If the demon did manage to ..." Mia still couldn't use the term, and Duncan needn't have been psychic to sense the woman's foreboding. "What exactly would it do with me once it had control?"

"The same as any other deranged spirit," Duncan said. "Wreak havoc on God's proudest creation."

***

"Mia, are you absolutely sure about this?" asked Nathan.

Mia nodded while handing over Louisa's suitcase. "Take care of our daughter, okay? And please make sure she knows why I had to do this. If anything happens to me ..."

"Don't talk like that." Nathan shook his head fiercely. The dampness of his freshly washed hair reflected beneath the streetlamps, which gave his face a yellowish hue that made him look even more sickly than he did already. "I should stay. Regina will be fine with the kids, won't you?" He looked pleadingly at his wife, who brushed the backs of her fingers lightly over his cheek.

"For once, I agree with Mia," she said. "Louisa needs her father, and you're in no fit state to tackle this ... *monster*." There was still a dubiousness about the woman, but whether it was down to her unwillingness to accept the truth or outright terror ... well, Mia could resonate with either.

"B-but I've already failed my family once." Nathan's voice wobbled with emotion. "I'm sorry I didn't listen to you, Mia. I'm sorry for Casey and Jamie and –"

"Nate, shut up and get into the car." Mia pulled open the passenger door of the Ford that Regina had driven up in. The plan was for Nathan to pick up his four-by-four in a couple of days when, fingers and toes crossed, all this would be over.

Finally, Nathan gave up and slipped into the car.

"Good luck," said Regina, strapping herself into the driver's seat. "Make sure you give us a call soon, yeah?"

Mia nodded at her with an unvoiced appreciation. As the car started up, she took a last look at Nathan slumped in the passenger seat with his coat draped over his shoulders, staring through the windshield like an escaped mental patient. God, she hoped he didn't end up like Paul.

As the car rolled away from the curb, Mia waved at her daughter through the back window until they were out of sight. Words would only further distress the girl, and Mia wasn't planning on saying her goodbyes just yet. She headed back to the house feeling strangely unemotional to what she was about to undergo. Louisa was safe, she had Duncan in her corner and as long as they kept a tight restrain on their emotions, the demon was virtually powerless.

"Do you think they'll be okay?" Jamie said, as Mia closed the front door.

Mia smiled, an expression she'd almost forgotten. "Of course they will be. I'm going to make sure of it."

"How?"

"First, you're going to get yourself around to Brenda's. I can't do anything while I'm busy fretting about you."

"What?" Jamie drew back her head, a scowl crimping her forehead. "You seriously expect me to leave you alone with this thing?"

"I won't be alone, and I've already spoken to Brenda. She rang me after hearing all the commotion with Regina, said she had to stop Paul from charging over here with his camera again." Mia had to chuckle at the scene in her mind, but this only seemed to agitate Jamie further.

"No way, the bastard has already done its worst to me and I'm still here. I know what happened wasn't real ... at least, not all of it. What more can it do?"

"You tell me, because I've been confused about the whole thing from the start. Did you know that Regina thought there was something going on between you and Nathan?"

Jamie cringed. "Please, that'd be like incest."

"Don't worry, I've put her straight. But whatever did happen in the past, I'm sorry you felt that you couldn't talk to me about it. I know I've been a little preoccupied since we decided to put Mum away, but you don't have to bottle it up anymore. From now on we deal with things together, as a family."

"Ladies?" Duncan's voice sounded from the living room, where he stood in wait. "It's time."

Mia nodded at him, before saying to Jamie, "Last chance to back out. You know I wouldn't blame you."

"She stays." Duncan spoke for the girl. Mia looked at him, bemused.

"She stays," he repeated, softer this time.

Jamie said, "You heard the man. I'm going nowhere."

"Fine, but if you want to be here for me now then you have to let me do the same for you when all this is over. Deal?"

Jamie agreed and, hand in hand, they made for the living room.

CHAPTER TWENTY-NINE

"Are you comfortable?" Duncan Lowe seated himself on a dining chair that he'd brought in from the kitchen. Just in front of him, Mia was reclined on the sofa with a mound of cushions padding her head and upper back. She looked to her sister, who was sitting in the armchair across the room, and forced a nervous smile.

"I reckon I'd get a better night's kip on this thing than in my own bed," she joked, although it was wasted on both Jamie and the psychic.

"Now, then," Duncan began, "as I explained to you earlier, in order to face the demon we must force it to reveal itself – no tricks or facades – but it must be on your terms and in a territory you feel comfortable with. That's not to say it won't do everything in its power to weaken you, though. I'd offer to take your place if I thought it would be of any success, but the demon is too firmly latched onto you now."

"Why are we doing this here, then?" Jamie wanted to know. "Surely, the freak's home is the least safe place on the planet."

Duncan rotated in the chair so he was facing the girl. "Your sister will be here in body, but my job is to help her open up her psychic channels in order for her mind to access the spirit realm, exactly as I do when performing an exorcism. To do this I must put her in a light hypnotic state, similar to that of meditation." He turned back to Mia. "That should allow you to call forth the demon, but remember that you being in control doesn't necessarily mean it will play by the rules; after all, this is their world you are about to enter."

"What if it doesn't want to play at all?" Mia questioned. "What if it comes here instead and tries to take over me or something? How can I defend myself if I'm off in Never-Never Land?"

Duncan smiled, although it could have been a constipated grimace for all the effort it took, and even then it didn't quite reach the affliction in his eyes. "Have faith in yourself, my dear, because everyone else does. And I will be right here watching over you."

Jamie said, "She'll still be aware of what's going on, won't she? I mean, she'll be able to hear us?"

"Of course, all she has to do is focus on the sound of my voice and allow it to guide her. You do trust me?" The last part was directed at Mia, who nodded in response. "Then, when you're ready I want you to take slow, gentle breaths: in through the nose, out through the mouth. In ..." Duncan performed the exercise with her, "... and out." He blew out a steady stream of air.

"Feel the tension drifting from your body and mind. Block out any distractions and concentrate purely on my voice. Place your focus on trying to reach your inner self and your own spirit guides, forgetting who they might be or how they appear. Just let it come naturally."

Mia's breathing was now a slow and steady rhythm, her only movement coming from the gentle undulations of her chest. Duncan removed his glasses and placed them on the coffee table, leaning forwards on the chair with his hands clasped in between his knees.

"Now, close your eyes and visualise a place in which you feel that you truly belong. Somewhere safe and secure, where your mind is able to flow freely. It could be a beach, a field; a place you visited as a child or even one that you don't recognise – perhaps somewhere that has become lost in your subconscious." He allowed a few moments for this to sink in. "Now then, Mia, describe to me what you can see before you."

It was an even longer while before Mia was able to reconnect her mind to her physical self, eyes darting about under their lids like trapped beetles. "I-I see a building," she said.

"What kind of building? Is it big, small; brick or stone? Really concentrate on the details."

"It's wooden, I think ... at least, part of it is. Some bits look different – stonier. I can't tell if it's been painted or ..." Her eyelids rucked up as she tried to get a clearer image. "Wait, I think ... yes, it's Godestone."

"Godestone?" Jamie blurted out. "That's the manor house where she works – where Edward's sister killed herself. Why would she –"

"Sshh!" Duncan hissed. Then, as if he could picture exactly what Mia was talking about, he went on to ask her, "Do you know if there's anyone inside the manor?"

Although Mia knew the building in front of her was Godestone, it wasn't how she remembered it. Most of the walls, interior as well as exterior, were completely dilapidated and stained with age. And the roof ... well, there was no roof – just creaky, weather-beaten support beams. The whole construction was like a skeleton.

"I can see figures roaming the grounds," Mia explained. "They're a little hazy, but it looks like they're wearing robes of some kind. I think it's the monks that used to live there."

"Very good, you're starting to connect to the spiritual realm. Don't worry about who's there or what it looks like, just go forwards and enter the manor."

"I-I can't, there's no door. And it's dark ... *God, so dark* ... I can hardly see anything." Mia felt her body shivering but was convinced it must have been a psychological reaction.

"The demon is trying to prevent you from accessing that innermost part of your mind, the place where you hold all the power. Remember, this is your subconscious. *You* control what happens. If there is no door then visualise one. Believe it and it will be so."

Mia shook her head, which quickly escalated into wild thrashing motions. Her hands clawed at her throat, leaving welts that felt like fire. "I can't b-breathe." She gasped. "Ch-choking ..."

"Oh, God – Mia!" Footsteps thudded across the carpet, but they were cut short by the sound of Duncan's voice.

"Quiet, child," he commanded.

"But it's killing her! We can't just sit here and –" *Moan.* "Oh, no ... please ... no!"

By now, Mia felt as though she was breathing through a straw. Wheezing, she tried to open her eyes but it was like waking herself up from a nightmare. A familiar aroma diffused through the air which, coupled with Jamie's sobs, could only mean one thing.

"Mia, if you won't heed my advice then I cannot help you!" Duncan was yelling. "You must enter the building. It can't hurt you in there."

It was the explosive scream that eventually smashed through Mia's subconscious, sweeping her back to reality. Her eyes popped open and she sat up before Duncan could restrain her. The whole house seemed to be convulsing. The television vibrated on its stand, ornaments rattled – some hopping off their resting places and crashing against the floor. She could even hear cutlery and glassware in the kitchen chinking away. And the stench ...

Mia couldn't have escaped it even if she tried, for she might as well have woken up in a mass grave, surrounded by death and decay. She heard a low fizzing sound that reminded her of a coke bottle being opened for the first time. Glancing around, she saw that it was coming from a dark brown patch on the wall where the paper had blistered up. There was another stain above the mantelpiece that was oozing a sludge-like matter.

"You must go back," Duncan implored. "This is nothing more than a decoy. Trust me, it won't hurt Jamie because it is afraid of you. It's *afraid* of you, Mia!"

Another wail receded into frantic whimpers. Jamie was on her knees at the far side of the room with her torso hunched over, hands clasped protectively over her crown. Something towered over her: a thin, nebulous shape that was becoming denser by the second. Mia's lungs expanded, and the rest of her body felt like it was being wrung out by the hands of Satan himself. Soon, she was able to discern the straggly white tufts that looked like they'd been pasted onto his scalp with lard. His eyes were like pools of black ice, one deformed by a scar that ran down the side of his face and forked over his cheek; both inundated by rings of shadow. He'd have passed for nothing more than a gangly old man if it wasn't for his abnormal height and the misty black aura surrounding him. Whether it was Duncan's psychic influence or not, that the demon was able to manifest in its most basic form told Mia she'd made a mistake that could cost her her family's lives.

Edward's thin, bluish lips peeled back over his gums like a retracted foreskin to expose a manky, gap-toothed grin. Jamie squealed as his gnarled hand came swooping down, gripping her ponytail and hoisting her up until her knees were lifted off the ground.

"Get away from her, you bastard!" Mia shouldered her way past Duncan and almost bowled him off the chair. Despite her frenzied rage, she was surprised when her hands locked around a wrinkled throat and she brought the man-demon crashing to the floor. Somehow, during the impact of the fall Edward managed to swing himself on top of her with a strength that transcended that of an elderly man. He clamped his hands around either side of her head with a paralysing effect, fingers boring into her temples and skewering her brain. Its wizened face – she could no longer refer to it as 'he', for there was absolutely nothing human about it – came down to her level, a whiff of putrescent meat adhering to her face.

"*We meet at last, cunt.*" Its voice was more a hiss than a whisper, but Mia's agony was so intense that she couldn't tell if the words had been telepathic. "*This is where I make you kill your whole wretched family.*"

The pain radiated through Mia's skull, down into her chest and torso and finally to her limbs. It felt as though every bone was broken. Every muscle had been torn from her body and her organs continuously battered with a meat tenderiser. She waited for the little black specs and the sirens in her ears, but all that came was a swift blackness as she sank into a deep oblivion.

CHAPTER THIRTY

A crack of lightening illuminated the sky like the flash from a nuclear blast. Mia awoke with a gasp, the chill from the wooden floor sinking through her clothes and numbing her to the bone. It was night outside and she couldn't see an awful lot in the room, not due to the layers of shadow but because it was majoritively empty apart from a tallish construction next to her and various other statuesque shapes dotted about. She hauled herself up using the wooden altar, checking herself for injuries but feeling only the searing pain in her head. Waddling to the oblong window, one of two in the old chapel, she peered up at the cloudy, starless sky and the rustling tree line that skirted the lawn, confirming in her mind what she'd already suspected.

"What the hell am I doing here?" she whispered to herself. The last thing she remembered was preparing for the hypnosis with Duncan Lowe by her side.

Thunder crashed in the humid air, and it felt like her brain was being used as a gong. She clapped her hands over her ears, at the same time feeling around her skull. There was no blood or swellings, and most of the tenderness seemed to be coming from within. Whatever the reason for her waking up in Godestone Manor, she couldn't have been unconscious for more than a day or else one of the staff would have found her by now.

Hovering at the window all night isn't going to solve anything, a voice inside prompted. Regardless of how much she loved the place, tonight there was nothing familiar about it. It wasn't bursting with vitality, charm and history; it was completely defunct. In fact, it wasn't much more inviting than the crumbling wreck she'd seen while under –

"The hypnosis," Mia mumbled. It had taken place after all. She remembered that choking sensation, as if her throat was somehow being crushed from the inside, but memories beyond that point were nonexistent.

What if that's because there were no memories? she pondered. What if she was dead and this was some twisted version of hell? She almost didn't want to leave the chapel – if any part of the manor was going to be safe then it had to be there. But something, perhaps that faint voice in her subconscious, urged her to proceed. It occurred to her that if she made a run for it then she could reach the car park in under a minute where, hopefully, her Corsa would be waiting.

Mia fumbled for the light switch and flicked it several times, but the wall-mounted bulbs didn't give so much as a spark. Either a fuse had blown somewhere or the storm had caused a power cut – there were no other buildings in the vicinity to make a comparison. Fortunately, she knew the layout so well that she could have found her way around blindfolded. With only the sporadic streaks of lightening to guide her path, she left the chapel and headed along the eastern corridor towards the reception area. Ignoring the Great Hall opposite, she tried the door to the main entrance. Locked.

Mia felt in her pockets for her set of keys but found nothing – not even her mobile phone. She rattled the oak panelled doors knowing full well that it would take a battering ram and at least five burly men to break it down. Next she tried the fire exit adjacent to the staffroom, but the panic bar was jammed.

"Jesus Christ ..." She stared into the heart of the building with her most chilling thought yet: if she hadn't locked herself inside then someone else must have done.

There was nothing for it, she'd have to smash through one of the windows and figure out her excuses later. On her way past the staircase, Mia realised the sounds she'd been hearing for the last few moments wasn't the wind howling through various cracks and crevices, but more like subdued whines or sobs. She canted her head a little, as if listening for clues in the air. It was definitely human over animal, and she was almost certain that it was coming from above. Another lightning bolt irradiated the staircase, as if to lead the way.

"Okay," she whispered to that voice in her head, which she liked to call her intuition. "No more running. No more hiding. It's time to end this."

She climbed the stairs with quick, nimble steps, avoiding the creaky ones to keep any echoes to a minimum. If someone was playing tricks on her then at least she'd have the edge of surprise. She held back on the landing and listened again. The sobbing was louder now, and it seemed to be coming from one of the rooms on the right-hand corridor. She tracked the sound, passing one of the smaller bedrooms and continuing on to the bathroom – or 'stool chamber' as the medievals would have called it – that also linked to the master bedroom. The door was already open.

Mia stuck her head inside, followed by her torso and finally her legs. This room only had a letterbox of a window, so she had to rely mostly on what poor light filtered in from the landing. She hadn't seen a hint of the moon on her journey through the manor – of all the nights for there to have been a storm, fate had chosen this one.

Mia could hardly make out the bench-like construction that ran along the back wall, where the garderobe – basically, a hole for one to stick their backside over – was built. If it wasn't for the crying, she might not have perceived the inky silhouette tucked away in a corner of the room. She could tell it was too big to be a child and curled her fists in preparation to defend herself.

"Who's there?" She spoke in the most commanding voice that her nerves would allow.

A cold silence followed. Gulping, Mia gentled her tone. "Hello?"

There was a shuffling sound, as if the stranger had had their back to the door and was turning round to see who was there. "M-Mia?"

Mia squinted her eyes, trying to penetrate the opaque shadows. "Jamie?"

Again: "Mia!"

"Oh, thank God." On the sprint across the room, Mia caught her foot on something sprawled over the floor. It was solid but not so weighty that it didn't budge when she kicked it, and if her sister hadn't been standing there then she'd have reeled headfirst into the wall.

Ignoring the obstruction, she threw her arms around Jamie and hugged her for longer than time permitted, making sure she was real and not some phantom impostor.

"Where have you been?" Jamie exclaimed.

"Sorry, I just woke up and ... Jay, what the hell's going on?" Mia tried to keep her voice to a whisper, but her consternation made it impossible.

"I was so scared," Jamie whimpered. "I didn't know if it was real or ... just another illusion."

"What are you talking about?" Mia cradled Jamie's face in her hands, feeling warm tears beneath her fingers. Her liquid eyes looked like diamonds in the gloom.

Another fulmination of thunder sent shockwaves through the building. It sounded even more deafening now she was on the upper floor, and the room flashed with a purple-blue radiance. In that two-second blink of light, Mia glimpsed a crimson pond on the floor by their feet. Only then did she feel the tacky substance daubed to her arms from where Jamie clung onto her.

"Shit, what happened? Did someone hurt you?" Mia said. She could see Jamie shaking her head.

"It's not my blood," came a hushed reply.

"Then, who –" Remembering the object that had almost sent her nosediving to her death, Mia searched the ground behind them. It was a few seconds before her eyes focused enough to make out something that resembled human legs poking out from behind the door.

"Jamie, what did you do?" Looking back at her sister, Mia realised that if she cogitated hard enough then she probably already knew the answer – or part of it.

"You see him, too?" Jamie almost sounded relieved. "I-I didn't mean to do it. He followed me to the bathroom. I said no but ... he wouldn't listen."

"Who was he?"

"Kerry said her cousin, Tariq, was having some mates over at his house and that he'd invited us for some drinks. I just wanted to forget about everything: Mum, the fire, my stupid exams – if only for a few hours. She said they were cool."

"Is this the cousin who gave her the weed?" Mia wanted to clarify.

Jamie nodded. "The guys started to get lairy – they were wasted before we even got there. Kerry didn't want to leave, so I pretended I felt sick and went to the bathroom. I didn't know what else to do."

"Are you saying he ..." Mia swallowed while trying to neutralise the fury that billowed inside her. She tried again. "Did he force himself on you?"

"Sometimes I wish he had. At least that way, he'd have been the one in the wrong and not me."

"What happened?" Neither of them questioned why events from the past appeared to have transpired all over again, in that very room, for it was obviously some kind of ruse and they were both used to it by now. But that didn't make it any less disturbing.

"Tariq's mate ... h-he had his hands all over me," Jamie spluttered. "I pushed him away, but it must have been too hard because he slipped and hit his head on the toilet. He didn't move afterwards. I thought he was taking the piss until I saw the blood - pints of it, there was. I went downstairs and pretended like nothing had happened. He must have been up there ten minutes before anyone realised he was missing. Now he's in a coma because of me. The other night when the demon attacked me, I really thought he'd tracked me down. I even texted Kerry to ask if he'd woken up, but as far as she knew there'd been no change."

"My god, I really wish you'd come to me sooner. Didn't the paramedics ask questions?"

"They put it down to a drunken accident - everyone did. Kerry's dad gave me a lift home because you were at work. Nathan came to drop Louisa off and I completely broke down. If I'd known how much trouble it'd cause then I never would have kept it a secret, but you had enough to deal with and I didn't want to disappoint you."

"It wasn't your fault, Jay - none of this is. The sooner you stop blaming yourself, the sooner you'll see it for the accident it was. Besides, there's still every chance that he'll make a recovery."

"And what'll happen to me then? It doesn't matter whether he lives or dies, I'm screwed either way."

"Let's not worry about that right now. Even if he does grass you up, any jury would see that it was self-defence. Better him than you, right?"

Jamie sniffed and nodded, but her expression was lost in the shade. Mia glanced down at the body again. She half expected it to leap up, completely zombified, and chase them down the corridors with a hunger for their flesh, but that was *too* fantastical - or so she hoped.

"Come on," she said to Jamie, "we can't stay here. How did we get locked inside anyway? Did the hypnosis work?"

"You don't remember?"

"Remember what?"

Another voice wafted in from the upstairs landing. "*Mia ...*"

Both women fell into a petrified silence. Although the voice had been quiet, almost cautious, they could tell it was close, as if whoever had called out was afraid of being heard.

Again: "Mia, where are you? ... Hello? ... Jamie?"

The voice was nearing with each word. Jamie made to speak but Mia cupped a hand over her mouth, seizing her from behind as if taking her hostage. The footsteps outside would pause every so often, as though someone was checking the neighbouring bedrooms.

"That voice," Mia whispered. "You recognised it, too?"

Jamie nodded beneath the weight of her hand. Mia gradually released her and slinked across to the open door.

"Mia –"

"*Quiet.*" Mia briefly faced the girl. "Stay here, it's probably another trick. Nothing is as it seems anymore."

The storm sounded like it was beginning to subside now, and the rain was falling fast and heavy, thrashing the windows and roof as though the clouds were firing out grit. At least the constant pattering sound made creeping around the manor less of a necessity.

However, when she emerged onto the landing, nothing could have braced her for what happened next. Even though the voice had belonged to Vivian, to see her standing just a few metres away in the blue nightgown that Mia had bought for her last Christmas propelled her thoughts into disarray – so much so that she'd forgotten about the rest of the world.

"What are you doing here?" The question came automatically. "How did you ... How did I ..." Mia shook her head while taking a wary step back. "This can't be happening."

"Mum?" Jamie came creeping out of the stool chamber, her damp face opening up to heart-filled relief. "Oh, Mum!"

With no time for a warning, Mia had to physically stop her from approaching the woman by grasping her elbow. Jamie lurched backwards with a yowl.

"Ouch! Mia, what are you doing?"

Mia stared into her sister's rumpled face. "It might look like our mother, but who's to say it's really her – that it even exists?"

Vivian extended both of her arms, like melted candlesticks poking out from the short sleeves of her nighty. Mia was surprised they weren't spurting fountains of blood much like the very first nightmare she'd had of her mother. At least that would prove she was a figment of their imaginations and they could concentrate on getting the hell out of there.

"Girls, you don't have to be afraid anymore. Everything is going to be all right. We're all going home together." The thing might have sounded like Vivian, but it *spoke* nothing like her.

"Where exactly do you think 'home' is, the local cemetery?" Mia retorted. "Because that's exactly where we'll end up if we believe a word you say."

Jamie yanked her arm out of Mia's tenacious grasp. "What's wrong with you? Can't you see that she's as real as you and me?"

Mia's eyes remained anchored to the woman as she replied, "Our mother is mentally ill, in case you'd forgotten, and this thing seems perfectly lucid to me. Was it you who locked us in here, you freak?"

"Mia, stop!" Jamie walked in front of her so they were standing face to face. "If anyone's a mental case around here then it's you. *You're* the one who brought us here."

"What?"

"You came out of the hypnosis completely crazed, said this was the only place we'd be safe until Duncan found another way to get rid of the demon. We picked Mum up on the way here and then you just disappeared."

Jamie's summary of events failed to evoke a single memory of the past few hours, and the uncomfortable sloshing motion in Mia's gut strengthened to a tidal wave of dread. "I ... don't remember any of that."

Jamie replied, "You need help, Mia. Just give me the keys so we can go home."

"I haven't got any keys!" Mia checked her pockets again, even frisking herself to make doubly sure. "Something's not right here, I know it."

"This isn't a trick," Vivian promised. "Jamie has told me all about what's been going on at Billy's house. I'm sorry I couldn't be there for you both, but I'm here for you now. Let me try and make it up to you while I'm still able."

"It's okay, Mum, we don't blame you." Jamie fled across the landing before Mia could stop her and slotted herself in between the woman's arms.

All Mia could do was stand and watch, part of her longing to join in with the reunion; to bask in their mother's love, but it was as though her feet were buried in a puddle of cement. Even when Vivian reached out to her, waving her over with that skeletal hand, Mia didn't succumb. She wouldn't allow herself to believe it.

"See?" Jamie twisted to face Mia, a joyous smile overwhelming her face. "I told you she was real. It's her, Mia. It's our m-*ugh!*"

It wasn't a grunt or a yelp but something in between. An involuntary sound that accompanied a loud crunch, like a child biting into a stick of rock. Mia had been too flummoxed to notice Vivian's other hand sneaking up behind Jamie's skull. What she had seen was her sister's neck being wrenched at a lethal angle to her body, but her thought process ended there and she couldn't determine whether it was down to shock, incredulity or total inner destruction – possibly a combination of all three.

"This is all your doing, Mia Reynolds." Vivian's tone became deeper, more gruff – almost masculine. It was ill and strained, like a man on his deathbed whose only sustenance was his hatred for mankind.

When Mia looked up it took a while to register that her mother's face had also changed, perhaps because she'd known all along that whatever form the demon took on was a lie. It was the teeth she noticed first, like chippings of stone coated in moss. His papery skin had a white-yellow tinge and was so stretched over his cranium that it punctuated the gauntness of his face. As for the rest of Edward Perkins ... his body, his clothes ... it was all a blur.

"Your mother left you in charge and you've let everyone down," the demon taunted her. "You let this happen, and now you will suffer the consequences."

Mia could feel the tears rolling down her cheeks and blobbing onto her chest, but the reflexive body shudders had been replaced by a creeping numbness. "This isn't happening." Even her voice sounded hollow, distant, as if her body was on a different plane to her mind. "I'm not really here. I'm not even awake."

But the images in her head were gradually merging into scenes no matter how hard she tried to discard them. She remembered being forced out of the hypnotism and lying helplessly as he, that barbarous *thing*, had effectively defiled her brain.

"Your pathetic mind games did not work." Edward spoke as if to verify her thoughts. "All the seer did was open up the doorway to your soul – a door that I've been banging on for so long, but until now have only managed to knock ajar. Perhaps, when we –" Mia assumed that by 'we' he meant himself *inside* her rather than *with* her, "– return home, I should thank Duncan Lowe personally."

"I-if what you say is true then why did you bring us here? And what the fuck did you do to my mother?"

"I had to lead you away from the seer, his body may be weak but his mind more than compensates for it. What you saw in that room with your sister was, of course, a reminder of what a lousy guardian you've been. And Vivian? Well, that old crone is better off in the ground anyway – just like Uncle Billy."

Mia kept on shaking her head, willing Jamie to get up. Praying for the nightmare to end. The longer she endured it, the more convinced she was by the harrowing sight before her. She could almost picture herself bundling her mum and Jamie into the Corsa and whisking them away to their doom, although it wasn't quite poignant enough for a memory. What she did remember was walking in on Jamie during the sexual assault. Seeing her lying on the bed, naked and catatonic, just as she lay before her now. Mia hadn't believed it then either.

Ringing – no, pop music – sounded through the landing, making the surreal experience far too substantial. Too real. Too goddamn random for any of this to have been a dream under the control of a ruthless fear demon. Edward bent over Jamie's corpse, a concept that Mia was still struggling to come to terms with, and took her mobile phone out of her jacket pocket.

"I think it's for you," he said, sliding it across the wooden floor. Mia gazed down at it tentatively.

"Go ahead," the demon urged, "say your goodbyes. By the time anyone gets here it will be far too late."

Her eyes skipped from the phone to Edward and back again. Picking it up off the floor, she tried to steady her hands enough so she could read the name that showed up on the screen.

"N-Nathan?" she answered.

"Mia? Is that you?" She sensed an urgency in the man's voice, but it was also laced with something else. Something cold, morbid. Something that gave him an air of reluctance. In fact, he sounded exactly how Mia felt internally.

"Yes, it's me," she confirmed.

"Where have you been?" *Sniff.* "I've been trying to get hold of you for ages. Something ... something terrible has happened."

Edward's grin broadened with each second the conversation progressed, and Mia was sure he could hear the voice on the other end of the line. She turned away from him, unable to stomach his grotesqueness any longer – nor could she bear to look at the heap of limbs by his feet. Horror and death were all around her: she could hear it in the silence, feel it in the air. She tasted it in her mouth and it lingered in her nostrils like gas.

"Nathan, please tell me you're still at the house." It was a last attempt to shake herself from this perpetual nightmare. "Tell me Jamie's there and that you're all okay."

"What are you talking about? You know me and Regina left with Louisa this evening. Christ, I wish you hadn't made us go. None of this would have happened."

"What do you mean? ... *Nathan.*" What she heard next was not so much sobbing but the parts in between: the gasps, the hiccups, the snorts and the snivels. Mia guessed he must have been in that state for some time.

"It's Louisa." Nathan spoke once he was able. "We had an accident on the motorway. It's n-not good, Mia."

The entire landing had just got bigger, wider, longer – as if it was some colossal jaw preparing to swallow her up. Forgetting all about the demon, Mia teetered backwards, only the banister railings preventing her from tumbling to her death. "Don't say it, Nate – don't you dare. The demon's tricking you. I know because it's trying to do exactly the same thing to –"

"Christ, woman, I saw it with my own eyes – half the pissing motorway did! Regina, sh-she was so shaken up after what happened at the house. She shouldn't have been on the road. None of us should!"

"Where's Louisa?" Mia's impatience spiralled, her voice cracking with premature grief. "Tell me what's happened to my little girl!"

"The impact was so severe ... so many tubes sticking out of her ...

doctors are doing tests ... say there's a lack of oxygen to the brain ... might have to turn off life support."

Mia wasn't sure if Nathan was purposely leaving blanks so he could squeeze in the crucial stuff, or it was actually her that kept zoning out. It wasn't long before his frantic babbling was drowned out by the sound of Edward's deep, raucous laughter. She let the phone slip from her hand and descended with it, her knees thwacking the hard floor a second after the phone had clattered through the banister railings, where it bounced down the stairs and eventually shattered somewhere below. She doubled over thinking she needed to vomit, but only managed to cough up a string of saliva. Tears coursed down her cheeks, snot dangling from her nostrils like slimy entrails.

Gazing across at Jamie, Mia had an impulse to reach out and stroke her beautiful hair one last time. To tell her how sorry she was, how much she loved her and all the other things that the teenager would never get to hear; but the innate desire to stay strong for her family was as pertinacious now as it had ever been. She sensed Edward's shadow drifting over her like a looming depression, his laughter reverberating through the manor as though it was an empty chasm, and almost begged that he took over her. At least that way she'd be spared the heart-fracturing pain that racked her entire body.

"We both knew how this was going to end," said the demon, with its usual simper. "Don't worry, I will treat your body with the respect that every sad, worthless bitch deserves."

"Go ahead." Mia spoke in a murmur, head sagging wearily against the banister. "Do what you want with me. You've taken everything that means anything in my life, you piece of shit. Now there's nothing left."

It was as she said those last two words – 'nothing left' – that she felt a supreme cleansing of her mind. A surge of brilliant white light that absorbed all of her anguish and her terror, and then flushed it into the atmosphere. *Is this what death feels like?* she wondered. She'd been preparing herself for an eternal blackness, not this. Not freedom.

It wasn't until after this divine revival that her inner voice spoke again, echoing that dismal but effective phrase and screaming at her that there was literally *nothing* left. No one to hurt and therefore nothing to lose. The end was dawning and Mia welcomed it, she yearned for it. For the first time, not only in the last month but in her twenty-six years of existence, she felt empowered. She felt fearless. And there was a wrathful hatred burning inside her that would have sent tremors through the Dark Lord himself.

"Well, what are you waiting for?" When Mia glanced up, she could have sworn the demon quailed from her. He – it – was nothing more than a mentally-scarred, debilitated old man with rotten teeth. If he'd been human then a kick in the shins from Louisa would have snapped his tibias in half. Without willing her muscles into action, Mia stood up and faced the demon.

"I *said* what are you waiting for?" She inched towards him, not fully apprehending how her trepidation had leaped from her body into his but glad of it nonetheless. "Come on, put me out of my misery. This is exactly what you wanted, isn't it? Well – *isn't it?*" She lashed out, thrusting Edward backwards as if he was all rags and no substance, which in essence was all he'd ever been.

"Surrender yourself to me and all of your heartache will be forgotten," the demon snarled.

Mia cackled then, his incapacity made even more evident by the desperation in those smouldering eyes. "You can't do it, can you? Not now you no longer have mine or anyone else's hardship to feast on. All this ..." she parted her arms while giving a turning sweep of the landing, "has been for nothing. You've fucked yourself, you vicious old twat."

"This is not the end!" Edward vowed, his voice thick with rancour. Features twisted and knotted so he looked even more hideous, even more hateful. "I will find a way to destroy you, be it through your children, your children's children or anyone else who may be unfortunate enough to bear your love. No one lives fearlessly-ever-after – not even you, Mia Reynolds."

"They don't have to if they're dead." Mia started to move backwards. Small, deliberate strides across the landing, away from the stairs and her sister's body. "What will you do without me, Edward? Fester in that house until the next victim comes along? Good luck with that, because now Duncan knows who and what you are, he will find a way to defeat you."

Edward mustered a slight but knowing grin. "I have a feeling the seer won't be around for much longer, and now that my sister is dead there's no chance you will ever find what she hid."

Mia eased her pace, almost coming to a complete stop. "Missy was the one that bound you to the house?"

"The bitch tried to have me locked away in an asylum and then had the nerve to take over my home after I'd passed. She'd all but moved in until my wrath aided me in clawing my way out of the underworld. She knew exactly who and what I was, and being the conniving wench she was, thought up a clever way to prevent me from following her; after all, the house was my prison in life so why not in death also? All along I've been biding my time. I knew she'd come in useful at some point, the tricky part was gathering enough energy to reach her – to reach all of you."

"Of course ..." Mia could have chuckled at this new clarity, however overdue it was. "It all makes sense now, but we both know that none of it matters anymore. Jamie's gone, and if there's the slightest chance that Louisa will live then I promise you'll never get to her again. That goes for my mum as well."

"How can you be so sure if you're not going to be around to protect them?"

"Because it's me you want, and if you were going to latch onto them then you'd have done it a long time ago. Whatever or wherever that item might be, my death will buy Duncan enough time to find it. He'll take it to consecrated grounds and you'll be burning in Purgatory for the rest of eternity."

Mia proceeded to slink backwards, knowing exactly how much ground she had to cover before reaching the furthermost end of the landing. Edward's eyes shifted to the tall rectangular window behind her, then they dilated like ripples expanding across a puddle's surface.

"You haven't got the guts," he hissed.

"But I have, and it's all thanks to you. Goodbye, Edward Perkins ..."

"Stop –"

"... and good riddance."

"*Nnnooo!*" With a long and deafening roar, the demon lunged at her. It wasn't so much a run as it was a swooshing glide, and Mia wondered if his feet had been touching the ground at any point that evening.

When Edward was just a couple of inches away, her arms encircled his torso in an iron hold and they both careered into the landing window. Mia's back cracked the glass, the full force of the collision causing a tremendous explosion of huge crystal shards. Then gravity took over.

Mia's screams merged with the demon's howls, and the last thing she saw was that yawning mouth – like a black, bottomless cavern – as she waited for the impact. For the shattering of her spine and the explosive agony in her crushed skull.

But neither came.

CHAPTER THIRTY-ONE

Mia opened her eyes to a dozen cloudy blobs floating above her.

Wait, not that many. They gradually fused together to create four ... three ... finally two pale ovals. She heard what sounded like voices, only the words were all mingled and distorted, as if someone was speaking into a milk bottle. Blinking, the clouds started to develop contours, tones – features.

Features she never expected to see again.

"Jamie? ... *Jamie!*" Mia tried to push herself up from ... well, the environment didn't come into it, but her arms felt like they were weighted down with bricks and she couldn't lift her head much higher than her chest.

A man spoke to her soothingly and she felt hands gently elevating the backs of her shoulders, helping her into a sitting position. She didn't know if she was dead or dreaming but supposed diving out of a first-floor window could have resulted in either. In all honesty, she didn't care as long as her family was there with her. That thought alone was paradise enough.

Mia leaned forwards over her knees and rested her forehead against the palm of her hand to support the giant spinning boulder attached to her shoulders.

"H-how ... Where did I ..." The questions interflowed in her jumbled thoughts.

"The demon accessed your mind, tried to gain control over it," the man – Duncan – explained. "You fought it with everything you had, just like I knew you would."

Mia took a few moments to absorb her surroundings. There were no cold, dingy corridors. No golden gates or celestial beings – not even a cubical filled with machines and medical staff. Instead, it was her own wreckage of a living room – not quite hell but near enough.

"Oh, Mia, thank God you came back to us." Jamie slumped against Mia's bosom and wrapped her arms around her width.

"Am I ... was I dead?" Mia asked the psychic. "Was any of it real? Is *this* real?"

Duncan replied, "You were neither alive nor dead. Your spirit was trapped in the astral plane between worlds, a sort of limbo. The hypnosis made you vulnerable to the demon's attacks, but it also gave you the strength and resources required in order to defeat it."

"We were guiding you the whole time," Jamie added triumphantly. "Did you hear us? Could you feel me there with you?"

"I don't know." Mia stretched her thoughts back to Godestone Manor, remembering that inner voice she'd daubed as her intuition, always encouraging her not to give up. Only now she was back in the real world did she realise how influential it had been. "I knew something wasn't right all along, but it's like I had to go through it in order to come out the other side. I don't think I'll ever be able to explain ..."

A wave of fatigue swept through her and almost knocked her back into unconsciousness. She pushed her hair away from her face and winced at the stinging pain in her cheeks. Numerous claw marks decorated her flesh, presumably from where Edward had manifested in the house and attempted to possess her. Everything up until that point had been hauntingly real, and Mia was surprised she remembered anything thereafter, her brain was so fried.

"You need plenty of rest now," Duncan advised. "Your mind needs time to recover from its ordeal. We psychics usually ground ourselves after something like this, it helps us to reconnect with the earth. I can teach you if you like?"

Mia shook her head. "No more mumbo jumbo – no offence. You knew this would happen, didn't you?" She didn't mean it condemningly, but more in admiration for this man and his astonishing gift. "That's why you didn't want Jamie to leave earlier. The plan all along was to use her as bait. You knew I'd give my life to protect her and that she was the one person guaranteed to bring me back."

Duncan eyed them both ruefully over his glasses. "I'm sorry you had to go through all that you did, but the only way to sever the demon's tie was to strip you of your fears – to eliminate their roots. By destroying yourself in your mind, you effectively quashed the power it had over you."

"And Louisa?" Mia almost daren't ask. Even though she knew her time in Godestone had been some mystical world created in the dark recesses of her mind, that earth-shattering moment when she'd received the call from Nathan would shackle her heart forever. "Sh-she's okay, isn't she? I don't even know how long I was out."

Duncan held one of her shoulders. "Your family is safe and the demon has no reason to go after them again. At least, not for the meantime."

A surreptitious look passed between them, and Mia gave an acknowledging nod. Unless they unearthed whatever it was that bound Edward to the house, the odds of him returning were pretty much guaranteed – if not in a month then in a year, perhaps when some other unsuspecting family moved in. Even now she could feel a pleasurable lightness in the air, as if the evil had been sealed away into some dark cellar or attic space. Mia had hoped that would be enough. Now she knew it would never be.

"Gosh, I feel like I've been hit by a train." Mia's sigh prolonged into a yawn.

"Battling the forces of evil will have that effect." Duncan pushed himself up off his knees, stretching his arms out behind him while rotating his neck and shoulders so every joint clicked and cracked. "I shall leave you to recover now. Well done tonight, Mia, and remember that the strength within you is always there to be called upon when needed."

"I will." Mia looked up at him, a glow of hope swelling in the empty chasm behind her breast. "Won't you stay for a drink or some food? It's the least I can do."

"Not for me, thank you, sleep is my best healer. I wish you and your family well, and if there's anything else you need then you know where we are. Do let my nephew know how you get on, won't you? I believe he'd like that very much."

Mia found it odd that he should mention Max at such a time, but the thought soon dissolved.

"Duncan ..." She reached up for his hand, almost letting go when she felt the cool clamminess of his skin. Come to think of it, he had turned a corpse-like grey. "Take care of yourself, won't you?" she said.

Duncan smiled. "Always."

Mia embraced her sister once more. Neither of them heard the psychic leave.

***

"Did you get through to Nathan okay?" Jamie asked, as Mia joined her in the kitchen.

"Yeah, they got home a couple of hours ago." Mia set her mobile down on the table. "I told them the good news, but I think it's going to take a while for it to sink in. I still can't believe it myself. I keep expecting to see something ... hear something ... even though I know it's over."

"You really think we're safe now?"

"What, you don't feel it?" Mia glanced curiously at her sister.

"Feel what?"

"Absolutely nothing, and if Edward does try to resurface then it won't be through us. That much I can guarantee."

"I guess." Jamie stubbed her toe against one of the cupboard doors, as if trying to deflect from her uncertainty. "So, what happens now? Not just with the house but ... you know ... what I did. Are you really not mad at me?"

"Forget about what I think, it's whether or not you can forgive yourself. If that means reporting it to the police then I'll back you whatever the outcome, but I reckon all this has been punishment enough. Why don't we call it tomorrow's problem?"

"Yeah, you're right," Jamie said, a little more upbeat. "I am sorry, you know."

"Me, too." Mia stroked her arm on the way over to the food cupboard. "Think you can manage something to eat now? I know we've got stuff to sort out, but it's all I can think about."

"Maybe later. Am I okay to grab a quick shower? It sounds weird but I can still feel that thing's hands on me."

"Sure, I'll come up and wait –"

"Mia, you don't have to babysit me anymore," Jamie insisted. "If you say the demon's gone then I believe you. It can only hurt us if we let it, right? I'm not about to make all you've done for us be for nothing."

"Well, okay, if you're sure." Mia smiled. If she'd learned anything from this ordeal, it was that Jamie had far outgrown the child she remembered her as.

Jamie finished her glass of juice and then headed upstairs, leaving Mia to scout through the cupboards for something to eat. She couldn't remember the last time they'd been to the supermarket, or anything they'd done as a family since moving to Bramley. She prayed they would recover from this in time and that any damage caused wouldn't be irreversible, but Mia was confident that, together, they could find a way to overcome anything.

A bang from above left her staring up at the ceiling, but the creaking footsteps that followed reassured her that it was only Jamie closing the bathroom door.

"Goddamn you, Edward," Mia cursed. If she couldn't let events over the last month glissade to the corners of her mind then everyone else was bound to pick up on it as well. It also occurred to her that, in all the mayhem, she'd forgotten to ring the care home.

She glanced over to her mobile. *Don't do it!* her mind screamed. It would only be giving nourishment to the seed of dark energy that still lingered, and then the whole night might as well have been rewound.

Having desisted from making the call, Mia made a detour to the fridge. Duncan had cleaned up most of the mess left behind from Casey's execution, although she had no desire to find out what he'd done with the remains of her mangled head. The only trace of the incident was a pinkish tinge on the tiles, and callous as it sounded, Mia knew it could have been a lot worse than losing the family pet. It could just as easily have been Louisa's body wrapped up in bin bags by the back door.

Mia peered through the kitchen window with her hands resting on the edge of the sink. She was scanning the lawn for a suitable grave plot when she noticed the bare patch of soil amid the thicket that lined the fence dividing next door's garden. Mia remembered the dog's obsession with destroying the lawn and could have kicked herself for being so quick to neglect the signs. Even though it was night, she could see that most of the hole had collapsed in on itself by now, with a little assistance from the wet weather they'd had of late.

"What were you trying to tell us, girl?" Mia pondered aloud. Animals were said to have a sixth sense, much like children, only they didn't have the capacity for speech. But that didn't mean they couldn't communicate.

"Oh my god ..." Mia's eyes could have punctured holes through the glass as Edward's words repeated in her mind: 'Now that my sister is dead there's no chance you will ever find what she hid.' If there was something in the house then it was likely to have been found and removed long before now, whether accidentally or not. She tried to convince herself that it was her brain overthinking matters, but if she'd acted on her instincts sooner then maybe the dog would still be alive. Maybe Jamie wouldn't have been the victim of yet more degradation and her daughter would be at home where she belonged, not hiding out with her traumatised father and stepmum.

Mia took a torch from the cupboard under the sink and then unlocked the back door. The kitchen fluorescents shed their light over the nearest half of the garden, but the rest of it looked like a solid black wall until she switched on the torch and the wilderness flared to life. Tree branches rocked in the wind, an army of shrubs whispering words of warning – urging her to go back inside. It had been over a week since Casey had last ventured outdoors, apart from to do her business; and even then she scarcely ate or drank enough to justify the visits. Weeds around the disturbed patch of soil wilted over the top of it to create a prickly umbrella, which Mia pushed aside with the head of the torch. They were so wasted that they didn't spring back into place, but the soil was too thickly clumped and matted to dig up with her bare hands – especially without knowing how deep she'd need to go before she found anything. *If* she found anything.

Mia returned to the house, where she slipped on her rain mac before fetching the key to the plastic storage container outside. Back in the garden, she removed the padlock from the container and fished out the spade that she'd bought from the store a few weeks ago, when clearing out the garden had been a priority. Positioning the torch on the grass so it acted as a spotlight to the area in which she had to dig, she plunged the spade down into the edge of the soil. It was relatively easy to turf up the earth, which had been softened by the intermittent rain spells. She tossed the contents of the spade to one side and then drove it back into the ditch, pushing down on the steel head with her foot and using her weight to cut through the harder layers below. It had only just occurred to her that she was wearing her fluffy slippers but she was too impatient, too eager to stop now. Grunting, she scooped up another huge clod of soil, taking a cluster of weeds with it, and repeated the process. Before she knew it, the mound of earth next to her had grown as high as her knees. The freshly dug pit was about wide enough for her to sit in, but there was still no indication of anything buried below.

Mia stabbed the spade into the grass by her feet and draped an arm over the handle, resting her head on her elbow while taking a moment to recuperate from the labour. She could already feel the sweat dribbling down her back, and the plastic material of her mac only made it worse. Her slippers were also drenched and majoritively brown instead of white: they resembled a pair of dead rats in the scant torchlight. She dreaded to think what she must have looked like, digging up the garden in the pitch-dark, but at the very least it would make a decent grave for Casey. She wondered if Louisa would ever be able to look her father in the eye without having flashbacks of their mutilated pet. Mia, for one, considered him a permanent reminder, and she felt a warm tear mingle with the rainwater drizzling down her face.

Jerking the spade out of the lawn, she shovelled out more soil. Worms wriggled frenetically, trying to burrow back into their shelter as they were flung onto the mud dune. Again, and again, and –

Dink.

The spade would go no deeper. *It could have been a rock*, she supposed – or a brick. She tapped the object with the flat edge of the spade, lightly at first; but as her anticipation bloomed into excitement, she moved it around over the surface until it made a dull clunking sound. Throwing down the spade, her breaths no longer deep with exertion but quick and shallow – almost a pant – she grabbed the torch and directed its shaft into the pit. There was something down there all right, and it was too flat, too smooth for stone. Mia reached into the hole, which was roughly two-feet deep, and scraped away the crumbs of mud that scattered the top of what she could now discern to be a box of some sort. *Could this be it – the key to ending our nightmare once and for all?* she thought. It almost seemed too easy.

With the torch wedged between her shoulder and ear as one might hold a phone while chatting to a friend, she used both hands to feel around the edges of the box, carving out soil as she went. Dirt caked under her fingernails and tiny legs skittered over her hands. With a bit of tugging, the box finally came loose. There was nothing obviously unique about it: just plain, weather-worn wood with no engravings, plaques or anything else to identify it. Actually, it was more like a chest than a box – about big enough to fit a small cat inside. Turning it around in her hands, she found a rusty padlock on the front and yanked it forcibly.

"Damn it," she muttered. Even if she did have a key, it would be useless seeing as the keyhole was clogged with dirt. Mia laid down the chest with the torch balanced on top. She reached for the spade and aimed the head at the looped part of the padlock, then gave it a good sharp jab. It fractured easier than she'd anticipated, and after a second strike the padlock snapped in half. Dropping the spade, Mia took the torch in one hand and wrenched open the tiny latch on the front of the chest, then flung the lid back on its hinges.

She immediately closed it again.

"Jesus bloody Christ." A hair-bristling tingle crept over her, and this time it wasn't the insects. This time it came from within. Deep beneath her flesh, frosting in her blood.

As if not quite believing what she'd seen, Mia slowly raised the lid and shone the torch upon the greyish powder inside. She had to stop herself from dunking a finger into it, although she could not for her own sanity think of why – the very sight of it caused her gut to clench up like a fist. No wonder Edward was so attached to the house: his body had never left it. The chest contained his goddamn *ashes*.

A noise from behind hacked through the night. A distinct *snap* that sounded like a twig being trodden on by something big and heavy. Mia whizzed round on her knees, the torch beam landing on a burly torso not a metre from her. She guided the light upwards to a neck that was thick with bristles and matted hair that looked like wet tar in the rain.

"Shit," said Mia, with a short expiration of air. "Paul, you scared the bejesus out of me."

She was trying so hard to gulp down her throbbing heart that it took a while to realise that, despite the glare from the torch, he hadn't blinked once. She put a hand to her forehead, using it as a visor to shield her eyes from the marble-sized raindrops as she tilted back her head to look up at him.

"What are you doing here?" she asked, having momentarily forgotten about the chest and what it contained.

Paul stood as still as the woody trunks at the back of the garden. His arms were rigid by his sides with a slight bend in the elbows, fists loosely curled. Although his head was dipped towards her, the heavy rain glistened in the torchlight, creating a bleary screen in front of his face. His top was soaked through and clung to the arcs of his upper arms and chest. Even though they weren't particularly muscular, the guy was so big that he didn't need steroids to look menacing.

"Paul, are you okay?" Mia spoke louder in case it was the weather distorting her speech. He wasn't a stealthy man, so she had no idea how he'd managed to clamber over next door's fence undetected. It took her back to their first night at the house, when she'd caught Paul staring through the kitchen window with that same barren expression. If she'd known back then what she knew now, there's no saying how she might have reacted.

Mia flicked her tongue over her lips, a nervous reaction more than anything. It was the coolness of the rainwater that shocked her back to the present.

"What's wrong? Is it Brenda? Has something happened?" Keeping her eyes on Paul, Mia fumbled behind her for the spade, her movements slow and measured. With any luck it was so dark that he would have been able to see very little with the torch shining in his unusually pallid face.

"Talk to me, Paul." She continued to distract the man. "You're starting to freak me out."

She couldn't be sure if it was the patterns from the light reflecting off his wet face, but Mia swore she saw teeny muscle spasms either side of his jaw. She started to feel behind her more frantically, fingers scuttering about like spider's legs and losing themselves in the grass. "Why don't we get you home so you can dry off, yeah?"

Paul's eyes gradually came into focus, wintry hollows now gleaming with a palpable loathing. Sliding his neck forwards, a single word leaked through his clenched teeth: "*Bitch.*"

It was so muted over the constant pitter-patter of rain splashing her hood that she actually had to lip read. At the same time he lunged at Mia, her hand fell upon the spade's handle. She took her chance and swung it at the man, not aiming for any body part in particular but just enough to ward him off. Paul caught the spade below its metal head, fingers closing all the way around the shaft and prising it from her grip as though it was a weightless cardboard tube. Mia was too busy concentrating on the tool to have noticed the huge fist that came plummeting towards her, cuffing her on the side of the jaw. It wasn't a fatal blow; nevertheless, her body was flung sideways and she landed face-first in the dirt heap before rolling onto her back. Her face was so numb that she couldn't feel much at all. She might even have blacked out, for one minute she was spitting out a mouthful of soggy soil and the next she was dodging the sharp edge of the spade that came sweeping down towards her neck like a homemade guillotine.

Mia executed a swift logroll to the left and then, almost spontaneously, she rammed her slipper into Paul's kneecap, but it was about as effective as booting a lamppost. Sneering, Paul yanked the spade out of the ground from where her severed head might have lain and then swung it back over his shoulders. This time, her foot disappeared into his groin. The man doubled up, one hand leaving the spade to nurse his swollen genitals. Mia contemplated snatching the weapon and clobbering him to unconsciousness, but with her body running off adrenaline, she grabbed the wooden chest and scrambled over the muddy heap; soil shooting out from under her feet like grit from spinning car tyres as she made a sprint for the house.

Her sodden slippers squeaked against the kitchen tiles, and she had to do a skidding half-spin in order to shut and lock the back door. Bracing herself against it, she waited for the sound of fists pounding against wood but there was nothing – not even a rattling handle. She scooted over to the window to find that he was already there, that venomous grin now a permanent feature on his face. Yet it was the eyes that gripped her: giant black eddies that could patently see her even though she could see nothing remotely human in them, let alone living.

Mia glanced down to the chest and then back at Paul – at least, it had the face of Paul. And the body, shell, host – whatever the term for it seemed irrelevant now. It was what dwelt within that caused Mia to step away from the window, her dread sinking way deeper than blood, nerves or even the intuitive mind. This thing had had a taste of her soul, and for that reason alone they would be forever connected. Now she'd chained the doorway to her subconscious, all it could do was peer in through the windows. Mia finally understood what Duncan had told her all along: that it was up to her to keep that door locked.

"What are you doing?"

Mia screeched and twirled round. Jamie was standing behind her in a dressing gown, her hair wrapped in a towel that was bundled onto her crown. Her gaze sprang from the muddy footprints smeared all over the floor to the bright red blood dribbling down Mia's chin.

"God, what happened? Are you okay?" Jamie reached out to examine her face. Mia ducked back, wincing as if she'd suddenly remembered about the throbbing ache in her jaw. She threw a quick glance to the window. Paul had gone.

"Oh, no," Mia mumbled.

"What's wrong? And ... what is that?" Jamie scowled at the object clutched in Mia's hands, suddenly less eager for answers.

"Take it." Mia held the chest out in front of her while casting anxious glances at the window and wondering why Paul hadn't smashed through it.

"No way, it's all mucky and gross!"

This time Mia didn't ask, and instead she thrust the chest into Jamie's arms, giving her no choice but to take hold of it as she dashed over to the window. Mia leaned over the sink and pressed her face against the glass to get a full view of the garden.

"Where did you go, you bastard?" she said.

The storage box outside was still open, providing plenty of tools to break in with – unless he didn't want to alert the neighbours so he could slaughter them both in peace. There was no path leading around to the front of the house, so unless he'd given up and gone home then he had to be out there somewhere.

"Mia, you're scaring me," Jamie was saying. "What were you doing out there? Why are you bleeding?"

"It's Paul, he's gone crazy." The metallic taste in her mouth becoming more and more bitter, Mia waggled her tongue around to check for any loose teeth. All she found was a flap of skin from where she must have bitten the inside of her cheek during the fall. She spat a bloody mixture of dirt and saliva into the sink before rinsing her mouth out with water, groaning at the swelling in her bottom lip.

"W-what do you mean?" Jamie worried. "He's always been crazy, hasn't he?"

"Not like this."

Mia scooped her mobile up off the kitchen table and dialled Brenda's number. Her phone was switched off. It was after ten – they were probably tucked up in bed, completely unaware of what Paul was up to. Either that or the alternative.

"No." Mia wiped the thought from her mind. "He wouldn't – not his sister."

"What are you talking about?" demanded Jamie.

"Brenda and Wesley, I think they might be in danger. Christ, she's never going to forgive me for this." Mia punched triple nine into the keypad. "Hello – police, please. My neighbour's just attacked me and I think he's trying to break into my house."

Jamie's face became more and more bleached as Mia reeled off her name and address before hanging up the phone. She followed Mia into the living room with a bombardment of questions: "Why is Paul doing this? What does he want? What's in the box?"

"It's him – Edward." Mia made a gap in the curtains and peeped out onto the front garden. Nearly all of the houses were in darkness apart from Keith's opposite and another one further down the street.

Jamie said, "But I thought he couldn't hurt us anymore?"

"Not in spirit form." Mia closed the curtains again. "This is his last resort, he's latching onto whoever he can while he still can. Duncan warned me about this. Why couldn't I have waited until the frigging morning?"

"Oh, God, not again." Jamie staggered back like a toddler taking its first steps, the chest tipping in her arms.

Mia rushed over, straightening them both before saying resolutely, "It's going to be okay, I promise. As long as we've got this."

Jamie's eyes followed Mia's hand as she placed it on top of the chest. "Do I even want to know?" she said.

"You'll find out soon enough. I want you to take this around to Brenda's while I distract Paul – *Edward*." Mia was confusing herself now. "Tell them what's happened and that you need to take it to a churchyard – not a cemetery, okay? It has to be consecrated grounds."

"And then what?"

"Then you bury it deep, somewhere no one will find it. I don't care how long it takes or how far you have to travel. I'll make sure Paul doesn't follow until the police get here."

"What if they're too late? Won't they arrest him? It's not his fault, Mia. Remember, if it wasn't for Paul then there's no saying what that thing would have done to me."

"I know, but better he's in a jail cell than trying to kill us both. We'll deal with that later, I'm not prepared to lose you after everything we've been through." Mia steered Jamie into the hallway and unlocked the front door. "If you get no answer from Brenda then bang on everyone's door until someone answers. You'll be a lot safer with them than you are with me."

"You will be okay, won't you?"

"Don't worry about me." Mia opened the door.

It was Jamie who screamed first, leaping backwards so her heel caught the bottom of the staircase. With the chest clutched to her torso, she had nothing to balance herself with and collapsed onto her backside, the towel on her head falling askew so one corner flopped down in front of her face. Mia attempted to close the door but a mud-caked boot was wedged behind it, and a force that multiplied her strength by a zillion crashed into the exterior side, ploughing both Mia and the door into the adjacent wall. Her hand rose instinctively to protect her face from being crushed beneath the wood, and the agony that shot through her wrist caused a yowl to spring from her lips. This was soon stifled by the hand that grasped her throat like one of those steel claw machines on building sites, pinning her to the wall as if trying to drive her right through the concrete. Paul must have taken a detour through Brenda's house and walked straight out of the front door.

Jamie steadied herself on the stairs and pushed away the towel that was now dangling from her head. "Mia!" she cried.

Paul's head jerked round, his 'eyes' sinking from Jamie to the chest and then tapering into gleaming crescents. His hold on Mia's throat slackened enough for her to splutter out the word: "*Ruuun!*"

With the chest tucked under one arm, Jamie turned and hurtled up the stairs. She wailed all the way to the top, the towel plopping off so her wet hair bobbed about wildly behind her. Mia kicked and punched the giant, twisting and tugging the arm that restrained her as if trying to give him a Chinese burn. In one powerful motion, he swung her round so she toppled into the hallway and ended up sprawled on her front. As Paul strode past her, Mia hooked her arms around one of his ankles, at the very least hoping to slow him down, but he merely glared at her with that demented grin. "Your time will come soon enough, as will that brat child of yours. But first ..."

Yanking his leg free, Paul thundered up the stairs. His long legs reached over at least three at a time, hand gliding up the banister as though he was on a leisurely stroll. Mia tried to push herself up, but the tendons in her injured wrist felt like a knot of twisted wires and she was more dazed from the punch to the face than she'd thought. Poised on all fours, she could see into the kitchen where there would be plenty of weapons – knives and blades that she'd wanted to avoid before. But if she had to make a decision between sparing Paul and saving her family, well, there was no competition. That's if she could get to Jamie in time.

***

"*Oh God oh God oh God!*" Jamie came to a skidding halt on the landing, turning in frenzied half-circles while searching for somewhere to hide. The footfalls on the stairs were getting rapidly closer and she thought about surrendering, giving the psychopath what he wanted, but there was no saying what he'd do to her afterwards; especially now he had a fit and healthy body. That she was as nude as a stripper beneath the dressing gown didn't help matters. Memories that were too fervent to evanesce into nightmares consumed her and, cliché or not, she made a dive for the bathroom and bolted the door behind her.

Rattle, rattle.

Jamie squealed when the door handle flipped up and down as if it was possessed.

Thump, thump, bang!

The entire door quaked from the force of the blows. She used her own meagre weight to secure it, digging her heels into the tiles. Mia had refitted the lock after the paramedics had forced it open to get to Kerry, but it didn't look like it would hold for long.

Crack!

The wood splintered, and a huge vertical slit formed at about face height. *Christ, what was this nut job on?* Jamie thought. Paul was big all right, but it sounded like there was a herd of elephants trying to break in. When a fist came bursting through the door, almost clipping her cheek, Jamie screamed while staggering across the room. A veiny arm protruded from the crevice in the door like a human cuckoo clock, muscles bulging and blood from his split knuckles blotting the paintwork.

Jamie balanced the chest on the toilet seat and flipped open the lid. At first she couldn't for the life of her figure out what was so special about the sandy substance inside.

"What in the name of ... Oh, gross!" she moaned.

The strikes on the door came as slow but regular booms. Dust flaked from the panels, and Jamie had to cover her ears with her hands.

"Go away!" she howled.

Biff ... biff ... biff. The bolt started to rattle. A screw popped out. He was trying to kick the door down.

"Where are you, Mia?" Jamie began to weep. "Please, somebody help me ... *please!*"

The bolt sprang from the wall and clattered across the tiles right next to her bare feet. The door flew open, and Jamie could only stare at the giant that obstructed the doorway. She was about to scream when another figure leaped up behind him, yelling obscenities that were too raving to comprehend while plunging something long and silvery into the back of Paul's shoulder. His eyes scrunched up, a deep and guttural roar spilling from his mouth. He reached up over his shoulder, and as he stumbled round, Jamie saw the handle sticking out of his trapezius muscle and the expanding blotch on his top that the rainwater had turned a crimson red. Paul thrashed his torso from side to side while attempting to grab the knife, groaning and hissing like a rabid drunk. The material shredded as he finally wrenched the blade from its fleshy sheath, then he grabbed the front of Mia's mac and slammed her hard against the landing wall.

"Fight it, Paul!" Mia shouted, the tip of the blade only millimetres away from piercing her eyeball. "I don't want to hurt you, and deep down I know you don't want to hurt me either."

"Tut, tut," Paul rasped. "You should have finished the retard off when you had a chance. Even if I have to spend an eternity in hell, it will be worth it knowing that I destroyed your whole fucking family."

"Oi, shithead!" Jamie waited until Paul faced her before dangling the chest over the toilet with its lid wide open. "You want them? Go and fetch them!"

"Jamie, no!" Mia coughed, but she'd already upturned the chest. The three of them watched the ashy stream pour down the toilet, turning the water a cloudy grey.

All it took was a flush of the handle, and in less than ten seconds Edward's remains had swirled away. It was that simple. That quick. So goddamn effortless that, when compared to the week upon week of torture and despair, Jamie almost wished it had been grander.

Paul released Mia, letting her slide down the wall into a crumpled heap before charging at Jamie. She dropped the chest and threw herself into a corner, arms up in front of her; eyes shut for what she thought would be the last time she ever closed them. Halfway across the bathroom, as if someone had flipped an 'off' switch, Paul collapsed onto his front – he didn't even stop beforehand. Jamie heard the staggering thud as his body smacked the floor, but she still couldn't bring herself to look. Not until she heard the second person that came shuffling into the room.

Mia crawled over to the man and put two fingers to his neck while checking for a pulse.

"I-is he dead?" Jamie whispered, afraid she might wake him.

Mia shook her head and rolled back so she was leaning against the side of the bathtub. Clutching her swollen wrist, she looked as drained as Jamie felt. Her adrenaline was quickly starting to dwindle; her body was shutting down and there was nothing she could do to stop it. No words were exchanged between them for the next few minutes, each reminiscing over their individual experiences. So grateful to have kept their lives that they couldn't begin to come to terms with the trauma of not only the last few hours, but all the days and weeks before that. As for the memories, Jamie knew hers would never fully heal.

"Should we call an ambulance?" she said, after a while.

Mia shook her head. "The police will be here soon. They'll deal with it."

"What are we going to tell them? What'll happen to Paul?"

"I don't know," was Mia's answer to both questions. "To be honest, he's the least of my worries."

Jamie followed her stare towards the toilet, dread surging once more.

"I-I didn't know what else to do. He was going to kill you."

"We've done all we can do now. Edward has been weakened, that's why he took control of Paul in the first place. Let's hope he rots in those sewers until the end of time."

"And, what, we just pretend it never happened?"

"No, we start rebuilding our lives like we always do. The sooner that happens, the sooner we can put all of this behind us."

Jamie drew her knees up to her chest, mumbling, "That doesn't even seem possible right now."

"One thing's for sure ..." Mia hooked an arm over the rim of the bath and grimaced as she found her footing, "if Edward Perkins ever has the guts to return then we won't be ready for him."

"No?"

Mia shook her head while glaring down at the defeated man. "We'll be waiting."

CHAPTER THIRTY-TWO

The air was brisk as Mia stepped out of the car onto Penny Street. She slipped on her leather gloves, moving aside as a swarm of children – not that you could see their little faces beneath the hideous masks, face paint and headwear – raced past her with their parents lagging behind, yelling at them to slow down and watch the roads. It was a little early in the day to start trick or treating, but then Halloween did only come around once a year. Listening to their cheerful laughter, Mia remembered a time when her own daughter would have fitted in amongst them; but today Louisa's reserve of costumes were stuffed away at the back of her wardrobe, never to see the 'darkness of night' again. Mia wondered what those kids would have done if a real Frankenstein walked around the corner, or a cackling hag flew past on her broomstick. Even as she chuckled at the daydream, deep inside, she knew that anything was possible.

Mia combed her fingers through her curls, plumping them up at the roots. Her rouge lip stain made her feel slightly overdone, but she was looking good and that was a bonus considering all that life had flung at her this last year. Walking past the other parked cars, she arrived at Secret Realm and pushed open the main door. *Strange, no squeak,* she thought. But that wasn't the only difference, for while everything looked the same, something about the shop felt uninhibited. Something was missing, and it wasn't due to the lack of customers.

"Long time no see." Mia heard the voice before she saw the body half-concealed behind an empty display stand. The chain on Max's jeans jangled as he strolled into view, dust floating about behind him in the light streaming in through the window.

"I hope you're not up to your old tricks again," Mia said, stopping in front of him.

"Nah, just having a bit of a move around before it gets busy – you've got to keep the whole feng shui vibe going. It's good to see you looking so ... well." Mia blushed when he ran an admiring eye over her body. At least her effort was appreciated.

"You, too." Strange how true that was considering their first meeting. "I was just passing and it occurred to me that I never got a chance to thank Duncan properly for everything he did for us. It was on my list of things to do, but it's been a pretty chaotic month."

"But everything's okay, isn't it? No more bumps in the night?"

"I wouldn't know, we decided to move on in the end. My daughter's staying with her dad, and a work colleague has taken Jamie in while I find us somewhere else to live. It's not ideal, but it's only until we can find a buyer for the house."

"And you?"

"I haven't gone far, just crashing in next door's spare room. My friend's brother was recently put into a psychiatric hospital, so we're kind of supporting each other. I owe her a lot."

"Is this the guy you mentioned before – the one who encountered the demon?"

Mia nodded without going into too much detail. It was something close to a miracle that everyone including Paul had survived the night of the attack. By the time Brenda and Wesley had realised what was going on, the police had already arrived at the scene, shortly followed by an ambulance. Of course, none of them had said a word about what really happened. That Paul had been labelled as psychotic was bad enough.

"Do the docs think he'll make a recovery?" Max wanted to know.

"It doesn't matter what they say. What slim chance he had of leading a normal life has been completely stripped away, but at least he can't hurt anyone while he's in there – or himself."

"Probably the best place for him right now," Max agreed. "If you're in need of some more space then there's a perfectly cosy flat upstairs. I'd even give up the double bedroom for you – just until you get yourself sorted, like."

"Thanks, but I doubt your uncle would be too pleased if he found out that you've been letting his home out to strangers. Did he decide to take another break in the end? I've tried calling him a few times, but the number he gave me seems to have been disconnected."

"Er, you could say that." There was a gloomy pause before Max explained, "He actually passed away. The doctors put it down to one of those freak deaths, but his friends and family all know the truth."

"Gosh ... I-I'm so sorry." Mia noticed a heavy slump to the man's shoulders, and the greyness in those eyes was like a winter sky. She had an urge to rush over and comfort him, but shock prevailed.

"When did it happen?"

"A few weeks back. His body just gave up on him."

"Weeks? But that would have been just after he ..." Mia recalled having slept for a whole day after the exorcism, and even then it had been like trying to recuperate from years spent in a coma. She might as well have handed Duncan a loaded pistol and told him to blow his brains out.

"Oh, Max, I don't know what to say. Have you had the funeral yet?"

"Yeah, I was going to invite you but then I thought it might have sounded a bit weird. Besides, I knew you'd feel bad about the whole thing and I didn't want you to go blaming yourself."

"Of course I feel bad – mortified, in fact. You warned me about his health, and if I hadn't asked him to –"

"Look, Uncle Duncan was old and ugly enough to make his own decisions. Something like this was bound to happen sooner or later, he knew that and it never stopped him. He might be dead but that doesn't mean he's gone."

Mia moved unwittingly closer to the man. "You mean you've felt him?"

"No, but he did leave this place to me in his will and something tells me he ain't going to stand back and watch me fuck it all up." They both chuckled at this, before Max said, "I know Duncan was practically a stranger to you, but seeing as you missed the funeral, why don't we go out sometime and raise a glass to him? If you can fit it into your schedule, of course."

"Max Lowe, you're not seriously using your uncle's death as a pulling technique?" Mia spoke in a stern but playful manner.

"No, ma'am, but if pity works then I ain't complaining. It's just that I could use a pick me up, and you were one of the last people that saw him alive. Drinks are on me?"

"Sorry, I doubt I'd be much company at the minute. Maybe in a few weeks when we're a bit more settled then ... yeah, why not?"

Max smiled, sunbeams bursting through that mist in his eyes. "Have you still got my number?"

***

Knock, knock.

The door to Vivian's bedroom opened and carer, Sally, waddled in, her portly figure swaying from side to side like a penguin on a tightrope.

"Hello, Vivian, I've brought you your coffee and biscuits," she said, setting a mug and saucer down onto the foldout table next to Vivian's armchair. She noticed fragments of broken porcelain scattered about the carpet and sighed. "Oh, dear, has someone been clumsy again?"

Vivian watched her kneel down to gather up what was left of the shattered plate. "Sorry, love, he gave me a start popping up like that. I was just having a doze and must have knocked the table."

Sally paused to ask her, "Who gave you a start?"

"The chap that came by. He said he was an old friend of Billy's, but I told him my memory isn't what it used to be."

"I think you must be confused, Vivian. You haven't had any visitors today."

"Yes, I have. He was right there as plain as you are now."

"Maybe you were dreaming." Sally laughed. The foldout table almost tipped over as she used it to heave up her bulk with the particles of plate stacked in her other hand. "Right, I'll go and fetch the hoover from downstairs. Don't go walking around because we don't want you cutting yourself, do we?"

"I won't move an inch, love."

Sally continued to scan the floor on her way out of the room. Vivian waited until she'd closed the door before getting out of the armchair and crossing over to the bed. She tossed back the duvet and slipped a hand under the edge of the mattress. When she withdrew it, she was clutching a long ivory shard that had once made up the base of the plate; one end running into a smooth, sharp spike.

She looked towards the corner furthest from the window, where the light from outside didn't quite reach. "Oh, you're back. Why do I need to keep this?" She held the shard up in front of her.

The answer came, but Vivian was unable to comprehend it.

"Who shouldn't I trust?" she asked the stranger. "They do love me ... Billy wasn't poisoned, it was his heart ... Why would they do that? I'm their mother ... No, I don't believe you!"

Vivian turned furiously from the shadow, eyeing the weapon in her hand – at least, that's what *he* called it. A weapon of 'self-defence' because, apparently, her family had condemned her to this place for one reason, and it wasn't the one they'd stated.

"Stop it!" Vivian tucked her head in between her arms to obstruct her ears. "I won't do it, she's just a little girl! ... I'll tell them about you ... Yes, they will believe me ... I'm not crazy!"

The bedroom door clicked open. Vivian spun round, shoving the porcelain fragment under the mattress and then smoothing the duvet back into place. She dived into the armchair as Sally lumbered in from the landing with the hoover bumping and scraping against the door.

"Right, I'll just give the place a quick once over because your family has arrived." Sally plugged in the device. "Don't let your coffee go cold."

Vivian took a digestive from the saucer and dunked it into the dark, steaming liquid. Holding it between her forefinger and thumb, she watched the coffee dissolving it like some kind of acid until the bottom of the biscuit melted off and plopped into the mug. She placed its remains back onto the saucer and said, "I don't think I want it anymore."

Leaning back in the armchair, she glanced across the room. Even obscured by the shadows, she was surprised that Sally hadn't seen the man standing there. It was as if he was invisible, a ghost. It crossed her mind that she might have imagined him, but he seemed to know an awful lot about Billy and her family – things even she didn't know, or had forgotten about.

Hearing more voices approaching from outside and the sound of a child's sprightly footsteps, Vivian painted on a smile and turned round in the chair.

"Hello, dears," she said. "Come on in."

THE END

View other Black Rose Writing titles at www.blackrosewriting.com/books

and use promo code PRINT to receive a 20% discount when purchasing.

BLACK ROSE
writing™